SUMMER'S REVENGE

EMMA K. C. COUETTE

SUMMER'S REVENGE

THE FIDALIAN CHRONICLES
BOOK 1

ELGIN HOUSE
— PRESS —

ALSO BY EMMA K. C. COUETTE

The Guild Trilogy

Silent Night
Sacred Ruse
Solemn Vow (February 23rd, 2021)

The Fidalian Chronicles

Summer's Revenge

PRONUNCIATION GUIDE

Appalachia: app-a-lay-shia	(Capital city of Winter)
Areevia: a -ree-vee-a	(Isan and Sky's mother)
Arkenier: are-ken-yay	(King of Summer)
Asmund: az-mund	(eldest son of Lord Arrath)
Fidal: fee-dal	(creator of Fidalia)
Fidalia: fee-dal-ee-a	(the name of the realm)
Icaria: eye-sair-ee-a	(Princess of Winter)
Isanfier: eyes-an-fire	(Prince of Summer)
Kallen: kal-lin	(King Frost's general)
Sancia: san-see-a	(Goddess of Summer)
Snowdon: snow-done	(Prince of Winter)
Skiansy: sky-an-zee	(Princess of Summer)
Widonia: wid-own-ee-a	(Capital city of Summer)
Wylla: will-a	(Goddess of Winter)

Created By Rachael Ward

*To my younger sister, Megan,
who helped this story come to life and tolerated all my endless
rants about this book for eight years.*

You're the real MVP, kid.

Once, an old God had a dream
Of a land that would be forever at peace.
This God's name was Fidal and
He created the realm of Fidalia.

Fidalia was wondrous
And its people were beings of grace and light.
Yet, Fidal was unhappy.
They were not like him and he was still alone.

From far across the winds,
A new Goddess heard the yearnings of his heart.
"Why are you sad?" she asked.
"My name is Madge and I would like to help you."

Fidal told her his woes
And together they rebuilt his broken heart.
They used magic and life
To create four goddesses to join Fidal.

Soon after, Madge vanished,
But Fidal would never forget her blessing:
Four daughters to rule with,
Four souls with which to share his grand creation.

SUMMER'S REVENGE

Wylla was the eldest.
She had snow-white hair and brilliant blue eyes.
Winter was her domain,
Goddess of death, travellers, sleep, rivers, and the moon.

Audria came second.
She had hair like fire and eyes of orange.
Autumn was her refuge,
Goddess of fire, forests, war, darkness, and love.

Sancia was the third,
Skin of rich earth and hair like raven feathers.
Summer was her palace,
Goddess of the sun, the sea, animals, plants, and hunting.

Stella was the youngest.
She had wispy, brown hair and eyes like fresh grass.
Spring was her festival,
Goddess of children, art, fertility, healing, and light.

. . .

Those who live a good life
Will join Fidal and his daughters when they pass
To live among the stars.

Those who don't pass his test
Find their soul in a tree, a silent watcher
Until the end of time.

Part One: Sorrow

"May our sorrow of today be our momentum for tomorrow."

—Anon

1
RAGE AND REMINISCENCE

My arm burned and the armour was covered in dents, but I didn't care. I couldn't stop. I had to persevere, had to keep pushing back the emotions clamouring for attention. I focused on swinging *Ember* over and over again, like my life depended on it, like my sanity depended on it. There was more truth in the latter.

In the back of my mind, I knew the illusion wouldn't last. I knew reality was destined to return eventually, but still I persisted. It was the only way to gain even a touch of relief.

My sword stuck in the armour on the next swing. I cursed and yanked at the blade, but she wouldn't budge.

"Come on," I urged.

I had to keep going. I had to.

I pulled on her with all my might. "Come on!"

Panic set in as I felt reality returning. Emotions poked at the back of my mind.

Stop.

"Get out! Get out!" I screamed at my sword, but that was it. It was too late. The walls I had built around me came crashing down, burying me in rubble. Tears streamed down my face and I sank to the ground in defeat, leaving my sword, *Ember*, where she hung.

I let my emotions go, knowing that was the only way to truly free myself. I cried for what once was and what might have been. I cried until there was nothing left, until my heart was but an empty husk, yearning for a hope it would not receive.

When my eyes finally dried, I dragged myself out of the bottomless pit of sorrow and began sifting through the rubble of my thoughts.

Twelve years ago…

I couldn't finish the thought, as if thinking the words would make it true.

Say it, Isan. Denying it won't change a thing.

I took a deep breath. "Twelve years ago today, my parents died," I whispered to the courtyard. My heart contracted and my eyes teared up again.

Every year, I expected the pain to fade and every year, it was like a fresh blow to the chest.

"Well, would you look at this," a voice crowed. "Our mighty Crown Prince, bawling like a baby."

I turned to see Asmund Arrath entering the courtyard. He hadn't changed a bit in appearance since I'd last seen him. He wore the same tailored military garb, and the same arrogance was etched into his deep brown face.

My eyes narrowed in his direction as I got to my feet.

What's he doing here?

Uncle said Lord Arrath's children weren't due for another week.

"What's the matter, Isanfier," Asmund went on, "did Skiansy beat you in a duel? Or did you lose to the dummy?"

I wiped my eyes with the back of my shirt sleeve. "Neither," I replied. "Today is the anniversary of my parents' death. You should show some respect."

Asmund snorted. "Real men don't cry, Isanfier. It's been well over a decade; pull yourself together."

Fidal give me strength.

That was why I hated him. Every encounter was a lecture, as if I was fourteen years younger than him instead of four.

"You of all people should understand," I told him. "How long has your mother been gone, Asmund? A couple months? And here you are telling me how to grieve? At least you still have a father."

At least he had proper memories of his mother. The memories I had of my parents were hazy and fading more with each passing year. Soon, they would be gone forever.

Sancia save me then.

"My mother was always a frail woman," Asmund replied. "It was only a matter of time. I spent years grieving her absence before that sickness took her."

"At least you have closure," I retorted. "My sister and I still don't know who killed our parents or why. Twelve years have passed and Summer is no closer to the truth."

Asmund shook his head, his long dreadlocks swinging. "You still don't believe it was magic, do you?"

"How can I? They were found with their throats slit, Asmund, and magic doesn't wield swords; men do."

"Men can wield magic," he reminded me. "The sorcerers could make it look like a sword too."

I let out an exasperated breath. He was just like the rest of them, always talking me down. The only one who believed me was Sky, but she had even less influence than I did.

"Forget about the murder weapon," I went on, "the murderer is more important."

He held up a dark hand. "Yes, yes I know. It was Winter, of course."

Am I that predictable?

"Think about it," I urged him. "Who in Summer could possibly want them dead? They were cherished by the people. Winter is the only kingdom cruel enough. Generations of Summer royalty have fallen to their hands. What more proof do you need?"

"Isan, please, I've heard it all before."

"I could be next, Asmund," I replied. "You won't be laughing then. They've had plenty of time to plan in the past twelve years. We should attack now, before it's too late. We—"

"Enough," he bellowed. "This is madness and you are in danger of falling to it. Be grateful Fidalia has been so quiet. Don't go looking for trouble where there is none." He turned to go. "I will pray for your family tonight, those in mourning and those already gone."

He left me there in the courtyard, dismissing me and my ideas as if I were some servant rather than his future king. His promise of a prayer was just to keep me from calling him out on his disrespect.

It didn't matter anyway; I knew I was right. I knew Winter was out there, lurking beyond our borders, waiting for the right moment to strike. I wouldn't let my guard down. I wouldn't let another person die because of them. I wouldn't let another person become like me.

Cold and angry and afraid.

• • •

My footsteps echoed in the quiet of the castle, the only sound that could be heard. As usual, I resisted the urge to talk to myself, if only to create the illusion that the place wasn't so empty. The castle had bustled with life before my parents' death, but balls, feasts, and any type of social gathering died with them.

Noblemen rarely came to visit anymore. Our staff had reduced after the tragedy too. Many rooms sat neglected in their absence and entire wings of the castle stood forgotten.

Our remaining servants would've had some excitement with the arrival of Lord Arrath's progeny. The guest wing needed some work to be presentable again, though I suppose, being from a military city, Asmund and his siblings would be used to a bit of dust.

I rounded a corner and entered a once-ornate section of the hall. White columns lined both walls, spaced evenly apart and stretched into arches that spanned across the ceiling to meet their sisters on the other side. Painted ivy snaked up and around them. Nestled between each pillar was a painting, though some of the spaces were empty, awaiting future masterpieces.

A part of me wanted to turn back, didn't want to face this, but today was a day of mourning and this hall was a memory of days long past. Some of the artwork dated back centuries and the canvases were as faded as the scenes and people they depicted. Balls, banquets, and coronations were forever preserved in the vibrant colours on the left side of the hall. On the right, the faces of my ancestors stared back at me.

My dead ancestors. Winter killed them all save for King Henri, but he had been even frailer than the late Lady Violette Arrath. Magic, disease, and all the other dangers in Fidalia could be the end of you, but in my family, it was Winter you had to watch out for. There was a whole kingdom full of people who wanted you dead.

How much safer Fidalia would be if Winter was wiped off the face of it.

I shoved that thought aside and regarded my family. Some smiled, as if they were glad I was there, and others glared at me, as if they could hear my thoughts and were wondering why I wasn't doing anything to avenge them. All of them were brown eyed, some with intricate braids and others letting their dark locks hang free. Each one of them upheld the trademarks of Summer people: brown eyes, dark skin, and hair that was never cut short for anything.

When I reached my parents' portraits, hanging side by side, I averted my gaze for a moment. I wanted to walk past, but this day belonged to them and I wasn't selfish enough to deny them that.

I looked up to meet my mother's smiling face and tears welled up in my eyes. She was so beautiful. Her skin was a rich, earthen brown and her hair cascaded around her face like an ebony waterfall. The painter had done such an impeccable job.

I brushed my hand across her face, trying to ignore the difference in our skin tones. "I wish I could've known you longer," I whispered to her. "I miss you."

I wiped away a tear that escaped.

You have to be strong for them.

Even so, I looked away from my mother. My father's portrait hung to her left. He smiled at me too and I couldn't help but smile back. I could see Sky in his facial features. No one would ever doubt they were related. I could imagine them standing side by side, laughing together. My most prominent memory of my father was his infectious, booming laughter.

My chest tightened at the thought.

I would never hear his laugh again and someday I would forget the sound.

I choked back my tears and closed my eyes.

"Blessed Wylla," I whispered to the realm, "watch over my parents on this day and every day. Audria, send them my love. Sancia, be with them always. Stella, help me to heal and to be more forgiving. Fidal, I am grateful for the life you have given me and continue to sustain. Fidalia forever."

I opened my eyes. My parents' death day was the only day I prayed to all four goddesses and Fidal with any measure of seriousness. It wasn't that I openly renounced them other times, but that day was the only one that truly mattered.

Summer was Sancia's domain, but I prayed to Audria, the goddess of love and Stella the goddess of healing. I tried never to utter Wylla's name, the patron goddess of Winter, but she was the goddess of death, so who else would listen? It seemed like a fitting match for Winter.

My mourning over, I moved to the end of the hall to where the latest portrait of Sky and I hung. It had been done two months prior, upon our sixteenth birthday. Sky's features mirrored the rest of the portraits, unlike mine. My dark brown hair was cut short, barely over my ears. The portrait depicted me with medium skin, like Sky, and the typical Summer brown eyes, but it couldn't be further from the truth. I was paler than a sheet and my eyes were a piercing, unnatural blue.

I was told it was some childhood disease that caused my strange complexion, but I couldn't help but feel like an imposter and an outcast, especially when walking the hall of my ancestors. I never felt like I belonged, but that I was a mistake that might one day ruin everything.

"Isan?" a voice called out to me, echoing throughout my end of the castle. It was a voice I would recognize anywhere.

"Sky?"

She didn't return my call, but I heard footsteps a few moments later and she rounded the corner in front of me. My twin looked resplendent in a deep green dress that matched the emeralds in her tiara. Her long, brown hair was braided over her shoulder, gold stars woven between the strands. Her darker skin seemed to glow in the presence of such finery.

"What's the occasion?" I asked. "You actually look like a princess."

She pulled at her skirt. "Oh, this? I visited Mother and Father this morning and I... I thought they'd like to see me in something nice." She gave me a small smile, but I could tell it was forced. Her eyes were rimmed with red and she looked a bit dishevelled behind all her splendour. Today was hard for her too, but she still tried to keep up appearances.

My coat, on the other hand, was covered in dirt and my hair was slicked back with sweat. I wouldn't doubt there to be tears tracks visible down my face as well. I looked more like Sky's lowly servant than her brother and heir to the kingdom. She always made me look even more out of place. It was the one thing that stood between us.

"How are you faring?" she asked me.

I shrugged. "Well enough. I had a run-in with Asmund earlier. He and his siblings have arrived early."

She scowled. "Lovely, and what did he have to say?"

"Nothing pleasant."

"I would expect nothing less," she sighed. "I suppose *he* was invited to the Council."

I raised an eyebrow. "Council?"

She nodded. "That's why I came to find you. I was having tea with Aunt Mag when she mentioned Uncle had called a Council. I thought it odd, since you hadn't mentioned one, so I investigated myself. They're holding one as we speak."

I frowned. "Without me?"

"It would seem so. Shall we go see what they wished to keep from you?" She gave me a mischievous grin.

I smiled. "Indeed we shall."

• • •

We heard the voices before the study even came into view. They were clamouring over each other, arguing about something.

"What in Fidalia is going on in there?" Sky wondered aloud, a bit out of breath from our rush over there. She didn't wear corseted dresses often enough to get used to them.

"Let's find out," I replied.

We approached on light feet, following a pattern we'd memorized as children to avoid squeaky floorboards, and took up places on either side of the door. Then I nudged the door into the room about an inch. Any further and the hinges would creak, a fact Sky and I had learned the hard way. We couldn't see much, but we could hear everything.

"Do you believe Lord Byron's claims that Widonia is in danger?" one of the knights was saying.

"How could I not?" Uncle replied. "Byron has no reason to lie to me and he has been a trusted nobleman for years. Besides, I would be a fool to assume Widonia is safe based solely on its status as the capital city. We are not without our limits."

"Perhaps not, your Majesty," another knight said, "but is a war with the Wyllans the best course of action?"

I raised an eyebrow.

War?

After all this time, they were finally considering it. I wished we hadn't missed the first part of the conversation. I wanted to know what prompted the action.

"I am more concerned about whether or not it is the *right* course of action, Sir Warmund," Uncle replied. "The Wyllans have done many things to earn our ire. This time, it will not be tolerated. It cannot."

"So we're going to sacrifice the lives of our people because you are too proud to show the Wyllans mercy?"

It was Asmund who had spoken this time and I marvelled at the audacity of his words.

"Mercy must first be deserved," Uncle replied. "Until then, we must defend our honour and our people."

"I don't think—"

"Enough," Uncle snapped. "You are here because your father is not. You are not yet a Lord, Asmund son of Arrath. Do not push my patience or you will never be one."

I took a step back at that. Asmund had been the favoured heir of Skar for over a decade. His brother Arran couldn't fill their father's shoes and as for Aramina… She was too wild. Besides, Uncle would never choose a female when there was a perfectly suitable male in the picture.

"Master Asmund may be out of line, your Majesty," Sir Warmund went on, "but his heart is in the right place. A war with the Wyllans would threaten our way of life."

"So you'd rather ignore the threat and have our people cut down one by one by Frost's assassins?" I could hear the frustration in Uncle's voice and began to count down the seconds before it boiled over.

It was never long.

One.

"No, Sire, I'm not saying that, but I do think we have to be more…tactful with this decision. A lot hangs in the balance."

Nine.

"Sir Warmund is right, your Majesty. This could be a ploy to get us to attack. We need to bide our time and —"

"Bide our time?" Uncle bellowed, as I reached fifteen seconds, his anger finally snapping. "King Frost had my sister murdered twelve years ago! I will not watch another Sancian be slaughtered by those Wyllan fiends!"

I sucked in a breath.

What?

The hallway seemed to expand with my lungs, as if the castle itself was waiting to see my reaction.

I turned to Sky. "Did he just…"

She only nodded, her face a pale semblance of the rich colour it usually bore.

He'd been lying to us all this time. He'd known the truth all along. I had been cheated and betrayed all in the name of keeping a non-existent peace.

The hatred between Summer and Winter traced back as far as any of our records went. Our ancient feud wouldn't end until one of us lay dead and desolate, until one of us destroyed the other.

2

Agree to Disagree

My body moved forward of its own volition as I swung the door open the rest of the way and stepped into the room.

All eyes turned from Uncle to me and then Sky, as she followed me in.

"Isanfier?" Uncle said. "Is something wrong?"

"Is something wrong?" I echoed, shaking my head. "You excluded me from a Council meeting and then admitted to lying to Sky and I about our parents' death since we were children. Why? Why would you keep us from the truth and let me believe my theories were delusional?"

Uncle dragged a hand down his face, pulling at his scar as he realized Sky and I had heard everything. "The truth has little bearing, Isanfier," he replied. "It can't change what happened. It can't bring them back."

"It could've brought us some peace, Uncle. It could've kept you from breaking our trust."

Uncle hung his head. "I am sorry for that, but I did what I thought was best. Tragedy is hard for everyone and I didn't think putting a face to it would ease your pain."

I sighed. I didn't want to accept his apology, but to refuse him in front of the Council would be seen as the highest disrespect, so I nodded and said, "I pray Fidal will help me find forgiveness."

A silence fell in the room then and I looked around the table at the knights, searching their faces for any sign of guilt. None of them had been surprised at Uncle's words, so they must've known as well.

Asmund was likely the only ignorant one among them, but he wouldn't apologize for mocking my claims, even though I had been right all along.

I looked back to Uncle. "I have one more question, if you will allow it."

He nodded his head, as if to say, *go on*.

"Why now? If you knew the truth from the moment they were found dead, why have you waited until now to declare war? It's been twelve years."

"I could hardly lead this kingdom into a war right after taking the throne, Isanfier. It would not honour your parents' memory to throw their kingdom into chaos any more than their deaths already had. Actions like these take time and we were *trying* to show the Wyllans mercy, but that opportunity has passed. They have revoked it."

"Pardon my intrusion," Sky said, "but what exactly have the Wyllans done this time?"

It was almost unheard of for her to attend a Council, but I was glad she was there to stand by me.

Uncle let out a breath, relieved to be moving on, and said, "Why don't you two have a seat and I'll tell the tale." He waved to my empty seat at his left and then looked to Asmund. "Master Asmund, if you would?"

"Of course, your Majesty," Asmund said, getting to his feet and offering Sky his empty chair.

I could sense Sky's irritation, but she took the seat anyway, taking a moment to straighten her skirts and figure out where to put her hands. Asmund hovered behind us and it was enough to make my skin crawl.

As soon as we pulled our chairs in, Uncle spoke again.

"This morning, I received a letter from Lord Byron telling us of an attack Mensden suffered a few nights ago. A group of Winter knights had snuck into the city and made an attempt on his life. They were unsuccessful, but several of Byron's guards were lost during the attack. The assailants escaped and Lord Byron fears they will head here next." He paused, as if gauging our reactions, and then continued. "There are men out searching for the culprits now and when they are found, they will await a fate much worse than death."

Sky's eyes widened. "Do you speak of torture?"

Uncle waved a hand. "They may receive that in time, but not from me. No, they will be sent back to *their* king to tell him that—because of them—Summer has declared war on Winter."

There it was again. That word.

War.

It had so few letters, but they each spoke volumes. They carried such an incredible weight. The Council was right to be wary, but for now, I was on Uncle's side. Winter had to pay for its crimes.

Uncle looked around the table, at all his knights, at Asmund, at Sky and me. He levelled us all with his even gaze, a gaze that told us not to be afraid, a gaze that told us this was our right, a gaze that promised our victory.

"All of you will have a part to play in this," he said. "It will not be an easy task and I do not ask this of you lightly. I ask because I know it can be done."

The men nodded, and I supposed they had all come to a silent agreement that war was the only way, come what may.

"Sir Kent will stay behind and oversee the kingdom's affairs in my absence," Uncle went on, nodding at his Captain of the Guard seated opposite him, "and each Lord shall govern their own section of the army." He looked to Asmund. "Your father will be eager to see some action."

Asmund nodded, but said nothing.

"What would you have *me* do?" I asked Uncle, eager to see some action myself.

"You and your sister will stay here," he replied, "safe and sound in the castle."

I bristled, but didn't let the emotion reach my face.

"You are the future of this kingdom," Uncle continued. "If I should perish… We will need the two of you alive. If I do not return, Isanfier, you will be King. You have my word."

His words echoed in my head.

If I do not return, you will be King.

I always knew being King was my destiny, but somehow it seemed like a distant, almost impossible event. It was easy to ignore. However, Uncle would die eventually—as everyone must—and with war looming on the horizon, the transition could be much sooner than I'd anticipated. I was lucky to have him between me and the throne at all. In decades past, he would've served as advisor to me and nothing more. I would've made all the decisions from a young age. He had saved me from that burden, but one day it would come to pass.

Could I handle the responsibility?

I didn't know if I was ready, but if my people needed me, I would not stand idly by.

I nodded, recognizing Uncle's vow. "I will rule honourably with Sancia at my side."

"I pray you do," he replied. The matter settled, Uncle turned back to his men. "We leave in a fortnight."

Everyone's eyebrows rose at that, but none of them dared to say a word against it, not even Asmund.

Sky however, had other ideas. "What if we don't find the Winter assassins by then?" she asked.

Uncle's eyes reflected his outrage at her audacity. "You dare doubt our men?"

Sky, realizing her mistake, backtracked quickly. "No I... I simply wondered what would happen if that was the case. We can hardly send them to Winter with the declaration if we don't have them in our custody."

"If that was the case," Uncle replied, his words slicing the air, "we would leave anyway. Winter does not need to know we are coming. I intend to give them one last kindness, but they can easily do without. Sancia knows they would not extend the same courtesy."

Sky nodded. "I suppose."

The discussion moved on to more details of the war then: preparations, plans, provisions. Sky and I stayed silent. I barely listened to what was being said and I doubt she did either. It didn't concern us. We were to stay in the castle, like caged animals. We were to do as we were told.

What a foolish notion.

Uncle couldn't keep us there. We had the right to fight for our kingdom, the right to avenge our parents. I could not stand by any longer. It was time to prove myself, to act, to do something worthwhile. I understood Uncle's sentiment. Sky and I were the future, but what future would we and Summer have if we lost this war? I'd rather die defending my kingdom than live to rule a desolate place. How long would my rule even last if Winter won?

No, I could not sit back and watch this conflict unfold, but now was not the time to protest. Sky and I would have to discuss it first and we'd have to wait for the right time to approach Uncle. I did not wish to quarrel with him in front of the entire Council again, not to mention Asmund. It would have to wait. I would have to be patient.

At long last, the conversation came to a close.

"Tomorrow, in the town square, I will announce our declaration of war to the people," Uncle said. "Sir Kent, see to it that the word gets out. I want everyone present at this gathering. That is all for now. You may go."

I stood up, almost knocking my chair over in my haste, and was halfway out the door when Uncle called out, "Prince Isanfier, a word please."

I groaned and turned around.

The Council filed out and Sky shut the door behind them, giving me an encouraging smile as she did so.

"Yes?" I asked Uncle, taking a few steps closer to him.

His deep brown eyes stared into me. "I truly am sorry for trying to keep you away from this meeting, Isanfier, but it was your day of mourning and I did not wish to burden you further."

I nodded. It was a decent excuse, but it felt empty somehow.

"I would like you and Sky to accompany me to the gathering as well," he went on. "We need to stand united against our enemy and I ask that you refrain from wearing your usual black attire."

I frowned. "Why?"

"It leaves a bad impression, especially considering who we are going to war against."

I sighed.

He was right, but I didn't like it.

"And another thing," he said. "As you can see, Lord Arrath's children have arrived. It is poor timing, but that can't be helped. I want you to ensure their stay is comfortable, all three of them. I would also like you to report any unusual behaviour."

I scrunched my face. "Unusual?"

"I want to choose Lord Arrath's successor before we head off for war, in case neither of us survive it. I need to know if any of his children slip up during their time here. I want to know if..." He looked around the room, as if afraid someone might hear us. "If any of them practise magic."

I snorted. "Those three? Magic? They're too rigid for it."

"You'd be surprised," Uncle replied, leaning back in his chair. "It can show up in the most unexpected places. Their mother had it."

"What?"

"Lady Violette Arrath. She had magic. She could make flowers grow out of nothing." He shuddered. "She swore not to use her 'gift' after I banned the use of magic, but if her children inherited her powers... They might not choose the same path."

I nodded. I thought the war on magic was madness and unjust, but I would do what he wished. It may gain me some favour with him. "Of course, Uncle, I will see to their stay and their...activities."

Uncle smiled. "You are dismissed then. I will see you at dinner."

Sky was waiting for me in the hall, as was Asmund. He was kissing her clasped hand when I joined them and I coughed pointedly.

It was no secret that Asmund coveted my sister; that was one of the many reasons I hated him. He didn't want her because of who she was. He wanted her because of *what* she was. The princess. Royal blood. Power. If he couldn't be Lord of Arrath, he would settle for Prince Consort. If Sky were ever to take the throne, Asmund would become the second most powerful person in Summer.

If it was my choice, I would choose anyone but Asmund to marry my sister. Sadly, only the monarch had that privilege. I would have to hope Uncle chose Asmund as heir to Skar. He could either be Lord of Skar or Prince Consort of Summer. He could not be both.

Asmund let go of Sky's hand and she let it fall. "It is good to see you again, your Highness," he said.

I snorted.

Your Highness. He never uses such frivolity with me.

Sky forced a smile. "I trust you have been keeping well?"

"Most well," he replied. "I was knighted this past spring."

"Good work," I chimed in. "It took you long enough."

He turned to me with a scowl. "You are just jealous."

I shrugged. "I don't need a title to tell me I can fight."

Sky cut in before we could start a scene. "Where are Arran and Aramina?" She was always the peacemaker when we were children.

"They are resting in our rooms," Asmund replied. "They'll be joining us for dinner."

Marvellous.

"I am sure it will be a pleasant evening," Sky said, "but I must be off now."

I suppressed a smile; I knew she had nowhere to be.

Asmund gave her a half-bow, his hair nearly scraping the marble floor. "It was a pleasure."

"I will see you after lunch?" I asked her. "At the usual place?"

She nodded. "Don't be late."

I grinned. "I wouldn't dare."

She flashed me a smile and walked off with a swirl of green skirts, leaving me with Asmund.

How generous.

"That smile was different," Asmund remarked as Sky disappeared around a corner.

I turned to him. "What?"

"The smile she gave you was different than the one I received."

"Mine was genuine, you mean."

His eyes narrowed in distaste.

"Face it, Asmund," I told him. "You are not well liked in this castle. You may be the favoured Son of Skar, but you lack friends here. Neither Sky nor I will make it easy for you to pursue her, so perhaps you should focus more on winning the King over. It would be in your best interest."

He scowled at me. "I will do as I see fit."

I shrugged. "Do as you must, but I have warned you. Remember that."

Remember to tread with care.

I may have been a weak man in his eyes, but I saw my emotions as strength. I would protect my sister at whatever the cost. She meant too much to me to watch her marry a man she despised.

• • •

I looked up at the sun's position in the sky, directly above my head. The light beat down on me but I shrugged off the heat.

Any minute now.

The courtyard stood empty and silent, save for me and the quiet *shing, shing* as I eased my sword in and out of her sheath, growing more impatient by the second.

Where is she?

Sky had admonished me for lateness and there she was, standing me up.

Then something whizzed over my head and I heard the unmistakable *thwack* as an arrowhead struck the stone wall beyond me.

I turned on my heel in the grass and there she was, crouched in the archway of the courtyard wall, her bow, *Tempest*, aimed at my head.

I put a hand to my heart. "Fidal's breath, Sky. Don't you have anything better to do with your time than giving me grey hairs?"

She grinned and hopped down from the ledge. "Nonsense."

She had changed her outfit. Gone was the gown and the tiara; taking their place was a white tunic, brown leather pants, and high brown boots. A shortsword hung on the belt around her waist and a quiver of arrows was slung over her shoulder.

Sky took to wearing pants whenever she could and I didn't blame her. She'd thrown one of her dresses at me once, and the thing nearly knocked me over, it was so heavy.

"I'm trying to keep your senses sharp," she went on, "and you clearly need more work." She poked me in the forehead with the end of her bow.

I rolled my eyes. "At least I wasn't late."

"Late? My dear Isanfier, I have been watching you for ten minutes."

She turned away from me as I gaped at her, and walked over to the other side of the courtyard to retrieve her arrow.

It was harrowing to think Uncle had once tried to keep her from this. He'd nearly fainted ten years ago when she asked him if she could learn weaponry with me. Uncle subscribed to the traditional idea that women were too delicate to wield weapons, but Sky had thrown such a fit he had eventually relented. She was only allowed the use of sword and bow, though, but that suited her just fine. Sky was born to be an archer; her arrow never missed its mark.

Sky and I had received our training from Sir Warmund himself with the aid of a few castle guards. He had taught us about weapon lore as well, how they were considered extensions of our wills. It was he who had told us of an ancient magic that bound man to weapon, so that weapon would serve them all their life.

The ritual was simple, but powerful and Sky and I had both undergone it. I did it for *Ember* and Sky for *Tempest*. The five letters of *Ember's* name were etched into the fuller of the sword, signifying to the entire realm that she was mine.

Our claimed weapons were our greatest secret. No doubt the ceremony would be considered part of the forbidden magic everyone was so afraid of those days. I found it ridiculous. How much more dangerous was magic than a sword? Both could kill; both could protect. People chose to take up arms; they did not choose to be born with magic.

"So," Sky said, interrupting my thoughts as she joined me again. "What do you wish to practise today?"

"Why don't we start with some simple sparring?"

It was her turn to roll her eyes. "Sparring is never simple with you."

I crossed my arms. "I think you owe it to me after your attempt on my life."

"I think next time I won't aim to miss," she replied, but then she shrugged off her quiver and placed it and *Tempest* against the wall before walking over to stand in front of me.

We nodded in acknowledgment of one another and drew our swords together, mine ringing softly as I pulled it out of its sheath.

We waited for the space of three breaths and then charged.

Ember sliced down at her and she blocked, our swords clashing with a shriek of metal on metal.

Her sword reached for me and I dodged, spinning away at the last second.

I knocked her off balance with that move, but she recovered before I could use it to my advantage.

We dodged, ducked, and parried as we fought to gain the upper hand, trading moves back and forth for several minutes before I saw a hole in her defences.

I sent *Ember* under her arm and poked her in the ribs.

"Ow!" she gasped, jumping back.

"I win," I said with a grin, "and you are now dead."

She sighed and sheathed her sword. "I only lost because you are a master."

I nodded. It was true. From the moment I first picked up a sword, it was clear that was my destiny.

Every challenger fell before me. Even Asmund, trained in soldiering as he was, had never beaten me in a duel, though our blades had crossed several times over the years. It was one of his greatest annoyances and I took great pride in it.

"I could beat someone else," Sky went on. "I have before. Besides, in a real battle, I'd have an arrow through your throat before you could even raise *Ember*."

She walked over to her discarded bow and quiver then, picking up *Tempest* and grabbing a single arrow before heading over to the far side of the courtyard.

I trailed after her and we stopped directly across from the wooden targets.

In moments, she had the bow nocked and drawn, and with an exhale of breath, she loosed the arrow. It flew one hundred paces across the courtyard and hit the target dead centre.

She followed it up with two others in quick succession before relaxing her stance and holding *Tempest* out to me. "Your turn, little brother."

I refused her offer and crossed my arms instead. "We both know I was born first."

She frowned. "Were you?"

"Of course I was," I retorted. "Why else would I be the Crown Prince? In answer to your challenge, no thank you. I'll keep to the sword, wouldn't want to steal your glory."

"Steal my glory?" she scoffed. "We both know I'm the best archer in Widonia."

I raised an eyebrow. "*Are you?*"

She shook her head. "You're so…"

"What?"

"Nothing," she said, but I could tell she was trying hard to hide a smile. "Let's not argue. There was enough of that this morning at the Council." She headed over to the targets to retrieve her arrows and I fell into step beside her.

"What do you think of it all?"

"It's a foolish move," she replied. "Uncle is acting before he thinks. The others could sense it, but they don't carry enough weight to stop him."

"So, you don't want us to go to war?"

She turned back to look at me. "Does anyone ever want to go to war, Isan? It's a dirty and dangerous business. We may not be at peace with Winter, but Summer is quiet, thriving. That will change when the war starts. It will take decades to restore our way of life. I'm not certain I am ready to give that up."

"It doesn't matter if you are," I replied. "Uncle isn't going to back out now and risk being called a coward. He is too proud to admit his mistakes, even if the entire realm can see them."

"I suppose you are right." She leaned over and yanked her arrow out of the threadbare target. Sky had overworked it in the month since it had been set up, as she always did.

"The war is inevitable," I told her, "and I have decided I am not going to stand idly by while everyone else fights in it. I was hoping you'd feel the same."

She dropped the arrow. "Have you lost your mind?"

"We have to fight, Sky."

"No, we have to think this through." She fixed me in her earthen gaze. Always so steady and so…stubborn.

"I have," I protested. "I *have* thought about it and I can't live like this anymore. Uncle tells us our every move. People treat me like I'm stupid and you like you're nothing more than a prize to be won. We're forbidden from leaving Widonia, even. This city is more of a prison than a home."

I took a deep breath.

"We have to fight back, Sky. We have to show Asmund and the others our worth. What better way to win our freedom than fighting for our people? Isn't this the reason we've been training? Why spend our days practising the bow and sword if we refuse to use our skills to fight for what we believe in? What's our purpose, Sky, if not that?" I threw my hands out.

"It's not that simple, Isan," she insisted. "Uncle would never allow it. The entire royal family cannot fight. What happens if we all perish? Summer would be in chaos without a ruler. Are you prepared to wed and leave a pregnant wife behind to ensure the future of Summer? Because that might be the price."

I winced. "Sky, I don't think—"

"Exactly," she replied, crossing her arms.

"We have to at least try. This could be our only chance to…" I stopped myself before I could reveal the real reason I wanted to go.

She narrowed her eyes. "Our only chance to what?"

"Nothing," I said with immediate regret.

"Nothing?" she repeated. "It has to be something. What were you going to say?"

"Let it go, Sky."

"I don't think I will. Tell me or I'll start rumours that you're ready to pick your future Queen." Her brown eyes were as fierce and unforgiving as a mighty oak tree, refusing to break under the pressure of a passing wind.

I scowled at her, my blue eyes like steel. "Fine," I relented. "This could be our only chance to avenge our parents."

"Oh, Isan," she sighed. "Not this again. I've told you a hundred times; let it go."

"But I can't," I exclaimed, throwing my arms out in exasperation. "I've tried. I swear I've tried, but it's useless. The anger is like a fire burning me alive. I might explode if I continue to sit here and let their killer run free. I have to do something, especially now that my suspicions have been confirmed. The Winter King had our parents killed, Sky. Does that mean nothing to you?" My eyes burned into hers, but she didn't flinch.

"Isan, making him 'pay' isn't going to bring our parents back. Nothing good comes from revenge; it only leads to more death."

"He *deserves* to die."

She put a hand on my shoulder and squeezed. "I know what you're going through, Isan. I understand the hatred, the pain. Some days I want nothing more than to march into Winter and bring them to their knees for what they stole from me, but deep down I know it will change nothing. It will help nothing. We have to move on. By killing them, we are only sinking to their level. We have to stay strong."

I shook off her hand and stepped back. "By letting them win? I will not stand by and watch that unfold."

"Isan, stop this," she pleaded. "You're letting anger cloud your judgment."

"And you're letting cowardice cloud yours," I snapped.

She reeled back as if I'd slapped her and I instantly regretted my words. A physical blow might have hurt us less.

For a moment, neither of us spoke and it was difficult to face each other again, but we did. Her eyes were full of sadness.

"Isan," she said softly.

"Yes?"

"Please don't do this."

I looked at my feet again and she sucked in a breath.

"I have to do this, Sky," I told her. "I won't rest until I have my vengeance."

"So be it," she replied. "I will see you at dinner."

I looked up in time to see her walking away, her steps rushed, *Tempest* clenched tightly in her hand. Her arrow still lay at my feet.

I watched her go in silence. I didn't call her back or try to stop her, knowing it was futile. Neither one of us would change our minds, not easily anyway. It hurt to see her walk away, but I knew she hadn't abandoned me, not completely. Our bond was much stronger than that, but even still, the peace between us had shattered, like a vase struck by one of her arrows.

3
Feast or Famine

That evening, my feet were heavy as I headed down the stairs to the great hall. I had debated skipping dinner entirely. It was already bound to be painful with Asmund and the others, but with Sky and I not talking, it would be a nightmare. The only thing that convinced me to go was the thought of how Uncle would react to my absence. Staying in my rooms for dinner while we had guests would put me far from his good graces.

Even with my slow steps, I arrived early. Asmund and Sky were already in attendance. Sky was back in her emerald gown, tiara nestled in her braided hair again. I had changed into one of my nicer jackets and clean boots, but that was it.

Sky studied the plate in front of her as I walked in, but Asmund waved his hand in greeting, much more than I expected from either of them, if I was being honest.

The great hall had been decorated in honour of our guests, more attention than it had seen in months. Fresh flowers sat in bright pots around the perimeter and in vases on the table. The floor had been polished, and the wooden table and chairs shone. Seven places had been laid out and it was odd to see so much cutlery. The table regularly sat two dozen in my parents' time, but now it was more for daily family use than hosting parties.

I frowned at all the finery. So much for it being a day of mourning.

Though I enjoyed a little change of pace, it seemed wrong somehow to dismiss the past, as if the arrival of the Arraths was more important than honouring my late parents.

The vacant seat at the head of the table was Uncle's. I sat down on his right, across the table from Sky and beside Asmund, unfortunately. I frowned at the white tablecloth, certain I would spill something on it before the meal was through.

"It is good to be in Widonia again," Asmund said to nobody in particular. "I have missed it."

"It can't be that different from Skar," I replied, slouching back in my chair.

"Ah, but it is. It's livelier, kinder, more bright and colourful. Skar is dull. Nothing grows outside the city. It's no wonder we became known for our military. There's not much else we could offer Summer."

"Widonia too has its faults." Not that I had been out much to see them.

"Oh?" Asmund said. "Like what?"

I was saved from answering by the arrival of Arran and Aramina.

Aramina waltzed into the room, her bright green dress flashing in the light of the torches and candelabras. Her black hair was braided down her back, all the way to her waist, and tied with a gold ribbon. She flashed the three of us a wide smile, her eyes sparkling with mischief.

"Isanfier, Skiansy," she exclaimed. "It's been forever."

Arran shuffled in behind her, dressed in soldier garb, though the uniform was immaculate. He had one braid in his shoulder-length hair compared to Asmund's dozens.

"Arran, Aramina," I replied. "Good of you to join us."

"Yes," Sky said, speaking finally. "How was your journey?"

"Long," Arran replied.

"Exhilarating," Aramina added. "The open road is marvellous. So much to see." Her heart had always been full of adventure. It's why I didn't see her as ever becoming Lady of Skar or Queen of Summer at my side. She was too free-spirited to be tied down.

"I can only imagine," Sky said, a tinge of jealousy in her tone.

"Oh, you would love it out there, Sky," Aramina replied, lighting down in the chair beside her. "It's so open. Nothing but grass and wildflowers for miles. The roads are quite dusty this time of year, but I rode my horse beside them. You should come visit Skar someday!"

Sky smiled at her.

Asmund snorted. "I doubt the princess would want to leave this place for our dusty town, Mina."

Her face fell. "Right, of course."

"Nonsense," Sky said, glaring sidelong at Asmund. "It would be lovely. I'm just not sure when I could find the time, especially now with the war and—"

Arran looked sharply at Asmund. "War?" He had not yet taken a seat, but hovered behind Sky and Aramina's chairs. He walked around them now to properly face his brother. "You mentioned nothing of that."

Asmund looked oddly chastised by his younger brother. "I was waiting for the right time."

"The King invited you to his Council, talked about a war, and you entertained us after with meaningless details?"

Asmund scowled. "Arran, please. You're making a scene."

Arran was indeed gripping the back of his chair with an unparalleled intensity. He took a deep breath before unclenching his fists and taking a seat. "I will not forget this," he told Asmund.

"I'm sure he did not mean to anger you, Arran," Aramina said.

"Don't side with him, Mina," Arran shot back.

A long awkward silence filled the room. I'd never seen the three of them quarrel, not even when we were all wayward children. Arran had never spoken this much before either. A lot had happened since we'd last seen each other. Maybe their mother's death had done more damage than Asmund had let on. They may have seen it coming, but I doubted knowing beforehand made it hurt any less.

"Why if it isn't Arrath's three little soldiers," a new voice exclaimed.

I turned to see Aunt Mag entering the room and smiled, some of the burdens falling off my shoulders.

"Governess Magnolia," Asmund said as he saw her too. "It's so good to see you." He stood up and pulled out the chair beside him.

I scrunched my nose up at the use of her official title. It always sounded so cold and distant. Aunt Mag had raised Sky and I as her own after our parents' deaths, far exceeding the bounds of her duty as governess. She had become our mother in all ways but blood. In truth, she was our great aunt, the younger sister of Summer's late Queen Meadow.

"How have the three of you been?" Aunt Mag asked the Arraths as she sat down, straightening her plain dress and pulling her two braids over her shoulder. Streaks of gray were beginning to show amongst the ebony. "I was so sorry to hear about your mother."

Aramina and Arran hung their heads.

"We're doing as well as to be expected," Asmund replied. "Our father encourages us to focus on our lessons."

Aunt Mag nodded. "Distraction can do us good, but don't forget to let yourself mourn as well, else your emotions fester and create a larger wound. The goal is to heal, Master Asmund, not forget."

Asmund looked affronted, but Aunt Mag was right, as usual. She had learned quite a bit in her near-eight decades of life and people rarely argued with her. I wondered what she would have to say about the war. I opened my mouth to ask her when Uncle decided to grace us with his presence.

He strode into the room with his golden, ceremonial cape dragging behind him, his black boots clicking along the marble floor. His braids rivaled even Asmund's, though they were more of a dark brown than black. A long scar ran up the front of his face, narrowly missing his left eye, but he didn't look any less like a king for it.

Asmund, Arran, and Aramina stood as he entered and bowed deeply.

"Your Majesty," they said in unison. "We are humbled by your presence." It was the standard greeting given to a person above your station, though I doubted Asmund was ever humbled by anything.

"Please, have a seat," Uncle said, waiting for them before he did the same. "I am glad to have you here, even in such troublesome times." He picked up his fork and tapped it against the stem of his glass, signalling the kitchen staff to bring out the first course of our meal. "I trust Asmund has told you about the war."

Arran quaked in his seat but kept his voice even as he said, "Not as much as we would have liked, your Majesty."

I glanced at Aunt Mag, hoping to catch her reaction, but her weathered face was as calm as ever.

"Oh?" Uncle said. "That is a shame. It would have been better to hear it from someone familiar, I would think." He glanced at Asmund, disapproval clear in his gaze.

What are you doing, Asmund? Continue on this path and Arran will be chosen as your father's successor.

Arran of all people. Arran who used to follow Asmund around like a puppy and who didn't speak a word until he was six years old. Arran who seemed to have finally grown up.

Uncle explained our situation as the first course of dinner was brought in. He paused to say a quick prayer to Sancia and then continued on as the rest of us started eating.

"Planning will, of course, be crucial," Uncle was saying, "especially if we forfeit the element of surprise by sending the message back with the would-be assassins."

"It will still come as a surprise," Arran replied. "They will simply have time to prepare, though not as much as we will."

"That is true," Uncle said.

"Who will be fighting?" Aramina asked.

"All able-bodied men, of course," Uncle replied. "I won't force people to fight, but there will be some strong encouragement. Promises of a better future, rewards for those who do join. It will not be an easy task, especially for Fortude and Ne-Trol. They haven't seen the cruel work of Winter firsthand."

"Ah, but the mountain men hate Winter anyway," Asmund said, "always have."

"Will they fight, though?" Arran asked him.

"They will if I royally decree the existence of their elusive, yet somehow lethal, mountain trolls," Uncle replied.

He and the others burst into laughter.

No one believed the stories of the trolls living deep in the Summer mountains. No one outside of Ne-Trol had ever seen one and no one from Ne-Trol had ever been able to provide solid evidence of the creatures. The mountain men were considered paranoid and superstitious, but they were also incredible warriors. Working in the mines for most of their lives had given them strength the rest of us could never imagine.

"Ah, but I digress," Uncle said. "Your father is well?"

"Quite well," Asmund replied between sips of red wine. "He was reluctant to send the three of us, but I think the time alone will do him some good."

Uncle nodded. "Yes, time alone can be important. I am still incredibly sorry to have missed Lady Violette's service."

Asmund and the others nodded.

"Loss is hard on everyone, each in our own way. Losing a mother is difficult indeed. I have no doubt she passed on to the stars, though, and you will see her again someday."

Asmund forced a smile and so did I. Uncle had condemned the woman only this morning. He was lying through his teeth, but such was politics.

I hated it.

"As I'm sure you're aware, today is an especially difficult day for our family," Uncle went on. "Today marks the twelfth anniversary of the murders of our late king and queen, my sister and her husband."

"Our deepest condolences," Arran said.

"I will ask Sancia to send you peace," Aramina added.

I smiled at that.

"I would like to say a prayer now, if none of you are opposed," Uncle said.

"That would be lovely, your Majesty," Aramina replied.

Uncle bowed his head and closed his eyes. The others followed suit.

I kept my eyes wide open, wondering if the goddesses ever actually listened to our pleas. Did my parents beg to be spared? Did Sancia forsake them?

"Blessed Sancia," Uncle said, "may you watch over the people of this land as you have for centuries. May you lend us grace and dignity as we head into this unknown war. May you give peace to those who have gone before us and to those we may lose along the way. Make our hearts strong and our wills even stronger. Sancia forever, blessed are we."

"Blessed are we," the others echoed.

I stayed silent.

"The winds of change are coming," Uncle finished. "We will not be torn asunder; we will sway with them, but we will not break." He raised his glass. "To Summer!"

Arran, Aramina, and I were quick to follow suit, both Sky and Asmund hesitating a moment before joining us.

Aunt Mag left her glass untouched.

"To Summer," we echoed.

Now that was a sentiment I could agree with.

The rest of dinner passed in silence, broken up by small, jovial conversations. We ate three courses and dessert, Uncle and Aunt Mag bidding us all goodnight before the sweets were brought out. Asmund was quick to leave once Uncle was gone and Sky only ate one small piece of pie before retiring as well. She said goodbye to Arran and Aramina, but didn't even spare a glance at me.

Arran, Aramina, and I left the great hall together, leaving the servants to clean up the remnants of our meal. All in all, it had been a quiet affair, nothing like the feasts of the past. Being from a military background, I doubted the Arrath children cared.

If we'd been hosting Lord Byron's children or Lachlan's, it would have been a different story altogether. There would've been half a dozen courses, and music and dancing afterwards. I was always so tired when either of them came to call. Keeping up appearances was exhausting. Asmund might have been a pain, but at least I could be somewhat honest with him.

In the hall, Arran turned to me and bowed his head. "It was a pleasure dining with you, your Highness. I apologize for the altercation between Asmund and I."

I waved a hand. "Oh please, Arran, you don't have to walk on eggshells around me. My name is Isan and I know all too well how much of a pain your brother is."

Aramina laughed and Arran looked sheepish.

He rubbed the back of his neck. "Sorry, Isan, I don't mean to be..."

"Pompous?" I offered.

He frowned. "I suppose. Father has been...hard on me lately. Says I have neglected my studies too much."

"He thinks he's too quiet," Aramina added.

"Yes, that," Arran said.

"I happen to like quiet Arran," I replied, "though I did enjoy watching you stand up to Asmund earlier. The look on his face made my entire day." I grinned at Arran and he managed a smile in return.

"Glad to be of service," he said. He looked to Aramina. "We should go now."

"I'll be along in a moment," Aramina said. "I want to ask Isan something first."

Arran frowned. "Asmund would not like me leaving the two of you alone."

I rolled my eyes.

"Oh for Sancia's sake, Arran," she snapped. "It'll only be a moment."

"But a young lady such as yourself should not —"

I held up a hand. "Leave her be. I give you my word I will not touch her. I swear on my parents' graves and Sancia herself. Aramina is safe with me."

Arran looked me in the eyes, searching for the lie.

He would find none. Aramina did not interest me romantically. I saw her as more of a little sister than anything else.

"Very well," Arran said, "but only a moment. I will wait outside our rooms for you, so Asmund doesn't lose his wits."

Aramina squeezed his hand. "Thank you."

He shook his head. "I may live to regret it, but you're welcome." He walked off, leaving me alone with Aramina and the mysterious question she had for me.

"So," I said, "what's on your mind, Mina?"

Her eyes met my own and they seemed sad. "Does it get easier?"

I frowned. "Does what get easier?"

"Your parents have been gone for twelve years," she replied. "Does it get easier to go through your days? Does their absence ever stop hurting?"

Oh.

She carried herself with such grace it was easy to forget how much younger she was. Her mother's death would have hit her hard and I'm sure it severed the link to her childhood as well.

"I... I'm not going to lie to you to make you feel better, okay?" I said.

She nodded, wiping at her eyes.

"It still hurts," I told her. "It doesn't hurt as much, mind you, not every day at least, but it still hurts. I think the pain is there so you never forget them. Some days, it's like it never happened. Grief is a long process, Mina, but it will get better."

"Thank you," she said. "Sometimes..." She sighed. "My brothers don't like to talk about it. Sometimes, I feel like I'm alone, that I'm crazy for feeling this way, for continuing to feel this way."

"You're not crazy," I assured her. "People just don't like to see grief because it reminds them of their own. They think it's easier to ignore it, but like Governess Magnolia said earlier, bottling up your pain is a recipe for disaster."

"I think you're right," she replied. "Well, I should go. I wouldn't want to keep Arran waiting."

I laughed. "Not if you want to be allowed out of his sight again."

She smiled. "Oh, I sneak away a lot more than either of them realize."

I didn't doubt it.

She waved goodbye and then disappeared down the hall after her brother.

I wondered if they'd always been this hard on her, if it was their way of showing they cared. I wondered if I ever came across that way to Sky without realizing it. Maybe I'd been too harsh earlier, maybe that was why she'd reacted the way she did.

I still felt awful about our fight, especially considering her silent treatment during dinner, but I didn't know what to do to make it better. I couldn't take back what I'd said. I made a promise to my parents a long time ago. I'd vowed to do whatever it took to avenge them. I could no more break that vow than I could forsake Sky. I trusted her more than anyone else in this realm and the thought that I had broken *her* infallible trust made me sick.

Standing alone outside the great hall, I realized Aunt Mag was the only person left to talk to. She had been rather quiet at dinner, but I think she had been processing everything herself. Even still, she would have some solution regarding Sky; she always did. It was like she could see the threads tying the two of us together better than we could.

Her room was down the hall from my own and it didn't take long to reach it. I knocked once on the wooden door.

"Who is it?" her voice rang out.

"It's Isan," I replied.

"Oh, come in, child," she said.

I entered with a smile, shutting the door behind me. The room was a fair size, but sparsely furnished, the way Aunt Mag liked it. A wardrobe stood in one corner, a chest in another. Pressed up against one wall was a bookcase and on the opposite wall, the bed.

Aunt Mag sat on the bed, her long hair unbraided for the night, falling down her back in a continuous wave. She would've been a sight to behold in her youth, but her beauty still shone through her wrinkles.

I dragged her chest in front of the bed and sat down. "I'm glad dinner is finally over. Uncle really misses entertaining, doesn't he?"

"I suppose we all do," Aunt Mag replied. "Why, entertaining was once an integral role of a royal. Your father was more trained in table manners than he was in arithmetic."

I smiled at that. "It wouldn't have been so bad if Asmund had gotten himself lost on the way there."

Aunt Mag forced down a smile. "Now Isan…"

"What? You know he's despicable."

She gave me a look. "I know *you* have a habit of exaggerating, and that you're trying to lead the conversation away from what actually brought you here."

I frowned. "What?"

"Don't give me that," she chided. "I can always tell when something is wrong with the two of you. Tell me what's troubling you, child. You know that's what I'm here for."

I sighed. "I made a mistake, Aunt Mag."

"What happened?" She reached for my hand and gave it a squeeze.

I took a deep breath and told her everything that had happened during the day, albeit a shortened version. It was great to get it off my chest, to be rid of the burden that had been weighing me down.

For a moment after, Aunt Mag said nothing, but she looked to be deep in thought.

"Your Uncle was wrong to lie about Oaden and Areevia's death," she said finally. "The truth was bound to escape eventually. It's a miracle he kept it for so long, but he is a stubborn man. He does not bend easily."

I glanced up at her. "Did you know?"

She shook her head. "I could not know for certain, but I had my suspicions. I'm not sure if I ever told you this, but my sister was murdered by a Winter prince, long before she and her husband ever took the Summer throne. She died as a Princess Consort."

I raised an eyebrow. "She was never Queen? But all the history books—"

Aung Mag gave me a look. "History belongs to those who write it, but I know Meadow was murdered by a Winter prince because I found the body and the note."

My heart sank into my stomach at the thought. I couldn't imagine what I would be like now if I'd found my parents. Aunt Mag held so much grief in her small body and never once showed it. She was strong, much stronger than me.

She took a deep breath, as if to calm herself, and said, "So I agree with your plight, child. You have the right to fight back, the right to be angry with the people who killed your parents, but don't let that rage consume you. It is one thing to regret not doing enough; it is quite another to regret going too far."

I swallowed hard at her words, trying to digest them. I didn't want to lose myself either.

"As for Sky," she went on, fixing me in her sage, motherly gaze, "you needn't worry about her, Isan. She'll come around. I've watched the two of you grow up. As children, you hardly fought, but when you did, the matter solved itself before the day was through. You didn't like staying mad at each other and you always forgave. The two of you will be fine."

I pulled at the hem of my shirt. "You think so?"

"I know so," she said with a smile.

I stood up and gave her a hug. "Thank you, Aunt Mag. You always know what to say."

"You're welcome, child," she replied as she hugged me back. "Sometimes all one needs is to share their troubles with someone else. They don't so much need a solution as they need support."

"I suppose you're right."

I dragged her chest back to its spot in the corner and headed for the door.

"Now Isan," Aunt Mag called after me, "remember to not push her. Skiansy is stubborn and doesn't work well under pressure. Let her come to forgive you on her own and have faith that she will. Try to sleep well tonight too. Things will look better in the morning."

I nodded and bid her goodnight.

I left her chambers and headed down the silent halls towards my own. Torchlight flickered against the stone walls and a cool breeze swept in through the open windows. Fatigue pulled at me, a sudden and strange exhaustion dragging my steps.

When I entered my room, I pulled off my boots and flopped onto the bed, fully clothed. I thought vaguely that I should probably undress, but I dropped off before I could follow through with it.

That was the first night I had the dream.

4
Poison

Frost

The stone at Frost's back dug into his coat, but he suppressed the urge to stretch. It was his duty as King to never appear uncomfortable—at least, that was what his many childhood tutors had tried to teach him, back when he was an unruly, neglected child. In truth, the mild pain of the moment was the only thing keeping him awake, and the only thing keeping him from killing the man in front of him, if only so their one-sided conversation could end.

Lord Humphrey of Ollyn had spent the last half an hour detailing his qualms, but King Frost had no sympathy for him. He thought it was pathetic to have to ask for help. A man who could not take care of his own city was not worth Frost's time. His fingers itched to freeze the man where he stood, but Frost knew such a swift end would not satisfy his anger.

He counted the candles in the chandelier high above him—an old habit formed to quell his impatience—until Lord Humphrey finally quieted.

"Your Majesty?" the man asked after a moment. Frost remembered him as a portly fellow, but he seemed thinner than when they had last met. Indeed, his cobalt robe hung loosely about his frame, as if belonging to another man.

King Frost finally shifted in his throne, leaning closer to Lord Humphrey as he said, "Are we finished?"

"Yes," Lord Humphrey replied. "I believe I have said my piece."

"Then you may go," Frost told him, giving him a little wave as relief washed through his veins. His last meeting of the day was finished and there was no blood to clean off the floor.

Lord Humphrey regarded him with uncertain eyes and stayed where he was. "Will you send more food to Ollyn?" he asked.

Frost bit back his usual malicious smile, but excitement danced in his nerves at Humphrey's condemning question. Finally, he could have some fun. A long meeting was only worth whatever entertainment he received in return.

Frost met Humphrey's eyes with his own and simply told him no.

Shock and anger clouded the other man's expression. "*No?* What are we supposed to eat?"

"I haven't the slightest idea," Frost said, leaning back in his seat, "nor do I particularly care. It's your city, Lord Humphrey. You should take better care of it."

"But you're the King," he protested, "and it's not our fault you give us nothing. Our stores are running dry!"

"Well, you should've rationed it better then, shouldn't you have?"

"Rationed..." Humphrey clenched his fists. "We *did* ration it, but it's hardly enough to feed a family well for three months, let alone a year!"

Frost bristled at his tone, his hair standing on end. "Be gone! I will hear no more of this."

Lord Humphrey fell to his knees before him, desperation evident in his wild blue eyes. "Your Majesty, I beg of you! The people are *starving*. We had an entire family drop dead last week. The youngest was a month old. I myself skipped a few meals to help them, but it was not enough."

Disgust coiled in Frost's stomach at the words. No doubt Lord Humphrey thought his sacrifice was noble, but bleeding hearts had no place in the palace, unless caused by a knife to the chest.

"Well," Frost replied, his even tone still managing to ring through, "that's one less family to feed, isn't it?" The weak always succumbed so the strong could survive. It was the way things were meant to be.

Lord Humphrey paled at Frost's words and his eyes glazed over the moment he realized the King wasn't giving in, the moment he realized the King would *never* give in.

"You..." he spluttered, a few tears trickling down his pale face. "You *monster*," he spat. "You coward!" He picked himself up off the floor and pointed in the direction of the city. "There are people out there dying! *Dying* and you just sit there. Where is your heart?"

Frost stood up and stepped toward him until he was mere inches away. He showed absolutely no fear in the face of Lord Humphrey's searching eyes as he said, "I am the King of Winter; Winter blood, Winter to my bones. I *have* no heart. Now go, before I lose my patience."

Lord Humphrey yelled and lunged for the King, but the throne room guards were on him in seconds.

Frost waved a hand towards them as he returned to his throne. "Take him away."

"We'll personally escort him out of the gates, your Majesty," the guards said, bowing low even with the prisoner in their grasp.

"No, take him to the dungeon," Frost replied. "He needs to learn what *real* starvation looks like."

There was a strangled whimper from the former Lord of Ollyn.

"Yes, your Majesty," the guard replied. They bowed again and dragged the man out.

"Messenger!" Frost called out.

A short man in long, blue robes hurried to the King's side from his post near the doors, the fabric dragging across the icy floor behind him. "Yes, your Majesty?"

"Send a letter to Ollyn," Frost told him. "Congratulate Odette on becoming its new Lady. Tell her she better have more of a backbone than her father or she will soon join him."

•   •   •

That evening, King Frost found himself alone in the dining room. He stood behind his chair at the head of the table, leaning against it and twirling a knife in his hand as a slow anger built up inside him. He did *not* like to be kept waiting. His anger had reached a dangerous level by the time his children strolled in, ten minutes past the hour.

"You're late," Frost snapped.

Snowdon winced at his father's tone and hung his head, already giving up. It was pitiful. The boy was a disgrace to the family.

Icaria, on the other hand, fixed her father with a cold, hard glare.

Frost smiled, rising to the challenge and glared back, throwing all his anger of the day into it.

She had no chance against him and dropped her eyes a minute later, but at least she had done something. That's more than Frost could ever say for the boy.

"Where is your cousin?" Frost asked them.

"She's indisposed at the moment," Icaria replied.

"That's why we were late," Snowdon added.

"Does Clarice not have a timepiece in her chambers?"

The two glanced at each other, but could not come up with a suitable answer.

"I see," Frost replied. "Is she, perhaps, on her deathbed?"

"Well, no," Icaria replied.

"Then you have no reasonable excuse for your lateness."

"No, Father," they said.

"If Clarice is strong enough, she will recover, but the two of you must stay focused. You cannot allow emotional ties to get in your way. This world will test you and if you are bothered by the slightest wind, you will break." Frost pulled out his chair and sat down. "Sit, but I shall not forget this infraction and you *will* be punished."

They nodded, Icaria with a touch of anger behind the movement but Snowdon without any emotion at all.

Frost slammed the dagger into the table; Snowdon jumped.

"For Wylla's sake, boy, fight back! Don't just stand there."

"But you said—"

"I know what I said, boy, but I will not have you acting as if you are defeated before the battle has even truly begun. I will not have you tarnishing our family's reputation with meekness. Hold your head high and take advantage of everything. You're royalty, act like it."

He nodded. "Yes, sir."

"Good, see to it that you do."

Frost's voice hinted at an *or else*, but he didn't elaborate on it. Let the boy sweat a bit. A small piece of fear never hurt anyone. In fact, Frost was under the opinion that it made a person stronger. Weak in the moment, but stronger later when they overcame the fear and pushed back.

Good was the battle where one won without a scratch, but what did it prove? That they were fast and skilled, sure, but winning a battle after being bloodied and broken, that showed true strength, and Frost valued strength above all else.

The King gestured to the vacant seats by his side and his children finally joined him at the table. Then their food was brought out: five courses each exquisitely prepared and set out one by one.

Once the servants had placed the dishes on the table, Frost told them to bring the girl. They nodded and bowed deeply before disappearing back into the dark recesses of the kitchen.

It seemed like forever before they returned, dragging the food taster behind them. She was shackled at the wrists and ankles, dried blood painting them light crimson, and a dirty, ragged dress hung off her thin frame, accentuating how little she weighed, how little fat or muscle was left on her bones.

Her white hair was cut straight along her pronounced jaw and her eyes were a lightless blue that held no life. They told a tale of a girl who had given up, who had stopped fighting, but she had never begun.

The first day they'd brought her out, she had said nothing. She had not argued and had not refused. Frost was still unsure if she could even speak. She had given up even then. She was pathetic. She had tasted every dish, twice even if he asked, without complaint. She didn't tremble when she took the first spoonful, didn't stare at the King with wide, terrified eyes, like all the tasters who had come before her.

This girl had shown no signs of fear at all, but it wasn't fear that made a person a coward, it was lack of will to fight the fear or, in this girl's case, a lack of any will at all. She was the epitome of cowardice, a poison in Frost's own domain. The only reason she was still alive was because she was useful and he found her job ironic, amusing. How fitting for a poison to be tasked with sniffing out its own kind?

Yet, her time was up. This meal would be her last.

The servants unlocked the girl's wrists and she uncurled from her huddled heap and stood, staring at the royal family with those vacant eyes. She shuffled over to the table, taking care not to clank her ankle chains against the floor. Frost had remarked on the first day how much the sound annoyed him and she hadn't done it again. Now the *lack* of the noise annoyed him. It heightened her cowardice, her unfailing obedience.

She walked around the table as quickly as she could manage, tasting each dish with the spoon that lay beside it and placing the spoon back on the table. One servant followed behind her, picking up the discarded spoons and replacing them with new ones.

Frost watched Icaria shiver as the girl passed her. After all these years, the girl still repulsed her.

He remembered the reaction Icaria had the first day—the refusal, the tantrum, and finally the question. Why did she and Snowdon have to be there when the tasting was done?

Frost had explained to them that it was a lesson, that the girl was an example of cowardice and she served as a reminder to them, a reminder of what happened when one let fear rule them or refused to fight back.

Icaria had not complained again, but the girl still disgusted her, still made her uncomfortable. As well she should.

The girl *was* something to be afraid of; *cowardice* was something to be afraid of. Every day in this room was a test. Every day when the royal family saw the girl and feared they would one day end up like her, they fought a battle. When they looked straight at the girl and vowed to never end up like her, they won, but every day the battle began anew. It was an endless cycle; fear chasing down discipline, which in turn chased down fear. The battle, for the girl at least, would come to an end that day.

When she had finished, she turned to the King for dismissal.

Frost said nothing to her, only signaled for the servants to re-chain her wrists. They obeyed and then he dismissed them.

The girl stood alone with Frost and his children. He saw the first faint flicker of fear in her eyes, but it was gone in an instant.

Still, Frost smiled.

The final battle had begun.

A second later, the girl clutched her stomach. Then she dropped to her knees, curling in on herself for a moment before rearing up to look at Frost. Fear danced in her eyes and it was sweet.

"Help me," she gasped, her voice hoarse from years of disuse. She was screaming in pain before the King could deign to answer her, writhing on the ground as the poison ran its course.

Several times, she tried to drag herself to her feet, but it was much too late to run, to fight.

Icaria and Snowdon watched it all in silence, looks of horror plastered on their faces. No doubt they thought someone was trying to kill them all.

Finally, the girl quieted and grew still, her battle coming to a close.

Frost called out to the guards beyond the dining room door and told them to dispose of the body discreetly. They did as they were told without question and once they were gone, the King faced his children again.

"Don't eat the turnip," he said, and then he dug into his meal.

Icaria, always the curious one, picked up the bowl and smelled it. "Nightstalk?" she asked.

Frost nodded.

"Is this some sort of…?"

"Test?" he finished for her. "No. Lesson? Yes."

She raised a white eyebrow. "And what might that lesson be?"

"It doesn't matter how much discipline you have to fight the fear if the battle is already lost. Will only matters while your heart still beats. So always fight back. You never know when the next great battle might be coming, a battle of life or death." Frost gestured to the bowl Icaria still held.

Poison, the perfect end to cowardice, a poison all its own.

5
Dreams and Denial

I woke up alone in an unfamiliar, torch-lit corridor. The walls were made of stone, but there were no doors set within them, at least not that I could see. The only thing that stood out to me was the window at the end of the hall. The sky outside was dark.

I decided to walk in that direction, hoping the window would be able to shed light on my whereabouts, but I had only taken a few steps when a cold wind gusted down the hall. It blew out the torches and threw the space into darkness.

I let out a squeak of fear as the hair rose on my arms.

It's only a little bit of wind, I told myself. *You're fine.*

Moonlight streamed in through the open window, pushing some of the shadows away, and I calmed down as soon as my eyes adjusted. I continued inching forward, keeping my gaze on the window, until it disappeared.

No, something is blocking it.

Wait, not something, someone.

A cloaked figure had entered the hall through the window and stood in front of it, blocking out what light remained. After a short pause, the figure began moving towards me. I pressed my back against the wall, willing myself to melt into the shadows, praying he hadn't seen me.

Apparently, Sancia was listening, because the dark figure strode past me without a glance. I waited until he was out of earshot before breathing a sigh of relief. Part of me wanted to pursue him, but I couldn't ask him what he was doing there when I didn't even know where I was.

I continued down the corridor through the almost-dark and finally reached the window. The night beyond was silent, a warmth hanging in the air. I was in a castle with a city nestled around it. Something about the layout of the streets looked familiar, but I couldn't say what until I saw the Summer Crest on a flag below.

I was in the Royal Castle and the city was Widonia, but where exactly in the castle was I? It had to be one of the abandoned wings if I didn't recognize it, but then, what purpose did the dark figure have?

What was he doing sneaking into the castle at this hour of the night? Who was he?

Before I could answer my questions, the world tilted, and the darkness caved in around me.

• • •

Sky was standing over me when I woke and I jumped at her presence, nearly smacking her in the face with my arm as I moved out of the way.

"What in Fidalia are you doing?" I gasped.

Sky froze at the sound of my voice. "Oh thank Fidal... You're awake. I thought... I thought maybe..." She let out a shaky breath.

I pulled myself into a sitting position. "What? What did you think? What's wrong?"

"You were sleeping like the dead, Isan," she breathed, her voice quavering. "It scared me terribly." She looked frazzled, fear shining in her eyes and sweat glistening on her brow.

"What do you mean?" I said.

She took a deep breath. "You missed breakfast, so I came to check on you. Thank Fidal that I did. You were hardly breathing, Isan, and I... I kept shaking you, but you didn't stir and your heart... I put my hand to your chest, but could barely feel it beating. I thought you were dying. I was afraid I was alone, that I would lose you like Mother and Father." Her voice broke on the final word and I looked up to see her crying.

I reached over and pulled her into a hug, letting her sob into my shoulder.

"It's okay," I told her. "I'm okay. Everything's going to be okay." I hated lying to her, but she needed reassurance, almost as much as I did.

It's not every day you fall asleep as soon as your head hits the pillow, have a dream that feels so real, and then wake up to have your sister tell you she thought you were dead. Something wasn't right about it at all and I was quite shaken by the whole ordeal.

Images from the dream flashed through my mind: the eerie glow of the torchlight, the light of the moon, and the black-clad man creeping down the hall.

A shiver passed through my body.

Sky pulled away from the hug then, bringing me back to reality. Her eyes were red now, but she smiled at me and I knew she was okay again.

"You're right, Isan," she said. "I'm overreacting. It's just..." She shook her head. "You know what, never mind. We'll talk about this later; we're going to be late."

"Late?" I asked. "Late for what?"

"The gathering, of course," she replied. "Don't you remember?"

She sounded panicked again, so I racked my brain for some recollection of her words. I found it unusual that I couldn't remember anything from the day before—I had a remarkable memory—but after a moment of concentration, the events in question came rushing back.

"Isan?" Sky prompted.

"It's okay," I told her. "I remember now. Uncle is telling everyone about the war today in the town square, right?"

"Yes," she said, sounding relieved. "I'll leave you to dress then and meet you in the entrance hall."

I nodded. "I shouldn't be long."

She smiled. "I don't suppose so. All your outfits look the same."

"Just the way I like them."

After she left, I dragged myself out of bed and turned to my wardrobe. I tried to fill my mind with positive thoughts, but I kept returning to the dream. I usually dreamt little and if I did, they were full of nonsense, events that couldn't possibly be real, but this dream…

It hadn't felt like a dream at all. I could still feel the cold press of the stones as I leaned my back against the wall, could hear the wind whistling down the corridor, and smell the warm smoke of the torches. Each blink of my eyes brought me back.

What if I'm still dreaming? What if I didn't wake up after all?

The irrational fear put me on edge and I jumped at the slightest of sounds as I made my way down to the entrance hall to join Sky.

When Sky saw me, she smiled a knowing smile. "Are you forgetting something?" she mused.

I checked myself over and was relieved to find I had not forgotten pants. "I don't think so," I answered. "Why?"

"Your crown, Isan," she replied. "You're not wearing your crown."

My hand reached up to pat my head. Indeed, she was right. While dwelling on the dream, I had forgotten the torture device.

Uncle said a crown marked someone as royalty and I countered that I hardly ever left the castle anyway, so why bother? The only real purpose it served was giving me a terrible headache, so I barely wore the thing. Uncle could only enforce it for official occasions and appearances like this one, but for the most part, the gold circlet stayed on top of my chest of drawers in the corner of my room.

Sky didn't like hers much either, but her tiara weighed a lot less than my crown, so she had nothing to complain about.

I retraced my steps to my room and grabbed the crown from my dresser. After hastily dusting it off with my shirt sleeve, I placed it on my head and raced back downstairs.

"Anything else?" I asked Sky as I joined her again.

She shook her head.

"Then let's go. The sooner we can get this over with, the better."

"Uncle instructed me to wait for Asmund and the others."

I groaned. "We have to ride with them?"

"No," she replied. "We'll have our own carriage, but he wants the five of us to arrive together. Something about preserving the image of unity."

I sighed. "They had better be prompt."

No sooner had I spoken than Arran and Aramina entered the hall.

"Good morning, your Highnesses," Arran said with a slight bow.

"I told you, Arran," I replied. "It's Isan."

"Good morning, Isan," Aramina said, heeding my words, "Skiansy."

Sky smiled and then turned to Arran. "Asmund must really be getting to you."

Arran scratched the back of his head, but didn't answer.

"Quite," Aramina replied in his stead. "I don't understand his attachment to formality, but I suppose he'll have to resort to it if he's appointed heir."

"All the more reason to be as informal as you'd like," I said. "Anything that bothers Asmund is a gift from above."

Aramina laughed and then turned to Sky. "I have to say you look simply wonderful this morning, Sky. That dress is a breathtaking colour."

"Oh, thank you," Sky said, glancing at the lavender ensemble. "It's not my favourite, but..."

I'm sure any girl in the kingdom would die to even have a day with Sky's closet, but most of her dresses hung neglected. Only the Arrath children's presence at the castle and today's gathering had prompted her to wear a gown again.

Aramina was dressed similar to last night and both girls had their hair up in intricate braids. Arran and I were quite dull standing in their shadows.

"Where is Asmund?" I asked.

"He should be along shortly," Arran replied. "He insisted on redoing his braids."

I was glad I kept my hair cropped. I didn't have time to spend on such frivolous upkeep. We had places to be. If he made us late...

Again, I spoke too soon.

"Sorry to keep you waiting, your Highness," Asmund said as he entered the great hall. He stopped in front of Sky, bowing before taking her hand and kissing it.

"I am here, as well, Asmund," I said, "but I'd like you to keep your hands to yourself."

He scowled at me and I returned it.

"Well, let's take our leave then," Sky said, hoping to break the tension. "We don't want to be late. His Majesty would be quite upset."

"Agreed," Arran said.

Sky headed for the doors and the rest of us followed her out. Four guards opened the solid oak doors that served as the grand entrance to the castle. They bowed to Sky and I as we crossed the threshold and descended the steps to the waiting carriage. Asmund, Arran, and Aramina received simple nods.

Sky and I took the front carriage, the one gilded in gold, the one everyone would be looking at. I was glad to be alone with Sky again. The Arrath children had barely been in Widonia a day and I was already growing tired of their presence.

As the carriage pulled away from the castle, Sky spoke. "Can we talk?"

"Of course," I said. "What's on your mind?"

"I wanted to apologize for my reaction yesterday," she started. "I was a bit...harsh with my judgment. It's only natural for you to be angry, but I just... I don't agree with an eye for an eye. It's not that I want to shrug aside our parents' murder, but I don't think they would want us to go to war over it."

I nodded. "I understand that, and I'm sorry for calling you a coward. Wanting peace is a strength, not a weakness, but the war is coming, whether we want it to or not. I believe it is our right and duty to participate. I couldn't stay here and wait for news for months on end. It would kill me, but I understand if you have to stay."

She wrung her hands in silence for a moment and then shook her head. "If you're going, Isan, I can't stay either. I've been debating it since our argument, but this morning when I thought you were dead... It put things into perspective. I realized that this war could take your life and I can't live with the thought of you coming back to me in a box. We have been through everything together, so I can't let you go alone. I'll be with you every step of the way, watching your back like I know you'll watch mine."

I smiled at her. "I am honoured to have you by my side. Sancia knows I'll need your expertise. Winter won't stand a chance against the both of us."

She smiled back, but it was tentative. I knew she wasn't exactly happy with her choice, but I was grateful she had changed her mind.

"So," I said. "How do you think we should break the news to Uncle? I planned on mentioning it today after the announcement, but if you have a better idea, I'm all ears."

She shrugged. "That time is as good as any. His reaction will be the same no matter when we tell him."

I nodded and she spoke again, using a ridiculous imitation of Uncle's voice.

"Preposterous I say! You two, fight? In a war? I've heard some ridiculous stories in my day, but this tops them all. You think I'd let a *girl* in my army? Over my dead body!"

And then we laughed; the two of us doubled over in the back of the carriage as it made its way through the city streets.

We arrived in the town square shortly after and the carriage stopped beside the covered pavilion in the centre, the Arraths' carriage following suit behind us. Ivy snaked around the pavilion's columns and plush chairs had been set out for us. It was the centre of the market when it came to the city, but it also served as a stage for all royal announcements.

Sky and I stepped onto the stage first and the Royal Herald called out to the crowd at our appearance. "I give you Crown Prince Isanfier and Princess Skiansy."

Quite a crowd had gathered for the announcement and the square filled with cheers and claps at the herald's words. I resisted the urge to frown; they couldn't *all* be that happy to see us. Even so, I bowed to the audience as Sky curtsied. Then we took our seats.

Asmund and the others were next.

"Please welcome Masters Asmund and Arran, and Mistress Aramina of Skar," the herald said. The people seemed confused at their presence and only a few clapped as they came to sit in the chairs to the left of Sky and I. "And now," the herald continued, "his Majesty, King Arkenier, shall give his speech."

Everyone fell silent as Uncle joined us on the stage. He wore a golden robe and gold beads were woven through his long braids. He seemed to glow. The sudden silence of the square unnerved me; it was not unlike the silence of the corridor in my dream.

I pinched myself before that thought could go any further, focusing on the pain as I watched our audience drop to one knee and bow to their King.

"Citizens of Widonia, I have called you here today to discuss a matter of some delicacy," Uncle began, his expression solemn. "I am grateful to be your King, but I cannot forget the events that led me here."

Everyone hung their heads as memories of that night and its aftermath flashed through their minds. We were fortunate Uncle had arrived when he did or the entire kingdom would be in turmoil.

"Twelve years ago, King Oaden and my sister, Queen Areevia, were murdered in their sleep. We have spent over a decade mourning their loss and searching for answers. I am here before you today to tell you that we now know who to blame for that merciless act."

Whispers travelled through the crowd like wind through a forest, a soft, yet ominous sound.

"After many years of careful calculation," Uncle went on, "we have come to the conclusion we suspected all along. Winter murdered our late King and Queen."

Angry and shocked gasps filled the area, some people throwing their fists in the air at the news. I noticed one lady in the front burst into tears.

"Yes, my friends," Uncle said, "this is true and now they have struck again. The night before last, five Wyllans stole into Mensden, ending the lives of three knights and making an unsuccessful attempt on Lord Byron's life. They are out there now as we speak, but make no mistake; we will find them and when we do, we will send them back to Winter with a message. We will tell them they have wronged us for the last time and now they will pay for their crimes. We will tell them to prepare their kingdom, for we are coming." Uncle paused for a second to clear his throat. "We will no longer stand by as they murder our people and invade our land. We all know what this means. This means *war!*"

The last sentence ended in a yell and the crowd erupted with cheers as they echoed him wholeheartedly.

"We shall depart for Winter in a fortnight. In the meantime, we must prepare ourselves for whatever this war might bring. We will need extra hands in the fields to double our food stores in case of a siege. Anyone with a cart or a horse they can lend to the cause can bring them to the barracks. All able-bodied men over the age of eighteen shall accompany us to Winter, save those we will choose to leave behind to protect the city. If you are not already trained in fighting, you shall begin today at the barracks. Today marks the beginning of Winter's end."

The people cheered and then dispersed at Uncle's dismissal. The knights would dictate various tasks and direct them to the barracks. There was a lot to be done in the next two weeks to prepare Widonia for war and I hoped to work as hard as everyone else.

Asmund, Arran, and Aramina were the first to depart the pavilion, bowing deeply to Uncle as they passed him.

I waited until their carriage had pulled away before getting to my feet. "Uncle, there is something Sky and I wish to discuss with you."

"Perhaps after dinner," he replied, waving a hand. "Today is a busy day."

"No, it can't wait," I told him. "It's about the war."

He sighed and crossed his arms. "If you insist, but make it quick please."

"We're going with you," I said before I could lose my nerve.

"What?"

I looked him straight in the eye as I continued. "We've decided we cannot stay locked up in the castle, doing nothing but waiting for your return. We want to be on the battlefield, seeking our revenge and protecting our kingdom."

Uncle's laughter died before it started when he saw the look on my face.

"We will not wait for your permission, Uncle. We'll find our own way to Winter if it comes to it, but we shall fight, one way or another."

"Oh, shall you?" he countered. "Isan, this is ridiculous. You two—Sky especially—are too delicate for battle. I tolerated your lessons as children, but this is out of line. You know little of weaponry and you cannot learn to master it in a mere two weeks."

"Sky is a better warrior than most men I've met," I argued, "and we know more than you think."

"I doubt that very much and it matters not." He started to walk away.

"Uncle, no!" Sky called after him. "Please, give us a chance. Let us prove ourselves."

I saw the exact moment something in him snapped and he gave in to his anger. He whirled on Sky, coming so close that his face was inches away from hers.

"You should be ashamed of yourself," he spat. "Consider yourself lucky I ever let you hold a weapon at all. War is a man's job; learn your place. And you," he went on, rounding on me.

I took an involuntary step back.

"Learn to keep your mouth shut in the future," he told me. "The first thing I look for in a soldier is obedience and in speaking against me you show you have *none*. You shall *not* fight in this war. You can be sure of that."

Then he stepped into his carriage and rode away.

I felt the flame of hope in my heart flicker as we watched him go, but it didn't go out, not yet. We would find a way. We had to.

"What do we do now?" Sky asked, still quaking from Uncle's rage.

"I don't know," I answered, but I was determined to find out.

6
Best Laid Plans

Our hopes dashed and feeling rather defeated, we returned to the castle.

"We have to come up with a plan," Sky said as we wandered through the doors, "a way to persuade Uncle or get around him, but a plan nonetheless. Uncle made the first move by telling us no. Now we must come up with a counterattack."

"We have to do *something*," I agreed. "He can't win that easily."

"Exactly," she replied. "We'll brainstorm ideas in my room. Meet me there in ten minutes." She headed off and I returned to my chamber as well, having nothing better to do.

I set my crown back on top of the dusty dresser. Then I sat on my bed and considered everything that had recently happened—the war, the dream, Sky's change of heart, and Uncle's refusal. So much had happened in so little time.

What has it been?

A day? Two?

The minutes moved along at light speed and I could barely keep up with them. The dream still haunted me, though.

Stop, I told myself. *Dwelling on it won't erase it from your mind. It was a dream, a one-time occurrence. You will forget about it in a week.*

I wished I could believe that.

Thankfully, I had other issues to worry about, like how in Fidalia were we going to get Uncle on our side? What could we do? His mind was set, but how could we go to war without his permission?

I sat there stumped for a few minutes before the answer appeared.

There *was* one way, but Sky wasn't going to like it.

• • •

"Do *what?*" she exclaimed, springing up from the bed to stand before me.

I held my hands out in surrender. "It might sound risky, but what else can we do?"

"I know we don't have many options, Isan, but don't you think this is a bit much? I mean, running away?" Her face turned up in disgust.

"Just for a bit," I argued, "and it's not running away. Think of it as scouting ahead. We'll get to Winter before everyone else and when they arrive, they'll have no choice but to let us fight."

"I don't know, Isan," she said, frowning. "Too much could go wrong. What if they send us back? What if Winter catches us? What if something happens on the way?" Her eyes shone with anxiety.

I waved a hand. "You worry too much. It's not going to be dangerous."

"Can you say that with certainty?"

I opened my mouth to reply, but closed it when I realized I didn't have an answer.

"See?" she said, putting her hands on her hips. "You can't. Isan, this is crazy. We can't just up and leave."

"Yes we can. We're royalty. We can do anything we want."

"Don't talk like that," she scolded, a scowl leaping onto her face. "We have boundaries too and we shouldn't abuse our status."

"We're not abusing it," I protested. "Uncle can't keep us here, Sky. We're well within our rights to leave. Widonia's not supposed to be a prison."

"I don't know, Isan," she said again, wrapping her arms around her chest. "When Uncle catches up to us, he's going to be furious."

"I'm willing to deal with that and whatever consequences that might come with it. I'm ready to act. Are you?" I gave her an imploring look.

Her eyes sharpened. "You can't expect me to make a decision right now," she objected. "I need time. I only just agreed to even join the war effort. This is another thing entirely."

"We don't *have* time," I replied. "We need to act before it's too late."

She didn't answer. She just sat back down on the bed and faced the window instead of me. Her eyes always sought the nearest exit when she was nervous, like a bird prepared for flight. More often than not, I was the one spooking her.

I didn't know what to do. I needed her, but I didn't want to force her to do something that made her uneasy.

"Look, Sky," I said after a moment, "I want you to have the choice, but I don't see another option. Uncle isn't going to bend; once he chooses a side, he stands by it. I stand a chance of sneaking into the barracks and posing as a peasant boy, but you certainly don't. I'm trying to find a path that works for the both of us."

She took a deep breath and looked back at me. "I know. I guess I'm afraid of change, afraid of what's out there, but what is running away when compared to fighting a war?"

She looked tense again and this time she stood up, walking over to the window and pausing in front of her desk. She gripped the back of her gilded chair as she stared out into the city. There were books and papers strewn about the desk, likely drawings and notes. My sister loved to create art for her books as much as she loved reading them.

I knew she'd always dreamt of adventure, but I'm sure she never imagined this.

"I don't wish to take back my choice to go with you," she said finally, "so if this is what we must do, then so be it. All I ask is that we take precautions along the way. I don't want to get eaten by a prairie wolf before we even reach Winter." She turned, giving me a look, and I smiled.

"Don't worry about that," I replied. "We'll keep to the main roads and I suspect your arrows won't let any beast get too close."

"As long as I don't run out of arrows," she pointed out.

"I'll make sure to pack plenty of extras."

She shook her head. "You know this is madness, right?"

"Perhaps, but it'll be legendary someday, if we survive."

"Uncle will denounce both of us when he finds out."

I waved a hand. "He can't; someone has to be heir."

She gave me a sly grin. "Perhaps he'll appoint Asmund."

"Over my dead body." My skin crawled at the thought.

Sky laughed. "All this is almost worth that look on your face." She took a deep breath and then sat back down on the bed. "What do we need to gather before we leave?"

"We'll need a tent, blankets, and a hatchet, some sort of lantern, saddlebags, and provisions for the horses," I replied. "It would be nice to have armour too, but we can't risk that luxury; we'd likely get caught if we tried to steal it. We went unnoticed when we were younger, but all eyes will be on our weapon stores right now. So we'll just have our swords and your bow for protection. I hope they'll be enough.

"I can convince the knights that Uncle wanted me to gather some provisions and I'm sure the kitchen servants will gladly give us food if we're polite, probably best if you talk to them though. I've nicked too much food from them over the years for them to trust me."

She nodded. "I assume you want to go as soon as possible."

"I was thinking tomorrow, if that gives us enough time. We'll sneak out of the castle before dawn and be gone before Uncle wakes. It's our best chance."

"Then we'll take it." She glanced towards the window once more. "We better start gathering those supplies; the day's growing old."

I nodded and added one more thing. "Tomorrow morning, I'll come to you. Gather whatever you need to bring and be ready."

"Okay."

I left the room with a smile on my face and my heart light, but I did not forget what lay ahead.

As I walked down the halls to the knights' quarters, I soaked in the warmth of the sun, the stone around me, and the marble beneath my feet. I wanted to remember every detail of my home, in case I should never see it again. The past was important, but today marked the end of my beginning. The following day would mark the beginning of the rest of my life.

• • •

That night, the dream came again, as vivid and real as the night before. Once again, I woke up before I could pursue the dark figure and was reminded it was only a dream. Yet, I couldn't help but feel it was trying to tell me something.

How often does one have the exact same dream two nights in a row? It shouldn't have been possible. It unnerved me, and, to be honest, it scared me a little.

Aside from that, it had kept me in bed longer than I had intended. Dawn was fast approaching and I wasn't even dressed yet.

Sky's going to be wondering where I am.

I threw the covers off, rolled out of bed, and dressed as hastily as I could, yawning all the while. My cloak eluded me for a few minutes, but I finally found it balled up on my desk chair and threw it around me. It would hide my face and sword, and shelter me from the fierce winds of Winter.

Speaking of which, I took *Ember* from atop my chest and attached her to my belt, pulling the cloak around her. I checked my reflection in the mirror before I left and was satisfied for once. No one would consider bothering me that day.

I grabbed my satchel next, which I had left by the door. It contained some food and a hunting knife, but we'd taken most of our supplies down to the stables at the far end of Widonia last night after dinner.

I took one last look around my room, before slipping into the hall.

The halls were still quiet at that time of day—only the servants were awake and working—but they had begun to lighten. Darkness lost its grip on the castle as sunlight danced in the windows and tickled the corners of rooms. People would be waking up soon. Sky and I had to hurry.

I arrived at her room a few moments later and was relieved to see her sitting on her bed, dressed and ready to go. She stood up as I entered, her evergreen cloak falling around her. It was loosely tied, allowing easy access to *Tempest* and her arrows if the need arose.

"Took you long enough," she said, slinging her bag over her shoulder. "I've been waiting for over twenty minutes."

"Sorry," I replied, "I overslept."

"Of course," she huffed, rolling her eyes. She marched past me to the door and paused with her hand on the knob. "Are you coming or not?"

I was still standing in the middle of the room.

"We've already wasted enough time," she said. "Let's *go*."

"Yes, yes," I mumbled as I followed her into the hall and ran into Asmund, standing outside the door with his sword drawn.

Sky jumped and I nearly drew my own sword before I recognized him.

"Fidal's breath, Asmund," Sky said, "what in Sancia's name are you doing?" She had a hand held to her heart.

I had stepped in front of her out of instinct and now stood between her and Asmund.

"Yes," I said, scowling at him. "What exactly are you doing outside the princess' quarters at this hour?"

"I could ask you the same thing," he countered.

"I am her brother."

"It was hard to recognize you in that black cloak," he snapped. "I mistook you for one of those Winter soldiers in the low light. I was following you, waiting for the right time to strike. I was not aware this was her Highness' room, only that a Winter citizen did not belong here."

"Well, you were clearly mistaken," I replied, my voice hard. "You may go now."

He showed no signs of moving. "You ought to be careful, Prince," he spat at me. "I might not be the only one who doubts who you are, especially in the thick of battle. I would grow my hair out if I were you, like a real man, like a Crown Prince of Summer should."

"I keep my hair short out of choice," I snapped. "I don't need a symbol to prove my identity, Asmund. I know who I am and you are out of line. Do not forget that you will answer to me one day. I will not forget this conversation; you can be sure of that."

He took a step back and sheathed his sword so he could cross his arms. "Where are the two of you going?"

"None of your concern," Sky told him.

I suppressed a smile. "You should be more worried about your own sister," I added. "I saw her yesterday meeting with some boy in the gardens." It was a lie, of course, but it would get him to leave.

His eyes grew wide. "Aramina? Meeting with a boy? Why didn't you tell me sooner? If our father finds out..." He half-turned away and then said, "I will find out what you're up to Isanfier, and I won't be upset if it costs you your crown."

He walked away then, his long braids swinging with every step. I longed to slice them off at their roots and see how confident he was in his own skin then.

I swear, he was the only person who acted as if Sky and I were mere peasants instead of royalty. One day, that treatment would cost him, but for now, I had bigger concerns.

"Let's go, before anyone else shows up to question us," I said.

"Oh I was so close to smacking him up the side of his arrogant face," Sky seethed, shaking a fist. "People are fools if they believe I would ever marry that buffoon."

"Don't worry about that," I assured her as we started down the hall. "Uncle asked me for information on each of them, in order to choose the heir of Skar. I'm going to tell him to pick Asmund, though I'd much rather say I caught him practising magic and have him locked away forever."

Sky laughed. "Isan, that's terrible."
"Not terrible enough I should think."
She just shook her head.

We crept through the castle corridors as sunlight took root in them, using minor halls and staircases to avoid guards and early morning maids. We knew every passage like the back of our hands and had memorized them at an early age. Our parents' death had given us a lot of free time and no motivation to do anything else but lose ourselves in the castle for hours on end.

It only took us ten minutes to reach the street. We left through a servant's side door and through an alleyway to the back of the castle. We were out. We were free.

•   •   •

Walking through the streets of Widonia in the early morning light like a regular person was illuminating. It was interesting to experience, even for a moment, how our people lived. The aroma of freshly baked bread wafted down the lane from the bakery and I salivated at the thought of waking up to that every morning. Children ran up and down the streets, embracing the day, and the sound of their laughter added to the shrill clang of the blacksmith's hammer.

The feeling of community was in every painted porch and open shop door. A slight breeze rustled the thatch roofs and sent dandelion seeds flying through the air.

For a second, I felt like I didn't belong there in that wonderful world. Then an old woman wished me a good morning from her front door and all was well again.

"It's beautiful, isn't it?" Sky said after a period of silence.

I didn't have to ask her what she meant, I just nodded.

"Don't you think it's a pity that we've never truly been out to see our city and now we're leaving it behind?"

"Yes," I agreed, "but we'll be back."

"Will we?"

"Of course, and when we return, I promise we'll spend a whole day out here experiencing everything Widonia has to offer."

She smiled. "I look forward to it."

Though it sounded like a fairy tale, I looked forward to it too.

7
Impeccable Aim

A little while after leaving the castle, Sky wandered toward a street vendor.

"What are you doing?" I asked her. "We're on a schedule."

"Well, *my* schedule suggests it's breakfast time and that bread smells divine." A smile lit up her face as she breathed in deeply through her nose. "The stables can wait, Isan, and so can Winter. I'm hungry."

I sighed. She was right; it wouldn't be wise to leave on an empty stomach, and the bread did smell good.

As we stood in line, I looked around the square. People bustled about, carrying wares and buckets of water. A horse and cart wheeled big bags of wheat through the crowd. The driver frowned at the group of children playing tag as he swerved to avoid them. My eyes swept past the cart as it left the square and that's when I noticed something amiss.

Two men dressed in black cloaks much like mine were leaning against the railing of a merchant shop on the street corner, their hoods obscuring their faces. There was something about them that made me take an unconscious step back.

"Sky," I whispered, elbowing her softly.

"What?" she asked, rubbing at her arm.

"Look at those two men."

"Who? The farmers?"

"No, no. The men in the black cloaks, by that merchant shop." I tilted my head ever so slightly in their direction.

Sky followed my gaze, trying her best to be discreet. "I see them," she told me.

"Good," I said.

"What about them?" she asked.

"Do they look suspicious to you?"

"Their cloaks seem out of place, considering the heat, but to be fair, so would ours."

"Yes, but there's something wrong about them. Can't you feel it?"

"No, Isan," she replied. "You're being paranoid."

"Maybe," I allowed. "Keep an eye on them anyway."

"Okay," she sighed, rolling her eyes.

I paid for our bread as Sky stood watch.

"Fine day, isn't it?" the baker said.

"Yes, always is."

"You don't look like you would know, son," he replied with a hint of a wry smile.

I frowned. "I'm sorry?"

He pointed to his face and as my eyes studied the brown hue of his skin, I remembered the lack of colour in my own.

"Oh, yes," I said, suppressing a sigh. "Took ill as a child. I'm lucky to have my life, so I try not to complain about being pale."

The man looked abashed at my answer. "I'm so sorry," he said. "I didn't mean to—"

I held up a hand. "Don't trouble yourself, sir. Have a good day."

He tried to muster a smile for me, but quickly moved on to the next person in line.

I tried to shake off the conversation as I walked back over to Sky and handed her a slice of bread. "Anything yet?"

"No, Isan," she said. "They haven't moved. Fidal's breath, you're even more uptight than usual today."

I ignored her comment. "Let's get a closer look." I headed off before she could protest.

We were almost across the square when I noticed something else. One of the palace guards had entered the area, sweeping quite close to the strangers. He was recognizable by his green uniform with gold buttons and polished, black boots.

Sky put a hand on my arm, stopping me in my tracks. "Is that Jerome?"

I took in a breath as I realized she was right. Jerome was one of Uncle's personal guards, which meant Uncle couldn't be far behind. If he saw us, we would be done for.

"We'll check the strangers out quickly," I assured Sky, "and be gone long before Uncle shows."

She followed me reluctantly. "If we get caught out here because of your paranoia, I will not let you hear the end of it."

I turned back to the strangers in time to watch one reach inside his cloak for something, something that flashed in the sunlight.

He was aiming for Jerome.

I reacted on instinct, racing those last few steps and launching myself at Uncle's guard. He would report our presence to Uncle for sure, but I could not let him die to protect our trivial charade.

I hit him with enough force to knock us both to the ground.

A split second later, something flew through the air above us. I heard a muffled clang as it collided with something else instead. The square descended into chaos. People scattered, their panicked screams in harsh contrast to the laughter of before.

I scrambled to my feet, keeping Jerome behind me as I faced the strangers once again.

"Are you okay?" I called back to him.

"I'm fine," he replied. "A little dizzy is all."

"Help the townspeople get to safety and alert Uncle if you have time," I told him. "Sky and I will keep these two contained."

"You and… Your *Highness?* What are you doing out here?"

I waved a hand. "No time, Jerome. Either help us, or get out of our way."

I didn't check behind me to see if he'd heeded my command; his sudden silence spoke for itself.

In his absence, I turned my attention to the problem at hand, the problem that couldn't possibly be happening in Widonia's peaceful streets.

Sky stepped up beside me, cloak discarded and *Tempest* drawn, ready to rain fury on the cloaked men. Her brown eyes seemed aglow.

The knife thrower and his partner drew full-length swords from hidden sheaths and walked toward us. I could feel their eyes boring into mine and knew they wanted a piece of me.

I tore my cloak off too and drew *Ember*, watching with great pride as the men halted where they stood. I took small, but calculated steps towards the man who had thrown the knife, *Ember* held at the ready. I studied him—his stance, the way he held his sword—as he studied me. Seeing he was right-handed, I switched *Ember* to my left. This would make it awkward for him but not hinder me at all; when it came to swordplay, I was ambidextrous.

Before we engaged each other, I whistled once—a signal Sky and I had created years ago.

Her first arrow was airborne in the space of a breath; so fast the man never saw it coming. It skimmed across his head and tore off his hood, revealing a shock of white hair and bright blue eyes, set in a face that saw little of the sun.

I let out a choked gasp.

Winter.

An instant later, Sky's second arrow was embedded in his chest and he dropped to the ground, stone dead.

My knees wobbled at the sight, but there wasn't time to panic. The death of his friend had urged the knife thrower into action and he charged me, shrieking a battle cry. I admired his nerve, but he would soon join his friend in whatever came after.

From the first move he made—an uppercut to my jaw—I could tell the fight was mine.

I pushed his sword away from my throat with a flick of my wrist, which sent him reeling to the side.

He recovered quickly, however, and came at me again. This time he aimed for my legs, but feigned to the left, hoping to distract me.

I didn't buy it, and, tired of playing the defensive, I advanced on him. I made a quick succession of thrusts toward him, holding my sword with both hands and hacking at him in order to look sloppy.

He fell for the act and blocked my attacks nonchalantly, casually waiting for a moment to end it. He wasn't in a rush and I could tell he wanted to see me flounder a bit before I lost. *I* was the one who'd made his knife miss its target.

It was his cruelty and pride that killed him.

It didn't take me long to find a hole in his defenses and, when I did, I sliced his right side open from armpit to hip.

He shrieked as his skin tore and his lifeblood started pooling on the cobblestones. The sight was enough to make me nauseous, but I swallowed it back.

I watched as he tried in vain to remain standing by pressing his hand to the wound, holding his chest contents in place, but the pain was too great and he'd lost too much blood. Defeated, he swayed once and fell to the ground. The sword he still held in his right hand clanked against the stones.

I could have left him to die in slow agony, but I wasn't a monster. I thrust my sword into his heart and put him out of his misery.

"Isan, look out!" Sky screamed.

I whirled around and felt the whisper of metal against my neck as another Winter knight nearly slit my throat. I took a few steps back and swung at him, my heart thundering in my chest.

He grunted and jumped out of the way just in time. The action knocked him off balance though and while he fumbled to regain it, I ran him through with *Ember*. He joined his comrade on the ground.

Panting, I looked around the square.

Blood stained the street, the vulgar taste of murder tainted the air, and five men lay dead. Three of them had arrows protruding from their chests. In the windows of nearby buildings, frightened eyes watched us.

I glanced in Sky's direction. She was unscathed, except for the haunted look in her eyes. I must have looked the same.

I stood frozen, thinking about the enormity of what I had done. I had ended two lives. Because of me, those men would never breathe again, would never be able to look at another sunset, and would never see their loved ones…

I started to shake.

Then I looked back over at Sky—Sky, who depended on my strength—and collected myself. I took a deep breath and ran over to her.

"Are you okay?" I asked, putting a hand on her shoulder.

"I'm fine," she replied, her breathing erratic. "You?"

"I'm all right. That last man nearly had me though." I touched a hand to my neck and was relieved to find it was dry. "Where did he come from?"

"As soon as you and the knife thrower started fighting, three more of them appeared. I managed to down two of them in quick succession, but the third was already behind you when I turned to finish him off. I couldn't get a clear shot."

"Luckily, I have good reflexes," I said, letting out a nervous laugh, though it was anything but funny. I shuddered at the thought of how close to death I'd come.

Sky nodded. "So I guess those were Lord Byron's would-be assassins."

"Yes," I replied, having come to the same conclusion, "but what were they doing in Widonia?"

"I believe they were after me," a voice said from behind us.

Sky and I jumped at the sound, turning to find Uncle and a dozen knights looking down at us from their steeds.

"We'll take it from here," Uncle said.

It turned out Jerome had been part of a small scouting party Uncle had sent ahead of him as he journeyed to the barracks to brief the new men. Jerome was the only one still breathing. He had found the other three abandoned in a nearby alley after he led the townspeople out of the square.

Uncle didn't seem shaken by the attempt on his life, but I suppose that was due to his distance from it. We had stopped the threat before he even knew of its existence.

As the knights moved the bodies of the fallen Winter soldiers and tried to calm down the people, Uncle turned to us. I was afraid he would ask what we were doing out in the city, but he merely said, "How did they die?"

Sky and I exchanged a look.

"We killed them," I replied.

Uncle laughed. "Nonsense. Don't lie to me."

"They're not lying, your Majesty," Jerome said, coming over to stand beside us. There was dirt on his uniform and a small cut under his left eye, but he didn't seem bothered by either.

"Come again?" Uncle asked him.

"They're telling the truth," Jerome answered. "The prince saved me from a knife and they both fought bravely until all the men were dead. I did not stay to watch it all unfold, as the prince urged me to protect the people, but the princess's first shots were impeccable and I would be like the others if not for their quick thinking."

Uncle narrowed his eyes, considering Jerome's words. "You swear that is what happened?"

"On my life, your Majesty," he replied.

Uncle nodded. "Thank you for your account, Jerome. You may go now. I'm sure the others could use some assistance."

Jerome bowed low before walking off towards the other guards.

Once he was gone, Uncle studied us more closely, noticing the bow Sky held in one hand and the blood beginning to dry on my sword, filling the engraved lettering of her name.

"Does Jerome speak the truth?" he asked us.

Sky and I nodded, not trusting our voices.

"Then consider it done," he said.

"Consider what done?" I asked.

"I'm granting your wish," he replied. "I want the two of you on the front lines of this war, reminding Winter of the sheer power of Summer." He paused. "I will see you at dinner tonight." Then he mounted his horse and led his knights out of the square.

Sky and I stared after him, dumbfounded.

I couldn't believe our luck. We had actually changed his mind, all by accident. We wouldn't have to run away.

The flame of hope in my chest burned brighter than ever as Sky threw her arms around me in celebration. Perhaps things would work out after all.

8
Discipline

Frost

Frost could feel the magic emanating from the room below as he descended the spiral staircase, torchlight flickering across his face at regular intervals. It had been a while since he had personally instructed his children during their training, but after their insolence the other night, he knew it had been poor judgment to grow lax. Some things had to be done yourself if you wanted them done right.

He slipped through the archway into the courtyard, ducking under some hanging icicles, and stood unnoticed for several minutes as he watched their progress. Clarice and Icaria were sparring with each other on one side of the room, wielding frozen swords. The occasional ice shard flew from one to the other, but they were both quick on their feet and remained unscathed.

It seemed Clarice had taken Frost's previous advice.

The girls' instructor stood off some feet from them and didn't offer much in the way of critique. Meanwhile, on the other side of the courtyard, Snowdon's instructor was shaking a fist at him as Snowdon stood empty-handed.

Frost shook his head. If the boy didn't show his magic soon, it would spell ill will for the entire family. It was just as well Icaria was the Heir Apparent and not him. The people would balk at a king who couldn't even summon a single flake of snow.

Frost turned his back on his son, deciding to see to his daughter and niece first, while his mood was still relatively pleasant.

He approached them on silent feet and froze their boots to the floor when he was a few paces away.

The two lurched forward but managed to stay upright and half-turn their bodies to face the oncoming threat.

"At ease," Frost told them, holding up a hand and relinquishing their bonds. Both turned to face him and Clarice curtsied.

"Father," Icaria said, her breath heavy from the fight. "What brings you here?"

"It has occurred to me that I have neglected your training as of late," he replied. "Your instructors are the best in the kingdom, but there are certain subjects only I am able, and willing, to teach."

She nodded. "We would be honoured to receive your guidance."

Frost turned to Clarice. "It is good to see you are well again. My children seemed to think you were suffering a terrible illness."

Clarice looked up at him. "It was but a headache, your Majesty. Icaria and Snowdon needn't have worried."

Frost frowned. Why couldn't his children be as well-mannered as she? Why were they so reckless and ignorant? Not for the first time, he wished their mother was still there; it was the one thing Clarice had that they didn't.

"What will you be teaching us today, your Majesty?" Clarice asked him.

"It is time to test your limits. I want you to encase your cousin in ice and then we shall see if she can get herself out."

Clarice blinked.

Beside her, Icaria's face was as deadpan as a wall, but her eyes betrayed her fear.

Frost smiled. This test was bound to be entertaining.

"I'm sorry, your Majesty," Clarice said, "but did I hear you right? You want me to use my magic to...trap her?"

Frost nodded. "I don't believe I could make my meaning more plain."

Finally, Icaria stepped forward. "I'm not sure I'm entirely comfortable with what you're planning," she said, wrapping her arms around her chest. "What if something goes wrong?"

"That is why I am here," Frost replied. "Worry will get you nowhere, Icaria. It only prevents you from seeing clearly, and you cannot afford the distraction. This is more than a test of magical ability; this is a test of wills. Clarice will be trying to maintain her control on the ice while you attempt to wrest it from her. The winner will be the one who wants it most. Now, let's get on with it. I have a meeting to get to in an hour and I've yet to deal with your brother."

The girls nodded. It was unwise to refute the king, especially in matters such as these. He wanted his daughter to be the best in the kingdom, so no one would dare challenge her if she ever took the throne.

Frost turned to Clarice. "Do not adhere the ice to her skin, keep about an inch gap. We will leave such a perilous task to another time."

Icaria swallowed hard but did not dare close her eyes as she faced her cousin.

"At your leisure," Frost told Clarice. He knew the words would spur her on more than anything else would.

The girl brushed her short, white hair behind her ears and then took a deep breath as she closed her eyes and raised her hands before her.

Frost was proud to see Icaria standing tall, accepting what awaited her. The defiance would begin once the ice surrounded her and Frost had no doubt she would prevail. Magic was stronger on his side of the family, and thus Clarice would never surpass her. They may be evenly matched at that moment, but Icaria was nowhere near her full potential.

Frost felt the pull then as magic cracked into the air, shards of ice forming a near-perfect circle around Icaria's feet and beginning to climb skywards, towards the arched stone ceiling high above them.

The ice grew as it ascended and was about three inches thick by the time Icaria disappeared underneath it. Her eyes flicked toward her father before she was swallowed up completely.

Frost checked his timepiece, marking the second. There wasn't much to watch now; the battle was between their mental strengths. He glanced across the courtyard and saw Snowdon wielding his axe. It seemed his trainer had given up on magic for the day.

Frost clenched his fists.

A blade would only get the boy so far. Magic was a weapon you carried wherever you went, whose power was only limited by your own mind and strength. It could not be broken or stolen or lost, and yet, Snowdon saw fit to neglect it and cling to his axe like a child clings to its blanket.

Behind Frost, Clarice groaned and he turned back to see sweat dripping down her face. A few small cracks had appeared in Icaria's prison and Frost knew it wouldn't be much longer.

Clarice gritted her teeth. "No, no," she muttered. "Must...keep..." She let out a sharp cry and fell to her knees as her ice creation shattered into a million pieces and Icaria emerged, gasping for breath.

Frost looked down at his watch. Five minutes. It seemed impressive, but he knew they could both do better.

"Once you recover," he told them, "switch roles. Then I want you to practise this once a week until you have perfected it. Is that understood?"

Icaria looked up and Clarice dragged herself to her feet. "Yes, sir," they both said.

Frost offered no further encouragement as he left them in the care of their instructor and trudged over to speak with his son.

Snowdon's instructor met him halfway. "Good morning, your Majesty," he said.

"Pitiful, isn't he?" Frost replied, nodding in Snowdon's direction.

"I beg your pardon, Sire?"

Frost waved a hand. "I would prefer it if you did not lie to my face about my son's progress. I am well aware of his complete lack of...anything. You are dismissed for the day. It is my turn to teach him a lesson."

The man bowed his head. "As you wish, Sire. I will return tomorrow."

When the instructor was gone, Frost turned to Snowdon—whose back was toward him—and flung out a hand. His magic froze Snowdon's boots to the floor, like he had done with Icaria and Clarice, but he didn't stop there. He let it continue to spread, let it suck the warmth out of Snowdon's body.

Snowdon half-turned toward him with wild fear in his eyes and Frost reined it in. A thin layer of frost coated his son from toes to hips. It had taken Snowdon too long to notice.

Frost scowled at his son as he marched over to him. "Utterly pathetic," he spat. "If I was an enemy, you would already be dead. Does that mean nothing to you?" He reached out and yanked the axe out of Snowdon's hands, throwing it to the stone floor behind him.

Snowdon winced but did not speak against the action.

"What good was that axe, Snowdon?" Frost asked him. "What good is it ever going to be against an enemy that can kill you from fifty yards away? Answer me!"

Snowdon hung his head. "It's not any good. I know that, but it's all I have."

Frost jabbed a finger in his face. "Wrong! You have magic in you, I know it. Your name is *Snow*don. You're my son for Wylla's sake! Our family has had magic for generations, on each branch of the tree, and if you think it's going to stop with you, you are gravely mistaken."

Frost was quaking in his skin. If this was truly what the divines had "blessed" him with, he could do without all of them. His son had to have magic in him; he just had to figure out how to reveal it.

"Magic manifests with strong emotions," Frost went on, though he knew Snowdon had heard it all before. "Your sister's trigger was sorrow. I don't know what yours is, but you need to find it." The only problem was that Snowdon showed no emotions with any sort of strength. He never put his full focus into anything.

"I don't mean to be a burden, Father," Snowdon replied. "I… I'll try harder."

Frost nodded. "You better, because until you do, this axe is mine." He bent over and picked it up.

Snowdon stilled. "Father…"

Frost's eyes snapped up to meet his. "You heard me. No more weapons training until you can prove you deserve a place in this family. I don't care if you meditate for hours. I don't care if it takes you a decade of training. Until you show your magic, you are not my son."

"Father—" Snowdon tried again, but Frost held up a hand.

"That's 'your Majesty' to you, boy. Now get back to work; I have a meeting to go to." Frost turned his back on Snowdon then, but not before releasing his magic and watching the boy fall to his knees on the stone.

It was difficult being a parent, but Frost was also the king and he had to do what was right for his kingdom, even if it shrivelled his heart smaller than it already was. One day, Snowdon would thank him. For now, Frost held his head high as he walked out of the training room and left him behind.

9
Temper and Training

Isan

That night, Uncle dismissed the Arraths from the dining hall early. They seemed confused but obeyed without complaint.

"Isan is welcome to join us in our rooms after, if he so wishes," Asmund said before he left. "Arran and I are going to stay up for a bit to discuss some current issues."

I raised an eyebrow, but nodded in acknowledgment of his invitation.

Aramina seemed sullen.

"Aramina could sit with me," Sky offered, noticing the girl's expression. "It's been so long since I've had another woman to chat with."

Mina's face lit up. "Oh, that would be lovely, your Highness."

"This is all well and good," Uncle said, "but I should like some time with my niece and nephew now. We have a delicate matter to discuss. They will join you when we are through. Goodnight."

"Of course, your Majesty," Asmund said with a low bow. He turned to his sister and brother. "Mina, Arran, let us go."

The three left without another word, abandoning Sky and I to our fate. Even Aunt Mag wasn't there to diffuse the tension. A dreadful headache had led to her taking dinner in her rooms.

I braced myself for what was to come. Judging from Uncle's frigid dismissal of the others, Sky and I were not in for compliments.

The door banged shut.

"Have the two of you completely lost your sanity?" Uncle snapped, slamming his hands on the table.

Cutlery rattled and Sky jumped in her chair.

"Did you think your victory today would hide your insolence? Did you think I would ignore the fact that you snuck out of the castle? Did you think I wouldn't discover your plans?"

Sky and I hung our heads. "No, Uncle."

I mean, for a few hours, I *had* thought we'd gotten away with it, but it was clear Uncle had let us think that, in order to make this moment even more painful.

"Your actions today were reckless," he thundered on, "and not befitting your station. You could've been killed. What if those Wyllan knights had recognized you before you recognized them? Winter has already humiliated us enough. You could've put the future of our kingdom in serious jeopardy. You were taught better than that."

He was right, of course, but it didn't make his words sting any less.

"Uncle, we—"

"No," he interrupted me. "I'm not finished. You will inherit this kingdom someday, Isanfier. You need to start acting like it. Irrational behaviour like this will cause the kingdom to collapse. Do you understand me? You may have this urge to fight for Summer and prove yourself, but that is pointless if there's no kingdom left. And as for you, Skiansy," he said, looking towards her. "I would hate to see you dragged down with your brother's terrible decisions. I thought you had more common sense than this."

"I... I was hesitant to agree with him," she tried.

Uncle shook his head. "Hesitant... Sancia save us all. You are lucky the two of you are as skilled as you claim or I would lock you in a tower until the war was over. Do you hear me?"

"Yes, Uncle," I said.

"We understand," Sky added.

"I don't want to be harsh with you," Uncle said, some of the hardness withdrawing from his gaze, "but no one else will. It is my job to prepare you for your future. It is my job to make the hard choices. That is what it means to be a king."

There was silence for a few moments, in which the three of us regained our composure.

"I want you to report to the barracks tomorrow morning. You will train with the other soldiers under Sir Kent's tutelage. Bring Masters Asmund and Arran with you, and give your weapons to Sir Kent upon your arrival."

I looked up. "Our weapons?"

He nodded. "That sword of yours and your sister's bow. He will be keeping them until you've finished your training."

"Whatever for?" I asked, shaking slightly. The thought of being separated from *Ember* was almost more than I could bear.

"It is part punishment, part learning tool," Uncle replied. "It will force you to learn other weapons and it will remind you that your actions have consequences. Go now, the Arraths are waiting. I will tell Sir Kent to expect you at first light."

I wanted to say something, anything, but I couldn't form the words and I knew it wouldn't do any good either. I didn't want to compromise my involvement in the war effort.

Sky was already at the door and she urged me on with a look.

I bid Uncle goodnight and left the room with her.

• • •

I was still fuming twenty minutes later, sitting with Asmund and Arran in the parlour outside their chambers. Apparently, when Asmund said "discuss current issues," he meant drink wine and gossip.

He was half-drunk already, lounging on the patterned couch against the wall, bottle in hand.

I sat in one of the chairs, Arran in the other, sipping his wine from a crystal glass.

My glass sat untouched on the table beside me.

"So, Isan," Asmund drawled. "Tell us about your glorious victory this morning. Sir Kent tells me you killed those Wyllan assassins all by your lonesome."

"Sir Kent is mistaken," I replied. "Sky dropped three of them. I only killed two."

Asmund sat up. "Skiansy? What on earth was she doing out with you, fighting the rabble?"

I shrugged. "She was doing what she does best."

He looked aghast and it took a great amount of effort not to laugh at him.

I think I've discovered how to improve my mood.

"She'll be joining us at the barracks tomorrow, you know," I went on, "and she'll be coming with us to Winter."

"The princess," Asmund stuttered. "We are talking about the same person, correct?"

"Correct."

Arran was back to his usual silence, his expression not revealing his opinion on the subject.

"But that's..." Asmund tried. "Why in Fidalia would the king sanction such a reckless act? She could get hurt."

"Of course she could," I replied, "but Sky can do more than hold her own. She outperforms any archer I've ever seen."

"Ah, but there is more to war than archery," he pointed out.

"Which is why she is also trained in sword and spear. Honestly, Asmund, do you think I would neglect her training? I do not wish to see her hurt any more than you do."

His dark face was waxy and a smile crept onto my lips at the sight of it. "This could ruin her reputation," he continued, desperate for me to see reason. "How will she ever find a husband if they know she hung around military men for months on end?"

I bristled. "You watch your tongue. If anyone questions her integrity, they will have the both of us to answer to. Sky is willing to lay her life on the line for this kingdom. Any man would be a fool to dismiss that. There is more to life than marriage anyway. It is the furthest thing from either of our minds."

"You have not chosen a Princess Consort then?" Asmund asked me.

"Sancia, no. It..." I stumbled. "Courting always seems so...trivial. Pointless. Lackluster. Besides, I have to focus on my studies and training. I don't have time to waste on romance."

Asmund took another swig from his bottle. "You're telling me the Crown Prince hasn't...dabbled?"

My stomach churned. "That's..."

"Oh leave him alone, Asmund," Arran butted in. "Perhaps we could choose a more favourable subject?"

"Nonsense," Asmund snapped, ignoring his brother. "You must've fancied someone, even once, even for a little while. It is unnatural for a man not to experience some form of desire for a woman."

"Fine," I relented. "There was a girl once, when I was younger, but it didn't lead anywhere and it's truly none of your business."

Asmund gave Arran a look. "Such fire our prince has."

"And you have a lot of nerve, Asmund, inviting me here only to ply me with spirits to spill my secrets," I snapped.

I wasn't a fool. I was well aware of his intentions.

"So you have never considered Aramina?" he asked me.

I stood up. "Are you even listening to me?"

He stared me down, not nearly as drunk now. His bottle had probably been filled with water. "Answer the question, Isanfier."

"No, I have not."

"So nothing happened the other night when Arran left the two of you alone?" He shot Arran a look.

I rolled my eyes. "Is that what this is about? She held *me* back, not the other way around. We spoke for a moment and went our separate ways."

"What did you talk about?"

I crossed my arms. "I won't break her confidence."

"Oh, you will, Prince, or I will tell the king you took my sister to bed."

"Aramina is thirteen, Asmund," I snapped, fire bubbling under my skin. "She's barely more than a child. I am disgusted at the thought of your insinuation."

"What did she say?" he demanded. "I won't ask you again." His voice was lethal.

I looked him straight in the eyes. "She asked me about the grieving process, if the pain of her mother's death would ever go away. She wanted someone to talk to, said the two of you aren't any help."

Asmund huffed. "She shouldn't waste your time with such trivial matters."

"Trivial?" I scoffed. "She is in *pain*, Asmund, and all you can think about is her physical preservation? What about her mind? Have you ever asked her how she's doing? Did you see the way her face lit up when Sky asked her to join her tonight? She wants someone to talk to, someone to see her as more than a possession. She misses her mother."

"I miss her too, but moping around isn't going to bring her back. We've been over this."

I shook my head. "You're heartless, Asmund," I told him. "I hope you know that. I would appoint Aramina as heir of Skar over you, if I didn't want to protect Sky from the possibility of being your wife."

For once, he had nothing to say.

"See, that's why Sky and I have such a strong bond," I went on. "I will always save her first, even if it means condemning this entire kingdom. That's the kind of loyalty Aramina craves. You might want to try talking to her for once, before you lose her forever." I turned to Arran. "It was a pleasure talking to you, Arran, but I must retire. Your sister looks up to you; don't disappoint her."

I left my full glass of wine on the table and a dumbfounded Asmund staring after me. I was sure I would live to regret the conversation, but at that moment, I felt better than I had in years. I just hoped Aramina wouldn't pay the price for my temper.

• • •

The arrow missed the target by an inch and I cursed. I'd been at it for hours with no improvement. Dozens of arrows lay discarded around the yard, some sticking straight up in the dirt, others snapped in half from the impact of an unintended target.

At least I hadn't accidentally skewered someone.

I sighed.

Why are they making me do this?

I already knew archery wasn't my strong suit and no amount of training was going to change that. Even Sky had written me off as a lost cause years ago, and she was the optimistic one.

"How's progress coming along, your Highness?" someone asked from behind me.

Lowering the bow, I turned to find Sir Kent—our Captain of the Guard—studying me.

"Not well," I told him. "Can I go now?" I knew I sounded like a child, but I'd had enough.

He regarded me with stern eyes. "No, you may not," he replied. "King Arkenier gave specific orders that you and the princess are to learn all types of weaponry, which includes archery."

I sighed. "I'm not good at this, Kent. Sky is my archer. She's the one picking people off from a distance. She's the one watching our backs."

"I understand that, your Highness," he replied, "but she might not always be there to protect you. The two of you could get separated. Your sister could pass on. You can't rely on her forever."

I shuddered, but tried to brush off his ominous comment. Sky wasn't going anywhere. Even still, Kent had a point. Sky had learned swordsmanship for me; the least I could do was put a decent effort into archery. Who knew? It could save her life one day.

Again, the thought of her death set me off balance, but I took a deep breath and turned back to the target.

I reached my hand back into my quiver of arrows, a move that felt awkward to me, and plucked an arrow from the bunch. Then I raised the bow and nocked the arrow, my muscles straining against the draw weight. *Ember* was heavy too, but it was a different sort of weight, not as steady.

Narrowing my eyes, I focused on the target, letting it fill my vision. I imagined Sky was doing it instead, reminding myself of her movements and stance as I took a deep breath and pulled back the string. Then, I exhaled and let the arrow fly.

It hit the outside ring, but it was a start.

An hour later, I headed to the main building for lunch, following the call of the sentry tower bell. A barrage of footsteps accompanied me, all the men hurrying to get a table before they were gone. The hard work of the morning had made them exhausted and ravenous.

I felt famished too, but the food was disappointing: dry bread, tough meat, and watered-down wine. It was tasteless, but I grabbed a plate anyway and made my way over to an empty table in the far corner of the room.

Most of the men sat together with their friends and knights they shared a battalion with. Sky and I sat alone, for we had no battalion and no friends other than each other. Sometimes Arran would join us, when he was feeling generous or when Asmund stayed late in the yard.

After our argument in their rooms, Asmund had made it his mission to make my life miserable, and Sky's too by simple association. He ensured that none of the men talked to us, that nobody liked us. He spread rumours that we were nothing but spoiled royals and that we'd used our status to gain our positions at the barracks.

It wasn't long before the men were talking about our supposed lack of valour and experience. Though they'd been told by Kent himself that we'd killed five Winter knights, they refused to believe it.

"Stories," they sneered. "Nothing but lies to make us think they're special."

Arrogant bastards, I thought. *I'll show them. We'll both show them. If only I had Ember, then I'd make them wish they'd treated me with more respect.*

I snorted. If I had *Ember,* I'd make a bid for Asmund's head.

I didn't have her though, and I wouldn't have her again until Uncle and Kent deemed me ready for battle. I felt as if they'd cut off a limb, but Uncle's choice had ultimately been for the best. He had no idea of the bloodshed he was preventing.

He wouldn't put a stop to the rumours either. We had chosen to join his army, had chosen this fate. It was now up to us to put up with whatever this experience threw at us.

Rage simmered in my veins, a slow-burning fire.

I clenched my fists, but told myself to calm down.

It worked, until Sky entered the room. She was the first-ever woman allowed to step foot in the barracks and everyone hated her. No one spoke to her as she received her food, but they sneered at her and muttered foul words as she walked between the tables towards me.

I gritted my teeth to keep from saying something I'd soon regret.

Sky remained calm and collected as always.

Then one of the men put a leg out into the aisle and she stumbled over it. To her credit, she didn't fall, nor did she spill her food, but still the men laughed.

My hand ached for *Ember* and the fire boiled in my veins.

"Watch where you're going, girl," the man who tripped her said. "Wouldn't want to ruin your pretty face."

Sky stilled and I could tell she'd had enough.

"No, *you* watch where you put your *foot,* you blithering buffoon," she snapped at him, whirling to look him straight in the eyes. Her tone conjured up the image of someone sharpening a blade. "Because next time, I might take a sword and cut it off."

The room had gone still and silent as death.

I unclenched my fists, the rage within me dying out.

Sky sauntered over to my table without another glance at the man. She sat down across from me and began eating without a word.

I followed her example and we ate in silence for a minute, until the chatter in the room started up again.

"So…" I started. "That was…violent."

She stabbed a piece of meat with her fork. "It was inevitable," she said. "I've had enough of their insults and humiliation. As a fellow soldier, I deserve recognition. As their princess, I deserve *respect*. They forget I could one day be ruling this kingdom, and if I do, you can count on me remembering all their kind words. I may pay them a visit and make good on my threat." Her anger rolled off her in waves and she clenched her wooden fork so hard I was afraid it might snap.

Slowly, I reached across the table and placed my hand over hers. "You're going to hurt yourself," I told her, looking into her eyes. "Breathe."

Finally coming to her senses, she released her hold on the fork and exhaled. The utensil clattered to the table and she took a deep breath.

The anger dissipated.

"Thank you," she said. "I lost myself for a minute. It's just… We worked so hard to get here—training twice a day since we were nine, having the courage to confront Uncle, and then killing those Winter men." She shuddered. "We *earned* the right to be here, but all they do is belittle us, because I'm a girl and you're the heir to the throne. We don't deserve this hate."

"I know," I sighed. "It's my fault. I never should've spoken against Asmund, but he was so… I wanted to put him in his place. Now we're both paying the price for it."

Sky shook her head. "The hatred was already there, Isan. Asmund just stoked the fires."

I sighed again. "You're probably right. We shouldn't let it get to us, though. The best way to combat criticism is to make the critic think it's falling on deaf ears. Once we fight together in battle, they'll realize our worth and their mistake, but until then, we have to pretend we don't care what they think of us."

"I suppose you're right," she said.

I grinned. "Aren't I always?"

"Don't push your luck, boy," she sneered, imitating the man who had tripped her.

We both started laughing and spent the rest of lunch talking and joking around.

The men may have insulted and humiliated us, but they hadn't broken our spirit—at least, not yet.

10
On the Edge

In the days following, the men left us relatively alone and, finally having some peace, we were able to focus on our training. A few days later, I shot a bullseye in archery and moved on to axes. A week after the lunch incident, Uncle added war tactics to our list of subjects to learn. Sir Kent lectured and quizzed us in the morning and oversaw our combat training in the afternoon. By the end of the day, we were both mentally and physically exhausted, yet I was denied a good night's sleep.

As soon as I closed my eyes, the dream was waiting for me, draining my last reserves of mental strength. It was the same each night, though after the first two instances, I learned not to waste precious time going to the window. Instead, I lay in wait for the dark figure and followed him to his destination, which was always the same wooden door.

The door was engraved with intricate symbols that were hard to decipher because of the swirls all around them. It fascinated me and I desperately wanted to know what lay beyond it. Yet, each night the dream ended before the dark figure could open the door. I would wait anxiously for the next night, only to have the same thing happen once again.

After the first few times, I grew frustrated and pushed my anxiety away, not allowing my nights to rule my days. Still, there was always a voice in the back of my mind telling me *this* would be the night the door would open. Of course, it never was.

With all my daydreaming and daily training, I hardly noticed the days go by. Before I knew it, we had less than forty-eight hours left. I could barely wrap my mind around it.

Time had run out and we would be marching for Winter in two days.

• • •

Sir Kent sent Sky and I back to the castle after one last duel, saying our training was finished and he would see us on the battlefield. As we walked through the doors of the castle, I couldn't help but think that it might be one of the last times we did so. It almost made me wish I was staying.

Sky headed to her room for some much-needed rest, but I sought out Uncle. I had yet to tell him my findings on the Arrath children and if I didn't do it soon, I doubted he would take my opinion into account.

I found him in his parlour, down the corridor from the dining hall. He was tending a small fire, various books spread out on the tables and chairs around him.

The door was ajar and I gave it a knock. "Uncle," I called out, not wanting to disturb him without his permission.

"Hmmm?" he replied. Then he looked up and saw me standing in the doorway. "Oh, Isanfier, do come in."

I closed the door behind me and walked over to him. There was nowhere to sit.

"How is your training?" he asked me, placing the fire poker back in its stand.

"Well," I replied, "Sir Kent says we're ready." My hand dropped to the familiar weight of *Ember* at my side. I was happy to have her back.

"Then you are ready," he said. "The Captain is rarely mistaken."

"I suppose not," I said, shifting on my feet. "You asked me to keep an eye on Asmund and his siblings," I went on.

He perked up, a sudden interest shining in his eyes. "Indeed I did. What did you find?"

"None of them use magic, as far as I can tell. Aramina is still young and untried. Arran seems to be coming into his own. Asmund..." I took a deep breath. "Uncle, can I be honest with you?"

He frowned. "Why would I want you to lie?"

"I just don't want my words to condemn me," I told him.

"Ah," he said. "I see. Tell me what you truly think, Isanfier. I will do my utmost to have an open mind."

I took a deep breath. It would have to be enough.

"Arran should be the next Lord of Skar," I said, "but I'm afraid if he does become heir, that you will marry Sky off to Asmund. I couldn't live with that, but I also hate the thought of Asmund becoming a powerful lord."

Uncle raised an eyebrow. "Would it be such a bad thing for Asmund to be Prince Consort? His family is one of the most reputable in Summer right now. The boy is smart and skilled with the sword."

"Asmund is cunning, manipulative, and cruel," I countered, my hatred for him spewing out. "He does not see Sky as a person; he sees her as power. He is the type of man who would try to seize the throne for himself if given the opportunity."

Uncle seemed amused. "Then who else should I give your sister to? Is anyone up to your standards?"

"Anybody but Asmund," I replied. "That is my only requirement. Arran should be Lord of Skar; Asmund should be forgotten."

"I will take your opinion into consideration," Uncle said. "Your sister's suitor will be chosen once the war is through. I wouldn't want to make her a widow before she's even a proper wife."

I nodded. "Thank you."

"I'll announce the heir of Skar at the meeting tonight."

He bent back over his papers then and I took that as a dismissal. I hoped I hadn't dug Sky an even deeper hole, but the promise of time was a gift I would not waste.

• • •

That night, after dinner, Sky and I attended a War Council in the study, which meant listening to Uncle and the knights discuss details like Winter's weak spot and the best places to strike first.

Arran and Asmund were both present this time, but they mostly listened and observed. I tried not to think about the glares I knew Asmund was sending me.

The Council was *so* boring. We weren't allowed any input and I doubted the knights would've listened to us anyway. Yet, they forced us to sit there and listen to *them*. I knew it was an honour to be invited at all, but being excluded lessened the prestige.

I gave a loud sigh and slouched in my chair.

Of course, this action didn't escape Uncle's notice. "Are we boring you, Prince Isanfier?" he asked, glaring at me.

"No, sir," I lied, sitting up straight.

"Good. Now pay attention."

I suppressed another sigh and tried to listen to the conversation. The men were standing around the table, leaning over a map, and pointing out the route we would take to Winter.

I took a moment to study it, locating Widonia first, beside Lake Lotus in the north end of the map. Then I mentally traced a line across the map from Widonia towards Winter in the south and stopped halfway. The centre of the map was a huge tangle of lines that stretched the whole width of it. They were so thick in some places the map appeared to be black.

A bell rang in my head at the sight and I remembered learning about it in my geography lessons. *The Edgewood.*

It's an impenetrable tangle of trees, hedges, bushes, and other plant life that stretches the width of our realm, my tutor had once said, *lying directly on the border between Summer and Winter.*

It stood between and around both kingdoms and was an ungoverned, wild land full of dangerous creatures, or so the stories said. It was a place to avoid at all costs.

"We aren't going through the Edgewood, are we?" I asked, addressing no one in particular.

"What was that, Isanfier?" Uncle replied.

"The Edgewood," I said, looking across the table at him. "We don't plan to go through it, do we?"

"Well, seeing as it surrounds the kingdoms, I should think that would be apparent." A knight from the other end of the table had spoken. His long hair was unbraided and he lounged in his chair.

"At ease, Quinton," Uncle said. "It is a fair question. The Edgewood has quite the reputation." He turned back to me. "People may say it's impenetrable, but there *is* a way to pass through unscathed. There is a path that runs through the wood, but it only reveals itself when the need is great. I'm sure it will deem our needs great enough."

"Will it?" I countered before I could stop myself.

Uncle's eyes hardened. "How do you think those Winter assassins were able to enter our kingdom? The forest let them through and I should think our cause is more noble than theirs could ever be."

I swallowed back my irritation. Of course, his answer seemed sound, but it was ridiculous that we were basing our entrance plan on the whims of a forest. It didn't sound like a great start to the war to me.

The Council continued on and I paid little attention to it. When it came to a close, I found I was less prepared than when it had begun.

"There is one more thing I would like to address before we go our separate ways and get some much-needed rest," Uncle said.

The men were all seated now and they looked at Uncle expectantly. He must not have informed them of his intentions beforehand.

"We have with us tonight the two sons of Lord Arrath of Skar. Asmund, Arran, please stand."

The two shared a confused look, but got to their feet.

"Gentlemen," Uncle said, looking around at his knights, "I am pleased to announce I have chosen Lord Arrath's future successor. Please join me in congratulating Master Arran in becoming the heir of Skar."

The knights erupted into cheers and banged their fists on the table. Sir Kent clapped Arran on the back.

Arran was dumbfounded, staring at Uncle with wide, confused eyes.

Asmund looked cheated, like he was about to go on a rampage. He did not congratulate his brother, only regarded him with distaste.

I couldn't believe Uncle had listened to me. I prayed he would follow my advice on Asmund as well.

Sky leaned over to me. "I didn't see that coming at all," she said, "but it's a sound choice."

"I agree."

I didn't tell her I had a lot to do with it. She knew as well as I that this left Asmund open to be her suitor and I didn't want her to think I'd condemned her. I would do everything in my power to see that didn't happen.

"All right, everyone," Uncle called out. "Settle down. Unfortunately, there is no time for celebrations now. Arran, I should like you to depart for Skar tomorrow with your sister. We need you safe, should something happen to your father and you'll need to finish your training."

Arran nodded. "I will not disappoint you."

"May Sancia guide you," Uncle replied.

The knights echoed him. If any disagreed with his choice, they did not show it. I'm sure most of them expected Asmund to be chosen, but they trusted Uncle's decision was sound.

"Asmund," Uncle went on, "tomorrow you ride with us. Your father's army will meet ours before we enter Winter and you can join him then."

Asmund only nodded, probably not trusting himself to use kind words if he should speak.

"I believe that is everything," Uncle finished. "I will see you all in the morning. May you be ready and may Sancia watch over us all as we embark on this great journey."

I caught up to Arran in the hall. Asmund had already stalked off, in search of something to break most likely.

"Congratulations, Arran," I said, facing him with a smile.

"Thank you, your Highness. I mean… Isan."

I laughed. "It's okay. You're probably a little flustered still. Be careful on your way to Skar. Try to fortify the city when you get back, in case something goes wrong with us."

He nodded. "I'll protect the city with my life. Oh, and Isan?"

"Yes?"

"I'll be watching over Aramina too. Maybe with Asmund and Father gone, she can take some time for herself."

I smiled. "I think their absence will be good for her."

Arran nodded. "I think it will be good for both of us."

He walked off then and I marvelled again at how much he had changed since his last visit to Widonia. I could see a lord in his words, in his steps. He would make this kingdom proud someday. I hoped I would be able to say the same.

• • •

The next morning, I awoke to darkness. Alarmed, I threw off my covers and raced to the window. The dream had only solidified my fear of the dark and I was worried it was starting to leak into reality. The answer was thankfully much simpler than that, but somehow just as sinister.

Dark clouds roiled overhead and an eerie silence clung to the castle like ivy to a wall. Not a bird chirped and nothing moved in the streets below. It was a bad omen, a storm on the day of war.

I grimaced as thunder rumbled in the distance and the rain clouds rolled in. Then the heavens opened and the rain came pouring down.

No, I thought. *Not an ideal start.*

I turned away from the window, trying to forget what I'd seen. Maybe if I didn't acknowledge it, it would go away.

As if that mentality had worked well for the dream.

I walked over to my wardrobe and got dressed—black pants and a black shirt accompanied by knee-high boots. The boots were made of black leather and were slim, lightweight, and flat-bottomed. They were made for the quick footwork involved with swordplay and were the only shoes I ever wore, though I owned dozens of other styles. I put my black cloak on over my clothes as I left my room.

Over half of my clothes were black, even though it was the colour of the enemy. As a prince of Summer, I was supposed to wear green and yellow gold, maybe the occasional white and brown, but I liked to wear black. It suited me. It made me more imposing. I wore black when I wanted to be left alone. That day though, my outfit matched my mood—dark, caused by the storm outside.

• • •

Uncle was absent from breakfast along with Aunt Mag, but she turned up just as we were about to leave to say her goodbyes.

"Oh please be careful, children," she said as she crushed us both tight against her. "I don't know what I'd do if I lost you."

"Well, you'd have more peace and quiet for one," I replied as she finally relinquished us.

She smiled, but it seemed bittersweet. "Skiansy," she said after a moment, "are you all right?"

Sky nodded, but from her tense posture and blinking lids, I could tell she was lying.

Aunt Mag could tell too and she gave Sky a look.

Sky withstood it for a few seconds, but then she burst into tears and threw herself back into Aunt Mag's arms.

Aunt Mag stroked her hair as Sky sobbed into her dress. "What's wrong child? Let us ease your pain."

"Oh, Aunt Mag," Sky gasped. "I... I'm so scared. What if we die? What if we never see you or Summer ever again?"

Aunt Mag nodded. "Fear is a natural emotion, Skiansy, and it's not too late to walk away, but you have to ask yourself what choice is best for you in the long run. Will you regret it more if you go or if you stay?"

Sky didn't answer. She let her tears run their course as Aunt Mag continued to hold her and murmur words of encouragement.

I stood there in awkward silence beside them, realizing I too had been neglecting my sister's emotional care lately. Events like this were supposed to bother her, were supposed to bother both of us. War wasn't an everyday trifle.

After a few minutes, Sky pulled away. "I'm okay now," she said. She brushed stray strands of hair out of her face and rubbed at her eyes.

Aunt Mag held an arm out to steady her in case she needed it.

"Are you certain?" I asked Sky. "I won't fault you if you want to stay."

She shook her head. "No, I want to go. I couldn't live with myself if I played a coward at the last second."

I nodded and Aunt Mag smiled, lighting up her weathered face. "You two have grown up much in these last few weeks," she said. "It makes my heart both full and empty."

Sky and I gave her a sad smile. Then we pulled her in for one last hug. I breathed in her familiar scent of flowers and sage, trying to commit it to memory. I remembered the hours we used to spend with her in the gardens when we were little, watering flowers and picking vegetables. I remembered her telling us that plants need help, but sometimes you have to step back and let them grow on their own.

"Thanks, Aunt Mag, for everything," Sky said.

"We'll make it home for you," I added, "whatever the cost."

"May Sancia watch over you always," she replied, "and may you make your parents proud."

• • •

Half an hour later and several pounds heavier, laden with our golden armour, Sky and I joined Uncle and the Council in the entrance hall. Asmund stood at Uncle's side and didn't spare us a glance. The rest of our army waited outside, a line of knights, horses, and carts snaking through Widonia's streets.

On Uncle's order, we marched out into the storm and were soaked through in seconds. The torrential rain pounded into us as we mounted our sodden horses and led the army out of the city. People cheered us on as we rode past, willing to brave the cold and wet to see us off.

The cheers came to a crescendo as we reached the wall and then cut off.

The enormity of what was happening hit me then. We were leaving Widonia. We were heading to war.

The city guards heaved the gates open and we rode into the world beyond.

I glanced back at the castle, its grey stone lost to the fog of the storm, and wondered if I would ever see it again.

11
Mire and Misgivings

We spent the day plodding through thick mud and braving the relentless rain, stopping a few times to rescue some of our carts from the sludge. Being Summer, it was a warm rain, but it was still unpleasant. It reminded me I had a dry room at the castle I could still be in.

I had never been in such a miserable situation in my entire life, but it was worth it. Sky and I had done it. We'd escaped the city. We hadn't been outside the wall in years and there we were, riding through fields, the capital but a distant speck on the horizon behind us.

The weather may have tried to dampen my spirits, but I revelled in the sweet taste of my newfound freedom.

We settled into bed with empty stomachs that night, as it was too wet for a fire to cook any meals and we didn't want to risk our dry food becoming wet and attracting mould. It was a new occurrence, being hungry, but then again, so was sleeping on the cold, hard ground.

You'll survive, I told myself. *Most of the journey will be the same, so you better get used to it.*

All in all, I thought a little discomfort was a small price to pay for the chance at adventure I'd been given.

The next morning, I woke up startled from yet another dream, though I could just as easily call it a nightmare. It was hard to tell. Nothing terrible had happened in it yet, but the atmosphere did not bode well for the future. I wished I could figure out what it meant, if anything. I had considered telling Sky about it, but I didn't want her worrying about me any more than she already did.

I yawned as I stretched my cramped limbs, shaking the dream from my mind. Wearing armour while riding a horse in the pouring rain, followed by a night on the ground, was not my favorite way to pass my days. My body didn't appreciate it either.

I sighed and dressed quickly, wincing when I turned the wrong way.

I tried to remind myself that this was what I wanted. The war was not going to be easy, so I couldn't give up before we even left the kingdom.

When I finally stepped out into the sweet embrace of warm sun rays, I realized it had stopped raining. A good sign; maybe everything would turn out okay after all.

I noticed more men around camp that morning as I attempted to start a fire. It had been a while since I'd last done it, so I was a bit rusty and it took several minutes before a spark caught.

Uncle's green and gold tent in the centre of our camp caught my eye as I worked. I doubted he would have the same luck, but I also doubted he would try. Though he had insisted Sky and I join the ranks of men as regular soldiers with no royal privileges, he didn't hold himself to the same standards. He'd brought several servants along and even had a proper bed, stowed away in his own personal cart during our travels.

I thought it was nice to shrug off our finery for once, despite the inconveniences, and I wished Uncle wouldn't throw his lingering luxury in our faces.

Someone slapped me on the back then and I turned, expecting Uncle, but found an unfamiliar face, though I did recognize the symbol of a leaf on the lapel of his uniform. It was a soldier from Fortude. Their army had joined us last night from Summer's most northeastern city.

I stood up straight and took a step back, distancing myself from the fire and the soldier. "What was that for?" I asked him.

He frowned at me. "I expected you to be more jumpy."

I narrowed my eyes. "Excuse me?"

"I was told I could find the Crown Prince around here, to watch for the white face and smell of inexperience." He grinned.

I faltered at his choice of words as I tried to remember the proper way to respond.

"I didn't believe Asmund Arrath when he said you tagged along," he went on, "but my eyes do not deceive me. There's only one man in Summer who looks as out of place as you do."

I winced inwardly at the intangible blow but mustered my courage and said, "I'm sorry, but have we met before?"

"I'm afraid not, your Highness, and I can't say I'm impressed with our first meeting."

I scowled. "Asmund put you up to this, didn't he? Well, you can tell him I'm not going to play his petty games. Go find someone else to berate before I put you in your place."

The man raised an eyebrow. "Is the Crown Prince threatening me?"

He expected me to stand down at the insinuation, but I didn't. Anyone who was friends with Asmund was an enemy by default. I didn't care what the consequences were; I wanted him to leave.

The man stretched then, as nonchalant as a cat. "It doesn't matter either way," he said. "You wouldn't hold a candle to me in a fight, but I'll walk away, save you the humiliation."

He was gone before I could so much as draw my sword and I sunk down on the log beside the fire as he disappeared among the throngs of men, a stranger once more.

Why can't Asmund leave me alone?

Yet, his trick had done its job. Slivers of doubt crept in through the cracks of my confidence as I watched the camp around me.

A large group of knights sat around the fire to my left, laughing as they clacked tankards of ale together. Their braids were long, brushing the grass behind them. To my right, an older knight was sharpening an ancient axe, sparks flying every few seconds. In the distance, two knights from Fortude were sparring as others looked on. Every single one of them fit into the backdrop of the tents and sodden ground seamlessly and my heart sank in my chest.

I didn't belong there, not like they did. I didn't have a place. I wasn't a knight. I was a sixteen-year-old boy who took more pride in his skills than he had to show for them. I might have killed a couple Winter knights, but that could've been pure luck.

Maybe Asmund and that stranger were right. Maybe Sky and I should've left the fighting to the others.

"What's on your mind, soldier?"

I jumped that time at the sound, startled from my thoughts, but relaxed when I saw it was Sky who had spoken. She was standing beside me, stretching her arms above her as she yawned.

I sighed. "I'm feeling inadequate, I guess."

She raised her eyebrows. "*You*, inadequate? Isan, you're the best swordsman I know!"

It was my turn to raise an eyebrow. "And how many swordsmen do you know, may I ask?"

"Not many," she admitted, sitting down on the log beside me, "but I've seen what you can do and it's truly extraordinary." She paused and gave me a searching look. "What happened, Isan? You seemed fine yesterday."

I looked down at my boots and debated not telling her, but if I kept it a secret, I would be giving it more weight than was necessary.

"Some random knight just came over here and...insulted me, I guess you could say. Asmund put him up to it and I know I shouldn't put much stock in what he says, but..." I shook my head. "He really knows how to get to people sometimes."

Sky's eyes were hard as she said, "Does he not have better things to do with his time? Honestly..." She sighed and put a hand on my arm. "You can't let him get to you, Isan."

I gave her a look. "That is brilliant advice."

"Look, Isan, Asmund doesn't know what he's talking about. You defeated your first knight when you were twelve years old and they haven't been able to best you since. If that doesn't count for something, I don't know what does. Plus, you killed those two Winter knights in less than a few minutes."

I knew she was trying to reassure me, but it wasn't working.

"That's just it," I told her. "I killed *two* Winter knights, only two. What happens in this war when there are thousands of them coming at me? What then? Winter soldiers are ruthless, seasoned killers. How can I possibly beat them?"

She squeezed my arm and barreled into me with her steadfast gaze. "They might be skilled, Isan," she said, "and they might be many in number, but you are different."

"And why is that?" I asked, ignoring the urge to look away from her fierce eyes.

She poked me in the chest. "You chose to be here; you wanted to do this. Most of the Winter soldiers won't have a say in the matter of fighting or not. Most of our soldiers are only here because Uncle told them to. These people are fighting for their kings and kingdoms, but you are fighting for a better world."

I raised an eyebrow. "And how do you figure that exactly? I thought anger was clouding my judgment."

She took a deep breath. "I did think that, Isan, but then I tried to look at it from a different light. If we end the man who killed our parents, then there will be one less immoral person in the realm. I'm told King Frost is a tyrant. Perhaps, if we kill him, we will not only be avenging our parents, but saving Winter from his wrath as well."

I raised a brow. "Save Winter?"

She gave me a look. "You heard me; they're people too you know, despite whatever crimes they have committed. As for you, if you're so worried about being inadequate, just work hard enough to prove Asmund and yourself wrong." She stood up and brushed off her pants. "I'll get us some breakfast. Don't brood too much while I'm gone."

I rolled my eyes at her back as she walked away.

She was probably right, but I didn't feel much better. I still worried I was in way over my head and that I would soon regret my choice.

The two of us were finishing our porridge when Uncle walked up to us, laden with armour that didn't seem to deter him in the least.

"It's time to pack up," he said. "Don't want to keep Winter waiting now, do we?" He gave us a smile before continuing through the camp, giving orders and words of encouragement to his men.

He made a good leader, despite not being born into the role. It's said he lived a simple life before my parents were assassinated, before he took on the role of caregiver and king. He hadn't dreamed of being either, but it all seemed so natural to him. It was hard to imagine him as anything else. In some ways, I was grateful he had been made king instead of regent. He handled the role better than I ever dreamed I could.

The men sprang into action around us as Uncle swept through their ranks. Sky and I followed suit, our conversation still hanging in the air between us.

I tried to ignore the discomfort as I donned my armour again and packed up my supplies. Then I mounted my horse, taking a deep breath as I mentally prepared myself for another long day in the saddle.

We rode farther into the plains, eating up the countryside as we drew closer and closer to our enemy.

• • •

We continued like that for several days, getting up at sunrise, riding all day, and stopping an hour before sunset. It didn't rain again, but the mud lingered.

On the fourth day, when Mensden's army merged with us and our numbers swelled again, I felt my confidence returning. I told myself we wouldn't fail, that Winter would pay for all the wrongs they'd dealt us. I'm sure Mensden agreed after the scare they'd had. Lord Byron headed his army with a look in his eyes that promised blood.

On the eighth day, after riding all morning, I noticed something strange. The sky was beginning to darken, though it was scarcely midday, and a deep sense of foreboding filled me at the sight.

It's not the dream, I told myself. *You're awake. This is reality.*

"Is it my imagination or is it getting dark out?" I asked Sky as I pulled my horse up beside hers.

She looked up and frowned. "I think you're right, but that's strange. There's no sign of rain and it's nowhere near evening."

"Then what's going on?" I inquired.

"Perhaps something is shadowing us?" she suggested.

I waved her off. "That's ridiculous. Nothing would be tall enough to shadow this much area. It—"

And that's when we saw it.

It came out of nowhere, rising out of the near-dark to loom over us. A stand of impossibly tall and absurdly gnarled trees stretched as far as the eye could see to the east and west. The trees were so twisted and interconnected that I couldn't tell where one ended and the other began. They were dark and menacing, like age-old sentries. They looked like they would come alive and strangle you if you let your guard down.

It was definitely worse than the stories said.

We had reached the Edgewood.

Uncle ordered us to halt and the entire army sat there on their steeds, marvelling at the forest standing before us, one that we would have to pass through in order to get to Winter.

Sky turned to me and said, "We're going through *that?*"

"It seems that way," I replied.

She shook her head. "This is insane."

The army waited for further instructions, not wanting to get any closer to the wood than we had to. Sky kept shaking her head and muttering about how stupid we were and how we were all going to die.

I couldn't agree more. I hadn't liked the idea when it had first been proposed and I didn't like it any better now with the Edgewood standing in front of me, promising certain death to all who dared to enter it.

A few minutes later, word was sent through that we would camp there, at the edge of the wood, until the armies from Ne-Trol and Skar arrived. Cargoff and Laurel's men were already present, a huddle of tents to the east. I hadn't noticed them at first, my attention taken by the wood.

I could admit we looked formidable, even without Ne-Trol and Skar, but would it be enough? Would Winter take one look at us and laugh? Had we stumbled into something we weren't ready for?

Wind rustled and the Edgewood seemed to whisper we had made a terrible mistake.

12
Miles To Go

"I can't do this," I confided to Sky two days later. Lord Norwell and his army had finally arrived from Ne-Trol the night before and we were preparing to enter the Edgewood. The energy around camp was fiery, but I felt nothing but nausea.

Sky glanced at me from her horse which was pawing at the ground, looking as nervous as I felt. "What do you mean?"

"I can't go in there," I said, pointing to the trees that weren't standing far enough away in my opinion. "There's a reason no one goes in it, a reason it's impenetrable. There has to be another way."

Sky looked at me with disappointment, like she expected more from me. Her long locks were braided tight behind her. I could tell she was ready and I found myself coveting her calm. "I suppose you can see what Uncle has to say," she replied, "but I doubt he'll be persuaded now. We've already come this far; he won't turn back."

She was probably right, but I wasn't going to go in there without looking into other options. I didn't care that the Winter assassins had survived the wood. I only found myself wondering if there had been more of them before the forest had taken them in.

I urged my horse onward, plodding through the masses to the front line with Sky following behind. I knew she didn't agree with me, but it also seemed she didn't want me to go alone.

The men made a path for us, our golden armour marking us as royalty if they didn't immediately recognize us. The Edgewood loomed ever closer. Uncle waited near the trees, set apart from the rest of the army, watching our approach. It was as if he had known we were coming.

We pulled our horses to a halt a few feet from him and I dropped to the ground.

Uncle followed suit, scrutinizing me with a sigh. "What is it now, Isanfier?"

I was quiet for a moment. Then, as I looked at the ground and worried at the dirt with my foot, I said, "Well, sir, I…. I was wondering if we…well, if *you* are certain about this? Could we not find a way around the wood or wait for Winter to come to us? I—"

"You want them to regard us as cowards?" he spat. "Weak men so scared they can't even tackle a Fidal-forsaken forest?" His scowl was dangerous, pulling at his scar.

"No, sir," I replied, trying to backtrack. "It's just… I don't understand how we plan to pass through the wood."

"You dare doubt me?" he said. "I *told* you there was a path and that it would reveal itself, so that is what will happen. We are going through this forest, whether you like it or not. There is no other way. It is merely an obstacle, one standing between us and our vengeance."

He stopped, giving me time to digest his words. What he said made sense, but I found it hard to believe the forest was only an obstacle. It looked more like a deadly foe that would tear you to pieces. I could feel it. Fidalian religion stated that if you did not live a good life, your soul became a tree in this very wood. How many of these trees had once been people, people now doomed to an eternity of nothing?

If the trees *were* lost souls, what kind of creatures lurked in the depths of the wood? Would we make it out alive or would we meet the same fate? Was it worth the risk?

I was seriously considering turning around and heading back to the safety of the castle walls, until Uncle said the one thing that would make me stay.

"Are you going to let a *forest* stand between you and your vengeance?" he asked me.

The words clicked in my mind and reminded me why I was there, to enact revenge for my parents who had been torn away from me. The Edgewood and all its potential dangers shouldn't matter, not as long as it brought me closer to Winter.

I turned to Uncle and said, "No, I won't. Apologies, sir, I was acting childish."

Uncle smiled as if I'd won the war singlehandedly. "It's quite all right, Isan," he told me. "Everyone gets knocked off their path at one point or another, but good people are always there to guide them back."

I nodded.

Uncle mounted his horse and turned to the army again. "All right, men," he bellowed. "Let's open the path to Winter!"

They roared in agreement, a cacophony of cheers running up and down the line.

Uncle looked down at me. "Isan, why don't you do the honours?"

"Me?" I said, shocked.

He nodded.

"I...uh... I suppose so."

"That's the spirit!" Uncle said, reaching down and clapping me on the shoulder.

I staggered a bit from the blow. "What do I do?" I asked him.

"It's not hard," he replied. "Legend says all you have to do is close your eyes, and visualize the path and where you want it to take you. If your intentions are true, the path will reveal itself."

I wanted to ask what would happen if my intentions *weren't* true, but he was already ushering me forward.

Slowly, I approached the Edgewood. When I stood about a foot away from it, I turned back.

"Wait," I said to Uncle. "Isn't this a form of magic?"
Isn't it forbidden?

"In a sense," he admitted, "but this magic comes from the trees, not from the person. I cannot fault you for what it decides to give you."

I nodded, but his answer did not comfort me in the least. I sighed and turned back to the forest, closing my eyes, letting my fears fall to the back of my mind. It wasn't easy. Images of spectres and reaching branches tried to catch me, but I pushed them aside.

I visualized a path through the trees and then I thought of Winter. I concentrated on those two images for a few moments, but when I opened my eyes, the forest was still there. It hadn't worked.

I glanced at Uncle.

"Try harder," he urged. "Think about why you need to go to Winter and the forest should listen to your call for passage."

"All right," I said, closing my eyes once more.

I tried not to think of the massive army at my back, watching my every move. I'm sure they were whispering about my incompetence, likely sparked by Asmund, but I tried to tune out any background noise and focus on the task at hand. The longer I took, the more their judgment would linger.

Again, I visualized a path, saw the trail snaking through the trees, and heard the dirt crunching beneath my boots. I visualized Winter too, tried to imagine the white snow, the biting wind, the absence of sunlight.

It was the same as the first attempt, but this time, I put my thoughts out there as well.

I need… I need to take revenge for my parents' death.

Was that a noble intention though? Planning to kill someone?

I thought for a few seconds more and then remembered what Sky had said our first morning out here.

Yes, I want to take revenge, to make them pay, I admitted, *but that's not all I want. I want to kill the assassin so he can't kill again, so no other families are torn apart like mine was. I don't want anyone else to experience my pain.*

I need to get to Winter, to stop a killer who will only kill again.

Cheers exploded behind me and I opened my eyes. A tunnel through the trees stood before me, cloaked in foliage.

I blinked, but it remained.

The path had revealed itself.

After Uncle congratulated me, he urged the men forward and into the tunnel. It was just wide enough and tall enough for three men to ride side by side. It would take hours for everyone to enter.

Uncle waited until about two dozen men had gone ahead before he rode forward, signalling for Sky and I to join him.

I hopped back onto my horse and sent Sky an encouraging smile as we turned towards the tunnel.

An intense feeling of unease enveloped me then, telling me something wasn't right, but it passed as quickly as it had come.

SUMMER'S REVENGE

By the time we reached the tunnel, I had convinced myself I had imagined the whole thing.

Yet, as we entered the forest, leaving Summer behind us, I couldn't help but ask myself the same question again and again.

Would we make it out alive?

• • •

It was as dark as dusk—like a mist constantly hanging in the air—and eerily silent in the Edgewood. Time moved differently. The minutes dragged by, as if moving through honey, and each second passed as an eternity. The trees pressed in on us and the further we travelled, the more trapped I felt. It was like walking through the belly of a beast—constricting, terrifying, and inescapable.

I didn't know what effect the Edgewood had on everyone else, but by the time we stopped to set up camp, I was thoroughly shaken.

"Isan…Isan?"

I turned my head. "Hmmm?"

Sky stood in front of my horse, head angled to the side as she studied me. "Are you going to dismount or are you sleeping astride your horse tonight?"

"Oh," I said. "Right." I thought about getting down, but my body didn't want to move.

"Isan, are you all right?" she asked me, a look of concern creeping into her brown eyes.

I looked away from her, to the trees that seemed to watch our every move. Earlier, when we were riding, the path had extended as the lead rider moved forward and closed up as the last rider moved. Now the men were making a clearing by approaching the forest on all sides of the path, forcing the trees to retreat.

The action proved my theory that the forest was more than it seemed. It was a living, breathing creature that moved as one, each plant and tree a part of the whole. The forest's collectiveness was unnatural and gave me shivers.

"Isan? You're scaring me."

I turned back to Sky. The expression on her face looked similar to the one she wore upon waking me up from the first dream. I hated to cause her pain like that again.

"I'm sorry," I said. "I'm just… I'm not enjoying this. I've never been so…uneasy. We're a long way from home."

She nodded. "I definitely never expected to find myself here."

"I hope to never find myself here again," I replied, "aside from the journey back to Summer, of course."

She smiled. "It'll be over soon. We'll be in Winter in no time and then we'll have the cold to complain about instead. Just remember, you can talk to me if you need to, okay? You're not alone."

I nodded. "I know."

"Give your horse a rest now and try to get some sleep. I'll see you in the morning."

"Okay."

She walked away then and I peeled myself off my horse, giving him a pat. I removed his tack and brushed him down for the night before tackling my tent. It gave me some trouble and most of the men had already retired by the time I finished and retreated into the safety of the canvas, glad to have the wood out of my sight.

It was more or less a relief when sleep came and the dream claimed me. At least I knew what to expect with the dream and it was a much-needed escape from reality.

When the dream pulled me under and I did not fight it.

• • •

I found myself in a familiar corridor, torch light sending shadows flickering across me, and settled into my nightly routine with ease. The torches blew out soon after, as they always did, and the dark figure appeared right on schedule. I waited in the dark for him to pass me and then followed in his wake.

It was clockwork, but that night, something changed.

The dark figure reached the usual door and started to pick the lock.

I didn't wake up.

I stayed to watch as the door swung open in silence and the dark figure crept into the room beyond. I waited a heartbeat before entering behind him, hardly able to contain my excitement.

I'm finally going to see what's behind the door.

I was disappointed, however, when I stepped into a parlour furnished with plain wooden chairs, a table, and a single wall painting. There was no sign of gold or any precious jewels for the dark figure to steal.

What in Fidalia is he after?

The dark figure didn't stop in the sitting room, though, and I trailed him through a warren of rooms and hallways before he stopped in front of another ornately carved wooden door.

Finally.

The dark figure bent to pick the lock, but then…

The door was fading.

No. I don't want to go.

Shadows swirled around my vision, distorting the image in front of me. The door became a man, became a face, became…

Nothing.

Nothing but blackness and a sense of urgency.

• • •

I jolted awake on the floor of my tent, slicked in sweat and tangled in blankets, cursing all the gods as I tried to right myself.

I had been so close. *So* close. Why did it have to end there? What did it have against me?

Clearly, I had lost my mind because I had started to talk about the dream as if it were a living thing, capable of making decisions, instead of a figment of my imagination.

What is wrong with me?

I needed help, and soon, but I didn't want to jeopardize the mission. If Uncle thought I had some sort of mental disease, he would send me straight back to Widonia. I would never see the outside of the castle walls again.

Don't lose your head, I told myself, *or everything you've ever worked towards will be gone, every loss and pain for nothing.*

I sat up then and focused on my breathing, trying to calm down and hold onto my sanity.

That's when I noticed something was off.

It was quiet outside my tent. I heard nothing, not the sound of chatter or booted feet tramping across the earth, not the rustle of the horses, not even the wind moving through the trees, but perhaps there *was* no wind in that unnatural wood. Unease crept through me, like fingernails on my spine.

Something was wrong.

I grabbed *Ember* and eased off my bedroll. Then, crouching low, I poked my head out of the tent flap, careful not to make a sound.

My stomach dropped to my toes.

No. Oh Fidal, please…

Yet, there was no mistaking what I saw.

13
Ultimatum

Frost

The king's best spy burst into the throne room one morning unannounced, sending the doors flying into the wall. They crashed into it with the sound of shattering glass but remained intact.

King Frost looked up from the throne and dismissed the small man he'd been talking to, who had been incredibly boring anyway.

The spy collapsed before the throne, out of breath and looking half-starved. "War, Sire," he gasped. "They are coming. Sum—" The last word was lost amongst a fit of coughing and he wheezed, struggling for breath.

"Guards," Frost called out.

Two of them ran forward from their places at the windows.

"Yes, Sire?" one asked.

"Bring this man some water," the King told him, "and make it quick. If he dies before you return, I'll have your head."

The man ran out of the throne room, his sword clanking against his armour-clad shins.

While he was gone, Frost pondered over what his spy had managed to choke out.

War? Has Summer finally lost their minds?

It can't be true. Summer wouldn't be brave enough to challenge Winter, to challenge me. There must be a mistake.

The spy was still wheezing at Frost's feet and he resisted the urge to shake him until he divulged everything. Patience was a constant thorn in Frost's side.

At long last, the guard returned, flask of water in hand.

"Hurry," Frost snapped at him. "This is urgent business."

The guard dropped to his knees beside the spy and helped him drink. With every sip, the spy relaxed, seemed to become real again.

The King waited until he'd emptied the flask before ordering every guard out of the room. He would not see rumours spread if any information the spy provided proved untrue.

Once they were alone, the man dragged himself to his feet. He was stable, but still weak.

What in Wylla's name had befallen him?

"I apologize for the delay, your Majesty," he said, bowing low before the King.

Frost nodded. "You have something to tell me?"

"I come with grave news." His voice shook when he spoke.

"Go on."

He took a deep breath and said, "I am afraid Summer has declared war on us."

Frost sighed. "What have we done now?" He knew full well their history was bloody, but they had never acted before.

"It was your assassins, Sire," the spy replied. "When they did not achieve their goal, they —"

"What?" Frost roared, standing up in sudden anger. His magic crackled in his veins, but he pushed it down.

Not yet. I need this man alive.

"The assassins did not achieve their goal, your Majesty," the spy repeated.

"Worthless idiots," Frost snapped. "How close did they get?" He fought to keep his voice even. It had taken him months to prepare that expedition and he had chosen his best for the task. All he had to show for it was a half-dead spy.

"They killed three Summer knights," the man replied, "but failed to even *find* Lord Byron, let alone kill him."

Frost's blood was glacial. "Can they do nothing right? Where are they now? They dare hide from me after such a colossal failure?"

The spy shook his head. "They are dead, your Majesty."

Frost raised an eyebrow. "Dead? How can that be?"

"They travelled to Widonia after their failed attack. I thought it was a shame; they could've easily escaped Summer without a scratch, but they had hoped killing the King of Summer might put them back into your good graces."

Frost shook his head. "Fools!" he spat. "They would never get anywhere *near* Arkenier."

"I agree, Sire, seeing as they were caught and killed in the outer streets of the city. They didn't even get anywhere near the *castle.*"

"Explain to me how they were defeated."

"The king had sent a scouting party ahead of him and they were killing them off one by one. However, they were not as discreet with their final target. The prince and princess were among the people in the square. The two intervened in time to save the guard and then finished off your men."

Frost's voice trembled as he answered, anger rocking him like a wave. "My men. Were killed. By the Summer whelps? How in the name of Wylla could that happen? My men were trained professionals!" If he had been seated at a table, his fist would've slammed into the wooden surface.

"The Summer whelps are incredibly skilled fighters," the spy replied.

"Impossible."

"I saw it all with my own two eyes," he assured his king. "The girl shot three of them through with arrows before they could even draw their swords and the boy... I have seen none more skilled than him."

Frost clenched the arms of his throne. "What good are assassins that can be defeated by children?"

"I don't know, Sire."

"I wasn't asking your opinion," Frost snapped.

The spy cowered before his king. "Of course, your Majesty. My sincerest apologies." He stood in awkward silence until Frost spoke again.

"I assume it was the failed assassins who sparked the war?"

The spy nodded. "King Arkenier arrived shortly after the killing was over and dragged them off, though the war was technically declared after their folly in Mensden."

Gears turned in Frost's mind as he tried to absorb all the information. "When exactly did this happen?"

"I left the day after he announced it. They were to ride to Winter in two weeks."

"And how long has it been?"

The spy trembled at that and hesitated. "Three weeks and four days, your Majesty," he said finally.

Frost shoved his magic down further as it tried to claw through his chest. "They will be halfway to Winter by now," he replied. "We barely have enough time to assemble our troops. Why did you not get here sooner?"

"I left as soon as I could," he assured the king, voice high in fear, "but the journey is long and arduous."

Frost slapped him across the face. "I don't want your excuses! I want results."

"Yes, Sire," he replied, hanging his head in shame.

"If you have nothing else to report, then leave me. Fetch Sir Kallen and Henrik when you go, but tell Henrik to wait outside until he's called. I will decide on your fate later; for now, I must think about our next course of action."

"There were no other developments in Summer," he said.

"Then get out of my sight," Frost snapped.

As soon as the doors shut behind him, the king looked around for something to throw, but could find nothing, which only served to anger him more.

So be it.

He let go of the tight hold he'd been keeping on his magic and sighed as it surged through the air. The pressure inside his chest eased as he shed the energy like a snake shedding its skin. The magic breathed a layer of frost around the room and sought out the closest living thing to torment.

There was a muffled crash in the hall outside followed by a cry of dismay. It seemed the king was in need of a new guard.

Frost smiled. Someone must always pay the price for angering him.

Calm once more, he returned to his throne and awaited the general's arrival. He came swiftly; scarcely five minutes had passed before the door opened again. Frost saw Henrik in the hall before the doors closed behind Sir Kallen.

Kallen walked up to the throne and dropped to one knee. "Your Majesty called for me?"

"Yes, General," Frost replied. "One of my spies returned today from Summer with terrible news. The Sancians have declared war."

Kallen's eyes widened as he stood again. "On what terms?"

Frost picked at his nails, dislodging some dried blood. "Apparently, a few of my assassins were discovered in Widonia after they killed three Sancian knights."

"Ah," Kallen replied, his expression grim. "So where do we stand?"

"We shall fight, of course. No Summer army will be allowed to defeat Winter while *I* am king. Time, though, is of the essence."

Kallen frowned. "How so?"

"Summer is already on the move," the king replied. "If my guess is right, they shall reach Winter in one week's time."

"What would you have me do, Sire?"

"I am going to send a message to Tamise. They will hold the border until the rest of our armies arrive. Messages will also be sent to the other cities, of course. Lupina and Raven Cliff will do their best to aid Tamise. We must ensure that Summer doesn't get too far inland. As for you, I want you to have Appalachia's knights ready to ride out in the morning."

He sucked in a breath. "The morning, Sire? But that's hardly enough—"

Frost slammed his fist against the arm of his throne, sending frost arcing across it. "Does it look like I care? We are at *war*, General. Sacrifices will have to be made. They are to be ready in the morning. Is that clear?"

"Yes, your Majesty," he replied. He seemed shaken.

"Don't look so disheartened, General," Frost told him. "We will finally be able to rid the world of Summer, once and for all. We shall make them rue the day they stepped foot in our land. We shall cover our snowy plains with their blood and hang their heads on our fence posts. I, for one, intend to enjoy this."

Kallen smiled meekly. "Of course, your Majesty."

"Now go, there is much work to be done. The knights should meet with their horses and supplies by the North Gate at dawn. Send Henrik in now, would you?"

Kallen nodded and took his leave.

Henrik waltzed into the room a few moments later as if it belonged to him, as if he wasn't there on the king's good graces and that alone. He was an insolent youth and only the power coursing through his veins kept Frost from crushing his windpipe every time he spoke.

"You called?" he asked, stopping before the throne and looking Frost straight in the eyes. His were almost so blue as to be black.

"I did," the king said, biting his tongue against the obscenities he wanted to scream at the boy for failing to greet him properly. "I need a message sent to Lady Celeste, Lady Helen, Lord Skandar, Lady Odette, Lord Everard, and your father. Oh, and to Sir Freid at Falco Point. Can you do that?"

Henrik rolled his eyes. "Of course I can do it, but who in Fidal's name is Lady Odette?"

Frost scowled. "I don't pay you to ask questions, Henrik."

He crossed his arms. "Since when do you pay me at all?"

"You live here in the palace, do you not?" Frost replied, refraining from clenching his fists. "You're still breathing. A lavish lifestyle is more payment than you deserve some days. Do not tempt me to take it away from you because I would do so in a heartbeat."

Most would hang their head after words like that, but Henrik continued to stare the king down. "What are the messages?"

"First and foremost: prepare yourself for war."

Henrik grinned. "Oh, I do like where this is going."

"Be quiet and concentrate. This is vital to our survival."

Another eye roll. "Go on."

The cold writhed in Frost's veins, but he ignored the bite and relayed his messages to Henrik one by one.

Henrik closed his eyes and sent them to the recipient, one thought word at a time until it was done.

Satisfied, your Majesty? His voice rang in the king's head.

Frost suppressed a shudder. Even through all his years as King, he hadn't grown accustomed to the feeling of having someone's thoughts in his head. He could feel the slime of Henrik's sarcasm, his disobedience.

"Yes," he replied aloud. "That is all."

Henrik gave him a mock bow. "Pleasure to be of service." Then, with a grin, he whirled around and strolled back out.

The temperature in the room plummeted upon his departure, frost snaking across the windows, climbing up the walls, making the doors creak, but the king did not let the magic leave the room this time. He kept it contained, under control. It was as much of an exercise of will as an outlet for his frustration.

One of these days, he would kill that boy, and he would not regret it.

Once Frost was certain Henrik was long gone, he headed for the doors. He had preparations of his own to make. An announcement needed to be written, his armour and weapons required work, and he would need to break the news to Icaria and Snowdon.

The lone remaining guard struggled to open the doors for Frost on his way out and he was forced to squeeze through a single door.

Frost gave the man a deadly look and regarded the downed guard with disgust. "It is not wise to leave bodies lying on the floor, boy," he sneered. "Someone might trip over them." He walked over the body and deliberately kicked it in the ribs as he did so.

The lone guard let out a dismayed whimper.

"Clean this up," Frost called over his shoulder, "and find a replacement."

He didn't reply.

The king strode on down the hall, confident in his ability to bend people to his will.

• • •

Around midday, Frost awaited his children's presence in the parlour. He had nearly finished his war preparations. Servants had packed his bags, polished his armour, and sharpened *Malice*, his long-sword. He had written up his speech and the announcement was scheduled for that afternoon. All that remained was to inform Icaria and Snowdon about the war and hopefully disappoint them.

Snowdon arrived early in an effort to please Frost and avoid punishment. "I am here, your Majesty," he said with a quick bow of his head. "What is it you wish to discuss?"

Frost turned away and rolled his eyes in disgust. Snowdon's unfailing obedience was almost as appalling as that of the serving girl he'd killed several weeks ago.

"Quiet," Frost replied. "I shall wait for your sister before I utter a single word."

That proved to be no small matter. Icaria was twenty minutes late and she was smiling when she finally strolled in. She had thought she was being clever, but she had crossed the line.

If she had been a servant, Frost would have killed her where she stood, but because she was his blood and the heir to the throne, he merely slapped her across the face, albeit hard enough to make her head whip back and her vision blur.

He waited for her senses to return before offering an explanation of his action. "A little rebellion I will endure," he told her, "but insolence I cannot stand. You are above these silly little tirades. You are not a child."

She hung her head. "Yes, Father." Her voice quavered. Clearly, she was in pain, but she did not cry and for that Frost was proud.

"Now that you are both here," he started, "I must tell you the wonderful news."

"What could that possibly be?" Icaria asked.

"Summer has declared war. They march for Winter as we speak."

"How is that *wonderful* news?" Snowdon inquired, glancing sidelong at his father.

"I have wanted war with them for a long time," Frost told them, "even before they murdered your dear mother, though that did nothing to quell my rage. It is high time they were destroyed. Forever."

"That *is* wonderful, Father," Icaria said. "We shall crush them and make them pay the price."

He grinned. "That's the spirit."

"When do we leave?" Her eyes were alight with her excitement.

"The army shall assemble tomorrow morning at dawn," Frost replied.

"So soon? I shall get my armour polished then and sharpen my sword. Oh, there is much work to be done."

Frost's grin widened. It was time to drop the axe. "Your preparations will be unnecessary, Icaria," he said, interrupting her next words.

She looked at him. "Why?"

"You won't be coming."

"What?" Her expression changed from shock, to sorrow, and then finally to anger. "No. That isn't fair!"

"Careful," Frost chided with a sly smirk, "you are sounding childish again."

"You can't do this to me," she protested. "*Why* are you doing this to me?"

"Remember that punishment I promised you the night the taster was taken away? This is that punishment."

She looked sick. "No. You can't keep me here. I want to fight!" The temperature in the room dropped as she began to lose control of her emotions, along with her magic.

"Well, you should've thought of that before you showed up late to dinner."

"But I didn't know there was going to be a war then," she protested, her voice breaking as if she was in pain.

"Don't give me such pitiful excuses," Frost replied. "What's done is done. I have made my final decision."

She shook with anger, but said nothing more.

Frost looked over at Snowdon. "As for you, boy, *your* punishment is to fight."

Fear flashed in his eyes, cold and glorious. "Father…"

"*Your Majesty,*" Frost snapped, "and I will not hear your protests. You had time to stand up for yourself and you didn't. This war will be a test. If you survive, I will know you are worthy of being my son. If you die, well, you'll be dead to me."

Frost laughed at his own pun.

His children didn't join him. They looked at him beseechingly. For a second, he expected them to fall to their knees and beg him to change his mind, but then they nodded gravely and awaited further instructions.

"Snowdon, get ready for the journey ahead," Frost said. "Have your armour polished and your sword sharpened. I expect to see you at dawn. Icaria, if I hear of you making preparations behind my back, you will receive more than a slap."

"Yes, sir," they replied in unison.

"You may go."

They nodded and took their leave.

Frost sighed.

One day they would understand why he treated them the way he did. If this war was a success, there would be two kingdoms for them to rule over and they would have to be strong to do so. Everything Frost did was for the future of their rule, their dynasty. They would rule all of Fidalia if it was the last thing they did.

14
Shadows Dark and Deep

Isan

The forest had encroached on us during the night. There was no clearing, no men, and no horses. There were only three tents: mine, Sky's, and one other.

We were alone.

Everyone else was gone and we were alone in the Edgewood.

My head whirled as a myriad of emotions sliced through me.

Fear of the future and the Edgewood; the forest had a mind of its own. Confusion: *why had we been left behind?* Above all, regret was the emotion that ruined me.

Oh how I regretted ever going into that forest, ever wanting to leave the safety of the castle and capital city. I wanted to go back, but we had made a choice and it couldn't be reversed.

I scrambled out of my tent and ran over to Sky's, yelling her name as I went.

"What?" she mumbled, still lost in the stupor of sleep.

"They're gone, Sky. Everyone's gone! What are we going to do? I—"

"Slow down, Isan," she said as she sat up and rubbed her eyes. "What do you mean everyone's gone?"

"Exactly as it sounds; *we were left behind.*"

That caught her attention, and, in a flash, she was out of her bedroll. She pushed past me, rushing out into the clearing or what was left of it.

I followed her out.

She looked around our campsite, turning in a small circle, and I saw the exact moment she realized the truth. Her eyes widened and fear clouded them, but she still tried to deny it.

"No, impossible," she muttered. "They wouldn't leave us."

And then she was screaming.

"Uncle! Uncle, where are you? Come back! Don't leave us here! I know you're out there! Please... Somebody! Anybody..."

She stopped then, choking on the tears streaming down her face, and dropped to her knees in the grass. I knelt beside her, draping an arm over her shoulder. Uncle and the others couldn't hear us; we were alone.

"What are you two going on about out there?" a gruff voice called from the other tent, across the small clearing. It was a voice I recognized and a stone settled in the pit of my stomach.

No. No, no, no.

Asmund was still complaining as he crawled out of his tent, but the words died on his lips as he beheld what had caused our uproar.

He froze, one foot in his tent and one out. "Fidal's breath," he gasped.

I couldn't believe it.

This isn't happening. This can't be happening.
Of all the people we could be stuck here with…

I looked up to the sky, or at where it should have been, but there was only a tangle of branches. "Is this some sort of joke?" I screamed.

There was no answer, from any of the deities.

Typical.

"What did you do?" Asmund snapped.

I turned to face his glare, getting to my feet. "Me?" I echoed. "I could ask you the same question! You're under as much suspicion as I am, so—"

His face was flush. "How dare you accuse me of this? You're the one who wants me gone so badly!"

I gave him a look. "Do you think I'd be stupid enough to endanger myself too?"

His smile was snakelike. "Do you want me to answer that question?

The verbal battle would've turned physical if Sky hadn't intervened. "Oh for Sancia's sake," she yelled. "Be quiet! The both of you."

We turned to her in surprise, and fear.

She was standing beside me now, her arms crossed and her eyes fiery behind the red rims of her earlier tears. "We are in this together, like it or not," she told us, "and we will have to work together to get out of it. I will not have you two at each other's throats the whole time. Do you understand me?"

I nodded.

Even Asmund was too lost for words and just mirrored me.

Sky threw her braid over her shoulder, brushing a few stray strands behind her ears. "Good," she said. "Now that's over with, we can get some work done. Let's focus on what we know."

"We're lost in the Edgewood," Asmund replied.

"We have no horses," I added.

"And we have very little supplies," Asmund finished.

"Okay," Sky said, hands on her hips. "So what are we going to do about it?"

"Keep moving forward, I guess," I replied, not too sure of my answer.

Asmund scoffed at me. "How do you propose we do that? We don't even know which way forward is. We never should've left Summer. This war is already a disaster and we haven't even reached Winter yet."

Sky shot him a look. "There will be none of that either," she said. "If you don't have anything positive to say, keep your mouth shut."

Asmund looked at her like she had grown a second head. Indeed, there were no traces of the royal Sky had pretended to be while around him. Asmund was finally seeing the true Princess Skiansy. I wondered if he still wanted her to be his wife.

"We'll have to pick a direction and stick to it," Sky went on. "The path should lead us out eventually."

I nodded. "I don't think we have another choice."

"Let's get to it then," she said.

Asmund didn't say a word.

The three of us were quiet—lost in the cacophony of our own thoughts—as we tore down our tents, and packed them and our few meager supplies into knapsacks. We had to carry everything ourselves, so we left much behind.

When we were ready, I picked a random direction, much to Asmund's dismay, and we headed back into the depths of the wood.

• • •

That night—if it even was night; it was hard to tell in this perpetual dusk—the three of us were fully exhausted. We skipped dinner and put our tents up quickly, barely saying goodnight before we let sleep take us away from our problems.

The dream unfolded in the same manner as the night before and I didn't understand why it had altered its path. Had I done something different or was it even something *I* had done at all?

Whatever the reason, I wished it would hurry up and end already. The *dream* was sucking the life out of me. At the same time, though, I was terrified I would not like the outcome, if it did end. I felt like it was water inside a dam, building up day by day, waiting to burst and flood me with the reality of the ending.

It might *not* end horribly, but I had a feeling there wasn't a happily ever after in store for me.

I put my head in my hands. It was too much to deal with on top of everything else we were going through.

"Rough night, Prince?"

I looked up to see Asmund standing over me, which did nothing to improve my mood. He looked...oddly sincere though, so I refrained from saying something nasty and merely nodded.

"Time to go," Sky said. Her bag was slung over her shoulder, a tired look to her brown eyes.

"Lead the way," Asmund said.

I stood up, grateful for the distraction, and followed them back into the eventide.

• • •

We were well into a day of walking when I noticed my feet growing heavier and my eyelids drooping.

Something was wrong.

I couldn't seem to move.

"Sky..." I said. I reached out to her, but the light was fading and I couldn't make her out. She and Asmund were dark silhouettes in the distance, getting smaller by the second.

I tried to say something, anything, but words failed me.

I vaguely heard somebody calling my name, but then my vision blurred, the ground whirled up to meet me, and everything went black.

I opened my eyes, disoriented for a second, and found myself lying on a cold stone floor, staring up at a dark ceiling. I shook my head to clear it and experienced instant regret as my skull started pounding like a racing heart.

I sat up, bringing my head to my knees, and took deep breaths, rocking back and forth until the pain subsided. Then I eased to my feet, wary of another attack of pain.

Swaying, I studied my surroundings and wasn't even mildly surprised to find that I was in a torchlit corridor.

I sighed.

Here we go again.

That time when the wind blew through the corridor though, it was different. It tore down the hall in a freezing whirlwind, consuming the torches and plunging the hall into darkness so black I could barely see my hand in front of my face.

This isn't normal.

The other dreams had been frightening, but this one seemed lethal, like a poison creeping through the cracks under the shutters and doors of a house to kill you in your sleep.

I shuddered.

What is going on?

Whatever it was, it didn't bode well.

Then, like a phantom materializing out of the dark on a moonless night, the dark figure appeared at the window. Only, this time, he didn't creep in and down the hall. Instead, he stepped off the windowsill and strode down the hall like he owned the place.

Where had his burst of confidence come from?

As he passed me, I stood motionless and thanked Fidal that he still couldn't see me. Even so, I took extra care in tailing him that time, remaining ten paces back. It was a good thing I knew where we were going because I couldn't see him at all in the dark.

We arrived at the door without delay. He picked the lock, gingerly swung open the door, and walked inside.

I followed tentatively as he wove through the warren of rooms and hallways.

When we finally reached the second door, I braced myself, waiting for the dream to extract me. Relief washed over me when I remained, for I would finally see the end of it, but terror crept through me at the same time.

My heart raced in anticipation as the dark figure opened the door, though I tried to remain calm. He was more cautious when he moved into the new room, and because of this, I was too. If the dark figure was wary, I should be twice as wary.

A single candle burned low on a table beside the door and I surveyed the new room—four walls, floor-to-ceiling bookshelves, and two night tables on either side of a four-poster bed.

At first glance, I perceived that the bed was empty. However, on second glance, I realized my mistake. A man and a woman lay in it, both of them sound asleep, unaware of the intruder.

I recognized them.

I knew who they were.

I had little recollection left of what they looked like in person, but I had their portraits committed to memory and would know their faces anywhere.

"Mother? Father?" I whispered, taking a step towards them.

I realized my folly in speaking too late and whipped my head in the direction of the dark figure.

He appeared not to have noticed and my parents hadn't stirred either.

I was quite suspicious of the situation then. What was the dark figure doing sneaking into my parents' bedroom in the middle of the night?

My heart sank as I realized what night it must be, as I realized why this section of the castle was abandoned.

As if reading my thoughts, the dark figure pulled out a sword. Even in the darkened room I could read its name: *Shadows*.

How fitting.

I unsheathed my own sword.

If he thought he could get away with killing my parents without a fight, then he was quite mistaken. I crept forward, raised *Ember*, and slashed towards him.

Ember sliced through his body as if he were made of smoke and—knocked off balance—I fell to the ground, dumbfounded.

That shouldn't have happened. My sword should not have gone through him like he wasn't there.

The dark figure, unaware of my attempt on his life, advanced on my parents.

"No!" I screamed, rising up off the ground and running at him, only to pass right through his incorporeal body.

Sancia's breath, this isn't working.

There has to be something I can do. Time is running out, but...

I turned and watched in horror as my parents were killed in front of me.

15
Goblins and Graves

"No!" I screamed.

I was crying hysterically, horrified by the image of my parents' throats being slit. I knew, from that moment on, that it would be burned into my eyelids. I knew that every time I closed my eyes, I would see them dying, over and over again. I would be helpless, knowing I couldn't save them.

I couldn't stop my tears. They poured out like I'd had them bottled up for years and was finally setting them free.

"Isan?" A voice cut through the fog of my misery. "Isan! Oh, Fidal… Asmund, help me!"

I felt hands grab my arms and I tried to pull away.

"No!" I screamed. "You won't take me too! Leave me alone!"

The arms held me down. "Wake up, Isanfier," a gruff second voice snapped.

"Isan, it's me," the first voice gasped. "It's Sky. You're awake. It's me."

Her words finally reached me.

I'm awake. It's over.

I stilled my flailing limbs and took a shuddering breath, finally noticing Sky and Asmund leaning over me. Asmund was pinning my arms to the ground.

"Isan?" Sky said softly.

I took another breath. "Is this real?"

Asmund raised an eyebrow. "Why wouldn't it be?" He let go of my arms and leaned back.

I could feel my tears drying on my face and wished Asmund hadn't been there to see me in such a state. "I need to be sure," I said.

"It's real, Isan," Sky assured me. "We're in the Edgewood with Asmund, heading for Winter, and you collapsed ten minutes ago with no warning. We've been trying to wake you since, only to have you startle awake yourself, screaming and crying like you'd just escaped death. What happened, Isan?"

I sat up. "This is not a happy tale." I glanced at Asmund. "I am trusting you with this information; don't take it lightly."

"On Sancia's shining light, I promise this stays between us," he replied, "but this is the only quarter I'm giving you."

I searched his dark eyes for a lie, but could find none circling the depths.

"Are you going to tell us?" Sky asked.

I nodded. "I've waited long enough." I continued my story before she could question exactly how long I'd been hiding it from her.

Starting and stopping, in bits and pieces, I told Asmund and Sky about the nightmares I'd been having. It was clear now that nightmare was the correct term. When I reached the latest one, I began to shudder, loathing the idea of having to relive it so I could tell them what happened.

I remained relatively calm until I reached the part where the dark figure and I entered the new room. Tears streamed down my cheeks again, and I raced through the rest of the story. Words tumbled out of my mouth in a streaming torrent as I fell down a waterfall of misery and nearly drowned in my sorrow.

"He *killed* them," I sobbed. "I couldn't stop him. I couldn't save them. I couldn't..." I trailed off, unable to continue.

I could hear Sky crying with me and looked up to see my own sorrow reflected in her brown eyes.

Asmund's eyes were dry, but his expression was grave.

"I want to know who did this to you," Sky choked out.

"*Who?*" I asked, bewildered.

"I want to know *who* or *what* did this to you so I can tear them limb from limb and make them feel the pain they inflicted on you a hundredfold. We already know our parents are dead, that they were murdered, but making you watch... Why would anyone do such a thing?"

She was furious, her hands balled into fists. She reached for *Tempest* where it lay on the ground beside us, but then stopped. She took a deep breath and uncurled her fingers. "I'm sorry," she said.

I wiped my eyes with my sleeve. "Sorry for what?"

"I'm sorry you had to go through that." She wrapped me in a hug that I somehow managed to return. "Isan, you didn't have to...you shouldn't have had to go through that alone. Why didn't you tell me?"

I shrugged. "I didn't want to burden you."

She pulled back from the hug and crossed her arms. "Isan, my brother needing my help is not a burden, and if it was, it would be a burden I'd carry gladly. Next time —"

I raised an eyebrow. "Next time? I sure hope there isn't a next time!"

"If," she amended, "something like this happens again, don't keep it from me. Tell me about it and we can work through it together."

"Fine," I whispered.

Asmund had remained silent throughout our entire exchange and I looked to him now. "So?" I asked him. "Considering rescinding your vow of secrecy?"

He shook his head. "Horrible as it seems, I believe that dream was sacred, a vision from the gods. It is your duty now to figure out what they were trying to tell you."

I only nodded in answer. I hadn't considered that. If he was right, I didn't know whether to be grateful or upset. Why would our so-called benevolent gods put me through something like that?

But Asmund was right. There had to be a reason for the nightmare.

"We should get going again," Sky said, interrupting my brooding. "We can discuss this more later."

I remembered our trek then, the endless trees and the lack of sunlight. "I don't think I can—"

"It'll do you good, Isan," Sky interrupted in her no-nonsense voice. "It'll be a perfect distraction, and besides, we have a lot of ground to cover. We can't afford another delay."

I sighed. "You're right. I don't want to spend more time in this forest than we have to."

She stood up then and I followed her slowly, refusing Asmund's offered hand. My legs were a little shaky, but I wasn't going to sacrifice my pride over it.

"I'll lead this time," Asmund said.

Sky and I simply nodded.

While we continued to trudge through the forest, I took my memories of the nightmare and the pain they brought with them, and buried them deep down in the recesses of my brain, never to be found again.

At least, that was the plan, though something told me it was a feat that would be easier said than done.

• • •

We walked for what seemed like an eternity before I noticed the change. The shadows were thickening, the canopy above us blocking the sunlight almost completely, turning dusk into nightfall. The trees around us became more twisted and menacing, if that was even possible. I imagined I could see faces in the peeling bark and gnarled limbs.

Branches rustled ahead of us and then silence reigned again.

Asmund came to a halt. He threw his hand out behind him, signalling Sky and I to do the same.

"What is it?" Sky asked him as we stopped side by side.

"We're not alone," he replied. "Something is out there." He kept his eyes on the forest ahead as he said it.

"What?" she said.

"I can feel it too," I told Asmund. "What do you think it is?"

He shrugged and shook his head.

"My imagination has lots of ideas," Sky chimed in.

"I doubt any of them hold much truth," Asmund replied, half-turning toward us. "*Something* is out there all the same, though. It's been stalking us for a while now."

"What do we do?" Sky asked. I could hear the fear rising in her voice.

"Nothing to do until it shows itself," Asmund said. "We'll keep moving for now, but pay close attention to our surroundings. Her Highness should walk between us. Isan, you watch our backs."

I nodded.

The three of us moved into formation and walked a few more minutes before we stepped into a clearing, one not caused by the path. Foliage still blocked the sky from view and I was beginning to wonder if I'd ever see its blue again.

We were halfway across the clearing when the rustling started again and our stalkers emerged from the trees.

We grabbed our weapons and fanned out as we prepared to face the threat, Asmund and I ahead of Sky, but the *threat* was nothing like I expected.

Out of the forest waddled a dozen grotesque little creatures armed with spears, bows, and an odd assortment of other weapons. They were short, barely as tall as my waist, and were all a sickly, greenish colour. They had big, bulbous noses and long, pointed ears. Their yellow teeth were sharp and rotted and they wore animal skins for clothing. I'd never seen the likes of them before.

"What are they?" I asked aloud without taking my eyes off them.

"I think they're...goblins," Sky replied.

"Goblins?" Asmund repeated, incredulous.

"Yes," Sky said. "I read about them in a book once. They..." She trailed off as the goblins advanced.

"What do we have here?" one goblin asked slyly as the group of them studied us.

My jaw dropped. They *talked*.

"I fink we have found us some human scum," replied another.

A third said, "Thems is easy pickings, chief."

He addressed the first who answered, "Yes, yes they is. We'll be feasting tonight, boys!"

The goblins began hooting and hollering in excitement.

Sky, clearly taken aback by the exchange, put a hand on her hip and said, "What makes you think you'll be getting away with *that*?"

The goblins scrambled, a few of them moving to hide behind their chief. "It speaks! It speaks as if it knows us!" they cried.

I shook my head; this scene was getting stranger by the second.

The goblins quivered as they studied us.

Their chief, however, was not fazed by Sky's words. He turned, looked her straight in the eyes, and said, "Oh, we'll be getting away with this, sweetheart. We *always* win."

Sky stiffened at being called sweetheart, but I was more troubled by the chief's faith in himself and the other goblins. He spoke with extreme confidence and I had a feeling they would be harder to beat than they looked.

Then one goblin piped up, saying, "That ain't true, chief. We was once defeated by…by the *Missing One*."

The goblins were on the move again, running and screaming.

"The Missing One?"

"The Missing One!"

"Where?"

"She'll kill us, chief! She'll kill us all!"

"Hush!" the chief snapped, raising a hand for silence. "She's nowhere near."

One goblin peeked out from behind the chief and said, "Are you sure, chief? What if…" He cleared his throat. "You don't think *they're* with the *Missing One,* do you?" He pointed to us and the chief narrowed his eyes in our direction.

"Well, are ya?" the hiding goblin asked.

I'd had it with these fiends. I opened my mouth to tell them no, to yell it, in fact, but Asmund stepped forward, signalling Sky and I to stay silent.

"You should listen to your man," he said to the chief. "It so happens that the Missing One *has* sent us here, to deal with the likes of you. She is not happy with your behaviour lately."

I narrowed my eyes.

What is he going on about? We're not...

The majority of the goblin horde stilled while the remainder glanced at the trees around them. "She watches us?" they asked.

They sounded chilled to the bone and that's when I realized what Asmund was doing. He'd recognized what they feared most and was trying to scare them off. For once, I had to hand it to him; this was genius. I guess he had learned a thing or two in that military city.

The goblin chief, however, was having none of it. "I *told* ya lousy ingrates that she's nowhere near," he snapped. "Get yer tails out from between yer legs fer crying out loud."

"She doesn't have to be near," Sky added, "not when we're here in her stead."

Asmund nodded. "Do you think she has the time to deal with you herself?"

The chief didn't look scared. In fact, he grinned as he replied, "The three of you are liars. I can smell it on you."

Sky and Asmund stilled. He had called our bluff and we no longer had any leverage.

I looked around, analyzing our options for escape, and that's when I noticed the lights—no, the *eyes*—in the trees.

Were they more goblins or some other unknown threat?

"Guys..." I said. I tugged on Sky's sleeve and pointed up to the trees.

She swore under her breath and had *Tempest* nocked and drawn in the space of three heartbeats, not thinking before she shot.

The first goblin hit the ground with a thump and the entire horde howled in fury.

"Enough!" the chief bellowed. "Get them!"

The goblins roared a battle cry and surged forward, the Missing One forgotten.

Asmund echoed them and the three of us reacted with a fury the goblins matched.

I killed three in quick succession, using their height to my advantage as I drove *Ember* into their skulls, but they soon learned from that. The next few to face me didn't dare come so close and thus it became a game of cat and mouse.

They came at me from all sides, but I was a flurry of motion, countering their strikes as fast as I could. If they gained the upperhand, their numbers would quickly overwhelm me.

I kept track of Sky's presence through the gold-fletched arrows she shot and knew Asmund was still alive simply because he was not a quiet fighter. His battles cries and cursing could still be heard over the din.

I leaned to the left to dodge an incoming spear and earned a club in the shoulder for my trouble. The goblins cackled as I cried out in pain, but the mistake only urged me on.

No goblin would be the end of me.

I ignored the ache in my shoulder as I pressed on, cleaving heads off shoulders and scrambling over the fallen. The goblins' screams were otherworldly and awful, but I told myself each one brought me closer to freedom and I was actually managing to gain ground until a searing pain blossomed in my left shin, dangerously close to my knee.

I'd been hit.

The thought shocked me for a moment, but then I reached down, pulled the spear out of my shin, and pressed on. I lunged for the next goblin in front of me, but stopped short as pain shot up my leg in a trail of white-hot fire, nearly bringing me to my knees.

I cried out and brushed my hand across the wound. It came back covered in blood. I forced myself to take deep breaths, gritting my teeth against the burning agony.

Keep going, I urged myself.

I couldn't stop until I was safe. If I did, I would be pulled under the goblin horde and torn apart, faster than Sky could shoot, faster than Asmund would think to save me.

The goblins around me sneered as my moves became less precise, but I would not die quietly and I would take as many of them down with me as I could.

I fought the goblins off with everything I could muster and did my best to ignore the pain slashing through my leg with each step I took. It wasn't long before I began to sway on my feet, but I ignored that too.

Keep going or die.

I was doing fine until I saw something horrific out of the corner of my eye. One of the trees had uprooted itself, launching dirt and leaves into the air. It moved towards me, seeming to float across the ground, its limbs reaching towards me like huge, misshapen claws.

I screamed and lashed out, even though I knew a sword wouldn't do much damage to its thick bark, but *Ember* passed through the tree and it vaporized into mist.

An illusion.

You're seeing things.

Don't pay them any heed.

It took a great amount of mental effort, but I managed to disregard the creatures and plants that came at me, multiplying and becoming more gruesome by the second.

I couldn't fathom how I was still standing; how an arrow hadn't yet pierced my heart or how I'd managed to avoid getting my head lopped off by a goblin, given the state I was in. And the goblins, it didn't matter how many of them I killed, they kept coming and coming. Surely there hadn't been this many before?

It was a losing battle. Sky, Asmund, and I would die here, and no one would know. No one would come to find us, and even if they did, there wouldn't be anything left to find, except perhaps a pile of bones scattered around the remnants of a goblin's fire. No one would tell tales of our heroic battle, how we fought the goblins, defiant to the end.

I sent up a silent prayer to Fidal; he was the only one who could save us now. Sancia had no influence in this forsaken wood and I was beginning to wonder if the gods had abandoned it entirely.

I lurched to one side to avoid another incoming spear and a wave of nausea washed over me.

Gravity finally won the battle and I fell.

Time slowed and it seemed like an eternity passed before I hit the ground with a *thud*. The sound echoed, like the realm was replaying my fall over and over again. I watched the world as if looking through a pane of cloudy glass, a blur of green and grey. The pain in my leg was fading, but that was because I was fading too. Numbness crept into my limbs and I laughed at the knowledge that, after everything I'd gone through, I was going to die of blood loss.

I'm sorry, Sky, I thought. *I'm sorry I couldn't hold on. Run. Get out while you still can. Don't come back for me. Don't try to avenge me; get to Uncle and Winter. I guess this is goodbye. Just…*

Death had its hold on me and I was losing my grip on reality.

I grabbed onto the last thread of thought. "Save yourself, Sky. Save yourself." I was too far gone to realize I'd whispered those final words aloud.

Death's icy fingers pulled me down towards nothing.

Part 2: Silence

"You are most powerful when you are most silent. People never expect silence. They expect words, defense, offense, back and forth. They expect to leap into the fray. They are ready, fists up, words hanging leaping from their mouths. Silence? No."

—Alison McGhee

16
Before I Sleep

For a while, I drifted.

Sometimes there was light and sometimes there was dark. Sometimes I was there, thoughts churning, and other times I knew nothing. If this was death, then death was...confusing.

Where were the stars people spoke of and the goddesses? Where was my eternal rest and celebration? Why was I stuck in limbo?

I should've been grateful that I hadn't turned into a tree yet, but the lack of closure was infuriating.

Just let me go, I screamed into the void. *I want to go back.*

I wasn't ready to die.

I needed to avenge my parents. I needed to return to Aunt Mag. I needed to protect Sky from Asmund, who I had left her all alone with.

Nothing answered my calls and so I drifted on.

• • •

Time had become irrelevant, but, eventually, a change occurred and it startled me from my lethargy.

My head felt fuzzy, like I was awakening from a long sleep, and I could hear...something. It sounded as if someone was talking to me from worlds away. I couldn't make out any words, but there was a voice, a person reaching out to me from the other side.

If only I could get to them.

I no longer had a sense of my limbs, but I tried to reach out, tried to push through the emptiness around me.

I'm not gone, I whispered. *Don't leave me here.*

The voice continued and I stretched my consciousness, as if reaching them could save me, until...

Something pulsed inside me, a steady beat.

I couldn't locate the source, but somehow I knew it would lead me to freedom, so I concentrated all of my mind on it.

I have so much more to do.

I can't die now.

I put my whole heart into my desire to live, willing myself to come back, concentrating on the pulse and that distant voice.

How long it took, I do not know, but sensation filled me again, spreading through my body until the numbness faded away. I could feel my limbs, could sense my fingers, and now that it was a part of me again, I could tell the soft pulse was coming from my leg.

My leg. Where I'd been hit.

What is happening?

I should have been dying still, but I...wasn't.

I heard the voice again and this time it was clear as day.

Sky was talking to me.

I'm here! I'm okay!

I gave my mind one last shove and opened my eyes.

Sky blinked once in confusion and then she whispered, "Isan?"

I tried to answer; I imagined my lips forming the words, but no sound came out.

Tears shone in Sky's eyes and dripped down onto my face. She turned her head and called out to someone behind her. "He's alive." She choked on the words, barely getting them out through her sobs of relief.

I wanted to smile, but something told me I couldn't do that either.

My vision distorted and my senses started to fade once more. I saw a blur of movement and colour beside Sky. Whiteness filled my sight and I wondered if we were in Winter, wondered how in Fidalia we managed to get there if we were.

I felt gentle hands pry my lips open and then blessed liquid enter my mouth. Though I craved it, it tasted rancid, and it was all I could do to swallow as it continued to drip down my throat.

Then the hands pulled away and I felt tired.

I should close my eyes and rest...

No!

Closing my eyes was dangerous, closing my eyes meant giving up, but I had no strength to prevent it. The last thing I saw was that blur of white as my vision faded and I knew nothing once more.

．　．　．

My waking moments happened off and on for a while. Each time I drifted off again, I was terrified, though each time I woke up, I was stronger.

Sky never said anything but my name, waiting for me to be strong enough to answer. She continued to give me water and I continued to make progress with my health.

Those days were the worst of my life, for I saw how much stress Sky was in, how happy she became when I awoke, but I was helpless to comfort her, to tell her I was okay and would continue to be. I wanted so badly to be able to reach up and dry her constant flow of tears and was frustrated when I couldn't, time and time again.

I thought of Asmund too. Was he taking advantage of my condition or was he actually taking care of my sister like any man should? I was glad I was recovering, almost simply because I hated the thought of leaving Sky alone with him.

• • •

I shook off the fog of sleep again and opened my eyes.

The world was full of colour and pain.

My limbs were stiff and hunger gnawed at my internal organs. Then there was my head… It was pounding, each beat like a blow by a large, blunt object.

I moaned and Sky was at my bedside in an instant.

"Isan?" she asked, worried about me. She was always worried about me.

"Yes?" I answered, my voice quiet and ragged. My jaw ached and the action didn't help matters. I never thought something as simple as speech could be so draining.

Sky's eyes widened and she flung her arms around me. "You're okay!" she exclaimed. "Oh Sancia, you're okay."

My whole body hummed with life and I hugged her back firmly, thrilled to be back with her in the land of the living.

She pulled back and stared at me in silence for a while. Then she started to cry through the smile tugging at the corner of her lips. "Oh, Isan, I could kill you for being so stupid, for scaring me like that. I hope you know that."

I shook my head. "Can't you just admit you missed me?"

"You scared me half to death," she snapped, hands on her hips. "How in Sancia's name was I supposed to return to Uncle without you? He'd have my head."

We both smiled at that and then we were laughing so hard I was crying too.

17
Rescue and Rest

When our laughter finally subsided, I gave Sky a stern look and said, "I thought I was dead. How in Fidalia did you manage to save me?"

She shook her head. "It wasn't me," she said. "It was Echo. We *all* would've died if it weren't for her."

I frowned. "Who?"

A girl walked into my line of sight as Sky cleared her throat and said, "Isan, this is Echo. Echo, meet my brother, Isan."

I looked at the girl called Echo and knew without a doubt she was a Wyllan. Her skin was pale, paler even than mine, and her hair was so blonde it was white. The long, wispy strands hung unbraided past her shoulders. She didn't look like much physically, but as soon as I met her eyes, I knew there was more to her.

Her eyes were the brightest blue I had ever seen, brighter than Lake Lotus, brighter even than the Summer sky, but they held an emptiness, a weight. I had a feeling this girl's past was fraught with heartache.

"Hello," I said, hoping I hadn't studied her for too long. I didn't want to make our supposed saviour uncomfortable, and if she really was a Wyllan, I didn't want to make her angry.

"Hello, Isan," Echo replied. "I'm glad you decided to wake up. Your sister here has been driving me crazy with the hysterics."

Sky shot Echo an indignant look and Echo laughed.

They must've had enough time together during my recovery to cultivate some sort of camaraderie then. I would've been jealous—even I couldn't play off one of those looks—but I was wary of how Echo might react.

"Anyway," Sky said, grabbing Echo by the shoulders. "This lady saved our lives. I don't know what we would've done if she hadn't shown up and scared the goblins off."

My eyebrows shot up. "*You* scared the goblins off?"

"Yes," Echo replied. "Evidently, I'm the Missing One."

I blinked. "*You're* the Missing One? I thought the goblins were going crazy about some fantasy. What did you do to make them fear you like that?"

She shrugged. "I have my secrets; I'm sure you can say the same."

I narrowed my eyes at the misdirection, but said nothing.

"It was impressive," Sky said. "There weren't many left by the time Echo showed up, but as soon as she did, the remaining goblins scattered."

I frowned. "Not many left? Sky, there were hundreds of them. We were doomed."

Sky looked to Echo, as if to say, *Should we tell him?*

Echo gave her a returning look I couldn't interpret.

"You were hallucinating," Sky replied finally. "The spear that cut you was poisoned. Your leg was purple when I found you, Isan, with green lines advancing up it."

I choked. "Poison?"

Echo nodded. "Sap from any tree in the Edgewood is lethal to humans. The goblins dip their weapons in it so that even if the hit isn't fatal, you'll die anyway. It's a guaranteed meal. Luckily, I know how to make the antidote."

"And I couldn't refuse when she offered to save you," Sky added, "even if she was a stranger who appeared suddenly out of the woods. So we brought you here to Echo's treehouse and we've been nursing you back to life ever since."

Echo must have been the white blur I had seen while in and out of consciousness. Again, I wondered if she was Wyllan. Both the hair and eye colour would suggest it, but if she was, what was she doing out here in the Edgewood?

"Where was Asmund while all of this was happening?" I asked.

"Well, he—"

"*He* is right here," his familiar voice said, and I turned in bed to watch him walk through the door. His right arm was in a sling and there was a long cut above his eye. He nodded at me. "Good to see you're still alive, Prince."

Sky rolled her eyes at him. "I suppose you want to tell your own story then?"

"Her Highness doesn't agree with my 'fanciful' recount of the events," he told me as he came to sit on the bed beside mine.

"That doesn't even begin to cover it," she said with a scowl.

I was glad to see she hadn't formed a new friendship with Asmund while I wasn't around.

Echo shook her head at the exchange. "Why don't you two call it a truce and I'll tell the story." She didn't wait for their replies and I admired that. "Asmund fought bravely, I'm sure, but got clubbed on the head moments before I arrived. I assume the goblins would have beaten him to death if I hadn't scared them away. Sky was the only one conscious upon my arrival.

We had to drag you and Asmund back here actually. Asmund woke up with minor bruising and a severe headache, but no lasting damage. You were the one we were really worried about."

"I wasn't worried," Asmund said.

Sky looked ready to beat him herself, so, to change the subject, I asked her how long I'd been out.

"A week," she stated simply.

I jumped in my skin. "A week!"

"Yes," she replied. "It was a couple days before we gathered the ingredients for the antidote and then four days for the poison to leave your system, though you woke up briefly on the third day and every day after. Do you remember that?"

I nodded.

"We took those opportunities to give you water, otherwise you would have succumbed to dehydration rather than the poison. It was a close thing."

I nodded again and then winced. The movement didn't do wonders for my headache. "It didn't seem like a week to me," I mused.

"You were unconscious," she reminded me. "I assure you, it was the longest week of my life. Echo was not exaggerating about the hysterics. I was so afraid you weren't going to make it...that you would die. I don't know what I would've done." She paused for a second, wrapping her arms around herself, and I noticed her hair was unbraided. An unusual sight. "Do you remember the morning after you had the dream for the first time?"

I met her eyes. "How could I forget?"

"I thought you were dead when I entered your room," she said, "but that was nothing compared to this. This time I *knew* you could die. I knew you were dying and I... I was terrified. Don't ever do that to me again, Isan, because that was pure agony."

"I'm sorry," I said. "I didn't know. It looked to me like we were being overrun. I thought it was a losing battle and I guess I gave up. I had been fighting it for a while, pushing on despite the pain. You've never known pain like that, but it wasn't the worst part."

She gave me a quizzical look. "What was the worst part?"

"It was when I thought I was dead," I replied. "I wanted to return to this world so badly, but I could do nothing. I've never felt so helpless or so alone."

She squeezed my hand. "You weren't alone. I would fight Fidal himself to get you back." She took a breath. "I'm sorry I didn't get to you sooner, that you had to think you were dead."

"You did the best you could," I assured her, "and you saved me in the end. That's all that matters."

Sky didn't reply and I looked towards Echo, who gave me a sympathetic look. There was pain in her eyes, a sense of...kinship, like she knew what I was going through. She knew pain, but I had a feeling hers was a much different colour than mine.

Before I could ponder further, Asmund stood up and said, "Enough with the melodrama. The man is clearly fine."

Sky pulled her hand back from mine and scowled up at him. "What matters is that we're all here. That's all we could ever ask for. I am grateful Fidal sent Echo to us."

"I would have to agree," I replied, looking over at Echo before adding, "How will we ever repay you?"

"Saving a life is all the payment I need," she replied with a smile. "From what I can gather, the realm has taken much from you in the past few weeks and I would not wish to add to it. All I ask is that you tread with care in the future."

"I'll do my best," I replied. "I certainly won't be asking any goblins for directions."

She and Sky both laughed at that.

Asmund merely crossed his arms. He was itching to be done with the conversation, itching to leave.

"Well," I said as I gave my arms a stretch. "What now?"

Sky frowned. "What do you mean?"

"What's the plan?" I replied. "Where do we go from here?" I figured Asmund already had something in the works. He was probably mad at me for delaying our travels, though I was surprised he was even still here. I wouldn't put it past him to leave both Sky and I behind.

"The *plan* is we're staying here and resting up," Sky answered.

"Here?" I replied. "But we have to get to Winter as soon as possible. Uncle and the others will be worried sick. We—"

"Isan," she interrupted. "You can't go anywhere. You won't make it two steps in the state you're in, let alone all the way to Winter. You need to lay low and recuperate."

"State I'm in?" I repeated. "Lay low? I don't think—"

"Yes, Isan," she said, cutting me off with a stern look. "You nearly died, remember? You can't ignore that. You can't jump back into the action like you suffered nothing but a minor scrape."

I opened my mouth to protest, but she held up a hand.

"No," she told me. "I'm in charge now and I say we're staying. I've already asked Echo and she says we can stay as long as we need."

Asmund grinned. "If I was you, I'd listen to your sister, Isan. Who do you think gave me this?" He pointed to the cut above his eye and then drifted out of the room.

I looked at Sky. "You did that?"

"Of course I didn't," she snapped, her eyes igniting. "He's just being insufferable, as always."

Echo laughed. "He's right about Skiansy though," she added. "I wouldn't cross her either."

"Fine," I said, caving. "We'll stay, but only until I'm better."

Sky smiled. "Good."

At that moment, my stomach groaned, sounding like some dying creature, and my headache returned to the forefront of my mind, pulsing in a frantic rhythm.

I closed my eyes against the agony and held my head in my hands.

"Oh," Sky exclaimed. "You must be starving; you haven't eaten anything since the attack."

I groaned. "Is that why I feel like my skull is going to cave in or is there something else you forgot to mention?"

"We tried to feed you," she said, "but you wouldn't swallow anything. Echo and I will get you something now. We'll only be a moment."

They turned to leave and I waved them off.

"Don't bother," I replied, "I can get it myself."

I started to get up and Sky rushed towards me. "No, no!" she admonished. "You need to rest. Lay back down!"

I ignored her and continued my effort to get myself into a sitting position, ignoring the pain in my head too. I was already out of breath though, and I'd barely lifted my back off the bed.

Sky tried to push me down and I gave one final heave.

Pain shot through me. I bit down a scream and fell back onto the bed with a muffled thump. My body shook as I lay there taking slow, shallow breaths in the wake of my stupidity.

"Oh, Isan," Sky chided, "why can't you ever listen? Your body endured a lot of trauma in the past week. You nearly *died*. How many times do I have to repeat that? You can't expect to be able to get up and walk around right away."

I sighed, which hurt a lot less than my attempt at sitting.

Echo sent me a sad smile and said, "Your sister's right, Isan. Considering what you suffered, I expect it'll be at least a week before you even *try* to get moving again."

"I can't lay here for a week," I protested. "I'll be bored out of my mind."

"Isn't that too bad," Sky replied.

Echo laughed. "It's better for you to spend the week in bed than to get up and run the risk of hurting yourself again. You need to give your body time to rest and heal."

I sighed again. "I suppose so, but…"

"No more whining," Sky snapped. "You're going to lay there in that bed for a week and you're going to do as you're told."

There was nothing mean in the way she said it, only a commanding tone to her voice that left no room for argument. She would make a great queen one day, a great leader of any kind.

"Echo and I will keep you fed, comfortable, and entertained," she went on. "Echo tells amazing stories and *I'll* remind you of all the stupid things you did as a child."

I rolled my eyes. "You're a twit, you know that, right?"

She shrugged. "That may be, but I'm the twit in charge."

We all laughed then—Echo's tinkling, Sky's wholehearted, and mine a bit strained because of my condition.

We're quite the bunch.

"It's great to be alive," I said, and I realized I meant it in the literal sense.

They both smiled at me, and, for a minute, we were all silent.

Then I cleared my throat and said, "So, about that food…"

"Yes," Sky said. "We'll get right on it. You stay put."

They rushed out of the room.

Then Sky's head peeked around the door. "Remember, Isanfier," she said, "I'm watching you. Any funny business, any attempt to get up again, and I'll know about it. Understand?"

"Crystal clear," I assured her.

"Good," she said, and then she left.

I relaxed into the bed and closed my eyes. Maybe some rest wouldn't be so bad after all.

18

Weaver and Wolven

Soon after, Echo came back carrying a bowl of soup on a makeshift wooden tray.

"That looks good," I said as she set the tray on the bedside table, "but how will I eat it? I can't sit up."

She gave me a smile. "Well, I had planned to prop you up with some pillows and feed it to you. Are you opposed to that? Skiansy tells me you're royalty. I wouldn't want to overstep boundaries..."

I waved a hand. "Oh, don't bother with that. I'm not *your* Prince and plenty of my subjects are nowhere near as polite to me as you've been so far. You've met Asmund, right?"

She narrowed her eyes. "I thought he was a relative."

I laughed. "Is that what he told you? He's a lord's son, but I guess that doesn't matter out here either. The point is, his opinion of me is shared by many."

She frowned. "That's a shame."

I managed a shrug. "I'm used to it. The life of a royal isn't all that it's made out to be. It certainly isn't as glamorous as you might think."

"Oh, I'm sure it isn't. Royalty are people too; they have their own problems."

I huffed at that. I had more problems than I knew what to do with.

"So, would you like to try the soup then?" she asked me.

"I don't see why not."

She grabbed an extra pillow from another room and—with a considerable amount of effort from both of us—she managed to get it under my head. It took us more than a few minutes and my cheeks flamed by the end of it. I couldn't believe I needed help to even move, but when we were done, I was vertical enough to eat the soup without choking.

Echo pulled a chair up to my bed and placed the tray on her lap. Then, she filled the spoon and lifted it to my lips.

I felt so helpless.

"Careful," she warned me, "it might be hot."

I sipped it.

The taste of mixed vegetables invaded my senses, along with a spice I could not name. It was different, but it was wholly satisfying, especially considering I hadn't eaten in days.

"This is good," I said between mouthfuls. My stomach rumbled its agreement, begging for more.

As I ate, I took a moment to finally study the room I was in. There had been too much going on earlier to get a good look.

The space wasn't large, just big enough to fit two small beds side by side and maybe half of a third at the end. The walls were rough wood, weathered by time, with nails exposed in several places. There was a long, red scarf dangling from one of them, barely hanging on to the metal. A wide, sawed-off log served as the bedside table and I smiled at the anomaly. It didn't feel out of place in a room such as this. Wispy curtains hung from the small window above my head, swaying in the breeze.

I felt safe there, like it was a place I could easily stay.

It was a slow process, but eventually I emptied the bowl of soup. I felt much better after, my stomach satisfied and my headache fading.

Echo set the bowl back on the tray.

"Thank you," I told her.

"There's no thanks necessary," she replied. "It would be cruel to let you starve after everything you've been through."

"No, not just for the soup," I said. "I mean for everything. Thank you for letting us stay here. Thank you for saving my life."

She shrugged. "I couldn't let you die, what with your sister sobbing all over me." She smiled.

I laughed. "I suppose not," I said.

"I should be thanking the three of you," she added. "You're the first visitors I've had since I came here. It's great to have someone to talk to."

I frowned. "It must be awfully lonely, living here by yourself." My tone was sympathetic, yet curious.

"It can be," she sighed, "but I've grown accustomed to solitude."

I raised an eyebrow. "You have to be starved for company if you're willing to take in a sobbing stranger, her dying brother, and their arch-nemesis. What are you doing in this wood anyway? You *are* a Wyllan, aren't you?" It felt like a question I shouldn't ask, but I had to know.

She looked away, though a slight smile tugged at her lips. "I suppose you could say I am," she said, "but my reasons for being here are a story for another time. Besides, the Edgewood has its own charms, its own freedom. It's a beautiful place, if you know where to look."

She offered nothing more, but my question had been answered, to an extent. More came to fill its place though, and others still lingered.

If she truly was Wyllan, why show kindness to three Sancians, noble ones at that? What were her motives?

They were questions I would have to answer myself, but not yet. My brain was too muddled and my eyelids were heavy.

I yawned and Echo said, "You should sleep. I'll see you in the morning." She stood abruptly, picking up the tray as she turned to go.

I blinked and she was gone.

The red scarf fluttered to the floor across the room and I wished I was well enough to pick it up.

• • •

I slept the whole night through with not so much as a glimpse of the nightmare that had plagued me for weeks. I woke up feeling rejuvenated and couldn't hold back my tears of joy at my freedom.

I told Sky the news when she came in to give me my breakfast and I was still smiling long after she left me to go practise her archery. She didn't want to get rusty while we were here and she was still wary of dangerous creatures in the woods. Echo apparently had no fighting experience, and, with me on bedrest and Asmund with a broken arm, Sky was the only one who could defend us. I hadn't seen Asmund since yesterday, which was probably for the best.

Echo knocked on the doorframe a few minutes after Sky headed out. "Can I come in?"

"Of course," I said. "I'm not busy."

She smiled as she walked in. "How are you feeling?"

"Much better, thank you," I replied.

"I wanted to apologize for my abrupt exit last night," Echo said. She had her arms wrapped tight around her torso, as if she was trying to hold herself together. "I'm not used to being asked questions, not used to people either. I don't mean to come off as rude."

"I don't think you're rude at all," I told her. "I can't imagine how overwhelmed you must be feeling. It's natural to slip up. Sancia knows my tongue can be sharp sometimes. I apologize in advance." I gave her a smile, and, much to my surprise, she returned it.

She took a breath. "I should leave you to your rest."

"No, please don't go," I said. "My mind isn't the happiest place right now. I'd rather not be alone. Could you stay, even for a bit?"

"I can try," she replied, "but I'm not the best company. I have little experience with entertaining."

"It's enough to have someone else in the room," I told her. "You could tell me a story. Didn't Sky say you're good at that?"

She blushed, the red giving her pale face colour. "Your sister was exaggerating," she protested. "I'm sure anything I could say pales in comparison to the books you have back home."

I shrugged. "I wouldn't know; I don't read unless I have to. Sky says it's sacrilege, but I don't have the patience. I'd always rather be doing something more exciting. Right now, on the other hand, I don't have much of a choice."

She frowned. "So you're saying…"

"I'm saying I have no concept of a good story or a bad one, so I'd like to hear one of yours, if you don't mind sharing."

She sighed and came to sit in the empty chair beside my bed. "I suppose I can give it a try, but you have to promise not to laugh."

I met her gaze. "Cross my heart and hope to die."

"Okay then," she said with a smile, "listen closely."

Then she took a deep breath and began.

Deep in the mountains of Winter, buried under eternal ice and snow, lies an ancient, frozen heart, or so the stories say. Some believe it is the heart of the First Queen, while others hold that it once belonged to Wylla herself, but you can't believe every story you hear under the light of a full moon, with firelight flickering through the darkness. One thing everyone agrees on, however, is that it is the reason the Winter Alps are cursed.

To wander too far into the mountains is to invite a terrible end, for none who venture into its snowy depths are ever seen again. Well, not as they were, not in a form anybody would recognize.

You see, Winter is watched over by a pack of ice wolves that guard the kingdom from harm, but that protection comes with a price. The mountains are their sacred grounds and if you step foot in their territory, you join the pack; you become lupine yourself and there is no going back.

It wasn't always that way. There was a time when nothing stood between us and the lands beyond the mountains, but the decisions of one man brought an end to that freedom, a man they call the Dream Weaver.

The Dream Weaver was a master of illusion, a well of magical power, but a darkness festered in his heart, an illness. He used his magic to wreak havoc, driving innocent people mad with his visions.

He was the First Queen's brother and though some say he is but a legend, those who believe in his existence say his anger stemmed from being cast aside by his father, from being denied the throne.

And so the Dream Weaver sought power elsewhere.

He found it in torturing people until their minds broke. He found it in tearing families apart with his mind games. He imagined it lay in the unknown lands behind the Winter Alps, a land he could conquer for himself.

But Wylla could not let that happen. She could not let his plague poison another land, though it was not her own, and so she interfered.

She came down from the heavens and killed one of Winter's precious wolves and took its heart, which she buried underneath the snow in a mountain pass, where none would ever unearth it.

That night, the heart and the wolf froze, and as the winds and snow of an almighty blizzard roared around them, Wylla's curse was cast.

From that moment on, all those who ventured into the Winter Alps transformed into wolves made of ice, never to walk among the humans again, never to escape the realm. They were named the Wolven and their origin story is almost lost to memory.

It is said that Wylla cried the day the curse was cast, that her tears fell to Fidalia and froze Waterfell. She did not wish to punish all her subjects, but the few would have to be sacrificed to keep the Dream Weaver contained. For he was not exempt from the curse, as powerful as he was, and so the lands beyond were saved from his malice.

Most regard the Wolven as watchmen now, revered souls who keep Winter from harm, but they are a lost people, waiting for someone strong enough to free them from their curse.

Waiting for someone to kill the Dream Weaver, for it is said that the curse shall remain as long as he draws breath.

Echo stopped then and a chill ran down my spine. The story was dark and terrifying, and despite her earlier words, Echo was an amazing storyteller. She knew exactly when to pause and how to make her voice sound dead to lend enough eeriness to the tale.

I'd never met someone like her before.

"So, what do you think?" she asked me, hesitant.

"You're... It... That was amazing," I replied, struggling to find the proper words to describe my awe.

She beamed. "You really think so?"

"Definitely," I assured her. "It gave me chills. I'm going to have nightmares for a week, even though I know it's just a story." I paused as a smile appeared on her lips. "It *is* just a story, isn't it?"

She shrugged. "Maybe it is, maybe it isn't."

"Don't tell me that," I protested.

She grinned.

"I'll never sleep again," I muttered.

"Sure you will. You just have to forget that the Dream Weaver is still out there, that even Wylla herself could not kill him."

"Stop," I exclaimed.

She was teasing me. It felt...natural.

"So," I continued, shaking off my fear, "now that I know you *can* tell stories, you shall tell me one once a day, even though they may lead to my early death."

She raised a white eyebrow. "Oh, shall I?"

"There isn't much a poor man can do when he is sick and bedridden," I told her. "All I ask of you is a single story a day to keep my hopes alive."

She laughed. "I suppose hope isn't much to ask for. You have yourself a deal."

19
Reconciliation

Frost

The horns of war woke King Frost from a deep sleep. They blasted through the silence of the night and he knew the enemy was upon them. He had only just crawled out of bed and dressed when a knight burst into his tent.

"Sire!" he called. "They are coming!"

Frost nodded. "Fetch my armour and have someone wake Snowdon if the horns didn't do the job."

"Yes, Sire."

The knight darted out and returned moments later to help Frost into his armour.

Once ready, Frost sheathed *Malice* at his side and stepped out to face their foe. It was snowing outside, the wind whipping it around their faces, a disadvantage for the Summer warriors who would be weakened by the cold.

All around the king, his men rushed to defend their camp, but they were headed south.

What in Fidalia?

Frost grabbed one of them by the collar as he ran past. "What is going on?" he demanded to know. "The enemy is in the other direction."

The knight shook with fear. "S-Summer has c-come around us, your M-Majesty. They are attacking f-from behind."

Frost cursed and let the man go.

He dropped to the ground and the king kicked him roughly.

"Get up! There is no time to lose. They must be pushed back."

"Yes, Sire," he said, jumping up and running off.

"Snowdon!" Frost bellowed, searching for his worthless child. So far, the boy had been nothing but a hindrance.

"Here, your Majesty," Snowdon cried as he ran up beside Frost. "I came as soon as I heard!"

"Silence," Frost snapped. "There is work to be done."

"What should *I* do?"

"Handle your sword with precision and fight to the end. We must not tarry. Come."

Frost followed his men southward, Snowdon trailing behind him, or not. At that point, Frost didn't know, nor did he care. Let Snowdon wallow in despair and fear. Frost would kill him himself, save Summer the trouble.

The men reached the battlefield before long and learned it was only a small number of men who had attacked. Summer must have thought they could surprise the Wyllans with stealth, and must have intended to thin out their numbers before they were noticed.

Well, they will soon see we aren't fools, Frost thought. *We aren't to be reckoned with lightly.*

Frost drew his sword and yelled, "For victory!" Then he launched himself into the fray.

His men followed and soon the entire wrath of the Winter army tore into the Summer scouts.

They never stood a chance.

• • •

Frost pulled *Malice* out of the knight's skull with the lovely squelching sound of tearing flesh. Blood glistened on the blade, made more brilliant by the snow that had melted on it as he fought. The last of the attackers had fallen.

The earlier blizzard had died out, though the wind still lingered, keeping his senses sharp.

A short horn blast signalled the victory and his knights raised their crimson-coated weapons in the air, yelling out their pride.

Frost smiled and wiped his blade on the dead knight's shirt. Then he walked away from the scarlet field.

"Sire?" one of his men questioned as Frost passed by.

The King nodded and said, "Show Summer what happens to those who attempt to trick us." He let a grin grace his lips, but his following laughter was drowned out by another horn blast.

The men looked around in confusion.

"What's happening?" they muttered.

"Your Majesty!"

Frost looked ahead and saw Snowdon standing between two tents. He was unscathed and his armour unbloodied.

"What is it now, boy?" the king asked scornfully. He was tired of his antics.

"More knights," Snowdon gasped. "They're coming from the north this time. The others were a distraction. We're being overrun!" His eyes flashed with fear; *Frost's* flashed with anger.

"To me!" he called and his knights assembled. "Onward!"

They ran north towards the next fight.

King Frost grabbed Snowdon's arm on the way. "Refuse to fight this time around and *I will kill you,*" he whispered into his son's ear. Then he let him go.

Once again, Frost charged into battle.

•   •   •

The second battle proved to be more difficult. The Summer knights kept coming. For every one Frost's army killed, two took their place, and three of his were slain. The King grew frustrated as the night wore on.

We will not be defeated. We will not.

His anger fuelled his next attack and he cut down the five knights who were surrounding him in one fell swoop. Behind him came a muffled cry as one of their own received a blow.

Frost ignored it and continued on, until a small, weak voice cried out, "Father!"

The king fought with himself for a second and finally whirled around furiously. It was pathetic that he should have to save Snowdon. It ruined any chance he had of proving himself.

The Summer knight never knew what hit him; one second he was plunging his sword towards Snowdon, who lay helpless on the ground before him, and the next his head was bouncing across the snow, leaving a bright trail of blood.

Snowdon let out a shuddering breath of relief.

"Thank you, Father, thank you," he gasped.

The words enraged Frost. "Silence!" he yelled, running *Malice* through Snowdon's left arm. It wasn't enough to kill him, but it *was* enough to render the arm useless for life and bring him unbearable pain.

He screamed and thrashed on the ground.

"This is your lesson for today," Frost told him. "Never speak words of gratitude, especially not for something you should have done yourself. It is appalling that I had to save you.

It shows no strength, only weakness. You are *weak,* Snowdon. The fear has won and from this day forth I shall look upon you in shame." The king had all but spat at his son's feet.

On the ground beneath him, Snowdon clenched his fists. Against the pain or against his failure, Frost did not know.

"If I am weak," Snowdon choked out, "it is through no fault of my own."

Frost raised his sword again, anger rattling his bones, but then something caught his eye in the pitch black of the night.

It was snowing, which wouldn't be an unusual sight, save for the fact that it was only snowing above his son.

By Wylla...

"Snowdon! Snowdon, get up," Frost demanded, resisting the urge to kick him.

Snowdon rolled over; there was blood and snow smeared across his face and armour. "Why?"

"I said *get up!*"

He jumped to his feet as fast as he could with his injuries; along with the arm wound, he had sustained a long gash on his leg. "What do you want now, your Majesty?"

Frost shook his head. The boy didn't even realize he was doing it.

"Can you not feel it, son?"

Snowdon's eyes widened at Frost's words but then they grew to the size of saucers as he finally understood. It seemed his lessons on magic hadn't been for naught.

"Fidal's breath," the boy gasped. "I...I'm doing it!"

"Yes," Frost said, placing a hand on his shoulder. "Now focus. You don't want to lose it. I just thought of a way for you to end this. We shall win the battle and Summer shall fear us, shall fear *you* from this day forth."

Snowdon trembled. "How?"

Frost ignored him for a moment as he turned to fend off a group of Sancians who were creeping up behind them. He made quick work of their feeble attack.

"Use your magic," Frost told his son as he returned to his side. "Turn this snowfall into a blizzard. Trap them behind walls of flying snow. Blind them until all they see is white and then... We shall kill all who do not flee in instant terror."

"But..." There was still a note of fear and reluctance in his voice. It caused Frost rage unlike any he had ever felt before.

"Do as I say, boy, or I will have your head!"

Frost hoped Snowdon saw the glint in his eyes, hoped he realized he was not bluffing, though the threat served more than one purpose. Rage seemed to be Snowdon's trigger and Frost wanted to stoke the fires as much as possible.

Snowdon squared his shoulders, took a deep breath, and splayed his hand out in front of him before closing his eyes.

The wind whipped up, the sky quaked, and soon snow tore through the air, blanketing it with white. The screams of the Summer army were lost in the shrieking of the wind.

Frost left Snowdon where he stood and ran to strike down the enemy while terror made them idle.

So it was that because of Snowdon, the Wyllans won the Battle of the Blizzard.

• • •

The next morning dawned bright and clear. The sky was blue and not a sliver of snow hung in the clouds above. The sunrise cast everything in a red light, accentuating the blood-covered fields. Countless Summer knights littered the snow; bloodied, broken, and headless. The posts surrounding the Wyllan camp raised their heads into the air for all to see, to see what became of those who attempted to trick Winter.

• • •

A guard poked his head inside Frost's tent. "Sire, your son has arrived."

Frost forced a smile through his usual instinct to sigh. "Send him in."

Snowdon limped his way inside and stopped before the King, bowing slowly. "You called for me, your Majesty?"

Frost did not look up when he answered. Instead, he focused on the quill in his hand, toying with it, as if it was more important than his son. "Manners will not aid you in escaping my wrath," Frost told him. "They only serve to dig you a deeper grave."

"Right," Snowdon replied, hanging his head. His hair fell into his eyes and Frost noticed the white strands were still flecked with blood.

"Why do you think you are here?" Frost asked, twirling the quill.

"You wish to tell me something."

Frost laughed darkly. "And what do you suppose that something is?"

"Not a good something," Snowdon replied.

"This particular something is a decision about what to do with you," Frost said. "You could say I have...decided your fate." He snapped the quill in his fingers as he said the last word.

Snowdon jumped.

Frost smiled and finally looked up at his son. "Do not worry, boy, you have escaped the noose this time, though it pains me to say it. You proved worthless in combat and could not muster the courage to save your own skin, but when it came down to it, you unlocked your magic and won the battle for us. Not all is forgiven, but it is a start."

Snowdon let out a breath. "What will my fate be then?" he asked quietly.

"You shall leave this camp and return to Appalachia, where I expect you to train ceaselessly with your magic until it is but second nature to you. You have a lot to catch up on." Frost pulled an envelope out of his coat. "Give this letter to your sister. She will dole out your accompanying punishment."

Snowdon took it and turned to go, but Frost was not yet finished with him.

"Snowdon?" Frost called after him.

"Yes, Father?" he answered, turning to face the king once more.

"You might be needing this." Frost reached under the table and pulled out Snowdon's axe, which he then held out towards him.

Snowdon looked from his father, to the axe, and then back again, as if he couldn't comprehend what was happening.

Frost was proud of him for not taking the gesture at face value; it showed growth and strength.

"Take it," he urged his son. "It is not a trick, but I expect to see some progress from you when I return to the capital. If not, you will lose it again. Is that clear?"

Snowdon nodded and finally closed his hand around the axe handle.

Frost saw something in the boy's eyes then that he hadn't seen before: a spark of determination. He knew his son would not take this opportunity lightly, not this time, and, for once, Frost was eager to see the path in life Snowdon would take.

20
Gardens and Guilt

Isan

For the week following my return to consciousness, Echo and Sky waited on me hand and foot. They fed me three meals a day, tended to my wounds, and made sure I was comfortable. Sky kept me company in the morning and Echo in the afternoon. As per our deal, Echo would tell me a story and then we talked until dinner.

The tale about the Dream Weaver scared me the most. The others were adventurous fantasies about kings, heroes, and fair maidens.

One was a legend of the trolls that supposedly lived in the mountains of Summer and I found myself asking Echo if they were real, to see if the mountain men had been right all along, but she wouldn't confirm or deny.

Other creatures that appeared in her stories—mystical or otherwise—were fairies, dragons, and the goblins of course, though she never told the tale of how she became known as the Missing One.

SUMMER'S REVENGE

All throughout the week, Asmund was a ghost. He never came to visit, which I didn't mind, but it unnerved me that I couldn't keep an eye on him. Sky said he'd been quiet, stuck in his room most days. She said he was upset about his broken arm and losing so spectacularly to the goblins, but I couldn't help but think it was more than that. I wondered what he was planning.

Yet, still being bedridden, there wasn't much I could do about the mystery. I supposed I should be grateful he wasn't badgering me all hours of the day.

One afternoon, as Echo finished her latest story, she leaned back in her chair and looked at me with a mischievous smile. "You know, I think it's your turn. I'd like to hear one of *your* stories."

"Oh, I don't think…" I started.

She waved me off. "You'll be fine. It can't be that horrible."

"I'm not a story-telling kind of person," I insisted, crossing my arms. "I don't read, remember?"

"It doesn't have to be made up," she said. "You could tell me about life at the castle, a favourite childhood memory perhaps or a time when you were scared to death."

I thought about what she said, about what story I could possibly offer as she looked at me expectantly, studying me with those brilliant blue eyes.

What could I tell her that could top anything she'd said?

It doesn't have to be better, I told myself. *It just has to come from the heart.*

I don't know why, but I trusted Echo, even if she was Wyllan. I could tell, somehow, that her soul was pure and she would never bring us harm.

Finally, after a moment of pondering, I had my answer. "Can I tell you a tale about Asmund?"

She raised an eyebrow and gave me a knowing smile. "Only if it's true."

I frowned. "The truth isn't nearly as entertaining as my imagination, but yes, this story is real. Would you like to hear it?"

There were many stories I could tell about Asmund and his siblings, truth and fiction, but this was the one that was most real to me, for it was the moment I started to truly despise him, despite my best efforts otherwise.

Echo nodded. "By all means, Isanfier, take the stage."

I took a deep breath and said, "Once upon a time, in a faraway land, Asmund and I were friends, or as close as we could be with the years separating us. He and his family used to call at the castle once a year and so the five of us children grew up together."

Confusion leapt into Echo's eyes and I paused.

"What is it?"

"You said five children."

"Ah yes, I was getting to that. Asmund has a younger brother and sister, Arran and Aramina."

She looked surprised, though she fought to hide it. "I never would've thought that with the way he carries himself," she said finally.

"Well, he is quite a bit older and was always preoccupied with becoming Lord of Skar, so I can see how the family tendencies could slip away."

"I suppose that makes sense," Echo said. "I'm sorry for interrupting. Do go on."

"Asmund's family was easier to get along with than our other noble visitors, as their military background gave them a certain...bluntness. There was no charade of power or luxury when they were among us, because we knew it didn't matter to them. So Sky and I were well acquainted with the Arrath children, but that wasn't meant to last.

"One year, when Sky and I were around eight years old, we were all playing hide and seek in the gardens at the castle. Asmund would've been twelve and Arran was seven. Aramina didn't hide herself, but she liked to be out with us and liked to look at the flowers. The rest of us, on the other hand, were highly competitive."

Echo cracked a smile. "Oh I can imagine."

I gave her a look. "Am I telling the story or not?"

She smiled wider and said, "I don't know, are you?"

I ignored her comment and went on. "We had been playing for a couple hours and were on our last round when everything took a turn. I had won all rounds but one, which had gone to Sky, and Asmund was fuming. He assumed his age should give him some sort of advantage, but I was a thin eight-year-old and could get into the smallest of spaces.

"Sky was the finder in that final round, having been caught by Arran the previous time, so I knew I had to be clever. She knew all my secrets, even then. Little did I know it was Asmund I should have been watching out for."

Echo grimaced. "What happened?"

I took a breath. "The horses were kept at the castle back then and the stables were just off the gardens, so I decided to slip inside, unaware that Asmund had shrugged off the game and was following close behind.

"I hid in a dark corner of the stables beside a pile of buckets and tack. When I heard the door open again behind me, I assumed it was Sky already and didn't dare move, but then, after a few minutes, I heard something else. The sound of hooves on stone and doors being pulled open.

"I realized quickly what was happening, but not who was doing it, so I leapt to my feet and yelled out to the person just as the door opened again and Sky actually walked in. She saw me immediately and called out her victory, breaking through the silence of the stable. She didn't notice the horses until it was too late. She had already spooked them. They shot towards her like an explosion had gone off and she was nearly trampled.

"Luckily, I reacted quickly enough to pull her out of the way with only a couple minor bruises."

I shook my head, feeling the weight of that day pressing in on me again. I hadn't even been all that angry at Asmund when it came down to it, just disappointed—an emotion I couldn't identify at the time.

"What did Asmund have to say?" Echo asked, pulling me out of my thoughts.

I huffed a breath. "He didn't even pause to see if Sky was all right. He just ran screaming after Aramina and I was too worried about Sky to stop him. Aunt Mag, our governess, and the guards were called out with all the commotion. The guards spent the next hour rounding up the horses and Aunt Mag dragged us all back into the castle, scolding us for our recklessness. She never asked if Sky was all right and I didn't question it at first, not until dinner." I shut my eyes.

"What happened at dinner?" Echo prompted me after a moment.

"Asmund's father, Lord Arrath, brought up the incident and Asmund blamed it all on me. He said I had freed the horses and Aramina was almost killed because of it. She was too young to refute the story and I had no solid evidence to prove otherwise. Uncle knew Skiansy would back me in any situation too, so her opinion meant little.

"That was the start of their family's scorn for me and the beginning of my feud with Asmund. I think he assumes I forgot about it—Arran and Aramina did—but I was old enough then to recognize the slight." I sighed. "I guess it probably seems petty to you, but everything has added up over the years and I can't bring myself to trust him again. Is that... Do you think that's stupid?"

I looked over at her again and she shook her head, her eyes glossy with sympathy. "It's not stupid. Someone could have been seriously injured, but I do think a part of him would have regretted his actions if someone had. It's easier to shrug off acts like that when there are no consequences."

I nodded. "That's what has always bugged me about him. He says and does whatever he wants, with no regard to how others might feel, and I just… I don't understand what I did wrong."

I hung my head then, lost in the emotion of my memories and the reality of my present day. I was stuck in the Edgewood with a man who hated me. We were no closer to getting out of the mess and even when we did, more trials would await.

A hand touched my shoulder then, bringing my thoughts to a halt and I looked up into Echo's eyes. Her hair cascaded down her shoulder, brushing against my arm, and goosebumps spread across my skin.

There was something so different about her, so refreshing. It was easy to forget the years of animosity that stood between her land and mine. Almost.

"You did nothing wrong, Isanfier," Echo assured me. "Sometimes we have to accept that people's actions are not directly related to our own. Asmund made a choice. You can't blame yourself for it, but I also think if you look closely, you might find he is not the same person now as he was that day in the gardens."

I pulled back from her touch. "I don't know about that."

She gave me a sad smile and then stepped away, giving me space again, though the room seemed smaller now somehow.

"It was a good story though," Echo said. "You could be a storyteller."

I managed a smile. "Thank you."

She hovered in front of the bed in silence for a moment before she said, "I'm going to go help Sky with dinner now. You rest up, okay?"

I nodded. "Thanks for listening."

She smiled. "It was my pleasure, but think about what I said, Isan. The world isn't always as black and white as it appears."

I didn't reply, but watched her go with a silent awe. For someone who was used to being alone, she had a way with people. Our conversations always left me feeling like I had something more to learn, but also left me with the confidence that I could master it somehow.

21

Magic and Misfortune

Slowly, through the stories and time spent with Echo and Sky, I began to get better. I gained more freedom of movement and the pain died down. On the tenth day of my recovery, Echo came into my room after lunch to find me sitting up in bed.

"Look at you!" she exclaimed.

"I know," I said with a wide smile. "I'm not even out of breath."

"It's a good sign. You might be walking in a couple of days." She smiled. "To celebrate, I'll let you pick the topic for the story today."

I grinned. "Sounds like a deal. Hmmm..." I tapped my fingers against my chin. "How about... Oh, could you tell me about magic?"

She raised an eyebrow. "Don't Sancians think it's treason to even speak of it?"

I shrugged. "You're not one of us and I don't agree with my uncle's choice to outlaw it. Besides, we're at war with

Winter and I'm told they use magic with abandon. If I want to survive this war, I should find out as much about my enemy as I can. The ban on magic has only put us in the dark."

"I fear you are right," Echo replied. "Winter has only grown stronger with its magic in the past decade. The king himself is a force to be reckoned with, as is the princess. Magic is almost considered more important than noble birth."

I leaned closer. "What can you tell me about it?"

"I'll start with the origin story," she said, tucking her long hair behind her ear. "Magic is tied closely with religion, so this is the origin story of our world too. Magic used to be considered a divine gift by all citizens of Fidalia. I'm sure your uncle met much resistance when he first implemented the ban."

"I wish I'd been old enough to resist with them," I mused.

"Well, you can't change the past, you can only look to the future." She paused, collecting her thoughts, and then began.

Long, long ago, in the beginning of time, Fidal created a realm which he called Fidalia. He filled it with plants and animals, and was proud of the people within, but he was lonely. A young goddess named Madge heard the longings of his heart and gifted Fidal with four daughters: Wylla, Audria, Sancia, and Stella, who were born of magic (Madge) and life (Fidal). Each daughter was given a kingdom and season to rule over.

Fidalia was destined to be a peaceful realm, watched over by the generous goddesses and the mighty Fidal, and it was, for a time. The Fidalians cooperated and there was no violence, but, alas, a perfect place like that cannot last.

One day, a dispute broke out between two families and a year later, the first mortal died by another's hand. Their blood seeped into the soil and the first tree in the Edgewood was born. With this first death, humans discovered revenge. In three months, five trees had joined the first. Two years' time found the land at war against itself.

Friend killed friend. Brother murdered brother. Lover slaughtered lover.

Fidal watched his realm fall apart and felt at a total loss as to what to do. It is said he was tempted to destroy his creation, but his daughters, who had fallen in love with their kingdoms and people, convinced him to give the realm another chance. Each daughter chose one brave man from their kingdom, a champion, to go out and fight the battle for peace, to bring balance back to the realms.

After countless years of war, full of untold horrors and unfathomable bloodshed, the four champions were able to return Fidalia to its former glory, much to Fidal's surprise. The war had ended, but now the Edgewood stood between the kingdoms, cutting them off from one another, as a reminder of what they had lost.

Each of the champions was rewarded for their efforts. Along with becoming the undisputed monarchs of their respective lands, Fidal gave them each a gift. Stella's champion was given immortality, so he could forever keep the peace. Wylla's was awarded that, as well as one small power to aid him. Sancia's champion was rewarded with amazing powers. Last, but certainly not least, Audria's champion was gifted both immortality and amazing powers, as he had been the leader throughout the wars.

The Wyllan and the Sancian fought the rest of their lives for peace, but the other two abused their powers and plotted a second war. They wanted dominance over all of Fidalia, as they believed themselves to be superior to mere mortals.

Audria, who had fallen in love with her champion throughout the years, was heartbroken at the path he'd chosen and it destroyed her piece by piece. This enraged Fidal, leading him to kill the Audrian champion and burn the Autumn kingdom to the ground. In her grief, Audria did not lead her people to safety and few survived.

The Stellan who also conspired against Fidal's will was allowed to live as he had only been a follower, but his kingdom was turned to ash as well. Stella saw to it that her people escaped the destruction.

So is the tale of magic and why only two kingdoms remain in Fidalia now, the Edgewood solemnly watching both in case tragedy should strike again.

Echo fell silent then, a sort of melancholy surrounding her. The tale was not a happy one.

"So that's the truth," I mused. "I wonder if Fidal will intervene in this war, if he will kill everyone this time and start from scratch."

Echo shrugged. "It's hard to say and I can't tell you whether or not the tale is strictly fact either. I read it in a book once. Details get lost over time, jumbled."

I nodded. "That's true. Who's to say the gods are even real? And if they are, who's to say they still care? But the magic must've come from somewhere..."

"Honestly, I don't know," she replied, "but I believe all stories are born from seeds of truth."

I smiled. "I like that. There's one aspect of your story that confused me though. If those people were born a thousand years ago, how come there's still magic today?"

"The champions' magic was passed down through their blood," she said. "There are five kinds of people in Fidalia: Mortals, Immortals, Magic Wielders, Gifted Immortals, and Immortal Magic Wielders." She ticked each off by raising the fingers of her right hand as she said them.

"Mortals are regular people, devoid of any magic. Immortals are descendants of the Stellan. They look like Mortals, but they live forever. Illness won't take them and they will not die of old age. The only way for them to die is through murder. They live normal human lives until they reach maturity and stop aging physically.

"Magic Wielders are the descendants of the Sancian. They are mortals who all share the same fundamental magical abilities and exceptional power, but their downfall is that they will die as nature intended.

"Gifted Immortals share the blood of the Wyllan champion and they are more interesting than the others. They stop aging at maturity, but discover their Gift at sixteen, which is one magic power given to them through their name. Take King Frost for example."

"The King of Winter?" I asked.

She nodded. "He's a Gifted Immortal. As his name suggests, he can create and manipulate frost."

I shuddered at the discovery. King Frost was the man who ordered my parents' deaths. If I wasn't daunted by the thought of facing him before, I certainly was then. At the same time, though, I marvelled at the fact that there were five types of people, some with powers beyond belief.

"Why were we never told about this before?" I wondered aloud.

"On the one hand," Echo replied, "it would have been cut from your studies because of the magic ban in your kingdom, though that will have done little to deter those with magic. On the other hand, those with magic don't want the mere Mortals knowing about their powers. They only divulge information when it suits them."

"That makes sense," I said. "How many people possess magic?"

She sat back in her chair. "More than you would think. A lot of people in royal positions are not as they seem, but most people are Mortals. I've been told the population is divided roughly like this: sixty-four percent of people are Mortals, five percent are Magic Wielders, ten percent are Immortals, and twenty percent are Gifted Immortals."

I raised an eyebrow. "So you're saying one third of Fidalians will live forever?"

"Hypothetically," she replied, "if they're not murdered. I've found that men always seek to kill those who hold more power than them. As well, there is a certain danger in possessing magic. If you do not balance magic and life equally, as nature intended, one will take from the other."

I frowned. "How do you mean?"

"It doesn't affect Immortals, but if a Gifted Immortal uses too much magic, it can steal from their life force until there's nothing left. Sometimes, the decay is gradual, but other times it's instant. The opposite can also be true; use too little magic and you will wither away."

My heart clenched at the notion. "That sounds awful."

She sighed. "Everything has a price. Magic users have a duty to themselves and the realm to keep their power in check."

We sat in silence for a few minutes as I tried to digest everything she'd said. I'd known about magic from a young age, but immortality was something I hadn't considered. I wondered if any of the champions from the first war still walked the realm.

"Wait," I said, realizing something. "What happened to the fifth type? You only listed four percentages."

She smiled. "I was waiting for you to catch that. The fifth type is the Immortal Magic Wielder, who counts for less than one percent of the population, much less. Immortal Magic Wielders are rare because the Audrian champion has no descendents. He was killed before he could father any children. The only way to become an Immortal Magic Wielder is to be a descendant of all three of the other champions. You need Mortal and Immortal blood and both the magic of a Magic Wielder and a Gifted Immortal running through your veins.

"Essentially, your parents would have to be a Gifted Immortal and a Magic Wielder, but even then they are more likely to produce another Gifted Immortal or Magic Wielder.

"Immortal Magic Wielders are the most powerful people in Fidalia. They are immortal, they excel at a specific gift, and they have an insurmountable amount of magic at their fingertips. Their power makes them a blessing as well as a curse, as shown by the Audrian champion's ascent to and fall from grace. Most Immortal Magic Wielders, though, are unaware of what they are or what kind of power they hold. Sometimes, they live their whole life thinking they are one of the other types."

I shook my head in disbelief. "This is all fascinating, like stepping into another realm." I found myself wondering how many magic users I'd unknowingly encountered daily. "Have you ever met a person who has magic?" I asked her.

"I have," she admitted.

"What were they like?"

"The same as you and I, but...different." She took a breath. "You see, magic can sometimes take more than a physical toll on the user. The people I knew... The power had corrupted them. They let the magic change them."

She looked incredibly sad when she said it and I wanted to reach out and squeeze her hand, but she had her hands tucked under her arms and was sitting too far away.

"I'm sorry," I said. "It must be hard to watch that happen."

She nodded, looking at me with those blue eyes of hers, as tumultuous as a rushing river. "It is. The worst part is being helpless to change it."

"Who were these people?" I asked her. "What happened to them?

She seemed to tense up. "I'd rather not say."

Strange.

"Okay," I said, "then how about you? Do you have magic or is your knowledge of it only from these people you used to know?"

She shot to her feet then, nearly toppling her chair. "No more questions," she snapped. "I... I've already said too much."

She headed for the door, and I realized I had overstepped. I had spent too much time on a topic she did not want to discuss.

"Don't go," I pleaded.

She stopped at the door, one foot already on the other side.

"I'm sorry," I told her. "I was curious to know more about you. I'm sure Sky told you all about me, but I know nothing of you."

"Maybe I want to keep it that way," she said, and then she left.

I don't know why, but I felt rather cold in her absence, rather empty. I'd grown to enjoy her company and I was sad to think I had torn a hole in our still-developing friendship. I just hoped her kind nature wasn't a facade to hide the Wyllan beast inside.

• • •

"Remember the day you climbed that tree and couldn't get down?" Sky asked. "Aunt Mag was absolutely livid."

We laughed.

Sky and I were sitting together on my bed the next morning. I'd finished my breakfast without the need for much help and Sky had decided to bring up the story of the tree. It hadn't been one of my finer moments.

"Yes, that was an interesting day," I replied.

"If I recall," Sky said slyly, "*I* was the one who had to climb up there and help you."

"You did not," I retorted. "I climbed down myself, after my fear diminished."

"That's not how I remember it," Sky protested.

"Well, that's how it happened."

We both crossed our arms.

We are *stubborn as mules.*

Echo joined us then and we forgot our quarrel, pausing to wish her a good morning.

"Good morning," she replied. She stood there, shifting her weight from foot to foot, looking as if she had something to say but was too nervous to say it.

I wanted to ask her what was on her mind, but Sky spoke first.

"I'm glad you're here, Echo," she said. "I think it's time Isan started walking again. I'm tired of waiting on him."

Echo laughed and I could tell she was glad for something else to focus on.

"I need your help to get him out of bed," Sky went on.

"I guess we can try," Echo replied. She looked at me. "If we can get you walking, Isan, we'll give you a tour."

"That would be great," I told her. "I'd like to see more of this treehouse you two keep referring to."

Maybe the previous night hadn't affected our friendship as much as I'd feared.

"Okay," Sky said to me. "Slide to the edge of the bed and swing your legs over."

I did as she suggested, moving slowly. I was breathing heavier when I finished, but it hadn't been too hard.

We waited a few minutes before I tried to stand.

I placed my feet on the floor and did fine, until I put weight on my bad leg and it gave out. Pain shot up the limb and I started to fall.

"Oh!" Sky gasped. She and Echo rushed to catch me and then lowered me back onto the bed.

I shook terribly, but clenched my fists to keep them from noticing.

"Clearly," I said, panting, "I won't be walking on that leg anytime soon."

"*Clearly*," Sky repeated. "I guess you'll have to hop around for a while."

After a few minutes, Echo said, "Do you want to try again? Sky and I will support you this time."

I frowned. "You shouldn't have to do that. Where's Asmund?"

Sky put her hands on her hips. "What? You don't think we're capable?"

"No, that's not it at all," I replied. "I just feel bad about everything the two of you have had to do for me. Asmund should pull his weight, but he'll probably milk that broken arm excuse as long as he can."

Sky sighed. "I know what you mean, but isn't it better this way? We don't have to hear him complain and besides, I wouldn't put it past him to drop you, so can you please let Echo and I do this?" Her brown eyes were pleading. Her hair was back to its usual braid, but there were pieces sticking out of it, like tufts of fur.

I realized then how hard the past few weeks had been on her. Getting lost in a forest, fighting goblins, nearly watching me die, trusting a stranger, and dealing with Asmund. She didn't need to add my unruliness to that list, especially if she wanted her hair to retain its colour.

"Okay," I told her. "You win."

"Thank you," she said. Then she and Echo grabbed hold of my arms, and I rose shakily to my feet.

I draped an arm each around their shoulders, keeping my bad leg elevated.

"That's it," Sky encouraged.

"Look at you," Echo exclaimed.

I was focusing on the wooden slats beneath my feet, but I knew they were both smiling from ear to ear.

"Time to show you around Echo's castle," Sky said.

"Oh, I wouldn't say that," Echo protested. "It's not much, certainly nothing like you're used to."

Sky reached across me and smacked Echo's arm. "Stop being so modest."

"Ladies, please," I said. "I was promised a tour."

"Of course, your Highness," Sky said. "Hold on tight."

The three of us shuffled out of the room, me hopping on one foot, and made our way around.

The treehouse was impressive. It had five levels and spanned across six trees. All of its many rooms were spacious and completely sheltered from the elements. The Great Room, located in the centre of the treehouse, was the only room open to the outside world. It had an amazing view of the sky above and was one of the only reminders we were in a tree. I had been conscious for over a week and had not been able to tell I was staying in a giant treehouse.

In one of the rooms, I made the mistake of looking out a window. The ground loomed far below and a queasiness filled my stomach. I swayed on my feet and Sky laughed.

"Are you going to be okay? We're pretty high up."

I gave her an indignant look. "I am *not* afraid of heights."

"If you say so."

I hopped away from the window and we continued our tour.

The treehouse had everything you could ever need: a sick bay—which was where I had spent the last week—many guest rooms, Echo's bedroom, a dining room, a makeshift kitchen, and even a lookout. I marvelled at its beauty.

"You built this?" I asked Echo as the three of us sat down at the dining room table. My good leg was aching a bit and my breathing was ragged.

"Not all of it," she admitted. "Someone built the main structure before I came along and I decided to spruce it up a bit, once I had the skill to do so."

"Do you have any idea who did build it then?" I asked her. "It's strange for a structure of this size to be found here. I don't imagine many people plan to call these woods home."

She shook her head. "Whoever it was left nothing personal behind. The only indication of occupancy are a pair of initials carved in the tree trunk, but O and S could be anyone."

Sky smiled. "Perhaps a lover's safe haven?"

"It could be, but I don't suppose we'll ever know."

"Still, the place is impressive, even if you had help," I said.

Echo smiled. "I had to teach myself carpentry before I could make an impact, but I've been adding to it ever since." She gazed around at the wood and decor. "When you have as much time on your hands as I do, you end up spending it in extravagant ways."

"So, you've lived in the Edgewood all by yourself?" I asked.

She nodded.

"For how long?"

"Since I was six," she replied.

Six?

"And you're sixteen," Sky said, not letting her shock show. "So that means...you've been here for ten years?"

Echo nodded.

"Ten years is a long time to be alone," I said. "How are you still sane? How did you survive it? How did you come to be here anyway?"

"That's what I wanted to talk to you guys about," she replied, running her thumb across her knuckles. "It's time I shared my own story." She turned to me. "Isan, you were right last night when you said I know all about you, when you know nothing about me, and I realized how unfair that is."

I nodded, trying my best to seem indifferent about it, but she had come around much faster than I thought she would. I figured she would keep us in the dark forever.

"If we are to be friends," she continued, "I need to be upfront. I don't want there to be any secrets between us."

"Okay," Sky said. "We're all ears, and no matter what you say, we promise we won't judge." She looked at me pointedly.

What? my eyes asked.

Behave, her eyes told me.

I rolled mine.

What does she think I am, a child?

I was just happy Echo didn't see fit to include Asmund in the conversation.

"All right," Echo said. "Get comfortable. This tale is far from happy. I'll answer your questions when I've finished. Oh, and if Asmund decides to join us, that's fine, but I won't fill him in on what he's missed. This story is difficult at the best of times; I do not wish to relive it twice in one day."

We nodded and she began.

"My story starts with Princess Icaria and Prince Snowdon of Winter. The two are twins, in their sixteenth year as we are. However, they are not like us in any sense of the word. Power and corruption are encouraged in Winter and many 'minor' criminals go unpunished while others are served an instant death sentence. Icaria and Snowdon are no different. In fact, they are worse.

"Icaria is the cruelest person I've ever known, aside from King Frost himself, though she may surpass him someday. She preys on people's weaknesses and thrives on their suffering. She's as volatile as a Winter storm when she's angry, and has been known to throw ice shards at people and encase them in ice for looking at her funny.

"Snowdon lacks magic himself, though his name suggests it is only a matter of time before that changes. For now, he makes up for his shortcoming with his ferocity as an axe-wielder. Some say he beheaded his first teacher for criticizing his footwork."

She took a deep breath and seemed to steady herself. It was obvious now that the Winter royalty were the people she spoke of the previous night, but I wondered how she'd known them.

"They weren't always like this," Echo went on. "Both Icaria and Snowdon were relatively nice, much to the dismay of their father, until their mother's sudden murder when they were six. After that, their hearts hardened and they felt they had no choice but to follow their father's less-than-civil teachings.

"Icaria was the one to find her mother's body and her sorrow was so deep, it unleashed her magic in an instant, a rare occurrence at her age, but that wasn't the only thing that changed that day. When Queen Cascadia died, half of Icaria died too and I was created. I was created out of the part of Icaria's soul that was good, the part she discarded in order to gain her father's favour and push away her grief. I am an *echo* of Icaria's former, kinder self. I am not sure why the realm chose to keep me here—it's never happened before, to my knowledge—but I try to remind myself that I *must* have a purpose, especially during the difficult days."

Echo met our gaze and I hope she saw understanding in our eyes, even through our shock. It was a difficult concept to grasp, but her mysteries were finally starting to make sense.

"I'm Icaria's mirror image," Echo continued, gesturing to herself. "What you see before you is exactly what the princess looks like at this moment. It would be impossible to tell the two of us apart, until one of us revealed our personalities.

"When I was created, I came here to live with the other 'halfies,' for all who reside here are creatures that are half-there or deformed in some way. Ghosts, ogres, and even your goblins; they don't have hearts, yet they live. That's the true reason it's called the Edgewood, not because it's on the edge of the two kingdoms—that happened by accident. No, it's called the Edgewood because it's home to all creatures who are on the edge of life and death. You may think there is a fine line between the two, but that couldn't be further from the truth.

"I may speak and move and look like a living creature, but I'm not truly alive. How can I be? I was created from a fragment of a soul. I was already six years old when I was brought into being, dropped into this murky wood with only the knowledge and skills of the girl I was fashioned after. I get flashes of memory from Icaria every now and again, and all they do is remind me of what I don't have."

She paused and looked me in the eyes.

"You asked me why I stay here, Isan, and the truth is that I am bound to this forest. If I leave, I will shrivel up and die as that piece of soul is whisked away in the breeze, because it's the magic of this forest that keeps me alive when I should be dead."

I nodded my head in recognition. "Magic and life must be kept in balance."

"Exactly," she replied. "Departure won't kill me instantly, but as soon as I step foot into either kingdom, my clock is ticking and my energy fades. I've made a few short trips to Tamise over the years, for luxuries like books and clothes, but each trip is harder than the last and I fear one day I'll cross the border and disappear."

She illustrated the motion with her hands and I shuddered at the thought. No one deserved to go like that, to just...cease to exist.

"The only way I can be free is for Icaria to die," she told us. "Then I will take her place as the version of us that lives on, but I don't think I could bring myself to do it. We are one, and I don't think I could make myself kill a part of me, even if that part is evil. So I am forever trapped, waiting for the day someone happens to kill her."

She paused then, gathering her thoughts or perhaps finding the courage to go on.

Her bright eyes were darkened by sorrow and her pain seeped into me, a dull ache in the back of my mind.

She was so strong to have endured this long alone. I realized then that I had underestimated her. She was more than a Wyllan girl in a dark wood. She was sewn together with magic and memory, but at the bottom of it all, she was human, just like us. She deserved so much more than life had given her.

It was then and there that I made a silent vow to help her, to do everything in my power to free her from this prison. Icaria may have been an even more formidable opponent than Frost, but it would be worth the risk to save a friend.

22
Hatred and Humility

"There is more to my sordid tale," Echo said, "but that's enough for today."

Sky squeezed her hand. "We respect your wishes; when you're ready to tell us more, we'll be here for you."

Echo managed a smile. "I am glad I met the two of you."

"I'm glad you decided to save us," I replied. "As horrible as the circumstances are, this forest is lucky to have you, Echo. You are the one bright light amidst the shadows of the wood. You give *balance.*"

She smiled. "I suppose there is a silver lining in everything."

There was a huff from the corner of the room. "If there is, I don't see one."

The three of us turned in our chairs to watch Asmund walk out of the shadows. My stomach leapt into my throat.

How long has he been there?

Sky was the first to speak. "What are you doing?" I could see the fear in her eyes and I knew Asmund could too. We'd been caught, but I don't know why I felt like such a criminal.

He laughed. "What am *I* doing? I was slipping outside for some fresh air when I heard the Wyllan witch spinning her tale. Since the three of you saw fit to keep me out of it, I thought I'd listen in and it's a good thing I did. We need to leave right now."

His expression was severe and I reached for my sword before I remembered I wasn't wearing it, before I remembered I couldn't stand on my own anyway.

Sky stood up, her chair skidding across the floor. "What are you talking about? And don't you dare talk to Echo that way."

Asmund jabbed a finger in Echo's direction and I was glad she was seated on the opposite side of the table. "She is the enemy," he snapped. "You heard it from her own lips. She is essentially the Winter King's daughter and here the two of you are, becoming her friend. The king's men could be on their way as we speak. We are in grave danger."

"She is innocent," Sky shot back, an untold fury in her eyes. "You heard the story, but did you listen to what she said? She was abandoned ten years ago. The Winter King isn't coming for her, let alone us."

"You trust she told the truth?" Asmund countered. "You're more stupid than I thought."

Heat surged through my veins. "Watch your tongue," I snapped.

Asmund's eyes fell on me. "Oh, and I see you're up and about. I guess nobody thought to tell me that either. You've known this girl for a mere week and a half and you trust her more than me, a fellow Sancian?"

"All due respect, Asmund, but it wouldn't take much for me to trust someone else over you."

"You're unbelievable, Prince." He looked at Echo. "Do you know he hates your people? Do you know he would burn your kingdom to the ground if he had the chance? If he's told you he's your friend, he's a Fidal-forsaken hypocrite. His only thought is towards his revenge, nothing more."

I looked to Echo. "That's not… Sancia's breath, Asmund, you like to wreak havoc wherever you go, don't you?"

He shook his head. Even here, in this wood, his dreadlocks were impeccable. "No, Isanfier, I like to be the voice of reason when no one else has their heads on their shoulders. Have you thought of your uncle, or anyone else since we got stuck in this forest? They're probably worried sick and here we are, consorting with a Wyllan. Fidal give us grace because if the king ever found out, he would not forgive us."

I hung my head. He was right about that. Uncle must never know about Echo.

"They could be dead, too, you know," Asmund went on. "Winter could already be storming the walls of Widonia and slaughtering your people. I bet you haven't thought of them either. Do you ever think of anyone but yourself?"

No one said a word for several minutes, even Sky, who I was sure would have leapt to defend me by then. Except, Asmund was right. I'd been more focused on my health and Echo's stories than the reason we were here in the first place. The war could be over. If Winter had won… Summer could already be reduced to ash. If Summer had won, Uncle could be naming another noble born as heir in my stead.

The thought made my skin crawl, but there I was, thinking of myself again.

I opened my mouth to say something, but Echo beat me to it.

She stood up from her chair slowly and met Asmund's gaze. "This is the very reason I did not wish to tell you," she told him. "I knew you would react this way. I knew you would judge me and then Isan and Sky by association. You do not have to take my word as truth, but I will not have you speaking ill of my friends in my home. Do you understand me?"

The look she gave Asmund was so intense that he immediately dropped his eyes. "Maybe you are the naive one for trusting them," he replied.

I curled my hands into fists, but Echo took the insult in stride. "You do not scare me, Asmund. I have dealt with far more malicious men than you and I have survived these woods alone for a decade. Your closed mind makes *you* naive."

I could tell his blood was boiling, but he looked from Echo to me. "I'll stay, Prince, but we are leaving as soon as you are capable. Do you hear me? Even if I have to knock you out and drag you behind me. The future of Summer may depend on the three of us." He gave us one last scathing look before storming back to his room, forgetting about the fresh air he'd been after.

As soon as he was gone, Sky met my gaze. "Where did that come from?"

"Does it matter?" I asked. "I knew the gods were trying to punish us when they let the Edgewood swallow him up too. I can't in good conscience let the two of you sleep alone now."

Sky gave me a look that said, *Really, Isan?*

Echo sat down. "He won't try anything."

I shot her an incredulous look. "Listen, Echo, we've known him a lot longer than you and—"

She held up a hand. "Yes, you met years ago, but I don't believe you truly *know* him, nor does he know the two of you. You never gave each other the chance. He is angry, that much is true, but he is also scared of me. It sounds ridiculous, but I think his prejudice will keep him from striking because he doesn't know enough about me to be certain I *don't* pose more of a threat than he does. He just needs to let off some steam. Being cooped up in this house can turn anyone. Trust me; I know."

"Are you sure?" I asked. I hated the thought of her getting hurt.

She nodded. "As I said to Asmund, I've dealt with far worse. A life like mine gives a person quite the perspective."

Sky finally found her voice again and said, "I'm sorry for Asmund's words and I don't think we are naive for trusting you. Our alliance is the smartest thing Isan and I have ever been a part of."

"And it is true, what he said about my feelings toward Winter," I added, "but it's not as black and white as he made it seem. Being here has taught me that maybe not all Wyllans are as evil as we're made to believe."

She gave us a rueful smile. "I don't need your apologies. Don't let his words make you question my trust. Nothing has changed between us. If anything, I trust you more for not choosing his side. In any case, I think we've all had enough excitement for one day. We should get Isan back to bed."

I frowned. "I thought my bedrest was over?"

"Not until you can put weight on that bad leg, or do you expect Sky and I to drag you around all day?" She smiled to lighten the words and I couldn't help but return it.

"Actually," Sky said. "I think I have a solution for that. You two wait here; I'll be right back." She left the room in a flurry, her hair streaming like shadows behind her.

I looked at Echo. "What do you think she's cooked up now?"

She shrugged. "Only one way to find out. Oh, and between you and I?"

I nodded.

"The Wyllan noble people deserve every bit of hatred that both you and Asmund possess. Don't downplay their villainy for my sake. I've witnessed firsthand what they're capable of, and remorse isn't on the list."

Before I could reply, Sky came back into the room, carrying a gnarled tree branch.

"What is that for?" I asked.

"It's for you," she replied with a smile.

I frowned. "What is it?"

She grinned. "A cane."

"No," I said. "Absolutely not."

"Oh come on, Isan," she prodded. "Let go of your pride and take it. You don't want to be bedridden? Well, this is your other option."

I heaved a sigh, but accepted the offer. It took several failed attempts at both standing and walking, but eventually, I was able to hobble back to my room on my own, leaving Echo and Sky in the kitchen.

I thought of Asmund in the next room over. His words had been nasty, but he had given me a much-needed wake-up call. Recovery should be my first priority. The gods didn't give me a second chance at life for me to waste it here. I still had parents to avenge. I couldn't let them down.

• • •

The sound of my bedroom door crashing open woke me in the dead of night.

I bolted up. "What in Fidal's— Sky?"

She was standing above my bed now and I could tell she was shaken.

My imagination ran with my thoughts.

Did Asmund hurt her? Did Asmund hurt Echo? Had the goblins found us and decided to attack despite the threat of the *Missing One*?

"He's gone," Sky gasped out.

I narrowed my eyes. "What?"

"Asmund," she said. "I brought some tea to his room as a peace offering and found his bed empty. Who knows how long he's been gone? Echo says he won't survive in these woods alone."

I rubbed my eyes. "And that's our problem because…?"

She smacked my arm. "We can't leave him for dead, Isan. We might have our differences, but we would be cruel if we didn't look for him. What would we tell Uncle?"

I sighed. "Okay, okay. What do you want me to do?"

"Stay here," she said. "Echo and I are going after him."

Ice water ran down my back. "By yourselves?"

"Who else is there? You're not going to be much help with that cane. Echo knows the forest like the back of her hand and I'll defend us with *Tempest*. I only told you so you wouldn't worry. We'll be back with Asmund soon, I promise."

I grabbed her arm. "Please, Sky. This is crazy."

"But it's the right thing to do," she replied. "We'll be careful and as quick as we can. Promise me you'll stay here."

I let go of her arm. "I promise, but if you don't come back, I'll never forgive you."

"I know." She took a breath. "We better go now before the trail gets cold."

"Fidal be with you."

She left the room without another word and my sanity left with her.

· · ·

I laid awake in bed the rest of the night, imagining the worst. When the sun finally rose, I grabbed my cane and wandered into the great room. I thought perhaps I could do some cleaning to pass the time, but I soon found that Echo kept the place impeccable. I couldn't even make a mess by eating. My stomach was too tied up in knots to even contemplate food.

What had Sky been thinking?

What had *Asmund* been thinking?

Sky and Echo might save him, but that didn't mean I wouldn't kill him on sight for his recklessness. His stunt was putting all of us in danger. What had happened to the three of us being the future of Summer? Clearly nothing that came out of his mouth held any value.

I clenched my fists.

My anger was getting the better of me. I needed a distraction, so I headed to Echo's small library. I loathed reading, but if her books were as interesting as the tales she told, then perhaps I could give it a try.

It only took a second to realize I'd opened the wrong door.

Echo's bed took up half of the space, neatly made with pale grey sheets and her closet stood open, revealing her familiar blue dresses.

I should've walked away, should've sought out the library, but curiosity overcame me and I stepped inside. A crooked side table sat beside her bed, a pile of books stacked on it, much like Sky's desk back home.

I smiled. No wonder the two got along.

I made my way over to the table to check the titles when I heard a shout from below.

They're back!

I rushed out of the room as fast as my leg and cane would carry me, meeting Echo and Sky in the entrance, hauling a bleeding Asmund between them.

"What happened?" I asked them. "Are you hurt?"

"Later," Sky gasped. "He needs immediate medical attention. Help us get him to the sick bay."

Asmund weighed a lot more than I did and I could tell the two of them were exhausted from carrying him this far. I tried to take as much weight as I could as the three of us dragged him the rest of the way and up onto a bed.

There was blood everywhere.

I didn't think Asmund was even conscious and I couldn't tell where the wound was.

Echo fired orders at Sky as she started tearing off Asmund's clothes. Her hands were already red.

"What do you want me to do?" I asked.

"Fetch some water," Echo said, "and then cut up some sheets to use as bandages."

I did as I was told and watched as she and Sky started putting Asmund back in order. There was a long gash down his chest and another across his head. The head caused most of the bleeding, but the chest was more serious. I heard Sky and Echo discussing internal organs and had to look away.

Finally, after what seemed like hours, Echo stood up, wiping her hands on a stray piece of cloth. "He'll live," she said and then she walked out of the room without another word.

Sky slumped on the opposite bed, totally spent.

I stayed glued to my spot on the floor, still trying to process the series of events.

Asmund lay on his blood-soaked bed, his breathing steady. Echo had covered him with a blanket, but his clothes lay ruined on the floor. He wasn't going to be happy about that when he woke up.

I looked to Sky. "Now will you tell me what happened?"

She took a deep, shuddering breath before sitting up and facing me. "I suppose you deserve to know. Asmund had made a path through the woods that hadn't completely closed yet, so we were able to follow him, but something else found him first."

"What?"

She wrung her bloodstained hands. "He was facing off with an ogre when we caught up to him. We arrived just in time. Unfortunately, our arrival distracted him and the ogre got him across the head with its fist. Echo ran to Asmund's aid and I was somehow able to make the impossible shot between the eyes to kill the ogre. Asmund had already sustained several other injuries. We patched him up as best we could, but we had to get him back here as soon as possible, before the smell of his blood attracted more creatures."

She went to hug herself with her hands, noticed the blood on them, then noticed the blood on her shirt and did it anyway. "It was a close call. We're going to be here longer because of it."

I hung my head. "I'm sure the army will manage a little while longer without us, though it is an unfortunate setback."

She sighed. "After Asmund's speech earlier, I hate the thought of lingering. We've been neglecting our duties, Isan. What will Uncle say?"

"We will have to ask for his forgiveness when the time comes. For now, you should go get some rest. I'm glad you're okay and I can't wait to see the look on Asmund's face when we tell him you killed the ogre."

That coaxed a smile out of her. "He's lucky neither Echo or I hold grudges."

"That too," I replied.

"Promise me you'll never go out in this wood alone?" Her brown eyes beseeched me.

"I promise," I told her. "I don't have any desire to meet an ogre."

"Oh, trust me, no one does. They're even uglier than the goblins. And less intelligent. Echo says they don't have any brains, which seems to defy reason, but..." She trailed off when she noticed the changed expression on my face. "What?"

I shook my head. "Only you could face off against a brainless creature and shrug it off like it was nothing. Any other girl would run away screaming."

"Maybe that's why Asmund wants to marry me, because I'm different."

I laughed. "When he learns that you saved his life, I doubt he'll still want to be your husband. It would ruin his pride."

She laughed. "I guess I have an ogre to thank then."

"I guess you do."

• • •

I was alone in the room with Asmund later that night when he groaned in his sleep.

I straightened up, leaning toward the bed in anticipation.

His eyelids fluttered and his face contorted in pain. He twitched for a few moments before a discernible sound escaped. "Help."

It took me a moment to understand what he said, but I grabbed my cane and limped over.

He stared up at me, brow slick with sweat, but I had a feeling he couldn't see me properly.

"Asmund, it's me, Isan," I told him. "What do you need?"

"Wa-er," he mumbled.

I frowned. "Wha— Oh. Water." I hobbled to the side table, where Echo had left a pitcher, and poured him a glass. Then I brought it over and held it to his lips. "Slowly," I told him.

He gave an unintelligible response, but I poured anyway, stopping after a few seconds to make sure he wasn't choking.

We went on like that for several minutes, until he had drained the glass.

I set it aside and watched as he relaxed into the bed.

"Isan?" His voice was drawn out, as if it took considerable thought to form each syllable.

"Yes?" I replied.

"What...happened?"

I sat down on the edge of the bed. "You almost died."

"How?" I could see him straining to focus on me.

"Close your eyes," I told him. "You're just causing yourself more pain. You don't need to see me to hear the story."

It took him a moment, but he complied.

"Sky and Echo went after you," I said. "Thank Fidal they did because you ran into an ogre and wouldn't have survived alone. The ogre knocked you out and you had a long gash on your chest that would've bled out long before you regained consciousness. The girls dragged you back here, after Sky killed the ogre, and spent hours patching you up while I stood by like a helpless idiot. So next time you think of them as lesser, think again. You owe them. Both of them. Echo might be a Wyllan, but she didn't hesitate to save you."

There was a long moment where I thought he must've fallen asleep, but then he said, "I'm sorry."

I sighed. "It's not me who deserves it. I'm not going to lie to you; if it had been up to me, I would have left you to your own devices. I doubt the two of us are ever going to see eye to eye, but if you want to make it out of this forest, you better apologize to Sky and Echo, and thank them for putting their lives on the line for yours."

He nodded and then winced.

"Careful," I chided him. "It looks like we'll be stuck here longer while you regain your strength. Try not to do anything stupid, again."

"I thought...I could...handle it...on my own."

"Even after everything that happened with the goblins?"

"My anger...may have...clouded my judgement."

I shook my head. "That's an understatement."

He ignored my comment and said, "I think...I know how...the mountain men feel." He was still talking with his eyes closed and it was a rather odd conversation.

I raised a brow. "What do you mean?"

"I faced an...ogre. No one will ever...believe me."

I laughed at that. "You're probably right. Maybe what happens in the Edgewood should stay in the Edgewood. Maybe in this godless place, our struggles are between us and the trees."

"I think so."

23
Sword and Song

Over the next fortnight, the four of us settled into a new normal. Asmund apologized to Echo and Sky, much to their surprise, and though there was still friction, there were no more outbursts. Asmund spent the first week in bed with a towel tied around his head so he wouldn't strain his eyes and stunt his recovery. Echo said it was a miracle the blow hadn't caused brain damage, but I thought that remained to be seen.

While Asmund was recovering, Echo, Sky, and I became closer than ever. It was the first time I felt like anyone—aside from Sky—knew the true me. There were no guards to comment on my posture or boisterousness, no Uncle to frown upon me neglecting my studies. I could be as improper as I wanted because the only people watching didn't care how I acted.

My own strength came back gradually. I relied on the cane for the first week, but could walk on my own by the second and threw the cane into our evening cooking fire so I wouldn't have to look at it again. My leg had healed nicely. Only a thin scar remained of the injury, though every once in a while I would be assaulted by a burst of pain like a line of fire up my leg.

Once I could swing my sword again, I added sword drills to my daily routine. I was a bit rusty at first, but the movements soon came back to me and I was glad to know I hadn't lost my touch.

One morning, as I paused for a short break in my drill, Echo approached me.

"Are you done already?" she asked.

"Hardly," I huffed, taking a drink of water. "I just needed a moment to catch my breath. Still getting used to being mobile again. My lungs enjoyed the time in bed too much."

She smiled. "I hope you didn't get too rusty."

"It doesn't seem so," I replied. "I didn't forget any of the moves anyway, but it's hard to gauge skill without duelling someone. That would be the real test."

"I could duel you, if you'd like."

I blinked. "What?"

"Oh this should be good," Asmund said. He had been collecting firewood, but he stopped now to watch the two of us. Echo had finally deemed his chest injury healed enough to lift things again.

Even Sky looked up from her work at Echo's offer. She was sitting at the base of the tree, whittling new arrows out of branches.

I ignored them both and gave Echo a sympathetic look. "I don't think that would be a good idea."

She put her hands on her hips and fixed me in her piercing gaze, a look she usually reserved for Asmund. "Why, because I'm a girl?"

I swallowed, recognizing dangerous territory. "Well, yes and no," I told her. "I've duelled with Sky before, but without the proper training, you might get hurt."

Her scowl deepened.

"Oh come now, Isanfier," Asmund said, "give the girl a chance."

I looked to Sky for help, but she only shrugged. "I don't see the harm in it, as long as you're both careful."

Oh honestly… Her and Asmund have never agreed on anything. Why now?

"Well?" Echo said, giving me an expectant look.

I sighed and stood up. "I accept your challenge, Miss Echo, but I must warn you of the peril you're now in."

She only smiled. "I'm not afraid of you, you know. In fact, I think it is you who should be warned."

"Oho," Asmund crowed.

I flashed him a glare before turning to Sky, pretending to ignore Echo's words. She had no idea what she was getting into. "Could you pass me your sword, Sky?"

"Certainly," she said, a smile hidden behind her eyes. I sensed she was up to something, but I didn't know what. She stood, grabbing the blade from its resting place against the tree trunk, and then threw it towards me.

I caught the hilt with my right hand a second before it would've hit my face.

Echo flinched, but I stuck my tongue out at my sister and then handed the blade to her. "This should be about the right length for you," I said. "How does it feel?"

She grasped it in her right hand and felt its weight, giving it a few experimental swings. "It feels okay."

I touched her shoulder. "Then you're ready."

She followed me as I walked out into the middle of the clearing, to give us the proper space. Asmund dropped his load of wood by the firepit and then sat down beside Sky, eager to see one of us lose.

"You call it, Sky," I called out to her and then Echo and I faced off, raising our swords before us. I expected Echo to be a little shaky with the unfamiliar blade, but she seemed comfortable with it, as if—

"Now!" Sky barked.

Her command caught me off guard and Echo took that as an opportunity to make the first move. She lunged toward me, sword pointed at my unguarded chest.

I pulled *Ember* up to block in the nick of time. The force of the impact vibrated through my wrist and up my arm.

I sucked in a breath.

Too close.

She lunged again, but I took a step back and slashed my sword towards her face.

She dodged it effortlessly and took a swipe at me.

I knocked her sword back, marvelling at her skill, and swung at her head.

She ducked and then we both paused, circling each other as we caught our breath. The duel should've been over in seconds, but here we still were. She was holding her own. I was both frustrated and intrigued.

I wanted to see how far she would go.

So I raced towards her again and we danced around the clearing, beneath a sky of foliage as Asmund and Sky looked on. We were a whirl of motion, of steel and sweat. She sensed my moves almost before I made them, but I still managed to keep my distance. Our swords crashed together again and again, each hit sending a thrill through my veins.

It had been years since I'd had this much fun in a sword fight and I expected it would be years until I felt like this again.

I picked up the tempo then, attacking her viciously.

She mirrored me and we were soon going at it like desperate soldiers defending the homeland.

I swung my blade toward her with considerable force, but she brought her sword up to meet mine and we strained against each other for several moments. She was incredibly strong for a woman of her size and age.

I pushed harder and so did she. Again, neither one of us could gain the advantage.

We pulled back, breathless, and tried a different approach. I was tiring and she had to be too, but we pressed on. We would not stop until one of us was disarmed or at the mercy of the other. At the rate we were going, though, I didn't think either one of us would slip up any time soon.

As I thought about it, I felt myself make a mistake. I didn't know if I turned the wrong way or angled my wrist too far, but it was enough for Echo to reach through and twist my sword out of my grip with her own.

Ember flew through the air and hit the ground five feet away.

I stood frozen, eyes wide in shock, as Echo took a step forward and pointed her sword at my throat.

She disarmed me. She won. I… I lost.

"You won, Echo!" Sky exclaimed and then she started laughing.

"Sancia's breath," Asmund gasped. "I don't believe it."

Echo bowed towards them both, basking in the glory of her victory for a moment, and then she turned back to me.

I was still standing there, gaping like an idiot.

"What's wrong?" Echo asked.

"Oh," Sky replied, "he's probably in shock. He's never lost before, much less to a woman."

"I've never even managed to make him sweat," Asmund added. "Where in Fidalia did you learn to fight like that?"

Echo ignored his question and gave me a quizzical look. "You've never lost?"

I took a deep breath, accepting what had transpired. "I haven't lost in a while, let's put it that way."

"He's the best in our kingdom," Sky added, "beat his first knight when he was twelve and can now fend off several knights at once. He is, you could say, our secret weapon. So secret, even our king doesn't know how skilled he is."

If Uncle had truly known, he would've sent me to Skar to hone my skills, like my father before me. Asmund and I would've seen a lot more of each other, so it was probably best I hadn't gone.

Echo looked impressed.

"So, to say I'm shocked at my defeat is an understatement," I went on, "but I accept my loss. You are an exceptional swordswoman."

She beamed at me, and despite my defeat, I couldn't help but smile back. She was full of surprises.

"Where *did* you learn to fight like that?" I asked her, repeating Asmund's question.

"Remember how I said I get glimpses of memory from Icaria?"

I nodded.

"Well, this is one of the perks. I was able to teach myself how to sword fight through the scraps of memory from her lessons. As well, due to our shared souls, some of our skills are transferable, as if in training her brain, she was also training mine. It's a bit hard to explain."

Asmund shrugged. "Complicated or not, you were able to beat Isan and the look on his face made my entire year."

She smiled again. "It was priceless, wasn't it?"

"I think your face was even better, Asmund," Sky added. "This was the best idea I've ever had."

Asmund and I shot her a look. "*You* put Echo up to this?"

Sky grinned. "Indeed I did, little brother. Echo told me about her skills *weeks* ago; we were just waiting for the right time to reveal them. I do have to admit though, I did not expect such great results."

The two of them high-fived while Asmund and I shook our heads.

"How about another duel to settle our differences," Echo suggested. "Sky and I against you and Asmund."

Asmund and I shared a look. "Deal."

And so we spent the afternoon locked in battle, laughter and battle cries breaking through the silence of the wood.

•   •   •

That night, the creak of a floorboard woke me up.

I sat up in bed, cocking my head to listen.

There it is again.

Wary, I rolled out of bed, grabbed *Ember*, and crept out of the room.

I stood in the doorway for a moment as my eyes adjusted to the dark and when they focused, I spied Echo creeping down the hall. Then I watched as she tiptoed over to the ladder and dropped from sight.

What is she doing?

Curiosity pulled me into the hall and down the ladder after her.

Once outside, I was afraid I'd lost her in the dark, but then I caught a glimpse of her white hair, slipping into the trees, leaving the clearing behind.

I trailed her through the forest, keeping about ten paces back.

What can she possibly be doing out here at this time of night?

My suspicions were high. What if she was up to something? Sky and I had chosen to trust her, but perhaps we were to be played as fools, perhaps Asmund was about to be proven right.

My thoughts came to a standstill, however, as we broke out of the trees and stepped into a different clearing.

A gurgling brook fed a small, rippling pond in the centre of the glade and breathtaking purple and white flowers grew along its bank. Above our heads was a break in the trees that bore the night stars for us to see. The full moon set everything aglow with a faint, white light; the flowers sparkled like priceless gems. Fireflies danced in the air, adding to the glory of it all, and I decided I could die happy here.

We had entered paradise.

I forgot what brought me there and stumbled in a small circle as I took it all in.

"What is this place?" I wondered aloud.

Echo inhaled a sharp breath and whirled around, nearly tripping into the pond. She placed a hand over her heart, alarm fading once she saw me. "Fidal's breath, Isan, you scared me half to death. How long have you been standing there?"

I shrugged. "Long enough to appreciate the beauty of this place. It's breathtaking."

"You followed me." Her tone was scolding.

"I wanted to see where you were stealing off to in the middle of the night. I certainly wasn't expecting this." I spread my arms out in front of me, gesturing to the glade. I expected her to be angry, but she didn't rebuke me further.

Instead she said, "I don't mind sharing it with you. It's peaceful, isn't it?"

I nodded.

"I discovered it a few years back and it's been my safe haven ever since, a place to go to forget my troubles. It reminds me that even in the most dismal places, like the Edgewood, you can still find beauty."

"It's a beautiful place, if you know where to look," I replied.

"Yes," she said and then a moment later her face scrunched up in confusion. "Wait, didn't I tell you that?"

"You did."

She raised a brow. "And you remembered?"

"Certain phrases stick with me," I replied, "and I can't seem to get most of yours out of my head."

"Oh?" she said. "I wonder why that is?"

I shrugged. "Who knows?" Then I noticed something familiar on a tree across the pond. "Is that…?"

As I pointed to the purple flowers, Echo followed my gaze and said, "That's a Wisteria vine. Are you familiar?"

"That's Summer's official flower," I replied. "They're everywhere in the capital. *Like a tall and bright Wisteria vine, I will never let you go. I will whisper my love into the wind, until Fidal calls me home.*"

Echo gave me a look. "What?"

"It's a Sancian song: Whispers of Wisteria." I hummed a few more lines and then held out a hand to her. "Would you care to join me for a dance?"

She looked at my hand as if it would bite her. "Here? Now?"

I shrugged. "Why not? We're in a beautiful glade in the middle of the night. This place deserves to be danced in. Let me share a piece of my childhood with you."

She hesitated a moment more, but then took a deep breath and placed her hand in mine.

I pulled her gently towards me, placing her other hand on my shoulder before putting my hand on her waist.

I began humming Whispers of Wisteria again as I led her across the clearing, the steps of the waltz coming back to me instantly. Echo was tense for the first few minutes, but she relaxed eventually and glided through the movements, even beginning to hum along with me.

We danced as if we'd done it a thousand times before, going through the song twice before twirling to a stop. It was an experience I wouldn't soon forget. A Summer prince dancing with a Wyllan princess under the light of the moon, in the middle of the Edgewood no less.

The entire realm would be baffled at the notion, but I felt at peace.

I let her go as the last notes died off and she twirled alone for a moment, before sitting down on a rock beside the pond.

I sat down beside her and the two of us sat in silence, lost in our own thoughts, until she turned to me and said, "Thank you."

I smiled. "You're welcome."

"You must have attended a lot of balls to be able to dance like that," she went on.

"Not as many as the monarchs that came before," I replied. "It was hard for people to celebrate after my parents' deaths. Feasts, parties, and balls are almost a thing of the past. Sky and I have only been to one actual ball in our entire lives, and that was the one they threw for our sixteenth birthday."

"Really?" Echo said. "Then how did you learn to dance so well?"

"Aunt Magnolia, our governess, made us take lessons. She wanted us to be capable if there ever was a ball, and she expected each of us to get married eventually. She insisted we'd have to dance at our weddings. She spent most of our early lessons dealing with my unruliness, though. I can still hear her telling me that men don't get to twirl."

I shook my head as I thought of her.

She must be worried sick by now.

Echo laughed. "Poor Isan," she said, "but this Magnolia sounds like a great woman."

"Oh, Aunt Mag's the best," I replied. "She read us stories, let us play outside the castle, and never spoiled us. She always wanted us to be humble and she raised us so we would be great rulers one day. She is the mother we never had, and we love her for it. I miss her."

Echo touched my shoulder. "Don't worry, you'll get back to her. I know it."

I leaned into her touch. "Thank you."

"What about the Wisteria song? Where did you hear it?"

"Oh, they play it every year at the Summer Solstice gala, the only gathering we still hold."

She frowned. "Why did they keep that one and not the others?"

"Well, it serves two purposes in one. Sky and I were born on the solstice, so the kingdom gets to celebrate the height of our season and our birthday all at once."

"I suppose that makes sense then," she replied. "You know, that's funny because it's actually the same as..."

She trailed off, going stock still, eyes widening in horror.

"The Curse," she whispered.

Then she disappeared right before my eyes.

24
Treachery

Frost

As the war raged on, Frost's frustration mounted. The two armies were doing nothing but dancing back and forth, waging battles that showed no favour to either side. Two steps forward, one step back, neither of them gaining anything.

Arkenier had yet to show his face—in his camp or in battle. Frost's sentries had yet to report seeing him, but they did point out the green and gold pavilion in the centre of the Summer encampment. The Winter King knew the scoundrel lurked inside, letting his men do the dirty work while he sat back and relaxed.

It made Frost furious. He couldn't see the war ending without either of them losing their heads, but Akenier knew that as well as he and wasn't going to leave his sanctuary. Frost cursed him every way he could think of and laid awake long into the night trying to find a way around it.

Exhaustion became Frost's new enemy. Thank Wylla the battles had grown few and far between and were over swiftly.

His stupidity would've killed him in earlier battles. Now, they could hardly be called that. They were mere skirmishes; each army only taunting, leaping over the flame but never into the fire. Arkenier and Frost were biding their time, making plans, but eventually time ran out.

Eventually you had to take a chance, a risk.

Eventually, you had to make a move.

The assassin was lounging in Frost's chair with his feet up on the table when Frost entered the tent. He was dressed all in black from his boots to his cloak and his hood was thrown back to reveal dark brown hair and deep blue eyes. He was the perfect assassin, born to blend into the dark, and he was annoying his king.

"Get out of my chair, boy," Frost said, not allowing his emotions to leak into his words.

The assassin smiled darkly and crossed his arms. "Make me."

Frost's eyes narrowed. "Do you want this job or not? Because insolence is not the way to earn it. You're not the only one in this tent skilled at killing people."

The assassin pushed the chair back, stood up, and had a knife to Frost's throat before the king could blink. "The name is Olwyn and I am not a child. I may not be the only murderer in this tent, but trust me; if you wanted me dead, I'd already be long gone and you would be in pieces."

His voice was like ice, cold and completely devoid of emotion.

It didn't scare Frost, but he could let the boy think it did. For now.

Frost swallowed against the blade and the assassin fixed him in a deadly stare for a few more seconds before stepping back and sheathing the knife.

"I... I am in charge here," Frost stuttered, letting just enough fear trickle into his voice.

The assassin took the bait. He laughed and sat back down in the king's chair. "No, Frost, you're not. *I'm* in charge and you'll respect that if you want the job done, and done properly."

Frost bristled at the boy's gall to challenge him, but said nothing.

"Now," Olwyn continued, "be a good little king and tell me who it is I am to kill."

Frost felt the temperature of the tent drop at his insulting tongue, but forced himself to ignore the urge to shove his own dagger through the boy's throat or freeze him where he stood.

"Arkenier," Frost told him. "I want the Summer King dead."

Olwyn nodded. "I thought as much. Desperate for the war to end? Trying to save your own head?" He grinned.

"My reasons are none of your concern," Frost snapped. "Can you do it or not?"

"Of course I can do it," Olwyn scoffed, waving a gloved hand. "It'll be like child's play. Do you want it to be quick and painless or slow and agonizing?"

"Do whatever you want as long as he's dead by morning and it's not traced back to me."

Olwyn smiled wickedly. "I was hoping you'd say that."

Frost rolled his eyes as Olwyn stood up, walking over to him and holding out a hand.

Frost shook it involuntarily.

"Pleasure doing business with you," Olwyn said.

"Let me know when it is finished."

Olwyn nodded. "I'll see you in the morning to collect my payment." Then he pulled his hood up over his head and slipped out of the tent without another word.

The king shuddered as he left and a new layer of frost sprang across the ground, across the table and chair.

The assassin's demeanour annoyed him and Frost found his lack of emotion unsettling, but he wouldn't let his own emotions take over. Frost was the *king* and he would not submit to cowardice.

"Henrik!" Frost bellowed.

Yes, your Majesty? his voice replied in Frost's head.

Frost clenched his fists, but some magic leaked out at Henrik's insolence, coating the entire inside of his tent.

Damn him.

"Do not make me wait, boy!" Frost snapped.

Frost heard the crunch of boots on snow outside his tent and then Henrik entered, shouldering through the now-rigid tent flap.

"Yes, your Majesty?" he repeated aloud.

"A boy dressed all in black exited my tent a few moments ago," Frost said, not bothering with pleasantries.

Henrik nodded. "I noticed."

"I want you to see where he goes. If he does not leave this camp tonight, bring him to me, by any means necessary, but I want him alive." The king's eyes bore daggers into Henrik, ensuring the boy understood his meaning.

"Of course, Sire," Henrik said, "and may I ask why?"

Habit urged Frost to dismiss him without an explanation, but this time he relented. "He is supposed to kill the Summer King tonight, but I don't trust him for a second."

Henrik's eyes lit up. "I am excited for either outcome, your Majesty."

The King sighed at Henrik's sadism and waved him along. "Leave me now, and tell my servants to bring me another tent."

Henrik bowed his head. "Until next time, your Majesty."

• • •

Frost counted the seams in his new tent as he listened to General Kallen's report. Each day it was the same.

Our numbers are dwindling, Sire. Our food is running out, your Majesty.

It mattered not to Frost. In war, sacrifices had to be made, and if the assassin followed through, they'd be celebrating their victory in the morning. If not…

Still, this was the reason Frost had a general. It was *his* job to deal with these problems.

"What would you have me do, General?" Frost asked, leaning back in his chair. It was more comfortable than his throne at the palace, which was an annoyance more than a respite.

"End the war as soon as possible, Sire," Kallen replied. "We can't hold out much longer." There was a certain desperation to his eyes that Frost disliked, but he supposed he couldn't blame the man. A lot was riding on their victory. Winter would be plunged into chaos if they should lose.

"Patience, General," Frost told him. "I *am* ending it."

Kallen raised a dark brow. "How?"

Frost leaned back toward him. "What if I told you that, by morning, King Arkenier would be dead?"

"I would be relieved, but not exactly confident in it," Kallen admitted, some stress falling out of his face. "We need a second plan, your Majesty. It does no good to put all your wolves in one den."

Frost sighed, but he knew the general was right. The chances of Henrik reporting good news tonight were slim; if Frost had felt otherwise, he wouldn't have sent him after the assassin.

Frost mulled over the problem in silence for a few minutes, before coming to a decision. He didn't like it, but if the assassin failed, what choice did they have?

"How much longer can we last?" Frost asked his general.

Kallen grimaced. "The food stores will last no longer than two weeks—and that's *with* the ride back to Appalachia."

Frost cursed under his breath.

"Here's what we must do then," he replied. "If Arkenier is not dead by morning, we shall plan one last battle for exactly six days from now. If we are unsuccessful, we will retreat over the ridge, grab what we need, and ride back to Appalachia. We'll lure the Summer army deeper into the country and when they attack the city, we'll be ready for them. They cannot win against us then."

Kallen bowed. "You are most wise, your Majesty."

"That may be, but it'll be your job to execute this plan. Spread the word amongst the knights, but don't tell them about Arkenier. I want his death to be a surprise and if it doesn't happen... Well, they need not know it was ever a possibility."

"Yes, Sire."

"You may go."

Kallen bowed once again and exited the tent.

Frost despised the idea of retreating and running back to Appalachia, but their chances of emerging victorious were far greater within their own city. The Appalachian sentries would pick the Sancians off one by one as they tried to climb the wall and if any made it over, the knights would make short work of them.

Frost felt confident that they could not lose, but something in the back of his mind prevented him from being certain. There was a flicker of unease, the feeling that something would go wrong, but that was the fear talking. Frost quashed it down and spent the rest of the afternoon imagining the different ways the assassin could kill Arkenier. Soon Frost would have his head and that was enough to put his mind at rest.

• • •

Night fell, but Frost couldn't bring himself to retire. He wanted to be awake for Arkenier's death. Even though he knew they were too far apart, he still hoped to hear the Summer King's final screams. As time passed, Frost grew anxious. He knew he would hear no news until morning, but he felt like something was amiss.

Frost's suspicions were confirmed when—at about half past midnight—Henrik's voice sounded in his head.

You were right, your Majesty. I have sniffed out a rather large rat. We'll be seeing you soon.

Frost cursed all the gods except Wylla and ruined his tent yet again, his furniture and some of his papers along with it. Then he sat down on his ice-crusted chair and waited for Henrik to bring the traitorous assassin to him.

It seemed a glimmer of hope had been too much to ask for.

Ten minutes later, the tent flap snapped open and Henrik dropped Olwyn at Frost's feet.

Henrik gave a half bow. "Special delivery, your Majesty. I apologize for the reek of deception that surrounds him, but, well, it's hard to get good help these days." He kicked the assassin in the ribs, eliciting a pitiful whimper.

There was blood on Olwyn's face and Frost wondered if Henrik had knocked some of his teeth out.

"How can you be certain he's a traitor?" Frost asked Henrik, not taking his eyes off the broken boy beneath him. He was sure Henrik was right, but mistakes could cost a fortune.

"He left his tent at midnight, dressed for a murder, but he wasn't heading in the direction of the Summer camp. No, his route was going to take him right to this tent, right to you."

Frost stiffened.

The gall.

"I caught up to him and he admitted everything, after a little...persuasion." Henrik grinned and then kicked the would-be assassin again. "Go on, Olwyn, tell your king what you were planning and why."

"That will be all, Henrik," Frost said. "I'll deal with him now myself."

Henrik looked crestfallen to miss the action, but nodded. "As you wish, your Majesty."

Frost waited until Henrik left before standing up and giving Olwyn a swift kick of his own. "Get up, you worthless whelp," he seethed, "and explain yourself!"

Olwyn groaned, but dragged himself shakily to his feet.

Frost noticed then that all his weapons were gone, save one dagger at his waist.

"You brought this upon yourself," Olwyn said finally.

Frost raised an eyebrow. "Oh? And what, pray tell, have I done to earn your pathetic ire?"

Olwyn smiled, a touch of his bravado from before sneaking into his expression. "You don't know who I am, do you? That's just how ignorant you are."

Frost bristled, but stamped his magic down. That would be too swift an end for his insolence. "It matters not who you are, boy. Now answer my question."

"You murdered my father, you heartless fiend," Olwyn snapped. "All he asked for was your help and you... You killed him for it." His eyes blazed with his fury. "I am Olwyn Humphrey of Ollyn and you will pay for what you did to my father."

The boy drew his dagger and circled the king until he had the blade at Frost's throat, his other hand holding Frost's left arm behind his back.

Yet, Frost only smiled. It was exactly where he wanted him. People's rage was a weapon you could use against them, for it blinded them to their own stupidity.

Frost shook his head slowly, careful not to knick himself on the dagger. "Your father is not worth this foolishness," he said.

"Treason is not the way to avenge the dead. It only leads to your own death."

"I'm not the one with a dagger at their neck," Olwyn countered, but Frost could hear the hesitance in his tone. There was a reason Frost wasn't dead yet.

"That is true," Frost replied, "but you're not the only one with a few tricks up your sleeve either."

Frost reached up and grabbed Olwyn's blade, letting his magic flow into it as he yanked it down from his throat and stepped away.

Olwyn stumbled and Frost turned to face him, holding out the dagger. Then, as Olwyn watched, he shattered the frozen blade in his bloody hands.

The boy stared at his broken weapon, stunned.

Frost smiled. "This is when you regret every decision you've ever made."

Olwyn blanched. "Please," he begged, holding his hands up in front of him in surrender. "Give me another chance. I'll kill him this time. I swear!"

Frost laughed; it hadn't taken him long to crack. "You're no assassin, boy," he snapped. "If you were, you'd understand why your father had to die. Besides, you've missed your chance and now you shall suffer the consequences."

Frost drew *Malice* and slashed it down the centre of Olwyn's face before he could make a move to defend himself.

Olwyn screamed.

Blood gushed from the wound.

Frost smiled yet again; his screams weren't Arkenier's, but they would suffice for tonight. The king kicked him to the ground and he fell without any resistance.

Olwyn was too focused on the pain in his face to fight back when Frost grabbed hold of his arm and shattered the bone. He screamed again, a shriek of pure, unadulterated agony.

The king went to work on him.

Olwyn pleaded with him, cried and screamed, but to no avail. Eventually, he succumbed to his wounds.

King Frost made him eat his own words; when he was done with him, Olwyn's body parts were scattered across the tent.

• • •

The evidence of what had happened was gone by the morning. No one questioned why the king was in such a good mood. Frost and Kallen went on with their second plan and nothing more was said on the attempted assassination of Arkenier.

25
Promises To Keep

Isan

"Echo?" I said. The glade darkened with her sudden absence. The fireflies were gone, dark clouds covered the moon and stars, and without the light shining on the flowers, they looked dull and dreary.

Wind whispered through the trees and my hair stood on end.

"Echo, what's going on?" I asked, fear creeping into my voice.

No answer came.

"Please come back," I urged. "Whatever I did, I'm sorry. I just—"

A crack sounded in the trees to my left, as if someone had stepped on a twig. I ran in the direction of the noise, spurred on by a sudden anxiety.

What if something took her?

"Echo!" I called out as I sprinted through the close-knit trees. "Echo, come back!"

I swore I could hear footfalls in front of me and so I followed them all the way back to the clearing and into the treehouse, only for them to fall silent.

"Sky, Asmund!" I called out. "Come quick!"

Sky barreled into the great room a few moments later, a yawning Asmund trailing behind her.

"What's this about?" he asked.

"Echo is missing," I replied.

Sky's face fell. "What?"

"I followed her out of the treehouse earlier to this glade and we talked for a while," I replied, my voice slowly getting more frantic. "She said something about a curse and then she disappeared. I followed the sound of footsteps here, but she's gone. I don't—"

I stopped my sentence short as Echo reappeared in front of us, materializing in the doorway as if she had been standing there all along.

Sky jumped, stifling a scream. "What did you do?"

"I— I can explain," Echo stammered, holding out her hands.

"You better hope you can," Sky said, "because I'm not in the mood for lies." Anger and fear rang in her voice.

I felt hurt too, but I was mostly glad Echo was safe.

Then Asmund smiled, which scared me more than anything. "You're a Gifted Immortal, aren't you?"

I looked at him. "What? How do you know that?"

"My mother was one too. She could grow flowers without a seed." His smile fell. "The one thing I miss most about her is how happy she was holding her creations in her hands. Your uncle's magic ban was what killed her, you know, not something as trivial as a disease. Not being able to use her magic destroyed her piece by piece."

My heart sank as I realized the truth in his words. For once in my life, I felt sorry for Asmund, but it wasn't the time. We were still waiting for Echo's explanation.

She took a deep breath. "Asmund's right."

I wasn't exactly surprised. It only made sense that she would be a Gifted Immortal if Princess Icaria was, seeing as they shared a soul. It also explained why she had shied away from my questions about her thoughts on magic.

"I have the power to become invisible," Echo confessed, "to disappear, leaving only an *echo* behind as proof that I was ever there, because I am an echo of Icaria and her past." She paused and tried to gauge our reactions.

Sky looked hurt.

Echo noticed this too and said, "I'm sorry I didn't tell you. I intended to, but I didn't know how. It's not exactly a normal topic of conversation."

"Regardless," Sky said. "You should have told us." She took a step closer to her. "We would have understood."

"I wanted to tell you," Echo replied, "I *did*, but I was afraid of what you might think. I mean, magic *is* outlawed in Summer. I didn't know how far your distrust of magic might run, despite Isan's interest in the stories. I'm sorry for the secrets, but I can't promise I won't do it again."

"I understand," Sky said, "but you don't have to worry about us."

I nodded. "We don't believe the nonsense our uncle spews about magic. It didn't kill our parents any more than he did. Winter is the killer, but Summer let our fear push magic aside and it became a scapegoat. You are not an abomination, Echo, you're a gift. You're special."

Echo smiled.

I turned to Asmund. "Your mother was special too. She shouldn't have had to hide what she was. She shouldn't have had to die because of it."

He nodded. "Thank you and I know."

The four of us were silent and serene until I remembered Echo's words before she disappeared and said, "You mentioned a curse?"

Terror crept back into Echo's expression at my words and she seemed to flicker on the edges.

Dread filled me at the sight.

"Well," Echo started, her voice shaking, "the Scholars say it is a prophecy, but I've only ever heard it referred to as a curse by the common folk." She wrung her hands and drifted over to the table to sit down.

Asmund, Sky, and I followed suit, a certain heaviness to our steps.

"It is said that when the fate of the kingdoms hangs in the balance, a set of twins will be born to both royal families on the same day," Echo went on. "Those children represent the imbalance in the realm; only two are meant to remain. The Elder twins must fight to the death and the Younger twins must do the same. The actions required to kill each other will restore the balance and save us all. For if they do not follow their quest, upon their eighteenth birthday, all four shall perish and our realm shall plunge into chaos."

Echo looked grim as she finished, but I was confused.

"I'm sorry," I said, scratching the back of my head. "This does sound...dire, but what does it have to do with any of us?"

Her eyes were sad. "You and Sky are one set of twins from the prophecy, Isan."

My heart dropped. "Pardon me?"

"You, Sky, Icaria, and Snowdon fulfill the criteria of the Curse," she replied.

"What?" Sky gasped. "That's crazy!" I could not describe the emotion swirling behind her eyes, a mixture of fear and anger and doubt.

"It's undeniable," Echo argued. "You are both royal twins and Isan just revealed to me that you were born on the same day, which cannot be written off as mere coincidence."

I felt the blood rush out of my face as I realized the truth of her words. "What does this mean for us?"

"It means that the four of you are now locked in a battle of life or death. Sky must kill Snowdon and you must kill Icaria, before the opposite becomes true, before time runs out and you all perish, bringing Fidalia down along with you."

I gripped the edge of the table, feeling myself sway under the weight that had been placed on my shoulders.

An ancient curse? A fight to the death?

It all sounded like heresy, but Echo had no reason to lie to us, not about this.

Sky reached for my hand and I let her, but didn't look over. I didn't want her to see the look on my face, to exacerbate her own fears.

Asmund spoke then, saving me the effort of trying to do so. "Why isn't this curse more common knowledge? I would think the two kingdoms would be on the lookout for such a birth."

Echo shook her head. "There is much that history can lose and there are few who were alive when last the curse was in effect. Perhaps your late king and queen knew, but they never had the chance to tell anyone."

My heart clenched at the mention of my parents. Had they known? Were they aware of the fate Sky and I would incur? Perhaps King Frost had known and he'd killed them to put us at a disadvantage, as if his magical bloodline didn't already do the job.

"How can we hope to win against them?" I asked, finally finding my voice. "Icaria has magic and you said it yourself—it's only a matter of time until Snowdon follows in her footsteps."

Echo's eyes were a source of comfort as she said, "Don't let your lack of magic discourage you."

Sky tore her hand from mine and stood up. "How can we not? How can we restore the balance when it is already tipped in their favour? This is madness, Echo. We..." She faltered and brushed a finger under her eye. "We didn't ask for this."

Echo held out a hand. "I know you're upset and scared. By Wylla, you have every right to be, but you can't give up before you've tried. You may lack magic, but you have other skills in your arsenal that you shouldn't discount. All you need is one clear shot and Snowdon is done for."

"You say that like it's easy," Sky said, her voice barely above a whisper.

Echo sighed. "I know it won't be, but I don't know what else you want me to say."

Sky sat back down. "I want you to tell me it isn't true, but I know you can't."

The look on her face was one of cold acceptance. She had always been the first one to take responsibility for anything we did, was always the strong one. I guess my greatest consolation in this was that we would go through it together. Perhaps our bond would be *our* advantage.

I took a deep breath and looked back at Echo. "Do you really think we can win?"

"I know you can," she replied, "but only if you believe in yourselves. The realm needs you."

Her eyes bore into mine and I knew then that I would not give up. She had faith in our victory, despite our short friendship, and I did not want to be the one to prove her wrong.

At the other end of the table, Asmund shook his head. "This could tear Fidalia apart. What was Fidal thinking?"

Echo shrugged. "It is said that this Curse keeps him from wiping the slate clean, after the events of the first war, but who can know for sure? He is a mostly benevolent god, but there are times when he acts out of anger and even he cannot undo his own actions. He is like us in that regard or perhaps, we are like him."

"Perhaps," Asmund allowed, "but our two kingdoms are already at war. Assassinating their prince and princess will only raise the conflict."

"Well, maybe..." Sky started, sitting up straighter in her chair. "Maybe this war is the imbalance we are meant to fix. Maybe Fidal is tired of us tearing at each other's throats."

Echo nodded. "Those are my thoughts exactly. The feud between Summer and Winter has gone on long enough."

Asmund huffed a breath. "I still don't see how more death will fix that.'"

"Only time will tell," Echo replied, "but the facts of the Curse remain."

Asmund stood then and turned to Sky and I. "I think the three of us need to discuss our next steps."

Sky nodded, glancing over at Echo. "Do you think you could excuse us for a moment?"

Echo managed a smile. "Of course, take all the time you need. I'll go make some tea."

She left us at the table then and the three of us stared at each other in silence for a minute before Asmund said, "We have to go."

The words were like a weight in my stomach, but I knew he was right. The Curse was only the last thing in a long list of reasons to leave.

Sky sighed. "You and Isan are completely healed, so I guess... I guess it's time."

"We've lingered too long already," Asmund went on. "Our army needs us and now the two of you have yet another quest, it seems." He turned to me. "Perhaps your dream is connected to this Curse?"

I shook my head. "I doubt it."

"Time will tell, I suppose," he said. "Let me know when you've decided on the details, Sky, but I for one would like to get some sleep."

Sky rolled her eyes at his back as he walked away. "At least he's on the same page, but we would've left weeks ago if he hadn't tried to go alone."

I nodded, my chest filling with a solemn acceptance. "How will we break the news to Echo?"

Sky sighed. "She knew this time would come and I'm sure it's what she expects after everything that happened tonight. We better go tell her now though, before I lose my nerve. Out of all the things I expected from this war, a new friend was not one of them."

"I agree, but I think a new friend was what we needed."

She smiled and the two of us headed to the kitchen where Echo was pouring three mugs of tea.

I guess she figured Asmund wouldn't join us.

"Are you two all right?" Echo asked as she handed us the mugs.

I let the warmth seep into my fingers as I took a deep breath, trying to calm my mind.

Sky took a sip of hers before she said, "We've decided it's time to finish our journey to Winter. We have a war to fight and promises to keep."

Echo sighed. "I was afraid you would say that." There was a deep sadness in her voice.

"Our uncle must think us dead and we wish to ease his mind," Sky went on. "Aside from that… Well, there's this Curse now and while we're still unsure of where it might lead, we figure we might as well start off on the path that was written for us."

"If you must," Echo said. "I won't stand in your way." Tears built up in her eyes, but she held them back.

"It's not because of anything you did, Echo," I assured her. "It's something we have to do. Please don't be angry."

She shook her head. "I'm not angry, and I completely understand. I knew this day would come, I just wish we'd had more time. When do you leave?"

"We leave tomorrow," Sky said. "Can you take us to the Winter border?"

Tomorrow?

Echo managed a smile. "It would be my pleasure. Fidal knows you wouldn't make it there in one piece yourselves."

We drank our tea in relative silence and then bid each other goodnight. I staggered back to my room, feeling a little lightheaded as I tried to process everything that had happened.

My head was pounding by the time I collapsed onto my bed, a mixture of stress and fear beating an incessant rhythm into my bones.

Too much had changed.

It was just this morning Echo and I had duelled. Just this morning everything was peaceful and now... Now we were leaving the Edgewood, returning to war with the Curse looming over our heads like a dark and ominous cloud.

My, how things change in the blink of an eye.

Aunt Mag's voice echoed in my head. It always came to me when I was feeling overwhelmed and in need of guidance. A part of me wished she were here, but I knew she was much safer at the castle, far from goblins and ghosts and bloodshed.

Far from the unknowns that plagued me.

I missed her.

How long has it been?

I counted the weeks in my head and the answer shocked me: two and a half months.

That can't be right, can it?

Yet, it was the truth. It goes to show how time flies when you're having fun and that's what we had been doing, having fun. We had been relaxing for the past couple months and now that we were finally joining the action, I wasn't sure I was ready for it.

• • •

The next morning, we woke early and packed our meager belongings. Then we ate a quiet breakfast, said goodbye to the treehouse, and headed back into the woods.

Echo spent the first half of the journey telling Sky and I what she knew of Snowdon and Icaria's weaknesses, and we prepared ourselves mentally to face them. Sky learned that Snowdon relied more on physical strength than mental strength, so it would be best to try and outwit him. I learned that Icaria's anger often distracted her from her real goals.

It was nice to have some sense of direction, but the four of us grew more quiet the closer we drew to our enemy. I knew it would be difficult to say goodbye when the time came, to leave the Edgewood behind and step foot into Winter. Yet, I also knew it had to be done.

• • •

"This is it," Echoed announced one afternoon.

It was five days into our journey and we stood in a sparse section of the wood, trees metres apart, leaves curled as if lacking moisture. A speck of white lay in the distance.

Echo looked at us sadly. "This is where I leave you."

Sky, Asmund, and I said nothing; we just stared into the remainder of the forest, what stood between us and Winter.

"Keep walking in this direction and you'll enter Wylla's domain," Echo went on. "You can probably already feel the shift in temperature."

Indeed there was a crispness to the air that I had never felt in Summer, a chill. The leaves rustled above us as a breeze curled through the wood.

"Thank you, Echo, for everything," Sky said finally. She walked over and gave Echo a hug. "You're a great friend, the sister I never had. I'm sad we have to leave, but we will meet again, I'm sure of it."

Echo smiled. "I'll miss you too."

Asmund nodded in agreement. "I know I wasn't the most gracious guest, but I recognize what you did for us, despite not knowing us. I will not forget your kindness."

I stared at him in disbelief. He'd certainly never spoken to me with such respect. I pushed him aside as I stepped forward to say my own goodbye.

"I owe you more than words, Echo," I told her, "but I hope they will suffice for now. Thank you for saving my life. Thank you for the stories. Thank you for being a friend."

She smiled. "As I said before, having people to talk to was repayment enough. You owe me nothing, Isanfier of Summer, but I do hope to see you again someday. Perhaps next time, you'll be the victor of our duel."

I laughed. "Perhaps next time I won't take it so easy on you."

Asmund and Sky groaned, but Echo smiled wider. She truly was a remarkable person. Perhaps the forest had taken us in for the sole purpose of meeting her, of finding someone different from us and yet the same.

26
Winter's Chill

As Asmund, Sky, and I walked for those last few minutes in the Edgewood, the forest changed even more. The trees became leafless and a white powder covered the ground. We crunched it beneath our boots, packing it into the earth.

It took me a minute to realize what it was; you would never see snow in Summer.

I knelt down and grabbed a handful. It was cold, though not unbearably so, and soft as sand. I tilted my hand, letting the snow fall, and a gust of wind carried the flakes away.

"Oh, that's freezing," Sky gasped, pulling her cloak tighter around her. "We must be close."

A hundred yards ahead, the trees parted and gave way to Winter. Nothing but snow, as far as the eye could see, save for a few dark masses that hinted at Winter woods. The barrenness of the land gave us a perfect view of the armies camped in the distance, a black dot on the horizon.

"Looks like they haven't made much progress," I said.

Sky crossed her arms. "What makes you say that?"

"We can still see them; they haven't gained any ground."

She frowned. "But the war's gone on for over two months now."

"It has," Asmund agreed, "but time doesn't translate directly to progress in a war. The Winter defense must be exemplary. We better catch up to them though, in case the situation changes."

Sky sighed and started walking down the snow-covered hill before us. "What I wouldn't give for a horse."

• • •

Several hours later, we had almost reached the camp. Our legs were sore from walking and Sky wasn't looking so good. We had underestimated the chill of Winter and hadn't dressed for it at all. Most of our suitable clothing had been lost when we'd been left behind, but we were paying the price for our foolishness.

It affected Sky more than Asmund and I, and I felt horrible for her. We had already given up our cloaks to wrap around her shoulders—Asmund a little worse for wear because of it—but it wasn't enough. She was red in the face from the wind burn and shivers wracked her body with every step. I had one arm around her for support. She used all her remaining strength to keep putting one foot in front of the other.

I set my mind on reaching the camp. It would be Sky's salvation and it was only a few hundred paces away.

Now that we were closer, I could see the soldiers as they milled about, doing idle chores to keep themselves busy. The camp in itself was impressive, filled with hundreds of tents. A trench had been dug around the perimeter and wooden spikes had been erected along the outside of it. There was also a watchtower, poorly constructed from stray pieces of wood and metal, but it served its purpose. From its top, one would be able to see the comings and goings from all directions.

It was from that watchtower that a bell began to ring.

The camp erupted into chaos, men grabbing for their weapons and running in all directions.

"Which way are they coming from?" someone yelled.

"The north!" was the response.

The north? We're coming from the north.

I whirled around, practically dragging Sky along with me, but there was no Winter army behind us. That meant...

"They're after *us*!" Sky exclaimed with what energy she could muster. "What do we do?"

"Don't worry, they'll realize their mistake," I said, as much to comfort myself as to comfort her.

"W-will they?" she asked.

I winced at her quivering voice. "They have to," I replied, trying to sound confident.

"I wouldn't bet my life on that," Asmund retorted. "Be ready for anything."

We continued to make our way forward as the soldiers assembled along the northern trench. The archers pushed their way to the front of the line, and following unknown orders, took aim.

Sky froze in her tracks and I stepped in front of her.

Then, as the archers tensed up and readied to shoot, Asmund lunged forward and cried out, "Hold! Hold! It's the prince and princess. *Hold!*"

I forgot to breathe, wondering if they would listen to him, but then one by one, our men lowered their weapons.

Mutterings of "The prince and princess?" traveled through the crowd.

I returned to stand beside Sky and she sagged against me, exhausted. Asmund stayed in front of us, as if planning to defend the three of us on his own, if it should come to it.

Two knights jumped on horses and rode out to meet us. They stopped a few feet away but remained on their mounts.

"You!" one knight called, addressing me. "State your name and business."

"I am Prince Isanfier," I replied. "This is my sister, Princess Skiansy, and Master Asmund, son of Lord Arrath of Skar. We have returned to fight in the war." I did my best to stand up straight and look him in the eye.

"Is that so?" he said, raising an eyebrow. "How do we know you are who you claim to be and not a trio of Winter spies?"

I sighed; these men didn't even recognize their own prince and princess. It emphasized how sheltered Sky and I were. Most of the knights had never even met us; they had only seen glimpses. On the other hand, I suppose Winter could have people with magic able to make someone look exactly like us, so the knights were right to be cautious.

"Tell me something only the prince would know," the knight demanded.

I thought for a second, and then said, "Arran, Asmund's younger brother, is to be the next Lord of Skar."

I could almost feel the heat of Asmund's annoyance coming off him at the reminder and wished for only a moment that Sky was leaning against him instead.

The two knights were quiet for a moment as they considered whether or not a Winter spy could possess that information.

Then they dropped down to one knee and bowed their heads, saying, "Your Highness; Sirs Leif and Henley at your service."

Apparently my answer had satisfied them.

I told them to get up and they did so, apologizing for questioning me. I said not to worry about it; Sky and I understood.

"We need to get to the king," I continued, "and my sister here is in need of some warmer clothes. Any longer out there and I fear she would've frozen." I looked to Sky, who was now barely awake, and the knights nodded vigorously.

Even Asmund looked chilled to the bone.

"Of course, your Highness," they replied. "It shall be done."

Sir Henley lifted Sky onto his horse and she leaned against him as he rode the short distance to the camp.

Asmund and I walked beside Sir Leif, the one who had done the talking, as we followed Sir Henley.

When we arrived at the camp, Sir Leif brought us to one of the many fires they had about. Sky and Asmund weren't the only ones in danger of becoming an icicle; we all were. Sancians were not built for the cold as Wyllans were not built for the sun.

The three of us warmed ourselves by the heat of the fire as Leif barked out orders to a pair of foot soldiers. They came back a few minutes later with extra thick, ankle-length fur cloaks for Sky and Asmund. Sky quickly traded mine and Asmund's for the warmer one and flipped up the hood to protect from the biting Winter wind. Asmund didn't even react when she let his cloak fall to the snow. Someone passed them each a pair of gloves as well that they accepted with much gratitude.

Sky held my cloak out to me. "Here," she said, her voice steady, "you can have this back now. You must be freezing." She regarded me with worried eyes, and that, if nothing else, assured me she was going to be okay.

I shrugged, but took it anyway. "I'm fine actually," I said, "and besides, you needed it more than I did."

"Thanks," she replied, "now put it back on before you catch your death."

I sighed, but did as she said, more to please her than because of the cold. I didn't really feel it, but maybe that was how numb it had made me.

I asked Leif about Uncle again, now that I knew Sky wasn't going to die on me.

He nodded and said it would be just a moment.

I turned to Asmund and Sky. "Can we agree to let me do the talking?"

Asmund frowned. "Why?"

"Because we can't screw up the details. Uncle doesn't need to know everything that happened. In fact, he shouldn't, for all our sakes. You're right about Echo being the enemy, Asmund. At least in the eyes of everyone in this camp, she would be. Uncle wouldn't trust any of us again if he knew the truth. We have to pretend it didn't happen."

Asmund smirked. "Are you sure you can, Prince?"

"I'll do whatever it takes to stay in Summer's good graces and if you're thinking about throwing Sky and I to the wolves as soon as we turn our backs, remember that you're incriminated too and that you owe Sky a life debt."

He sighed. "I'm well aware, but our little jaunt in the woods didn't change things. We're still not friends."

I laughed. "Oh, don't worry, *Az*, I wouldn't want to be."

He scowled. "Don't call me that."

Sir Leif saved us from further conflict, informing us he was ready to go. We stood and let him lead the way to Uncle's tent, though we could've easily found it ourselves; it was hard to miss with its gold fabric and green designs.

Leif paused outside the tent. "Your Majesty," he called, "you have visitors."

"Send them away," Uncle's voice answered from within. "I'm busy."

"But, Sire," Leif insisted. "It's your niece and nephew, and the Arrath boy; they're alive!"

"What?" Uncle said, shocked, and for a second, he didn't sound happy at all; rather, he sounded angry.

That's ridiculous, I thought. *Why would he be angry?*

"Then what are you waiting for?" Uncle's voice called out. "Send them in!"

"Yes, Sire," Leif said. He hurried us into the tent and took his leave.

Uncle sat in a straight-backed wooden chair in front of a small desk, looking over a bunch of papers. "Isan! Sky!" he exclaimed. "You don't know how happy I am to see you! We thought you were dead." His eyes were bright with awe as he looked from us to Asmund. "Master Asmund. Your father already said your last prayers."

"Is he all right?" Asmund asked.

"More deadly than ever," Uncle replied. "I thought you three had surely perished, having little idea of what creatures lurk in that wood. Yet, here you are. How did you survive?"

I tried to formulate a believable answer to his question and finally said, "I made another path to Winter and we followed it."

His brows furrowed. "If you made a path, then how come you've been gone so long?"

The lies came easier this time. "I was panicking when I constructed it and wasn't thinking straight, which the path reflected. It was winding and sometimes doubled back on us, but we had to follow it. It was our only hope."

"I see," he replied. "It must have been a traumatic experience for all of you."

"It was," I agreed, considering I'd almost died, but we couldn't tell him about *that* either. "How did we end up like we did?"

Alone in the Edgewood?

"Ah, yes," Uncle said. "I knew you would be curious about that. When we woke up that first morning in the Edgewood, the three of you were nowhere to be found. You had been swallowed up by the forest, tents and all. It had crept forward all night until it lay between us and you. We tried to get to you, but to no avail. The Edgewood wouldn't let us forge a path and we hacked at the branches only to have them grow back seconds later.

"After hours of futile attempts to save you, I told the men it was useless; you were gone. They would've tried indefinitely, but we had to get to Winter, to take revenge for your parents because you could no longer do so yourselves. I'm sorry we left you, but I hope you can understand why we did it."

"Yes, I understand," I told him, though I did not.

Why would they leave us? Why would they give up on us? Sky and I, at least, were the future. If we were dead, there would be no one to take the throne when Uncle died. Winter would surely step in and all would be lost.

"Well, now that we're here," I said, "we're eager to join the war and leave the past behind."

Yet another lie. I would never in a million years forget our time in the Edgewood.

"Of course," Uncle said, "we'll not discuss it further. Let's get your tents set up and everything settled. You can attend Council tomorrow. For now, you should rest. It must have been a long journey." He gave us a sympathetic look and we nodded tiredly.

"If I may," Asmund said, "I would like to go see my father."

Uncle nodded. "Of course."

Asmund turned to go, but I grabbed his shoulder. Our eyes met and I said, "Thank you, for your loyalty."

He nodded. "Thanks for not killing me in the Edgewood."

Despite myself, I smiled, and so did he.

Once Asmund left, Uncle called for Leif again and he returned promptly. "How may I be of assistance, your Majesty?" he asked with a bow.

"Find a suitable place for my niece and nephew's tents and help them set them up," Uncle told him. "Then, you are to tell everyone they are not to be disturbed until morning."

"Of course, Sire, it shall be done," Leif said. Then he turned to us. "This way, your Highnesses."

• • •

Most of the day passed in a blur, but after setting up my tent and being left alone, I finally took the time to process everything. We were in Winter now, right in the thick of a war that had been going on for months, while we sat idle in the Edgewood. I realized I had had plenty of time to come to terms with this, but it was as if nothing else existed in the Edgewood. The problems of the realm had become background noise, but now...

We could die tomorrow. This could be my last day as a living being. My brush with death at the hands of the goblins did nothing to deter my fear of it. If anything, it had reminded me of how much I had to lose, and now a quiet Wyllan girl had been added to the list of people I would leave behind if I should go.

Echo had done so much for us, but if we perished, she would never know.

I guess I'll have to beat Icaria then, so Echo can be free and discover our fates for herself.

I thought about Aunt Mag then too, about my promise to return to her. She would berate my thoughts of death and she would have just the right words to spur me on, to make me believe in myself again. Yet, she wasn't there, and so I brooded in silence as I sat at the fire outside my tent, staring into the flames.

I didn't notice the knight sitting across from me until he said, "Why so solemn, son?"

"Regret," I replied.

"Regret?" he repeated, raising a weathered eyebrow. "What does someone as young as you have to regret?"

"A lot of choices," I replied, looking up from the fire, "but the most pressing one being my decision to come here and risk my life."

"Ah, I see." He thought for a second and then said, "Is there a girl involved?"

I scrunched my face. "Yes and no. She's a friend, but I'm afraid to die and never see her again." I sighed. "It's not just that though. For months now, I thought I wouldn't make it to Winter, but now that I'm here... I fear I'm not ready. Is that stupid?"

He shook his head. "Only a weak man boasts that he is not afraid, and I promise you, you are not the only one new to war. It is only on the battlefield that you will truly see what you're made of, though I have a feeling it's more than you think."

I smiled, touched by his kindness.

"Besides," the man went on, "I should think you to be the least concerned of all of us when it comes to death."

"And why is that?" I asked.

"You're the future; the king won't let anything happen to you."

"I hope you're right," I said, trying to sound positive, but dark thoughts swirled in the back of my mind.

If we were the future, why would Uncle leave us for dead?

27

Leaping Over The Flame

The knight and I talked for a while and I asked him about his life and the war. He told me his name was Silas and that he had a wife, a son, and three daughters. He was an older knight, nearing his fiftieth year if I had to guess, but that made him more likable. Silas had honour in place of arrogance. He treated me like an equal through our entire conversation and never once used the condescending tone I'd grown used to from my elders. Even his use of lad and son to address me was familiar.

Silas didn't make me fish for information either; he was an open book when it came to the war. From him, I learned that Summer had been at that outpost exactly two months and, like I'd predicted, hadn't dealt with much.

"There have been several battles," Silas told me, "though I am hesitant to call them battles at all. Most of them are nothing but dipping our toes into the water. It is my personal belief that Winter is toying with us. Once a day, a dozen or so of them will ride up to the top of that rise over yonder and taunt us." His eyes shifted to the south, as if he could see the ridge through the darkness. "They make no move to attack. They just sit there, watching us, daring us to challenge them."

"Where is their camp?" I inquired.

"About half a mile past the ridge," he replied, poking at the fire before us. "It's a good place, as it allows them the element of surprise. They're not stupid, these Winter knights, and the sooner everyone else realizes that, the better off we'll be."

"Do you know our next move?"

He shook his head. "I do not, but I fear that's only because we don't have one. This war has become a waiting game. Both of us are afraid to make a move, lest it be the wrong one."

We sat in companionable silence for a while, until my thoughts turned dark again and I decided it was time to retire.

"Well," I said, yawning. "I think I'll turn in." I stood up and stretched.

Silas nodded. "You best rest up when you can, lad. You never know what tomorrow may bring."

I bid him goodnight and entered my tent where I took off my coat and boots and collapsed onto the cot.

It had been a long day. Not much had happened, but that was the problem. Time had flown when we were with Echo and now time dragged its heavy wings along the ground behind it, loath to go any further.

I wondered if Echo felt the same, if our absence made everything move in slow motion.

Anxious thoughts beckoned to me, but sleep tugged harder, promising me a chance to forget all my troubles, if only for a short time.

• • •

I woke up to the rumble of hundreds of feet assaulting the hard-packed snow, followed by shouting and the clanking of armour.

What's going on?

Better find out.

I rubbed my tired eyes and set about getting dressed. I was pulling on my boots when Sky burst into my tent.

"Isan, they're here," she gasped out. "They've come for us! I don't know what to do. Everyone's running around like chickens with their heads cut off. There's no order to the preparations and I..." She trailed off, running out of breath, and I took that as an opportunity to speak.

I held out a hand. "Slow down, Sky. Who's here? What's going on?"

"It's the Wyllans," she said. "We're under attack."

• • •

I ran through the crowd of soldiers, Sky following close behind. After Sky had filled me in on all she knew, we had donned our armour and weapons. Thankfully, Leif had brought the armour to us last night, along with our other lost possessions.

I had *Ember* in hand and Sky had *Tempest* half drawn. She had managed to find a couple extra full quivers in the chaos that hopefully wouldn't be missed.

We pushed through the soldiers, trying to find Uncle, trying to attain orders for ourselves. We had no idea where we should be stationed, but the crowd pushed back, dragging us in the opposite direction of the gold and green pavilion.

"Isan," Sky said, grabbing my arm. "There's no use in finding him now."

I looked back at her. "But we don't know where we're going."

"I don't think it matters where, Isan, so long as we fight."

I sighed. She was right. I was wasting valuable time.

I shook off her arm. "Come on then."

We turned around and headed to the battlefield instead, following the knights around us until they came to a stop. Then we stood at attention and waited, near the front of the line, all but invisible in a sea of armour. The morning sun was an orange glow to the east.

A dozen Winter knights stood opposite us atop the ridge, a herald for the army to follow.

At the sound of a horn, they rode over the ridge on their black steeds, the rising sun glinting off their silver armour. Malevolence rolled off them in waves and the temperature dropped even further with their presence. None of them wore helmets, leaving their short brown or white hair on display, refusing to hide.

The knights were similar enough that no man stood out from the others, except one. He rode front and centre on the only white horse. He radiated importance and his shock of white hair looked crystallized, as if it were made of snow.

That must be Frost.

I was within reach of the feared King of Winter.

This is the man who ordered my parents' deaths.

I wanted to study him more, to memorize every single detail about him, but Frost let out a yell and the Winter army surged toward us.

We let out a war cry of our own and ran to meet them.

They were on us in moments, our armies clashing together. Weapons were drawn and blood began to spill. The air filled with the sounds of clashing swords, twanging bows, and final screams.

Sky nocked an arrow to *Tempest* and I held *Ember* at the ready.

"This is it," I breathed.

"May Sancia make your sword light," she replied.

"And your aim true."

She let her first arrow fly and I lunged at the first Winter soldier in sight, felling him quickly.

The minutes blurred together and the battle raged on.

• • •

Our army had devastated their numbers; I could tell by the number of silver-clad bodies piled around me and the amount of blood soaking the snow. They were no match for us and by the time they realized that, it was too late.

Sky watched my back with her bow and I ensured no one came close to her; that is, until she reached into her quiver and found it empty.

She threw it aside, slung *Tempest* over her shoulder, and drew her sword.

"Are you going to be okay?" I called to her in a short moment of reprieve.

She sank into a ready stance. "I may be better with a bow, but if they think I'll be an easy target now, they're even more stupid than they look."

I grinned. She was right. She could easily hold her own.

"On your left!" she cried.

I turned and felt metal slide across my cheek. I hissed against the sudden stinging, but didn't let the injury deter me as I swung my sword at my assailant and carved a deep line in his breast plate.

I guess not all of them can afford decent armour.

We danced for a short time before he too succumbed to my blade, joining his comrades in the snow.

I whirled to face my next opponent in time to watch Sky get clubbed in the shoulder with a mace. She staggered back and the man struck her again, with enough force to send her to the snow.

My heart sank into my toes as she hit the ground and gasped for breath.

"Sky!" I called out, but then something smacked into my ribcage and I was caught up in a battle of my own.

Please get up, Sky, I begged her as I fought off my new opponent, letting my fury and fear fuel my moves. *Don't die on me now.*

It was only moments before I turned to face her again and I almost sank to my knees in relief when I saw Asmund standing over Sky's assailant, his sword through the Wyllan's back.

He helped Sky to her feet and they exchanged a few words I couldn't hear over the din of the battle still raging around us. We nodded to each other before the three of us lost ourselves in the fight once again.

Not long after, the call for retreat rang out, but I couldn't tell who it was for. Both sides ignored it for several minutes before the call came again and the Wyllans started to fall back.

Our archers shot a rain of arrows at their backs as they fled out of range.

Not all of them made it.

28
Hands Stained Crimson

A victory cry arose from our comrades, but it didn't mask the whimpers of pain from others. The wounded were many, the dead even more.

My breath was heavy in my lungs and it was a moment before I even thought to move. I could not tear my eyes away from that ridge, fearing Winter was not done with us yet. I was afraid to turn my back on them. I'd been in my element during the fight, but now anxiety rippled across my skin like a thousand ants.

So this is what war feels like.

A hand touched my shoulder. "Isan? Let's not linger."

I relaxed a bit, turning to face my sister. Her braided hair was in disarray and her face was flecked with blood, so bright I could see it against her dark skin. Her armour was dented in several places, severely enough on her shoulder that I worried about broken bones.

"You're okay," she told me. "We survived. Now, come on. This isn't the right place to rest." She started to walk back to camp, pulling me by the arm behind her.

I sheathed my sword and let myself be taken.

We walked in silence, stepping over and around the bodies scattered across the field, people who had been living and breathing only a short while ago.

I shuddered, wanting to close my eyes, but the least I could do was bare witness to the carnage I had helped wreak.

We were almost free when one body gave me a start and I jumped back, tearing my arm out of Sky's grip.

She whirled around. "Isan? What happened?" Her brown eyes were muddied; fearful.

My face felt ashen. "He looks so much like me," I choked out.

Sky followed my gaze, her eyes landing on the boy in front of us. A boy with the same pale skin, same blue eyes, and same messy, brown hair as me. We could be the same person, except his eyes were lifeless—wide open but seeing nothing.

"Oh, Isan," Sky breathed.

Still shaking, I looked around at the destruction the battle had left in its wake. There were bodies everywhere, both Winter and Summer. The once pristine, white snow had become a crimson puddle of death.

A wave of guilt washed over me.

I had done this. I had contributed to this bloodshed. I had killed countless Winter knights in the name of revenge, but not all of them could be guilty of killing my parents. I had killed innocent men.

Despite what Echo had said, I refused to believe all of them were evil. How many of them had a family to go back to, like Silas? They were normal people and I had killed them mercilessly.

I was a monster.

I glanced at the knights returning to camp ahead of me.

I'm not the only one.

I looked back at Sky. She was furiously trying to blink away tears, her expression laced with guilt and pain. I half expected her to fall to her knees and retch.

Was my guilt that noticeable too?

The two of us were alone on the battlefield, save for the dead. No one else had lingered. Did they not feel this remorse? Did it not weigh them down?

They must have all fought before and killed before. Did killing get easier over time? Did you eventually walk out of a battle without looking back? Did your conscience disappear slowly until no guilt could be felt?

If so, I couldn't—*wouldn't*—let that happen to me. If I began killing without feeling, I'd be no better than the enemy we fought against.

When we finally reached the camp, the bustle of activity served as a distraction from my brooding thoughts. Men barked orders, telling us where to put broken weapons and take the injured, and where we could get cleaned up if we chose to do so.

Sky and I ignored the first two orders, but listened intently to the third. We walked to our tents first to ditch our stained chainmail and armour. Then we headed to wash up.

"Washing up" consisted of a basin of water and a rag.

I dipped my hand in the water to test it. It was ice cold—melted snow. The temperature didn't deter me, though. It was oddly bracing. I submerged my arms up to my elbows and felt my mind clear a bit.

The world will move on. So will you.

I wiped at the cut on my cheek, soon realizing the blood had dried on my skin. I hoped it wasn't too deep, that it wasn't in danger of infection or scarring. It was my only major injury though, save from the blow to my ribs. I was lucky, but somehow I knew the emotional scars would run deeper than any blade.

I rinsed the rest of my body as needed and then changed into a fresh pair of clothes. The clean fabric against my skin felt wrong somehow. It did not calm my racing heart, could not mask the truth of what I had become: a murderer.

The Wyllans in Widonia had been different. They had threatened an innocent Summer civilian and then tried to kill me. The men today had done nothing wrong that I knew about; they were simply following orders, though I suppose I could say the same about myself.

I looked down at the wash basin; the water had turned red.

I grimaced.

I had been covered in blood. I was glad to get it off my skin, but I could never wash it off my hands. They would be stained forever.

I pushed such thoughts away, pulling on a pair of clean boots and my coat.

The world will move on.

I might follow.

• • •

I met Sky on the way back to my tent.

She smiled at me, but it looked forced.

I brushed my hair back from my face. "How is your shoulder?"

"It's been better," she replied, giving it a slow roll and grimacing at the action. "I might have to set *Tempest* aside for a few days so it can heal properly, but nothing is broken, thank Fidal. How about you? That cut on your cheek looks painful."

I shrugged. "I've had worse." Compared to the goblin spear, this was nothing. "What did Asmund say to you, during the battle?"

"He said the debt has been paid; he owes me nothing now."

I grimaced. And here I had thought he'd saved her out of the goodness of his heart.

We walked side by side in silence for a moment before I said, "Do you...want to talk about it?" She knew what I meant.

"Not particularly," she said, sounding exhausted, "but I do want to say that I just... I don't know if we should be doing this. I mean, I feel wrong for having killed those men, cold. They can't all be guilty of the crimes we've come here to punish. This war is already changing me. I was exhilarated out there, Isan, and that scares me."

"I know," I told her, "but what can we do? We can't abandon our men. We can't just go home after all we suffered through to get here."

Sky sighed. "You're right," she said. "We have to remember why we came in the first place. We're here to take revenge and that's it. We have to find our parents' killer. Once they're dead, we're done. The entire kingdom of Winter does not deserve to suffer for the deeds of one person."

I nodded. "It is not our place to judge their actions. Wylla will find justice for them, if it is needed."

Sky frowned. "I thought Fidal was the god of justice."

"Oh, you knew what I meant," I retorted.

She smiled. "No more wars after this one?"

"Not if I can help it," I replied. "I do not wish to kill like this again. Nor do I want to turn into a monster."

"Let's shake on it," Sky suggested.

I arched a brow. "Why?"

"As a promise to each other," she replied, "and a promise to ourselves."

I nodded and took her hand. "To peace."

"To peace," she repeated and we shook.

We parted ways after that, returning to our tents to rest up. The battle had taken a toll on us. My muscles were aching and my mind was still reeling, the sound of steel on steel echoing in my ears.

I looked forward to some quiet time, but my head had only just touched the pillow of my cot when someone burst into my tent.

I squeezed my eyes shut and groaned. "Sky, I told you I need to rest," I exclaimed. "Whatever you want to say can wait."

"I'm sorry, your Highness," the person replied.

Not Sky then.

I opened my eyes and sat up.

A messenger stood at the door. "I... I'll come back later," he said, turning to go.

I waved a hand. "No, it's all right," I told him. "Now is fine."

He turned back to face me.

"I apologize for my outburst," I said. "The battle put me on edge and I have yet to recover."

He nodded. "I understand, your Highness. It happens to the best of us. Why, I don't think anyone is exactly comfortable in this camp."

"I suppose that's true," I replied. "In any case, what can I do for you?"

"The king wishes to see you. I was told to escort you to him."

I sighed. "Now?"

The messenger fiddled with the hem of his coat. "He ordered me to go with haste. He does not know if you survived the battle."

"Then go and tell him." I tried not to let my irritation echo in my voice.

"Unfortunately, my word will not suffice, your Highness. His Majesty wants physical proof of your well-being and he also requires your presence at the War Council. It will be held shortly."

I sighed again. "Fine, I'll go, but let me get my sister first."

Sky kicked up a fuss when I arrived and I had to all but drag her out of her tent.

"I am not going to this Council alone," I told her.

"You're insufferable," she retorted.

We followed the messenger to Uncle's pavilion, forcing our way through the crowds of knights. We didn't want to be late. Uncle hated it when people were late and we didn't want him to start without us or proclaim us dead again. When we finally arrived, we were happy to see we weren't the last ones. Sirs Warmund and Quinton were already present, as was Lord Byron.

Uncle noticed us right away. "Isan, Sky!" he exclaimed. "I was worried when I couldn't find you before the battle."

"We tried to look for you," I replied, "but it was too chaotic."

He waved a hand. "It doesn't matter now. Did you fair all right?"

I shrugged. "As well as can be expected."

He grinned. "I heard you gave the Wyllans a difficult time."

"You could say that," I replied.

A harder time than most of them deserved.

Uncle clapped me on the back. "Good show! How did it feel to finally be a part of the action?"

"Great," I said, which wasn't entirely a lie. It had felt great in the moment, but after? Not so much.

He smiled wide. "I'm glad to hear it. Well, have a seat. We'll get started in a minute."

Sky and I took seats side by side near the middle of the table. I was surprised Uncle hadn't asked after her health specifically. I suppose he'd decided that if she wasn't going to act like a lady then he wasn't going to give her special treatment.

The other members of the Council trickled into the tent over the next five minutes or so: Lords Norwell, Arrath, Caldwell, Lachlan, and Maddix, as well as Sirs Delwyn and Saxon. Sky sat in the twelfth seat, reserved for Sir Kent, even though he was busy managing Widonia in Uncle's absence.

Lord Arrath's armour was still covered in blood and Lord Norwell had a bandage wrapped around his left arm. Lord Byron, on the other hand, looked like he had stepped right out of a painting, as if he hadn't set foot on the battlefield at all. I didn't have time to study the others before Uncle began.

"It is good to see you all," Uncle said as soon as everyone was seated. "What is our status?"

"A hundred wounded, two hundred dead, and twenty still unaccounted for, Sire," Sir Quinton reported.

Uncle nodded. "Sancia rest their weary souls. They will not be forgotten. We'll burn the bodies today and make sure to add to our list of the dead. See to it the wounded receive the necessary treatments. How about the Wyllans? How many of Frost's men lay dead?"

"Their dead outnumber ours by at least a hundred," Lord Byron said, his chest puffed with pride.

"Good," Uncle replied. "We have the advantage now, if they didn't outnumber us before." He paused for a second, as if he was trying to discern the exact number of Winter knights alive before this morning's battle. "What about our weapons?"

"They've all been retrieved, Sire," Sir Warmund answered.

Uncle rhymed off a few more questions.

How many of the wounded could still fight? Had we lost any horses? What were our rations like?

The lords and knights held all the answers. I tried to keep up with the onslaught of information, in case I needed it later, but their words were becoming nothing but letters and numbers.

I was jolted back to focus when Uncle clapped his hands together, signalling for silence.

"Your attention, please," Uncle said. "There is another reason I have called you here today, aside from the usual housekeeping." He cleared his throat and his tone became serious. "We need to consider our next move, gentlemen. My thoughts lie with continuing on to the Winter capital and forcing them into a siege."

My eyes widened.

Has he gone mad?

I could imagine Asmund's reaction to the suggestion.

"A siege?" Sir Warmund asked. "But, Sire, how will we manage that?"

Uncle leaned forward in his chair. "The first piece of the puzzle is already in place: the element of surprise. The Wyllans didn't merely fall back this morning, they fled. Their camp is abandoned, no soul left behind. I am certain they have retreated back to Appalachia to protect the palace. We simply have to follow their trail back to the city."

"A siege could take weeks, though, your Majesty," Lord Arrath argued, "months even. That is time I fear we do not have. The Wyllans have the advantage with this weather. Our men may not survive the conditions, especially as our supplies run low. Frost will simply wait for us to succumb to the elements before finishing us off."

I waited for Uncle to rebuke him, but Lord Arrath was the most versed in war at this table, having taught the knights at Skar's military academy for nearly four decades.

Uncle simply sat back. "What do you suggest then, Arrath?"

"We should invade the city instead and attack the palace straight on," he replied, "We'll surround Appalachia and storm the walls in the dead of night, not stopping until we reach our goal."

"Oh that sounds like a marvellous plan, Arrath," Lord Caldwell said, "if you want to get us all killed."

Lord Arrath scowled. "War comes with casualties, Caldwell, you know that. There is nothing else we can do."

"I will not send my men to be slaughtered," Lord Caldwell replied. "The Wyllans are not stupid enough to leave their walls unguarded and they will certainly notice the approach of a golden-clad army. They will pick us off like insects."

Lord Arrath opened his mouth to retort, but Uncle held up a hand. "Lord Caldwell does make a good observation. Perhaps there is a more subtle way for us to gain entry." He looked around the table. "Any thoughts, men?"

There was silence for a moment, enough that I could almost hear Lord Arrath's frustration. He was clearly miffed that his plan was being overlooked. It was easy to see where Asmund got his temperament.

Finally, Lord Maddix raised a gloved hand and Uncle nodded for him to speak.

"If we want to retain our element of surprise," he said, "then we will have to assemble a small team to go over the wall first. They will need to kill the sentries quietly and open the gates for us without alerting anyone else. Then one member of this team can notify us to move out while the others guard the gate."

Uncle nodded. "There is merit in that idea, Lord Maddix, but who would you choose for your team?"

"I have a few men in mind," Maddix replied, "but I would like to hear suggestions from the rest of you as well. We will need those who are quick and quiet; there will be no room for error."

"Then none shall be made," Uncle assured him. "Let's hear everyone's candidates then. We shall have no more than four or five."

I stayed silent as the men chose the members of their scouting party and then talked through the entire plan again, going into detail and working through the kinks. A plan of my own was forming in my mind, the puzzle pieces clicking into place one by one.

As the meeting came to a close, I raised my hand and asked when it would all transpire.

"We leave tomorrow," Uncle answered, "and the invasion starts whenever we arrive."

My heart leapt into my throat. Why was every timeline so thin as of late?

I supposed Uncle wanted the war to end as soon as possible, but I feared he was rushing it along, that his haste would bring with it a host of mistakes.

After we were dismissed, Sky and I walked in silence for a while, each of us lost in our own thoughts as we wandered aimlessly through the rows of tents. Some of the men were already taking stuff down and packing it away, preparing for the journey that awaited us in the morning.

I wondered if they ever questioned the Council's plans. I wondered if their loyalty lay with their king or with Summer itself.

Sky stopped in her tracks then and turned to me. "What are your thoughts on this plan, Isan? Am I the only one who is uneasy?"

I shook my head. "Lord Maddix's plan is far better than Lord Arrath's, but that doesn't make it foolproof. Even if the scouting team manages to open the gate without being detected, it won't be long before the Winter army converges."

She nodded. "We may believe the Wyllans to be beneath us, but they're not stupid. This plan buys us time, not lives."

"I agree, but there's nothing we can do about it."

"I know," she spat. "It makes me feel so *useless*." She kicked a chunk of ice so hard it flew several paces. "Uncle never listens to us, nor does anyone else of note. Our opinion is unimportant. If we brought up our doubts, Uncle would wave us off. He thinks the plan is watertight, simply because he helped construct it. He doesn't care, Isan. He doesn't care about us and he doesn't care that we're all going to die. All he cares about is getting to Frost. I can see it in his eyes when he says his name. He wants Frost dead more than he wants anything else."

"I don't know, Sky," I said. "I don't think it's Frost as a person; I think it's what he represents. If Winter loses its monarch, it will fall apart. At least, that's the hope."

"I guess so, but..." She sighed. "You know what, never mind. We can discuss it more later. I propose we create our own plan for this attack, one that won't get us killed."

I smiled. "I thought you'd never ask."

She massaged her temples. "Why do I have a bad feeling about this?"

"Because you never like my plans," I replied, "but listen, I think I've really got it this time."

She sighed. "Out with it then."

"This scouting mission has given us the perfect opportunity. We might not be included in the team, but that doesn't mean we can't follow them."

She frowned. "Why in Fidalia would we want to follow them?"

"They're going to get us into the city without having to face the bulk of the Winter army. From there we can part ways, sneak into the palace, and find Frost ourselves, ahead of Uncle.

Then, with Frost's knights preoccupied by the ensuing battle in their streets, we'll put an end to Frost for good. And who knows, we might run into Icaria or Snowdon while we're in the palace."

"That's not necessarily a good thing," she replied. "They're out to kill us, remember?"

"Perhaps they are as blind to the Curse as we were," I suggested. "Wouldn't you rather get it over with, instead of waiting for them to come to Summer or making another trip to Winter?"

"Yes, but I'm afraid we're not ready, Isan," she said. "There's too much going on. If we're going after them, it should be our main focus. Let Uncle deal with Frost. He doesn't have a god-given vendetta against us like his children do. Why kill him?"

I squared my shoulders. "You heard what Uncle said in the meeting room back at the castle. Frost had our parents killed. He did not hold the blade, but he gave the order and I will not let Uncle take my vengeance for me."

Sky took a deep breath. "You're not going to let it go, are you?"

I shook my head. "Lord Maddix's plan is dangerous, that much is true, but the main reason I came up with this plan is because mine ends in revenge and revenge is the reason we're here. We might die in the process, but I'll be damned if I go home now without at least trying."

Sky was taken aback by my words, but I wasn't sorry and I meant every word I said. I hadn't come all this way—hadn't almost died at the hands of goblins or killed innocent men—to abandon ship.

I would gladly die in my pursuit of justice and if that made me a fool, so be it.

Part 3: Vengeance

"None who go into the land of revenge and reason emerge with shoulders light of sin."

—L. L. Tyrrell

29
No Turning Back

The tolling of the watchtower bell tore me from a deep sleep the next morning. I dressed in a fog, still drained from battle, and set about the task of packing at a methodical pace. I folded my clothes and rolled my bedroll up tight.

The tent was easier to take down than put up and I finished just as the first true rays of sun began to sneak over the horizon, bathing the camp in a pale orange glow, as if it had been set ablaze.

I heaved my supplies onto my shoulder and wove through the masses to retrieve my horse. The stable tent had already been torn down and the horses had been tied to several posts in the general vicinity.

I found my horse quickly and secured my supplies to him along with his tack.

When I finished, the camp was all but a memory. Only a few remaining tents and the trampled, bloody snow betrayed our presence there.

The men had gathered beneath the ridge and I led my horse over, wanting to conserve his energy for the long ride ahead.

The sun was fully visible above the horizon by the time Uncle rode into our midst, full armour gleaming as he parted through the crowd.

The men bowed in his presence.

Sky and I mounted our horses.

Uncle gave a short speech and the men roared in response. Sky and I were too far away to hear his words, but I did not wonder at them. Words were unimportant. We needed action. We needed to *go*.

Finally, Uncle gave the order.

We turned as one and rode south, towards the horizon, towards Appalachia, and perhaps towards our doom.

• • •

The journey to Appalachia was arduous.

We rode without proper rest the first two days, only stopping long enough to eat something quick and wipe down the horses.

By the second night, when Uncle called a full halt, I was so exhausted that I nearly fell off my horse and so sore I could barely walk. Sky and I didn't even consider staying up to talk. We went straight to our tents and were all but dead until morning.

Uncle let us break every night after, but he still pushed us hard during the day, closer to our limits with each passing hour and gust of wind.

I told myself to be grateful it wasn't raining.

I wasn't sure if it *could* rain in Winter, not with the temperature consistently below freezing. The chill didn't bother me as much as it should; I found it was a nice respite from the scorching Summer days. The Winter wind was relentless too, tearing across the land, its power unhindered by trees. Every time it hit, I felt a sense of awe and relief, while everyone else pulled their fur coats tighter around them.

I pushed aside my thoughts on the weather to concentrate on more important issues, like how in Fidal's name was I going to kill Frost?

My plan had seemed promising at the time, but after days with nothing but my thoughts for company, I was starting to second guess myself. Who was I to think I could kill him? What was so special about me that I could kill the King of Winter, that I could kill a Gifted Immortal with nothing but my sword and my wits?

I convinced myself I would die attempting an impossible feat, but that was just it: I had to try. I wasn't going to be a coward anymore. I wasn't content to sit on the sidelines and watch, in hopes that someone would avenge my parents.

No one would do it for me. I had to do it myself.

• • •

The sun was setting on the seventh day when we rode to the top of a rise and finally beheld Appalachia.

It was glorious.

Houses lined the cobblestone streets — three-storey wooden and stone buildings painted in shades of blue, grey, and red. Everything had been dusted in a fine layer of snow and the city glistened. I'd never seen anything like it. In Summer, all our houses were one-storey plain wooden buildings. They were nowhere near as magnificent as what Winter had created.

A high wall encircled the entire city, constructed with pale grey stone and I noticed a lone gate facing north, the only apparent route in and out of Appalachia.

Finally, inevitably, I caught a glimpse of the palace and could not tear my eyes away. At first glance, it looked to be made of glass, but then I connected the dots and realized it was ice sparkling in the sun and reflecting the orange of the sunset. An entire palace made of ice, putting our stone castle to shame. It was breathtaking, the most beautiful thing I had ever seen.

I took an involuntary step forward.

The setting sun glinted off one of its spires, accentuating their lethal points, and I realized the place was as deadly as it was beautiful.

Most of our number was as captivated as I was, even Sky. She stared at Appalachia with open-mouthed awe.

I stifled a laugh and reminded myself to tease her about it later.

After a moment, the men managed to tear their eyes from the city and we turned our horses back the way we came, descending the rise. The hill stood between us and Appalachia. It would keep us hidden until nightfall when we would put our plan into action, however stupid it may be.

We established a small base, nothing like our previous camp. Uncle's was the only tent put up, leaving nowhere for us or the horses to rest.

The horses stood around, no one paying them any heed. Their obedience kept us from worrying about them straying, but I feared for their fates. They would remain at this base during the battle, for we had no need of them, but where would they go if we did not return? Would Winter come out and slaughter them like they slaughtered us?

I doubted anyone else shared my concerns, but just because they were animals didn't mean their lives weren't as significant as ours. Even now, they were huddled together for warmth, just like we would. Their big eyes stared into me, as if they could sense the danger, sense my anxiety. They were more than just muscle and bone to carry us wherever we pleased.

They were lifelong companions who would protect us in a heartbeat.

Someone tapped me on the shoulder then and I turned away from the horses, expecting to find Sky, but coming face to face with another soldier instead.

"Can I help you?" I asked him.

He held a sword out towards me. "We're distributing the remaining weapons, your Highness. I thought I would offer one to you first."

"Oh, well, thank you," I replied, "but I already have one."

The man nodded. "I can see that," he said, eyeing *Ember* at my belt, "but you might need another."

I shook my head. "I think not."

He frowned. "Sir, what happens if you lose your sword? Surely—"

"No," I said forcefully. "If I lose my sword, I won't be in need of another. If I lose my sword, I'll be dead."

The knight harrumphed and stalked off, clearly seeing me as nothing more than an obnoxious brat, but I had simply stated the truth. The only way someone could separate me from my sword was after death. *Ember* was my lifeline.

After the weapons were handed out, the extras were discarded in a pile on the snow and I scowled at the action. If any of those weapons were claimed, it was akin to throwing away pieces of our fallen comrades' souls. Where was the respect?

For once, I wished my prince status meant something more than mere privilege. I wished my opinion would be valued, wished I could voice my concerns and bring about change. I didn't care about being treated like a prince. I simply believed everyone was important and deserved to be heard. However, now wasn't the time to bemoan my problems. I had to find Sky and start putting our plan into action.

I wove through the ranks of men until I found my sister, leaning against her horse by the edge of the makeshift camp.

"Uncle just called Lord Maddix and the scouting team into his tent," she told me. "It won't be long now. How do you plan on sneaking away?"

I kicked at the snow. "Well, I've thought about it extensively, and I think we're going to have to ditch our armour or trade it for some that's less conspicuous."

Sky scowled. "Now? Isan, we don't have time to snag some, and if you think I'm going into that city without any, you've gone mad."

"Well, what else are we supposed to do, Sky?" I countered. "If Uncle catches us, we can kiss our vengeance and future freedom goodbye."

"If Uncle catches us," she replied, "I'm telling him it was all your idea, and he'll believe me. I will follow you to the ends of the realm, Isan, but this is *your* insane plan so it is up to you to figure out how to execute it."

I groaned and massaged my temples.

Why does she always have to argue with my logic, and why does she always have to be right?

"Something amiss, Prince?" a familiar voice drawled from behind us.

My skin crawled.

This is the last thing I need right now.

I turned around and gave Asmund an indignant shrug. "Even if there was," I told him, "it wouldn't be any of your business, now, would it?"

He bristled. A gust of wind had his braids swinging and I grinned as I watched a shiver pass through him, as I merely stood there and took it.

"There's the arrogant prince I remember," Asmund replied. "I'm glad our time in the Edgewood is over. It's nice not having to pretend anymore, isn't it?"

I rolled my eyes. "If I'm arrogant, I'm not alone."

"Oh Sancia, give me strength," Sky said.

I looked over at her. "What?"

"The two of you are exhausting," she replied. "All this posturing and back and forth… Why can't either of you admit you'd make better allies than enemies?"

I glanced from her to Asmund. "Allies. With him."

"Yes, Isan," she exclaimed. "He is a Sancian, is he not? He helped us in the Edgewood, did he not? And he kept his word to keep the details of our time there from Uncle. I know he's been a prick most of his life, but people can change. Experiences and tragedy change us."

"I can't believe you of all people are defending Asmund."

"I'm not agreeing to marry him, Isan. I'm just saying he might not be as bad as he once was."

Asmund cleared his throat. "You two do know I'm standing right here, right? I can hear everything you're saying."

We turned our heads in his direction.

"Oh, right," I said. "Sorry."

He scowled and I resisted the urge to stick my tongue out at him.

"Skiansy here thinks I should give you another chance," I told him. "What do you think?"

He shook his head. "Fidal save me, but she might be right. The three of us would make unlikely allies, but I can see how we might all benefit from it."

I rolled my eyes. "Oh you are such a people pleaser."

"Isan…" Sky all but growled.

"Okay, okay," I said, not daring to check the expression on her face. "I'll give you another chance, Asmund, but if you break my trust, I will not give it to you again."

Asmund nodded. "Likewise, Prince."

I held out a hand. "Truce?"

"Truce," he said, and then we clasped hands.

I'm not sure which of us squeezed tighter as we shook on it, but my knuckles felt stiff when we let go.

Sky smiled. "See, that wasn't so hard, was it? Now, why don't you tell him the plan."

My eyes widened. "Don't you think that's a little too far?"

Asmund clapped me on the shoulder. "Don't you worry, Isanfier. I may have overheard a conversation between you and Skiansy on the subject back at the old camp. I considered telling King Arkenier, but well, now that we have a truce, I'd like to offer my help." He grinned.

I glanced sidelong at Sky. "This is a terrible idea."

Asmund sighed and walked around in front of me. "Look, Prince, I understand your hesitation. You can think of it as a thank you for not leaving me behind in the Edgewood or for not killing me that day at the castle when we were drinking."

I bristled. "I don't think bringing up that memory will help your case."

Sky stiffened beside us. "The scouting team is leaving the tent. We don't have much time, Isan."

I cursed and then made a decision.

"Can you create some kind of distraction so we can slip away unnoticed?" I asked Asmund, a rock settling deep in my gut as I decided to trust him.

"On my honour," he replied.

"Then make it quick," I told him. "Sky and I have a king to kill."

30
Iron and Ash

Sky and I trudged over the snow-covered hill towards the city as the camp exploded to life behind us. I wasn't sure what Asmund had done, but it seemed to be working. The sky above was overcast, a blessing from Fidal himself; the moon would've given our presence away. The city itself glowed, giving us just enough light to see by as we followed the footprints left by the scouting team.

The wind buffeted us as we neared the wall, but we made good time and I felt a wave of relief rush through me as we rested our backs against the cold stone. No alarms had sounded yet, which meant the scouting team had met success thus far and we had not ruined their progress.

Sky turned to me. "I suppose we're climbing this barehanded then?"

I shook my head. "The scouting team was supposed to leave a rope in case they needed a quick escape. We'll use that."

"Oh, so you actually listened during the Council meeting."

I scowled. "Just follow my lead."

The two of us shuffled down the wall until we found the rope dangling in the wind. The night remained silent, still. I hated to admit it, but I was beginning to think the scouting plan might actually work.

"I better go up first," I whispered to Sky.

She shrugged. "As long as you don't get stuck halfway."

I ignored her comment and gave the rope a tug, testing its strength. It seemed solid, so I pulled myself up the first few feet, using the wall for leverage, trying my best to keep my armour from clinking against the stone.

Don't look down, I told myself.

Despite my many denials, I *was* afraid of heights and I didn't have time to deal with the immobilizing fear.

When I reached the top, I scanned the area for movement, and then dragged myself over the ledge. A quick glance below told me Sky was already following, and that was all I could manage. I studied my new surroundings as my stomach roiled.

The wall was about three yards wide and towers stood along it, fifty feet between each one, our access point to the streets below. The wall was a perfect line of defence and it had been well-guarded, until the scouting team did their work. I noticed two bodies propped up against the ledge a few feet away, arrows sunk deep into their chests.

Sky brushed herself off as she joined me at the top. "Let's not linger," she whispered. "I don't like being out in the open like this, even if the scouting team is as good as they seem."

I nodded and headed right, away from the two bodies and towards the nearest tower, praying it was no longer guarded either. Our footfalls were soft, but quick. We didn't have much time left before the rest of the army would attack, and then stealth would be impossible.

The watchtower was dark and I pushed open the broken wooden door to find a trio of dead Winter soldiers, heads against a table covered in cards and blood. A tankard of ale lay discarded on the floor.

Sky muffled a cough. "That smell..." she whispered.

I nodded. It was pretty gruesome. It pained me to see their lives ended in such a way, but there was no time to mourn or apologize, and we would not be the ones to honour their memories.

The staircase was empty and we encountered two more bodies before emerging onto the street. Our boots clicked on the cobblestones and I winced at each step as we headed in a southerly direction towards the palace at the base of the Winter Alps. The mountains loomed in the distance and I thought for a second about Echo's stories and the ice wolves.

Would they come down from their snowcaps to defend the city?

Sky and I had only made it one street over from the watchtower when a bell began to toll.

We stopped in our tracks and turned to see the Summer army flooding into the city from the open gate three blocks away, and then, like spectres in a haunted hall, the Winter army emerged from the shadows and side streets to meet them, a sea of silver and savagery.

Sky's eyes met my own and they begged for guidance.

The Summer army was closer, so I turned in that direction and ran, my plan evaporating from my mind as survival took its place.

We joined the ranks of Summer men just as the two armies converged and chaos erupted.

The night became a blur. As soon as one man fell, he was forgotten and I focused on the next. The battle brought on the same intense feeling as the goblin attack and my blood sang in my veins as *Ember* travelled from one victim to the next.

In some ways, this battle was easier than the goblin attack, and in some ways, it was harder. It was easier because I wasn't awkwardly trying to fight something half my size, but unlike the goblins, the Winter knights actually had brains in their heads, and they used them. I feared their numbers would overwhelm us, but I fought on, not letting that fear control me.

Eventually though, I felt the press of soldiers lessening.

Are we actually pushing them back?

It took a few more minutes, but I felled a couple more men and broke out into the open. The men were fighting in small groups now instead of the earlier mass and the battle had spread further into the city, though it was impossible to tell if anyone was winning.

I had lost Sky somewhere between the wall and where I had ended up, and panic set in as I finally realized her absence.

What if she's gone?

I shuddered at the thought. If Sky had died because I wasn't there to help her, I would never forgive myself.

My worry distracted me for only a moment, but it was enough. I didn't notice the knight behind me until it was too late. I whirled, raising my sword, but he had already swung at me with his axe and there was no way I'd be able to deflect it with so little time to prepare myself for the blow.

This might be the end.

I was about to close my eyes when my assailant collapsed like a puppet with cut strings. I jumped back at his sudden demise and noticed an arrow protruding from the man's neck. My heart skipped a beat.

Sky?

I looked around the area and there she was, standing on a rooftop, firing arrows into the crowd below.

She gave me a nod before returning to the task at hand.

I took a deep breath.

My worries were wasted on her; she could clearly look out for herself.

So I raised my sword and dove back into the pandemonium of the streets.

I fought harder, not giving myself time for distractions. Our army was certainly putting a dent in their numbers and they continued to give ground as we pushed forward, leaving nothing but carnage in our wake.

Bodies lay everywhere and the once-pristine streets were bathed in blood. The smell of iron and death hung in the air, so thick that if you breathed in too deeply, you might choke. Underneath those smells, almost imperceptible, was the smell of fear and…

Is that…smoke?

I looked around and saw that one of the houses behind me had caught fire. As I watched, the fire leapt from one house to the next and the whole street went up in flames. They danced in the wind of the night, orange fingers reaching up into the sky.

I dismissed it at first, but then I remembered there were people in those houses.

That's when the screaming started—horrible, high-pitched shrieks filled with agony and despair.

I winced as the noise grated on my ears and pulled at my heartstrings, as not a single soul came to their aid. The Wyllans were either completely oblivious or ignoring their citizens' cries.

Somebody do *something!*

I took an involuntary step towards the inferno and then another, and then I was rushing across the square. I skidded to a stop in the snow about a foot from the blaze, the heat seeping into my skin.

I didn't know what I planned to do, but I couldn't stand aside as innocents were killed.

What do I do? Think, Isan!

I was one person against a raging fire, but if I walked away, I would be no better than my enemies. If I walked away, the decision would haunt me forever. I felt like I was on the edge of a precipice and if I fell, I would never be the same.

Who will I become after this war? Who do I want to be?

All these thoughts flew through me in seconds as I stared at the burning houses, unable to move in either direction. Still, the screams persisted. Still, I was the only one who seemed to care at all.

A piece of timber broke off and hit the ground at my feet, sending burning coals and ash flying.

I raised a hand to cover my face and squeezed my eyes shut against the dust.

If I didn't do something soon, I would be too late. They would all perish, trapped in the inferno, but then, like a spark of hope, I saw two people emerge from the house beside me.

A mother and son ran out of the collapsing door, coughing and covering their eyes. The two fell to their knees in the snow a few feet away and I ran over.

"Are you okay?" I asked them, crouching down to their level. "Is there anyone else inside?"

The woman looked up. "We are fine, but the others..." She shook her head. "One of the support beams collapsed, blocking their escape." Either she didn't realize what side I was on or she didn't care, as there was no fear apparent in her eyes.

I hung my head. "May Wylla rest their souls. You two should head for safety. The fighting is going to be thickest near the palace, so stay as far away from it as you can."

She nodded and dragged her son to his feet. "You have been a great—" Her sentence cut off as her eyes opened in shock. I watched as a blade came through her stomach and then slid out again, leaving her covered in blood.

She crumpled to the ground, letting go of her son's hand, and I saw the Summer knight standing behind her, wiping his sword off on his pants.

Lord Arrath stared down at me, his braids covered in ash and his armour stained in red. "Ah, Prince Isanfier," he said, "good show in catching these two. They're the last of the survivors." He raised his sword again and turned towards the boy, who was oblivious to the danger, sobbing over his mother's body.

My shock at her death was still fresh, but I didn't hesitate to step in front of the boy and meet Lord Arrath's sword with my own.

The sound of the two blades clashing rang through the night.

"Run!" I called back at the boy. "Go now!"

I didn't have time to see if he obeyed. Lord Arrath was glaring daggers into my soul, as if I was an insect beneath his boots.

"What in Sancia's name are you doing, boy?" he bellowed at me.

"What you should be doing!" I replied. "These are innocent people. King Frost is our goal. We wouldn't even be killing the knights if they weren't standing in our way. This isn't like us. We are not savages who kill without mercy. Do our morals mean nothing now, Lord Arrath? Is it all a *farce*?"

I shoved hard against his blade and he stumbled backward.

"It's a little late to be worried about morals, don't you think?" he replied, lowering his sword.

"I don't think it's ever too late to re-evaluate. What is the point of winning this war if we lose ourselves in the process?"

He shook his head. "I told Arkenier you'd grow up soft if he didn't send you to the academy, but he wouldn't listen.

You'll learn one day, boy. War isn't about who is right, it's about who has what it takes."

Then he rushed away, in search of another target, leaving me alone in the square as ash rained down upon me. The fighting had moved further into the city, closer to the palace.

Lord Arrath might report me to Uncle when this was all over, but if that boy lived to tell his tragic tale, it would be worth it.

I followed in Lord Arrath's wake, each fallen enemy bringing me one step closer to my goal: King Frost, the man who had started it all.

31
Preservation

Frost

For the first time in his life, the King of Winter had been wrong.

Scaling the walls surrounding Appalachia and overrunning his men had proved no obstacle for Summer. His sentries had been useless against them and his knights couldn't keep them off the city's streets. The Wyllan numbers dwindled as the Sancians advanced on the palace like a pack of wolves.

From his balcony, Frost watched the battles raging in his once-quiet city streets and for the first time during the war, he felt fear.

We are going to lose. The thought rang in his head like a hammer on an anvil.

Frost knew what that meant. He knew what he had to do. He turned away from the balcony with a heavy heart and called out to his messenger.

"Yes, your Majesty?" the man said, poking his head into the room.

"Send for my daughter," Frost told him, "and quickly. Time is of the essence."

The messenger scampered off and Frost began to pace.

Countless scenarios ran through his mind, all of them ending in bloody defeat. He couldn't think of a way to prevail, a way to take back what was rightfully theirs, but he wouldn't rest until he found one. The future of his dynasty depended on it.

Frost still hadn't made any headway when the messenger returned with Icaria in tow.

"Ah, Icaria," Frost said, "we have much to discuss." He looked at the messenger. "Leave us."

The messenger bowed once and promptly left.

King Frost took a deep breath and turned to his daughter. "Icaria," he started.

"Yes, Father?" She sounded cautious.

Good girl.

She was learning.

"I am going to tell you to do something you're not going to like," Frost began. "In fact, you will probably loathe me for making this decision, but it has to be done. Someday, you will understand, but for now, you must listen."

"Of course," she said. "What is it you want me to do?"

"I want you to gather a meager amount of supplies and set forth at once for Desolace. Take Clarice with you and give my regards to Lord Everard and Lady Aerona."

Her eyes widened. "What?"

Frost ignored her and continued. "You will not return until it is safe. Do you understand?"

"No," she replied, her voice furious. "I most certainly do *not* understand. Why are you sending me away? I can help. I can fight—much better than Snowdon. Let me prove myself to you."

"No," Frost said, not liking the begging in her tone. "You have *already* proven yourself, beyond measure. This is not about your fighting skills. This is about the future of our land. From Desolace, you can watch and wait, in safety. You will be able to continue the Royal Line should I fall and I trust you to take back our kingdom if Summer somehow manages to seize control. You could become our salvation."

"But... But I can't just leave." Tears sparkled in her eyes. "I can't leave you and Snowdon."

"You can and you must," Frost told her. "Now is not the time for emotions. They ruin our calm, our concentration. They distract us from what must be done. Do not be selfish by letting your sorrow be the end of us."

Ashamed, she wiped her eyes and said, "I understand, Father. I shall do what you ask of me and rest assured, if ever the need arises, if ever you should fall, I will defend our dynasty until my dying breath."

The king nodded. "I'm sure you will. Now go; we don't have much time."

Icaria inclined her head in acknowledgment and Frost did the same. It was the goodbye they would never voice. They were both too proud for that. Saying goodbye would expose their doubts for the other to see and they could not show weakness to each other, even in those final moments—*potential* final moments.

Icaria held her head high as she walked out of the room without another word.

Frost shed a single tear that froze on his cheek.

Not too long after, guards came to inform the king that Icaria and Clarice had departed safely and were well on their way to Desolace. Frost doubted he would ever see them again, but he would not let emotions distract him either.

Frost locked his sorrow and fear into a little box and threw the key over the balcony.

32
Looks That Kill

Isan

A while later, I slowed to a near-crawl. The fighting had thickened and our progress was stinted. The men who challenged me were more experienced and put up quite a fight. However, I was the best in Summer for a reason and each of them fell in turn, though not without some leaving their own mark.

My armour was dented in several places and I had sustained several minor injuries, the largest of which was a glancing blow to the side of my head. The blood had already dried on my temple though and my mind was clear, so I wasn't worried about lasting damage.

As I shoved my way through the thickening crowd, I heard the unmistakable twang of five arrows being loosed and watched as the men in my direct vicinity dropped.

"Nice one," I told Sky as she jumped down from the shed she'd been perched on and landed beside me.

She shrugged. "I try. Are you ready to show these men what happens when they dare to challenge the Prince and Princess of Summer?"

I laughed and raised *Ember*. "Nothing would please me more."

She slung *Tempest* over her shoulder and unsheathed her sword. "Then let's do this."

We stood back to back and called upon our last reserves of energy. Swords flashing, we laid waste to Winter's army. Those that managed to escape our wrath scattered and fled.

We looked up and down the empty street.

"Where to now?" Sky asked.

"Where we've always been headed: the palace."

She sheathed her sword and grabbed *Tempest* once more. "All right then," she said, "let's go kill ourselves a king."

Not long after, we arrived at the palace, the place where Frost was born, had lived, and would ultimately die. I wasn't leaving until he was dead.

We were greeted by a group of Wyllan soldiers facing off against what was left of the Sancian army. They were lined up between us and our quarry, but they would die soon, as would anyone else who stood in our way.

Neither side advanced. They had reached a stalemate and I wondered who would be the one to break the standstill.

The palace looked even grander up close. Its towers reached up to the heavens, disappearing into the dark. The stairs leading to the front door were perfectly cut, and, like everything else, made entirely of ice. The palace's grand doors were a sight to behold. They had to be twenty feet tall and made out of a single slab of ice each. As long as I lived, I would never be able to deny the beauty of it.

As I studied the palace, I saw something out of the corner of my eye—a knight set apart from the rest. He stood at the top of the staircase, watching the confrontation below with detached interest, like he didn't care what its outcome was. Something about him was familiar, but I couldn't put my finger on it.

I pointed him out to Sky and a shudder travelled through her as she studied him.

Then his gaze swept towards us and the two locked eyes.

Sky went rigid.

I wanted to ask her what was wrong but then I remembered who it was that knight reminded me of: King Frost. He looked exactly like the man on the white horse that had led the Winter army into battle that first morning after Sky and I rejoined the army. No one had confirmed that man had been King Frost, but who else would he have leading his army?

The knight that faced Sky now at the top of the stairs looked just like King Frost. He had the same snowy hair and the same air of malevolence, though muted.

He must be Prince Snowdon, Frost's son.

It explained Sky's reaction. Snowdon was the one cursed to kill her or die trying, and judging from the look in Sky's eyes, she was not going to let him slip away.

They stared at each other for what seemed like an eternity.

Then Snowdon blinked and the connection broke. In moments, he had disappeared into the palace, as if he had never been there in the first place.

Sky started after him and I called out for her to stop, but my cries fell on deaf ears. All I could do was follow as she pushed her way through the crowd of Summer knights and into the empty space between the two armies.

The Wyllans took that as an invitation and surged forward. The battle recommenced, with Sky and I in the middle of it all.

33
Valor

Frost

The Sancians had finally reached the palace and a bloody battle was being waged far below King Frost. He watched it with a keen interest, as the results would directly affect him. So when the knock came at the door, it took a great deal of effort to leave the balcony and return to his room.

Frost took a seat in a red armchair by the window and said, "Come in."

A few seconds later, General Kallen entered. He closed the door firmly behind him.

"Your Majesty," he said, "you shouldn't be here." His eyes flashed with fear as he beheld Frost sitting totally relaxed and unbothered in his chair. He walked up to the king. "Come, we have arranged to evacuate you to Falco Point, you and the boy."

Frost laughed. "I shall not be leaving, General, and neither shall the boy. This battle is a perfect time for him to practise his new skills."

"But, Sire," Kallen protested, "it is not safe here. Any minute now the Summer army will burst through the doors. Our men cannot hold them back."

"Let them come and I shall face them," Frost replied. "I'd rather stay and die courageous, than run and live a coward. There is no glory in surviving, General, if it is because of cowardice."

Kallen nodded gravely. "Very well, your Majesty," he said. "What would you have me do instead?"

"I want you and the other knights to lead the Sancians to the throne room. Send some men ahead. We will have our final battle there, for that is where I will be waiting."

"But, Sire, they could kill you."

"And I am not afraid to die," Frost snapped, rising from his chair.

General Kallen took a step back.

Frost paused a moment to calm himself down, letting his magic curl back up inside him. "Fearing death is the ultimate cowardice. Only fools fear the inevitable, General. We will all die eventually, why not make it today? Rest assured, I will do my best to postpone it. Don't give up yet, for I surely have not."

The king sent out his magic then and frost settled over the room, over every curtain and chair. If he should die, it would be preserved for all eternity.

General Kallen smiled at his king. "Ah, so you have a plan?"

"I have the *only* plan," Frost told him, "and it is foolproof. We may yet win this war, General. Now go, lead the Summer scum to the throne room. I shall be waiting."

Frost walked past the general then and out the door, towards his future and his fate.

34
Snow and Arrows

Isan

I expected to be crushed between the two opposing sides, to be dragged down by the battle raging around us, but Sky was on a rampage. She shot arrow after arrow, carving herself a path to the other side.

I followed in her wake.

Only a few moments had passed by the time Sky broke free.

I scrambled to keep up with her as she sprinted up the staircase, the steps of sheer ice hardly posing an obstacle.

She didn't stop for breath at the top, but continued in through the open doors.

The interior of the palace was even more marvelous. We had stepped into a magnificent grand entrance hall. The ceilings were vaulted and I knew our every sound would echo in the space. Our features were reflected in each wall, the ice polished smooth until they were more mirror than barrier.

The shining version of myself beside me was unnerving and I looked away. I wasn't surprised to find the hall empty, with no sign of Snowdon. Three corridors branched off from the hall. He could be anywhere by now.

I wondered if he would run to Icaria, if the Winter royals were as close as Sky and I. Something told me they were not, but I prepared myself for the worst, prepared myself to face the other piece of Echo's soul, the person meant to kill me.

Sky paused for only a moment in the entrance hall before heading towards the corridor on the right.

I reached forward and caught hold of her wrist.

She turned to face me. "Let me go, Isan. We're wasting time." She tried to pull her arm away, but I didn't loosen my grip.

"We have to think rationally about this, come up with a plan. He could be anywhere, and so could Icaria. We could end up running into her instead."

She stopped and took a deep breath. "You're right. I'm sorry. I just have this… It feels like there's something tugging me away. I think I can sense where he is, now that I've seen him."

I raised an eyebrow. "Really?"

She nodded. "I'm being pulled towards the right corridor. It's an effort to remain stationary actually."

"All right, then we'll go that way, but try not to be too reckless. This is his home, so we're already at a disadvantage."

"I know. I'll try to be careful."

"Then lead the way; I trust you."

• • •

We ran down the corridors of the palace for what seemed like forever, turning this way and that until I had no hope of finding our way back again. Each time we came to an intersection, Sky chose a direction with confidence, but I couldn't help but doubt her.

How can she possibly know where she is going?

I had tried to keep track of where we were, but the hallways all looked the same and I soon gave up.

The hallways were deserted too, save for the two of us, and I wondered at the absence of guards. Where was everyone? How were we able to go this far into the royal household undetected?

Finally, when I was about to accept that we'd be running around in that labyrinth until we died, Sky stopped. She came to a halt so abruptly I ran into her, our armour colliding with a muffled clang.

I winced and Sky turned around to shush me.

"He's close," she said. "Try to be a little more subtle."

"Sorry," I whispered.

We crept down the corridor and around the corner as quietly as we could. At the end of the hall, a door awaited us. I was surprised to find that, unlike all the doors we'd seen so far, this one was made of wood.

As we drew closer, I noticed the door stood ajar. Wind rushed into the hall, carrying with it a flurry of snow.

Sky shivered as the wind passed by, but I was too excited to care.

That door must lead outside!

Sky tried to stop me, but I was already running for the door, following the wind that smelled like a crisp Winter morning and called me home. Sky muttered a curse and raced after me.

I reached the door and flung it open the rest of the way, eager to embrace the outside world, but was soon disappointed.

I was in a wide-open space, but there were walls around me and a ceiling above my head. The ground was cobbled and the walls were partially stone, the ice taking over after twenty feet. It reminded me of the courtyard at home, but if that's what it was, it had been forgotten, swallowed up by the ice palace.

I shuddered, but then I saw something that made my heart drop.

It wasn't the snow falling in lazy flakes from the ceiling or the cold wind curling around me. It was the person standing in the centre of the courtyard, staring at me with his ice-blue eyes.

Snowdon.

He had tricked me. He had lured me here with his wind, made me think I was going towards freedom when in reality I would only be more trapped. I had fallen for it, and Sky had lost her element of surprise.

I wanted to warn her, but as I turned to do so, she entered the courtyard, her eyes shooting daggers at me.

What are you doing? they seemed to say. *Are you crazy?*

She rushed at me and, for a moment, I thought she might tackle me, as punishment for being so brash, for running into the open like that, but then she saw Snowdon and stopped dead in her tracks once again.

She swore and Snowdon smirked, though it seemed forced.

The game was afoot. He had moved the first piece and so far, he was winning.

Sky glared at me. *This is your fault*, her eyes said.

Snowdon took a step forward and Sky swore again, fumbling for *Tempest* who was slung uselessly over her shoulder.

Snowdon saw what she was going for and stopped. He put his right hand up in surrender and I noticed his left arm hung at an awkward angle, as if it was no longer connected properly.

Strange, but maybe we can use that to our advantage.

"Easy," Snowdon said. "I don't know who you are, but I have this...strange feeling when I look at you. Have we met before?"

Sky's eyes narrowed at his words, but she lowered her hands.

I didn't want to buy his ignorance, but he looked genuinely confused. It seemed the Winter royal family was not aware of the Curse and for a moment, I felt bad.

"You seriously have no idea who I am?" Sky asked him.

"Well, I can tell you're a Sancian," he replied, "but other than that…"

Sky blinked. "I am Princess Skiansy of Summer and this is my twin brother, Isanfier. I am here…" She swallowed. "I am here to kill you, Snowdon."

Fear flashed in Snowdon's eyes and he took a step back, reaching for an axe slung at his hip.

I reached for *Ember* too, remembering Echo's words about that weapon.

"Why me?" Snowdon asked, his hand hovering over the hilt of his axe. "Why not my father? He is the true tyrant in this castle. He is the one you want."

Sky shook her head. "We have come for him too, but… Tell me, Snowdon, have you ever heard of the Curse, the one about twins restoring the balance?"

Snowdon narrowed his eyes in confusion, but then a moment later they widened. "Oh Wylla, no," he whispered. "That's why I felt so strange when I saw you, like someone was tugging me in your direction."

Sky nodded.

"Then… Then one of us must die here today."

"I wish there was another way," Sky replied, "but if we don't do it, then we shall both die a couple years from now and the whole realm will suffer for it. I am told Wyllans know little of sacrifice, but something tells me you are different, Snowdon."

He scowled. "Different enough for my father to shun me most of my life, but I suppose there is little time for talk. It will only make it harder for me to kill you."

He hefted his axe up in front of him and I jumped back.

I hadn't even seen him draw the weapon.

"I will make your death swift, Princess," Snowdon said, "though it will not make my father proud."

Sky wrenched *Tempest* free of her cloak, but before she could shoot, everything went white.

I was immediately disoriented. For a moment, it felt like I was floating in midair, for it was hard to tell what was up and what was down. A roaring wind buffeted against me, but I remained upright.

"Sky, are you there?"

"Yes," she said, her voice coming from behind me. "What did he do? It's freezing."

It hit me then.

It was snowing. Thick flakes swirled around us, falling in all directions, enclosing us behind walls of white.

Echo's voice rang in my head. *Snowdon lacks magic himself, though his name suggests it is only a matter of time before that changes.* This was Snowdon's doing. He had unlocked his Gift and now he was going to use it to keep us blind while he finished us off.

"Isan?" Sky's voice came again.

"Keep it down," I whispered. "He can't see us either, so we don't want him to hear us."

"I can't shoot with this snow," Sky replied.

"I know. We have to get rid of it somehow."

My brain was whirling as I tried to come up with some sort of plan, but the clock was ticking.

"I'm surprised you two didn't scream," Snowdon's voice called through the void. "My father says Sancians don't see a lot of magic. I feel bad that you two are at such a disadvantage, being powerless, but it makes it easier."

So he isn't aware that a conversation is a bad idea.

I turned to Sky again. "You circle around him. I'll try to keep him talking."

She didn't reply, but I heard her footsteps walk away, crunching softly on the snow accumulating beneath our feet.

I started heading in the other direction, hoping he wouldn't be able to track both of us at once. "I was told you lacked magic too," I replied, "but I guess you finally lived up to your father's expectations."

There was a thick silence for a moment and then he said, "You have some nerve saying that. You have no idea what you're talking about and it's none of your concern."

"I wish Sky and I had come upon you earlier, back when you were weaker. Killing someone who can't see you coming isn't anything to be proud of. It's a coward's way out, if you ask me."

"Don't say that word," he spat. "Do not say that ugly, Fidal-forsaken word. I am not a coward! I am simply trying to survive in this world that crushes you at every turn. Do you have any idea what it's like to live in your sister's shadow, to watch your father praise her every move while he spits at your feet?"

The snow picked up around me at his words, falling faster and thicker by the second. I blinked rapidly to keep my eyesight clear, though there was nothing around me to see. Sky was lost now amongst the snow and I hoped she was all right.

"I don't have any experience with that," I said, "but then again, I didn't know my father. *Your* father had him killed when I was four years old."

"I told you, he is the real villain," Snowdon scoffed, "and yet, thanks to Fidal, the three of us are here fighting each other instead of him. Our god is a cruel being."

I had to agree with him on that, but there was nothing we could do. Like Sky said, both options led to death in some form, but we all wanted a chance at life.

"You had sixteen years to stand up to your father, Snowdon," I countered, "but you didn't. Again, I smell cowardice."

For a mere moment, the snow around me flickered and I saw Snowdon silhouetted in the distance, Sky a dark shadow somewhere behind him, but then I blinked and the white was back.

What in Sancia's...

"I told you to shut your mouth," Snowdon roared. "I'm not fated to kill you, Prince, but maybe Fidal will make an exception."

I heard the sound of fast footfalls on snow and then I saw a shadow emerging from the blizzard.

Fidal's breath, he's after me.

I fumbled for *Ember* and drew her just in time to block the first swing of his axe.

The blow staggered me and I slid back through the snow, which was now up to my ankles.

Snowdon lunged for me again.

I tried to gauge the angle of his weapon, but it was difficult to tell in the blinding snow and I didn't judge correctly. His axe glanced along the side of my blade and hit me full on the collarbone, ringing against my armour.

I hit the ground hard, kicking up a flurry of snow, as pain blossomed through me, but I didn't give myself time to feel it. I rolled away and scrambled to my feet as Snowdon's axe came down again in the space I had vacated.

This is not going at all to plan. Where is Sky?

I turned to swing at him this time when the snow flickered again. I saw him in perfect clarity as we parried back and forth for a few moments before the snow closed in and I finally realized what was happening.

He's losing his focus. He won't be able to control his magic for much longer.

I heard an arrow hit the ground a few feet away from us and realized Sky had tried to take a shot in the short window she had.

I need to give her a longer one.

Snowdon and I kept fighting and I hit the ground a few more times before I finally made a significant hit, slashing my sword across his face.

He hissed and stumbled backward, his hand going to his face, and around us the snow vanished, painting the world in colour once more.

"You shouldn't have done that," Snowdon gasped, glancing in Sky's direction.

Her bow was pulled to full draw, but before she could loose the arrow, Snowdon raised a hand.

What is he doing?

Time suspended itself in midair as I watched the snow around Sky swirl to life, curling around her like a snake and burying her beneath the white. One moment she was there and the next she was gone, like a lantern snuffed out by the slamming of a door.

"No!" I cried out, lunging forward, my heart leaping into my throat.

Snowdon didn't hesitate to take advantage of my shift in focus.

The flat of his blade smacked against the side of my head and I dropped like a stone to the snow-covered floor beneath me, feeling a sting as the edge nicked my skin. My vision blurred and then the world tipped upside down.

The last thing I thought of before I slipped into unconsciousness was how dearly he would pay if Sky did not live.

35
Oblivion

Frost

A chill settled into Frost's bones as he opened the doors to the empty throne room. Darkness reigned inside, save for a pale beam of moonlight that dropped through the window, alighting on the throne.

The doors banged shut behind the king, echoing with certain finality. They knew as well as he that this could be the end, but neither one of them were afraid. The room had seen its fair share of death and carnage. It was only fitting that it was where the Wyllans should make their last stand. Frost almost smiled at the perfection of it. Almost.

He walked around the room, lighting the torches, until it glowed with an eerie calm. Then he walked up to the throne and took his place.

Frost waited.

Soon, dozens of knights joined him. They stood facing the doors, silent as death itself. Together they waited for Summer to come, for the remainder of their men to lead the Sancians to their doom. The Wyllans would not end today. King Frost could not allow it.

Finally, they heard the sound of pounding feet echoing through the quiet of their sanctuary.

It was time.

Frost closed his eyes and called on his magic. He bent it to his will.

The temperature in the room dropped thirty degrees.

Frost smiled.

The noise of boots on ice grew louder, a low rumbling like thunder. Frost's men tensed, preparing for the fight of their lives, but they wouldn't need to lift a finger.

The king called out an order to them and—without questioning—they shifted their positions, making a clear path from him to the doors.

There was a split second where time stopped and the realm grew silent. Then the Summer army burst through the doors and Frost let his magic go.

36
Darkness and Demise

Isan

I woke to the uncomfortable sensation of my head sliding against ice, and the sense of foreboding that comes with a lack of control. My head was pounding and I remembered the blow I'd received. I remembered what I had left behind.

Oh Sancia's breath, Sky. Please be all right.

Snowdon was dragging me behind him through the palace and I wondered briefly where he was taking me before I decided it didn't matter. I wouldn't let him.

I reared up and twisted my torso at the same time, startling him out of focus. It was a close thing, but I managed to tear myself free of his grip.

"Oh no you don't," he seethed.

I jumped to my feet and whirled around, though I soon realized my mistake in doing so. All the blood rushed to my head, accentuating my headache tenfold, and I wobbled on my feet.

It took little effort on his part to regain control and his axe was underneath my chin in moments, his torso pressed against my back. If I inched forward, I would draw blood.

Fire seethed under my skin.

This isn't how it's supposed to go. We aren't supposed to lose already for Fidal's sake!

"What do you want with me?" I gasped out when the room stopped spinning. "I am not your quarry or were you stupid enough to forget that?"

He applied more pressure and I winced. "On the contrary, Prince," he replied. "I've decided to divide and conquer. Once I've dealt with you, I'll return to your sister, if the cold hasn't already done the job for me."

"You're sadistic."

He stiffened against my back. "I am doing what has to be done. We all are. In another life, we could've been allies, but that is not the fate we were given, is it?"

I clenched my fists. "Duty or not, you can be sure your pain will be unbearable if my sister dies."

He laughed then, but there was no pride in it, only a cruel acceptance. "You won't live long enough to fulfill that promise. My father will see to that."

He started dragging me away again then, in an upright position this time, and it took me a moment to realize what he meant.

He's bringing me to Frost.

That thought coupled with his words should've shot fear into my heart, but I felt only satisfaction. I wanted a chance at the king anyway. It would be more difficult to kill him with Snowdon in the picture, but I would be damned if I didn't go out fighting.

So I relaxed against Snowdon, letting him think I was giving up so I could reserve what little energy I had left. Blood was drying against my face and pain throbbed in every muscle, but I wouldn't give up hope.

We were so close to victory, I could taste it. Frost would soon meet his demise and what a shock it would be to him when it came in the form of a vengeful, sixteen-year-old Summer prince.

I'm coming for you, Frost, I'm coming for you, and when I arrive, it'll be over before you even know what hit you.

• • •

Soon after, we arrived in a small, circular stone room that looked like a dead end, but then Snowdon brushed his hand across a symbol on the wall and the wall began to shake.

I tensed as a low rumbling sound filled the room, wondering what on earth he had set off, but then I noticed the section of the wall in front of us was moving. I watched in awe as the ancient stone moved back from its place and slid behind the rest of the wall. When it finally came to a stop, an archway stood in its place, as seamless as if it had been there all along.

Snowdon relinquished his grip and shoved me forward.

I caught myself on the doorway before I could fall and peered into the space beyond. It was dark without a torch, but not dark enough to miss the spiral staircase ascending into the unknown.

"Where does it lead?" I asked aloud, wondering why someone would hide an entire staircase.

"Up to the throne room," Snowdon replied, "where my father and all his knights are waiting, so I wouldn't try running if I were you."

I resisted the urge to give some nasty remark and started up the stairs, eager to get it all over with. Exhaustion was beginning to seep into my bones, each step heavier than the last.

If we didn't reach Frost soon, I doubted whether I would be able to stand and face him.

Snowdon fell into step behind me, his axe hovering at my back, and the wall slipped back into place, sealing us in.

The stairway was cold and dusty, full of cobwebs and other unpleasant debris and I wondered when it had last been used. It seemed to go on forever and I had begun to think that we'd never reach the exit, when I saw light not far ahead.

We climbed up thirty more steps and around the corner, the staircase ended, pale light leaking in from the room beyond.

My thoughts screamed at me to make a break for it, but I ignored them. Anyone could be waiting outside. At least with Snowdon's escort, my life couldn't be severely threatened until I reached Frost.

I thought of Sky then, somewhere in the depths of the castle beneath us and prayed she was all right. I knew she was strong enough to prevail, but my heart still clenched at the thought of her all alone. Did she think I was dead?

Was she…?

But I couldn't go there. She had to be okay.

Snowdon reached for me again and I let him, despite all my instincts fighting against it. I hoped my plan wasn't a fool's errand, that Frost wouldn't cut my head off on sight.

Snowdon pulled me up the last couple steps to where the stairway ended in another arch. A pair of knights waited in the room beyond, but that didn't deter him.

"Halt," one of them called out. "Who goes there?"

"Surely you recognize me, Sir Kallen," Snowdon replied. "I have a present for my father."

The knight scowled. "I am surprised you would show your face after your complete lack of courage in the past battles, but I will not stand in your way. I suppose his Majesty is in an agreeable mood."

I wondered what Snowdon had done to incur such scorn from his subjects. A part of me felt a sense of kinship with him in that moment, but it was overshadowed by the circumstance we found ourselves in. Like he said before, it didn't matter what could have been. We had all made our choices.

"I have done what all of you could not," Snowdon replied, venom in his voice. "I'm sure he will be more than pleased when I hand him the Crown Prince of Summer."

The knight, Sir Kallen, had nothing to say to that and I marvelled at his ability to keep his expression neutral as he waved us on.

We must have been in an antechamber before because Snowdon dragged me through a doorway into a room so spectacular and immaculate that it could only be the throne room. The ice walls sparkled and shone, and held countless windows through which the daytime sun would stream. Torches sat in sconces at even intervals around the walls, forming a circle of light along the perimeter, though the room was so huge the light could not reach the centre. The ceiling was a long way away, almost lost in shadow. It drew the walls in, tapering them to a point, and crystals of ice hung from it, forming a stunning chandelier. The room was breathtaking, but the vital piece stood in the centre.

Atop a carved snowflake dais stood the throne. It looked to be about three feet wide and nine feet tall and had been sculpted out of ice that was the perfect shade of Winter blue. The throne's back ended in a crown shape, the centre of which held a sapphire at least the size of my fist.

Frost sat before us on the throne, wearing his silver armour and a snow-white crown adorned with more sapphires. A host of Winter knights stood at our backs and he watched them with his cold, dark eyes. He turned as we entered, regarding his son and I with a cool disinterest.

"What's this?" Frost asked, his tone bemused.

"This is the Crown Prince of Summer," Snowdon replied as he dropped me at his father's feet, "or what's left of him."

My knees smacked against the ice and I winced at the impact, though I felt a trickle of confidence at his comment. I wasn't done yet, not by half.

Frost looked from me to his son, light dancing in his eyes. "I dare say I'm impressed. Where did you find him? Was he already battered when you picked him up?"

Snowdon crossed his arms. "Not at all. He and his sister came after me, actually."

Frost looked down his nose at me. "Is that so? My assassins weren't enough of a prize for you? You dared to threaten my son?" His voice was full of contempt and I decided I had better answer politely if I wanted to survive long enough to come up with a plan.

"No, sir," I said, hanging my head, though still trying to look dignified. It was a hard look to accomplish when on my knees before the King of Winter. "It was my sister's idea, initially."

"And where is she now? Look at me when I speak to you, boy!"

My head snapped up and my eyes met his as I said, "I don't know, sir." I resisted the urge to draw my sword against him and end his arrogant existence.

This was the man who had ordered my parents' deaths. I was so close and yet so far.

"I left her in the courtyard," Snowdon told his father, "under a pile of snow."

Frost smiled, a sight that chilled me to the bone more than the weather in Winter ever had. "Then she is dead or will be soon. Why did you not finish off the boy?"

I hated that they were talking over me and I hated the certainty in his words, the confidence.

She is not dead. She is stronger than that. She is coming for me and we will end you both together.

"I did not think it was my place," Snowdon replied.

"A wise choice," Frost said. "The death of Arkenier's heir deserves more fanfare than a swift beheading in the depths of our fine palace, I should think. This moment shall be remembered by our dynasty for centuries to come. The Sancians' final stand, all for naught."

He stood up, pulling a greatsword from his belt and the blood rushed to my head again.

No. Not yet. Not until I've killed him.

I surged to my feet and said, "This isn't over!"

He raised a pale brow, holding his sword loosely in his hand. "And why is that?"

"Summer will come for me, for you. We can still win."

Frost laughed. "My dear boy, they've already come. You missed the finale and I can tell you, your people failed miserably."

My heart sank to my stomach. "I don't believe you!" Defiance blazed in my eyes and Frost smiled.

"See for yourself," he said. He signalled to the knights gathered before him and I turned to watch as they stepped aside, revealing a hundred Summer knights standing like statues in the middle of the room. They were frozen mid-motion, some of their swords still raised, and I noticed they were all covered head to toe in snow crystals.

My heart skipped a beat. "What did you do to them?"

"They gave victory their best shot," Frost drawled, "but I was waiting. My magic is freezing them to death, a slow but inevitable end. A couple of their hearts have already stopped."

Nausea roiled in my stomach. Then I turned my head further and noticed one man standing by the edge of the dais, his arm extended out in Frost's direction. A couple more steps and he would've had a chance. It was odd to see him so still, to see his dreadlocks coated in ice instead of swinging in the wind.

You're a prick, Asmund, I thought, *but I'll be damned if I let you die like this.*

I turned back to Frost as he laid his icy eyes on me. "How would you like to die, Prince? Shall I unfreeze your army enough to make them watch?"

I drew *Ember*, a solemn resolve settling in my gut. I would have to fight this battle alone.

"I propose a duel, your Majesty. If you can land a killing blow, that will be my end, but none of your men can interfere." I glanced at Snowdon still standing behind me. "Not even your son."

Frost grinned. "You have fire, boy, but it won't save your life. In fact, I have no desire to cater to your wishes."

He flashed a hand signal and a moment later two knights had hold of my shoulders, shoving me back down onto my knees. *Ember* fell from my hands, clattering to the icy floor. Frost raised his sword in front of me again and my heart quickened, my mind running a mile per second as I tried to think of a way to break free.

Come on, there has to be something…

And then I watched as an arrowhead smacked against the hilt of Frost's sword.

Frost whirled around, but the knights did not relinquish their hold on me. "Show yourself," he called out.

"Let my brother go or my next arrow won't miss."

I couldn't see her, but I knew it was Sky, knew it the moment I saw the arrow.

She's okay! She found me.

She had come to save me and now the fate of the entire kingdom was in her hands.

"Those are confident words for one lady against an army," Frost replied, his attention now completely on her.

"Oh, I'm not here to fight your army, Frost," Sky replied, and I was shocked at the calmness in her voice. "I am here to save my brother, and I am here to kill your son."

At her words, the knights let go of me and jumped to protect their prince, but they didn't know Sky like I did. They didn't know she'd already loosed her arrow before she finished speaking.

I had heard the unmistakable twang after she'd said the word brother and I stood up in time to turn and watch as the arrow struck Snowdon in the chest.

Snowdon stumbled, dropping to his knees, and Frost cried out, "Someone fetch Henrik at once!"

Snowdon plucked the arrow from his chest and blood began to pool down his front. "No, this...can't be," he muttered. "I wanted...to win this time."

"No, Snowdon," Frost snapped, coming to stand in front of his son. "It's not over yet. Don't you dare give up this fight!"

Snowdon stared at him and said, "I'm sorry I wasn't enough." Then his eyes closed and he breathed his last.

The ensuing silence was deafening, until a battle cry shattered through it.

The temperature in the room sank even lower as the air seemed to crackle with Frost's rage.

I heard a cry from the other side of the room and turned to see Sky being tackled by a trio of Winter knights, who then dragged her in my direction.

"Let her go!" I cried out, lunging towards her, but suddenly I couldn't move; my feet seemed frozen to the floor.

"You are not going anywhere," Frost crooned as he came to stand in front of me. There were no tears drying on his cheeks, only a cold, hard fury writhing behind his eyes. "You will watch as your sister pays for what she did. You will watch as the light in her eyes slowly fades away to nothing and you will not be able to do a thing about it."

The knights deposited Sky beside me, though not close enough to reach out and touch. She struggled against them, her limbs flying in all directions, but as soon as her feet touched the floor, Frost froze them too and she was wrenched to a stop.

The knights stepped away and it was her and I against the King of Winter.

"Not so confident now, are we?" Frost asked her.

"I didn't want to do it," she told him. "I didn't want to kill your son." There were tears in her eyes, but Frost shook his head.

"You made your choice, girl. Now live with the consequences." He raised a hand.

An image of Sky lying lifeless on the ground flashed across my eyes and I couldn't bear to stay silent any longer.

"No!" I cried out. "Don't hurt her; kill me instead! Kill me and spare my sister."

Frost smiled. "How touching, but your pain only makes me want it more." He flicked his hand in Sky's direction and crystals instantly appeared on her. She screamed as the frost crept up her arms and spread to the rest of her body.

"No!" I screamed again. I tried to lunge for her before I remembered I couldn't move.

Sky continued to scream. "Help me, Isan, help me! I can't get it off! Please, help me!" She raked her nails across her flesh, trying to scrape off the frost, but it wasn't working. She shivered as it covered her.

I watched helplessly as she looked at Frost with tears in her eyes, tears that froze on her cheeks as fast as they were shed.

"P-please, stop," she whispered, her voice shaking as her lips started to go purple. "I-I d-d-don't want t-to die. I-I'm sorry."

Frost ignored her and laughed as I tugged at my feet, trying to pull them free, but to no avail.

Sky was dying and I couldn't get to her.

It was like the nightmare all over again—watching a loved one die but being powerless to stop it, except this was real. I wouldn't wake up from this.

What am I going to do? There has to be a way to free myself. I can't give up on her. I can't watch her die.

Think, Isan, think!

My thoughts stopped short as the torches around the room flickered and went out, but they were alight again before panic could sink in.

A new person stood before the throne, between Sky and I and Frost. They were dressed all in black with a hooded cloak that hung to the floor and something about them was familiar...

My eyes widened in recognition.

It's him. It's the dark figure.

I couldn't believe my eyes. The person who had walked my dreams for months was flesh and blood before me.

Frost may have had my parents killed, but this person was the weapon he had used to do the deed. Frost would still have to die, but the dark figure had become my top priority. All I had to do was free Sky and I. Perhaps the dark figure could distract Frost enough that his magic would let go, like I had done with Snowdon, but then again, Frost had been honing his skill for decades, unlike his late son.

I decided I would have to see how the confrontation played out.

Frost's face betrayed his own surprise at the dark figure's appearance, but he smiled and said, "Ah, cousin! Come to join me at last? Done hiding amongst the Sancians?"

Cousin? Hiding amongst us?

The dark figure laughed. "Frost, you are so *very* amusing. You still think that after all these years, that after everything I've done, that I'd want to *join* you?" He scoffed. "Why would I do such a thing when I've spent *years* plotting your demise?"

I raised an eyebrow.

That escalated quickly.

The dark figure carried on before Frost could reply. "That's right, dear *cousin*. I'm going to end you, just like I ended your wife all those years ago."

Frost blanched and I noticed the section of floor around him was coated in a new layer of frost.

The dark figure feigned surprise. "Oh, I do apologize. Had I not mentioned that yet?" He didn't sound sorry at all and something about his voice seemed familiar. He had never spoken in my dream, but I felt like I knew the voice.

"I guess you should know it was I who killed your wife," he went on. "A little poison goes a long way, don't you agree?"

Frost looked pained. "Why?" he snapped. "Why Cascadia? What did she ever do to you? This should've been a war between men! Killing my wife was a coward's move and you know it!"

The frost beneath his feet spread even further, crackling halfway up the walls before it stuttered to a halt.

The dark figure shrugged. "She did nothing to me, but her death was all part of my plan to take over Winter. Now, there's no one standing between me and the crown, except you. There will be no queen to plot a rebellion against me and I see your son has conveniently gotten himself killed, so you have no heir. Once you're dead, I'll go after the Sancian brats and then all of Fidalia will bow to me!"

He's after us now too?

It made sense, though, I supposed. If he had killed our parents for the throne twelve years ago, it was only logical that Sky and I would be next, but why had he waited so long?

Speaking of Sky...

I glanced over at her and was relieved to see her head was still free, though the frost was climbing slowly up her neck. She too was focused on the events in front of us, and so I stamped out my thoughts and looked away.

Frost was grinning at the dark figure's words. "Ah, my dear cousin," he said, "that is where you are wrong. Snowdon wasn't my heir. Icaria is my firstborn or did you forget about your niece? She is far away from your clutches now and she will return to reclaim her kingdom, if need be. You have not won, not by half."

I felt some part of myself relax, knowing she wasn't going to burst into the room at any moment. Two enemies to face was enough.

"She will fall in time," the dark figure replied, not giving any indication that the information was new.

"You'll have to go through me first before you ever lay a finger on her," Frost replied, raising his sword.

The dark figure followed suit, but Frost threw a hand out in his direction before he could take a step.

I watched the frost crackle against the dark figure's black cloak, but he only laughed. "Is that all you can manage? Is that all you are willing to do? Because I promise you, it won't be enough."

"I want you to be still when I end you," Frost replied, standing in a way that implied the dark figure was but an ant beneath his boots. "I want you to be still when I shove *Malice* through your heart and out your spine."

"Then you have failed," the dark figure said. Then he heaved up his sword, the one named *Shadows*, and threw it at the Winter King.

The blade sank into the unarmoured spot between Frost's torso and arm and he lurched back, his eyes bulging.

My feet slipped beneath me and I fell to my knees, the impact reverberating through my bones.

Frost's magic...

I watched the dark figure take a step forward before the room plunged into absolute darkness. It was like all light had been sucked out and it terrified me. The darkness suffocated me. The darkness was a living being, grabbing hold of me, pulling me down.

It's going to kill me.

Just as I began to fear that I'd never see the light again, it returned.

The light had been gone for a minute this time, though it had felt like hours. Yet, a minute had been long enough for the dark figure to accomplish his goal.

Blood dripped down the throne and pooled on the dais, where Frost's severed head lay. His blue eyes stared at us. They would never see again.

37

Until Sunrise

For a second, the knights stood frozen in shock, but then they started shouting, cries of outrage and despair. Several ran after the dark figure who had fled the room, while others rushed to their king's side.

As if they can help him now, I scoffed. *It's far too late for that.*

I was grateful, at least, that their attention was no longer on Sky and I.

Wait.

"Sky!" I yelled, pivoting in her direction. My feet were free and so I prayed she was okay too.

I almost fainted in relief when I saw her.

Water dripped off her and she gasped for breath, but she was alive.

I practically pounced on her, wrapping my arms around her and hugging her so tightly I doubted she could breathe properly. She was shaking and crying so hard though that she scarcely noticed.

"Oh, Isan," she gasped between sobs. "I...I was so afraid and it... It was so cold. I thought... I thought that was it for me...that...that I was going to die." She shuddered and broke into sobs again.

"Shhh..." I murmured, trying to comfort her. "It's okay, you're safe now."

Gradually, she calmed down and pulled away. My armour was wet with her tears and the melted frost.

"What now?" she asked, her voice small. "Frost's dead, but our army..." she trailed off, knowing I knew what she meant, but what she didn't say made me realize something.

"Our army!"

Sky jumped when I shouted.

"Sky, they were frozen too," I said. "You and I escaped, so maybe they..."

We whipped our heads in the direction of where the army had stood frozen. Just as I'd thought, they were no longer statues dying a slow death; they had begun to stir, brushing melting ice off their clothes and skin. A couple were on their knees, gasping for breath. They had come so close to death, yet Wylla had chosen not to claim them. Sancia had watched over them and they would live to tell the tale.

There was a chance we could still win. We were outnumbered, but the Winter knights had been distracted by their king's death and hadn't noticed our knights had been released from the king's spell. They didn't know that while their backs were turned, the enemy was recuperating. They certainly didn't know we were drawing our weapons and preparing for one final attack.

It was our last chance. If we did not strike at that moment, all would be lost.

Once again, we had the element of surprise and I was determined not to let it go to waste. Our knights gathered, but they did not move. They waited for an order. I realized then that Uncle wasn't there to give them one. It had to be me.

"For Summer!" I yelled, and they charged.

The Winter knights were caught completely off guard and several of them fell before they could even draw their weapons. In seconds, the two armies were locked in battle, the Winter King forgotten. This battle would be the finale and would determine the victor of the war. There was one last thing I had to do.

"Sky, listen," I said, "I need you to stay here and help the knights while I take care of something.

"Consider it done," she replied, "but can I ask where you are going?"

"I'm going after the dark figure."

"What? No, Isan, you can't!"

"Someone has to go after him, Sky. If we don't, it won't matter who wins this war. He's after both our kingdoms and I'm not spending my whole life looking over my shoulder, waiting for him to return. We have to find him before he disappears again."

"I understand what you're saying, Isan, but it's too dangerous. You saw what he did to Frost. Let someone else do it. Get Uncle to do it."

I sighed. "Sky, in case you haven't noticed, Uncle isn't here. The dark figure probably finished him off already, like he did Frost. Now both kingdoms are without a king, our thrones ready for the taking. I'm not going to stand here idly and let it happen." I turned to go, but Sky grabbed my arm.

"Please," she said. "Don't do this. There has to be another way."

"*There is no other way!*" I snapped. "Sky, he killed our parents!"

Silence reigned between us, but it was broken by someone clearing their throat.

We turned to find a sopping wet Asmund smiling at us, which was strange in and of itself.

I sighed. "Let me guess, you want to help."

He grinned. "Let me go with you, Prince. It'll put Skiansy's mind at ease and who knows, you might need me."

I snorted, but it lacked any lustre. "Oh, I doubt I'll ever need you, Asmund, but I'll allow your company."

"When I said I wanted you two to be allies," Sky said, "I didn't mean for you to throw yourselves to the wolves together."

Asmund gave her a look. "Then I suppose you'll have to be more specific next time."

Sky crossed her arms and I knew she burned with the desire to go with us, but I couldn't let her. I had to keep her safe.

Our parents would have wanted her safe.

"Stay here," I told her. "Win this battle and if we're not back by sunrise, leave without us."

"Isan—" she started.

"No. Promise me you won't come looking for us if I don't return."

"Isan, I—" she tried again.

"*Promise me*," I said firmly.

I locked eyes with her, daring her to say no.

For a minute, she said nothing and I knew she was searching for a way out of it. Finally, her eyes fell in defeat.

"Fine," she conceded. "I promise I won't come looking for you once the sun rises."

"Thank you," I replied and hugged her for what could be the last time.

She must have been thinking the same thing, for she hugged me tighter. When she finally released me, I turned on my heel and walked away.

I didn't say goodbye because goodbyes are forever. In fact, I said nothing at all. I walked away without looking back, trusting Asmund would follow.

By sunrise, I'd said. That left me one hour to find and kill the dark figure, to get revenge for my parents and all the pain their absence had caused us.

One hour to make up for twelve years of sorrow and anger.

One hour until I saw my sister again.

One hour.

I hoped it would be enough.

38
Into The Fire

Asmund and I dashed across the throne room and back the way I had come with Snowdon. We dodged arrows and swords as we pushed through the melee of Summer and Winter knights. I was headed for the antechamber and the spiral staircase I knew the dark figure had escaped down.

I'd seen him take his leave after Frost's murder. He had slipped into the antechamber while everyone was distracted by Frost's sudden death. A few Wyllan knights had headed that way as well, but I doubted they could kill him. I felt it was my destiny to do the deed. He was the one who had ruined my childhood, who had torn my parents from me.

As soon as I entered the antechamber, I began to run. I located the staircase and descended it with such speed I almost tripped over my feet and fell down it instead.

Asmund yelled after me, but I ignored him. It wasn't my fault if he couldn't keep up.

I skidded to a stop at the bottom of the stairs and peered into the circular room beyond. I wasn't surprised to find the dark figure absent, but I was surprised at the two Wyllan knights standing guard outside the door.

I took a couple steps back up the staircase and motioned for Asmund to be silent.

He stopped on the step above me. "What is it?" he mouthed.

"There are two Wyllans outside the door," I whispered in reply. "We're going to have to get past them if we hope to reach the dark figure."

"The dark figure is the man from your dream?" Asmund whispered back. "The one who killed the Winter King."

I nodded.

"Then you must get your vengeance. I'll distract the guards and you can sneak past."

I gave him a look. "Why would you do that?"

"Because this dark figure is the reason we're in this mess in the first place. The sooner he's dead, the sooner we can all go home. I'll kill the guards and be right behind you."

I took a breath. "If you insist, but don't get yourself killed, all right? I'm just starting to enjoy your company."

He smiled. "Likewise, Prince." Then he crept down the last few steps and into the room beyond as I stood watch, ready to run to his aid should anything go wrong.

It was strange to me how much our relationship had changed over the course of the war. Part of me was angry he had wormed his way into my circle, but the other part of me was relieved that I could let my guard down a bit. I was still worried it was all a game, but after everything we'd been through, he deserved a chance.

Asmund drew his sword as he walked, careful not to let the weapon scrape, and raised it above his head, stalking up to the first guard on silent feet. Then he drove the blade into the man's back before he had the chance to react, like he did when saving Sky's life on the battlefield a week ago.

The man let out a gurgle as he collapsed to the stone floor and the other guard leapt into action, but Asmund was quick. He yanked his sword out of the dead guard's flesh and slipped out of the door.

The second guard's axe clashed against the floor where Asmund had stood a second ago. Then he raced off after Asmund, not sparing a second to mourn his comrade.

This is my chance. I can't waste it.

I shuffled across the room and peered out into the hallway beyond. Asmund and the Winter knight were gone from sight, but I could hear them yelling not far off.

I headed in the opposite direction of their sparring, deeper into the Winter castle.

Something told me the dark figure hadn't gone far, but I wasn't certain until I rounded the corner and saw the first body.

The man was crumpled against the wall and his armour was soaked in blood. His own sword was discarded a few feet away, pointing towards another fallen knight.

I followed the bodies until the trail ran cold in a dead-end hall. The only way forward was through a single door.

He's on the other side.

This is it.

I tried not to let his swath of carnage concern me, but I was less confident in my abilities than when I had left the throne room.

If a host of Winter knights hadn't been able to best him, then how could I hope to?

However, there wasn't any time for doubt. It seemed I was both kingdoms' final chance at defeating a man who had plagued us all. I wouldn't take that for granted.

I took a deep breath and opened the door, *Ember* at the ready.

The room was dim, lit with a single torch, the light not reaching the corners. The dark figure was nowhere to be seen, but that was to be expected.

"Show yourself," I said, my voice raised.

Nothing moved.

I stepped into the room. "I know you're in here. There's no use hiding. Come out and fight!"

He didn't reply, and just as I was about to take another step forward, the torch went out.

Fear enveloped me. If I couldn't see, I was done for.

Calm down, I told myself. *You can't afford to panic either.*

I breathed in through my nose, not daring to close my eyes, and that's when I realized it wasn't completely dark. There was a window in the far wall through which moonlight streamed.

A chill ran through me.

Why does this seem so familiar?

Then it hit me.

The nightmare. Fidal save me. I'm back there. It came back for me.

But I didn't remember falling asleep.

Then a terrifying thought crossed my mind; what if I had never woken up?

I shook off that idea. It was crazy. This wasn't the nightmare. It was exactly like it, but it was real this time. He could hurt me; he could kill me.

The notion sent a quiver through my bones, but I couldn't let it get to me.

"Do you think the darkness will save you?" I asked. "I will still find you. So come out and fight me like a man. Only cowards hide."

Something moved in the corner of my eye and I turned to see the dark figure walking towards me. Finally, after all these years, my parents' killer stood before me.

It occurred to me then that I still didn't know who the dark figure was. He had walked through my nightmares every single night for a month, but I hadn't seen his face. I had never been able to identify him.

Even now, as he stood mere feet away, I could not begin to describe him. He wore a hood that obscured his face in shadows and his cloak covered the rest of him. I could not tell whether he was from Summer or Winter, how old he was, or if he was even human. The one thing I knew with utmost certainty was that he was tall.

Then he pulled back the hood, revealing a long, intricate, black braid and a scarred face.

I froze.

No, it couldn't be. There had to be a mistake.

It can't *be.*

His face was pale like mine and his eyes were blue instead of the brown I remembered, but the familiar scar revealed the truth.

"Uncle?" I said, all the blood draining from my face.

He smiled. "Took you long enough."

I couldn't move. I couldn't speak. I felt sick, like someone had punched me in the gut. All those years, everything…

It had all been a lie.

Uncle regarded me with false sympathy. "Oh, look at you," he crooned, "you've been betrayed."

I didn't understand. How could Uncle…? Why would he…?

"What happened to your face?" I managed to choke out. Not the most pressing question, but something I did want to know.

He laughed. "Clever, wasn't it? You see this"—he tugged at his braid—"was nothing but an illusion. I'll be glad to be rid of it. How you Sancians live without cutting your hair is beyond me."

Sancians…

"You're a Wyllan," I gasped.

"Clearly."

"But—"

"But I had dark skin and brown eyes, right?" he finished for me. "Well, magic can do the most wonderful things, Isan. You see what I want you to see."

In the space of a blink, his face changed again, back to the tones I remembered. Then his image distorted once more like a ripple through water and his true Wyllan features returned.

I gaped at him. He'd been masquerading as a Summer citizen for years. Even his race had been a lie. It was appalling. I may have looked different than my family, but I never pretended to be something I wasn't. I would never ask someone to make me look like Sky did, or Asmund even. It was wrong, but even worse was the fact that he had killed my parents.

"Why?" I asked him. "Why kill my parents? Why go through all this effort?"

"Because I was promised greatness when I was born, Isanfier, and I was cheated. I wanted the power that should've been mine. Your parents were merely a stepping stone in my plan to rule Fidalia."

"So one kingdom wasn't enough for you?" I asked, pain and sorrow wrenching through my insides. "You *had* power in Summer. No one would ever have known the truth of your origins. Why risk that comfort to come after Frost?"

"*Why?*" he scoffed. "Frost came for me, Isanfier. His assassins sought me out in my *own* domain. He stole everything from me and yet it was not enough for him. So no, one kingdom wasn't enough for *me*."

His domain.

Anger burned in my veins at the notion.

"Summer was never yours to exploit, Uncle, but I suppose I shouldn't call you that anymore, should I?"

He drew his sword with a wicked grin. "The name is Darkenier and Summer was ripe for the taking. It practically screamed for my salvation."

For the first time in my waking hours, I saw the name engraved along the length of his blade.

Shadows.

My stomach dropped.

That was what the dream had been trying to tell me, but I didn't know enough to connect the dots. Perhaps he had shrouded his sword's name in magic too.

Was there anything about him that was true?

"It's going to be as much fun killing you as it was killing your parents," my former uncle went on. "Say hello to them for me when you join them among the stars."

I blanched again and took an involuntary step back. Our talk was over and he was preparing to kill me. The realization brought me to my senses.

He might have been my uncle, he might have helped raise me to be the man I was today, but those facts had become meaningless. He had killed my parents. He had destroyed the peace between the kingdoms, and he would pay for both in blood. I had gone to Winter for revenge and revenge is what I would receive.

"Any last words, nephew?" he asked.

"Yes," I replied, leveling my own sword in his direction. "May Fidal spare you, because I won't."

He laughed. "You may have killed Frost's assassins in Widonia, but I assure you, your skills are nothing compared to mine. I let you accompany me on this war in hopes you would get yourself killed on the way."

I began to circle him and he followed. "Ah, so you tried to take the coward's way out. What happened, *Uncle*? Did you get too attached? Did you regret all this deception and destruction?"

His eyes darkened. "I regret nothing, save letting you and your sister live this long."

"Then try to kill me, Darkenier. See if your assumptions of me are true, but know this: I will not hold back."

At my final word, I lunged at him.

Darkenier didn't even flinch. In one fluid movement, he blocked my attempt and made a counterattack, thrusting *Shadows* towards my chest.

I leapt out of the way just in time. In seconds, I'd gone from offensive to defensive, but I tried not to let that impact me. He was going to lose. I would *not* let him win.

I aimed a blow at his feet, but he leapt back and swung *Shadows* at my head. I ducked and feinted to the side but brought *Ember* swinging up to his neck instead.

He didn't fall for the feint and his sword met mine halfway. He tried to push *Ember* away, but I pushed back harder.

As we strained against each other, Darkenier said, "You are a much better swordsman than your father. Never won a single duel, that man."

"Don't you *dare* insult my father!" I yelled.

Distracted, I had let my muscles ease and Darkenier was finally able to push *Ember* aside. He caught my face with the flat of his sword as it swung by.

I cursed—the pain was unreal—but I'd faced worse, a lot worse.

Focus, Isan, focus.

I'd managed to hold onto *Ember* and I swung her at him angrily.

He sidestepped it easily and smiled, saying, "You'll have to try a lot harder than that if you wish to beat me."

I said nothing and the duel continued in earnest.

We moved so fast that we'd barely blocked a hit before another came. Our swords would've been blurs to anyone watching. It'd be impossible to tell who was at an advantage, but so far no one was. We were evenly matched. Neither one of us gained ground, but neither one of us lost ground either. It was infuriating.

As we fought, Darkenier continued to goad me by insulting my parents. I didn't falter, not after the first time, but each insult stung. He told me my father never truly loved my mother, that theirs was an arranged marriage and my mother had been in it for the title.

"Do you have any lady friends, Isan?" he asked. "Your father had loads of them, even after he was married."

I cracked a little on that one. "Is that right?" I snapped. "How can I believe anything you say? How do I know you knew them at all?"

"You can't," he sneered, raising *Shadows* above his head, as if preparing to cleave me in half. At the last second, he swung her at my waist instead.

Distracted by his words, I didn't have time to block. His sword hit me full force, denting my armour and throwing me across the room. Pain blossomed in my midsection and then throughout my entire body as I collided with the stone floor and skidded to a stop against the wall.

My head rang from the impact and the room spun.

I tried to lift my sword, but then Darkenier's boot came down on my wrist and I froze.

His face came into focus a few seconds later and he scowled down at me.

"Pathetic," he said. "I always thought you were a waste, but I had hoped you would show more potential than this. Your parents would be ashamed of you."

Anger burned inside me, lighting through the pain still pulsing throughout my body. "Don't you dare tell me what my parents think of me," I snapped. "I *know* they are proud of me. Everything I've done in this war has been for them!"

He dug his heel into my wrist and aimed his sword at my throat.

I gritted my teeth against the pain.

"Yet, you are still going to die today," he replied, "without avenging them. What a disappointment that will be. Not to mention the fact that you left your sister all alone and unprotected, though I think her death will be a blessing."

I bristled. "Excuse me?"

"That girl has brought nothing but shame to your family," he replied. "She is a disgrace—fighting battles and prancing around in pants and armour. Her disregard for gender standing is appalling. Yes, her death would be a gift to Areevia and Oaden."

He had crossed the line. Insulting my parents was one thing, but my sister…

Anger raged up like a fire in me and I snapped.

The fire started in my heart and spread through my veins, igniting me in a blaze of fury. When it reached my hands, I felt the anger like a wave of heat, burning me to the core.

Darkenier swore and jumped back, distancing himself from me.

"By Wylla," he breathed. "You do have it."

"Have…"

Fidal's breath!

My hands were on fire. Not burning hot, but actually *on fire*. The flames danced and flickered as they crept down my fingers towards *Ember's* hilt, which I still somehow held in my right hand.

Seconds later, my sword caught fire and despite my shock, I managed to drag myself to my feet. I was battered, bruised, and confused, but I was still alive. I still had a chance.

I waved the burning blade in Darkenier's direction. "Still willing to face me?"

He rolled his eyes. "Your magic won't save you. It didn't save your parents in the end."

"What?"

He rushed at me without another word and I swung my burning blade, wondering how long the fire would last.

No, don't think about that. You can't lose your focus.

"Isanfier, look out!" a new voice screamed and I turned to avoid Darkenier's blade at the last second. The light in the room had dimmed even further and I wondered if he was attempting to darken the moon itself.

"Over here, you Fidal-forsaken murderer!" the voice shouted and I realized then that it was Asmund. He had finally joined me.

Uncle pivoted in his direction, blocking a blow Asmund had aimed at his head, and I saw my chance.

For once, I didn't hesitate. I shoved my burning sword into Darkenier's back and he stiffened, *Shadows* slipping from his fingers and clattering to the floor.

Then the fire flared up and Darkenier began to burn.

I sank to my knees, watching as the flames ate away at him. The heat from the fire should have been sweltering, but I knelt a foot away and felt nothing.

After a moment, I pulled *Ember* out of the pyre and her flames died instantly. Just as suddenly, the rest of the fire burned out.

There was nothing left of the so-called King Arkenier but *Shadows* and a pile of ashes.

39

Bittersweet Revenge

I stood, staring at his ashes, and felt the enormity of what I'd done.

I murdered my own uncle.

He was not the first person to meet his end by my sword, nor would he be the last, but his death was different. Part of me wished it hadn't ended this way. He had raised me, had given me a roof over my head and someone to look to for advice when life grew difficult.

I guess it wasn't his death that bothered me so much as the necessity of it. He had killed my parents. He was a traitor.

"Are you okay, Prince?" Asmund asked, bringing me back to the present. He was standing on the other side of the ash pile, a concerned look on his face.

"I'm fine, thanks to you," I replied. "I suppose I owe you a life debt now."

He shook his head. "I don't need it. That man...he was the king, wasn't he? And you...you just used magic."

I nodded, though I still couldn't believe either of those truths myself. "He admitted to killing my parents; he planned to take over the entire realm, though I'm still not entirely sure why. I don't even know if he was my uncle or not in the end. As for the fire I conjured… Can I trust you to keep that between us?"

He put a fist to his heart. "You have my word, Prince, not as your subject, but as your friend, if you will allow me to call you that."

I gave him a smile. "Don't hurt yourself, Asmund. Your word is enough for me, for now."

"Did you know there was magic inside you?"

I shook my head. "It just happened. He had me on the ground, my wrist pinned with his boot and his sword to my throat. Then he started talking about Skiansy, horrible things and…the fire just happened. It was enough to free me and reduce him to this." I gestured to the ashes beneath us.

"Well, as you told Echo, magic is a gift. The gods gave you this power and it is your right to use it. Perhaps, now that his Majesty is dead, you can restore magic to Summer."

"Perhaps I can." I sighed. "Let's get back to the throne room. Sky is probably worried sick."

"Agreed, we can discuss it all later."

I knelt down and picked up *Shadows*, loath to touch the blade that had killed my parents, but it was all that was left of Summer's late king and I knew the lords would want something to bury. Besides, it was claimed and would only be a detriment to the poor soul who came across it next. Better for it to be six feet under.

I slid the blade into the empty sheath on my right side, the weight a strange feeling, and then turned back to Asmund. "Ready?"

"When you are, Prince. I hope our army has managed to neutralize the Wyllans."

"So do I."

We left the room then and headed back the way we came, away from the carnage and the ghost of our pasts, away from the man who had started the war and put us all in danger.

• • •

Relief passed through me when Asmund and I returned to the throne room to find our knights resting by one wall, the remaining Wyllans guarded by a few others. The war was over. The final battle had been won and we had emerged victorious.

I noticed Sky talking to a familiar elderly knight and motioned the two over.

Sky's eyes lit up and she ran forward, flinging her arms around me.

I stumbled, but remained upright and returned her hug with the same ferocity.

"Thank Fidal, you're all right, and Asmund too," Sky exclaimed, turning to give Asmund a smile.

When she let me go, I turned to the other knight and shook his hand. "It's good to see you again, Silas. What's the situation here?"

He smiled. "Likewise, your Highness. The Wyllans surrendered to us soon after you left. Their king was dead and they saw the futility of continuing to resist."

I nodded. "A wise choice. How many men did we lose tonight?"

"We have not done a final count as there is a chance some retreated back to our camp, but we did not lose any lords at least."

"Good," I replied, but my heart sank at the thought of all the people who had died in vain.

"Your sister tells me you pursued the man who killed the Winter King," Silas went on, "that he is the same man who killed your parents twelve years ago. How did you fare?"

"He is dead."

"Do you have any idea who he was," Sky asked me, "and why he wanted to destroy both kingdoms?"

I winced at her question, not wanting to ruin her memory of Uncle, but she would find out soon enough and it was better she heard it from me.

"It was Uncle," I replied.

She stared at me incomprehensibly for a minute before my words sank in and her eyes widened in shock. "*What?*" she gasped. "That's ridiculous! Why would he...?" She shook her head in disbelief.

"That's exactly what my reaction was at first," I told her, "but he admitted everything and then he tried to kill me. So I was forced to face the truth. He wasn't even our uncle, Sky. He was a Wyllan. Everything he's ever said about our parents can't be taken at face value." I looked around at her, Asmund, and Silas, adding, "However, his true heritage should be kept a secret. To everyone else, he was simply a traitor."

The three nodded.

Sky was quiet for a minute. Then she said softly, "I can't believe it. All those years he was right there in our midst and we never suspected him. We trusted him..." She broke off, ashamed of herself for believing the man who'd killed our parents, but it wasn't her fault.

"You weren't the only one," I told her. "He had us all fooled; he planned it perfectly. He killed our parents and then showed up as the queen's brother right when the castle needed a leader."

Silas nodded. "The whole land saw him as our salvation and accepted him as King," he said to Sky, "though never in history has the *queen's* brother inherited the throne. It should have gone to your brother and a regent should have been appointed until Isan came of age. In fact, your uncle should have been the regent."

"He should not have been given power over us all," I agreed, "but the people shrugged off tradition and crowned him, never thinking about how convenient his appearance was. He raised us as if we were his own, thus ensuring we would trust him with our lives, that we would follow him blindly without ever once doubting his loyalties.

"Then, with the whole Summer army at his back, he rode to Winter under the pretense of revenge, but it was actually for his own ends. He wanted Frost dead and Winter conquered, and he had a loyal and unsuspecting army to do that."

Sky shook her head again. "I believe you, but it's a pity we're only realizing this now."

"I know. A lot of lives were lost for nothing. We could have avoided this whole war had we paid more attention to what was happening in our own city, but at least we caught our parents' killer in the end. Now they can rest in peace, knowing he won't kill again."

She nodded. "And we can relax, knowing we have avenged them. Are you happy now that you have taken your revenge?"

I sighed. "Not entirely. Revenge is bittersweet. He was a traitor and I'm glad he's dead, but at the same time, he was still family, in a way. I never exactly loved him, but I did care about him and I always thought he cared about me too."

"I assumed the same," Sky said.

We stood there in silence for several minutes, remembering the man we thought we knew.

"I guess that's it then," I said finally. "We're alone. Our family is gone."

"That's not true," Sky argued. "We still have Aunt Mag and each other, and as long as *that's* true, we still have a family."

"There is that," I agreed.

"You have me as well, Prince," Asmund said.

"I will stand by your side also," Silas added.

Sky and I smiled at them. "Thank you."

"Well, are you ready to address your men, your Highness?" Silas asked me.

His words caught me off guard, but I supposed they *were* my men now that Uncle was gone. "I'll try to be swift, so we can all get home."

He nodded and I headed over to the throne to get a better vantage point. Someone had removed Frost's body, but the blood still remained and I tried not to step in it.

"Your attention, please," I called out and all eyes turned to me, my remaining knights scrambling to their feet and snapping to attention.

I held up a hand. "At ease."

They relaxed at once, but were ready for any orders I should give.

"I have just returned from confronting the man who killed King Frost of Winter. He was also the man who killed King Oaden and Queen Areevia twelve years ago." I took a deep breath. "His true name is Darkenier, but he posed in our kingdom for years as King Arkenier."

The energy in the room changed as both sides came to terms with the revelation. I knew there would be those who wouldn't believe my story, but I wouldn't worry about them. The truth needed to be told.

"The King of Summer is dead," I went on, "killed by my own hand for his unforgivable deeds. His remains can be found at the end of the hall on the fourth floor, should any wish to confirm the fact. He is responsible for this war and he dragged us all here under false pretenses. Now that he is dead, we have no quarrel with the Wyllans, if we ever did."

"Liar!" someone yelled and I watched as Lord Arrath stepped forward, his armour covered head to toe in blood. I thought of the Winter civilians he had killed and cringed. Of course he would be the one to speak against me.

"Arkenier would never betray us!" he went on. "You merely wished to usurp the throne, to kill him while the rest of us were occupied. The true traitor stands before us now. You dare to besmirch his memory?"

I winced at each word, but knew his suspicions had weight, that I would wonder the same thing if I was in his shoes.

"I had no wish to take the throne from him before his time," I replied. "I only did what had to be done after he confessed everything and tried to kill me. He was a tyrant, Lord Arrath. He wanted to rule both kingdoms and crush whoever stood in his way."

Lord Arrath took a step forward and opened his mouth to speak again when Asmund stepped in front of me.

"Stand down, Father," he said. "I was with the prince when the king revealed his true intentions. His words are true and I will not listen to you accuse otherwise."

Lord Arrath looked affronted, but he did not say another word. I was glad their bond held enough for that, but I feared it would be severed now by Asmund's audacity to refute him.

"Does anyone else wish to argue against his Highness' claims?" Asmund called out to our remaining knights.

No one said a word and so I walked down from the throne, towards the captive Wyllans.

"I apologize for the pain we have caused you and your kingdom. I shall take whatever supplies I need for my men to survive the journey back to Summer, but I would like to return this castle to Winter."

One of the knights scrunched up his face and I recognized him as Sir Kallen, the man who had spoken to Snowdon in the antechamber. "You do not wish to slaughter us all and establish a base here, to destroy the wills of our people until they accept you as King?"

I shook my head. "That may be your way, Sir Kallen, but it is not mine. I have no use for your kingdom and wish to part ways peacefully, but don't take my word for it. You will see the truth in a few hours when we are long gone."

I turned to Silas then. "See to it they are left alive, but cannot follow us."

He nodded and I signalled to the men that it was time to leave.

A couple were hesitant, but eventually they began to move, following Sky out the door and down the hall.

I lingered a moment until Asmund clapped a hand on my shoulder and said, "Let us go, Prince. It has been a long enough day already."

• • •

It took the better part of an hour to get everybody together as I spread the news of Uncle's death among the men. They couldn't believe we were going to leave after all the trouble we'd gone through to get here, but since Uncle was dead, I was in charge. If there's one thing knights won't question, it's authority, and besides, if they stayed behind, what would they do? It wouldn't take long for the Wyllans to muster up more men and then they would be doomed.

We gathered the wounded, tending to them as best we could, and set fire to the dead. I made a mental note to host a proper memorial once we were back in Widonia. We left Appalachia as the sun began to rise and reached our small base camp a few minutes later, where our horses were waiting patiently for us. Uncle's tent still stood in the centre of the camp.

I told the men we should press on, but I gave them a few minutes to check their belongings and have something to eat.

I found my horse easily, leaning against him as I watched the men.

My *men now*, I reminded myself.

Sky came up beside me with her horse a few moments later. "It's beautiful, isn't it?"

"What?" I said, turning towards her.

"Sunrise," she stated simply.

I looked to the east, where the sun was rising above the horizon, and had to agree with her. It *was* beautiful and the colours were stunning. The sun itself was a deep orange, the colour of warmth and happiness, and it was rimmed with red and pink clouds. For the first time in a while, the red colour didn't remind me of blood. Instead, I thought of the red roses that would bloom in Summer when we returned, and I smiled.

Sky picked up on my smile and said, "What are you thinking of?"

"That the sunrise reminds me of the roses back home."

She looked at the sunrise with scrutiny and finally nodded. "You're right; those clouds are the exact same shade of red. *I* was thinking, though, about how much it looked like fire and what I wouldn't give for one right about now to warm me up."

At her words, I flashed back to my fight with Uncle and the fire that had erupted in my hands, the fire that had reduced him to ashes but left me without a single burn.

Suddenly, the sunrise didn't look happy anymore; gone were the memories of roses. All I could see now was death and destruction.

I shuddered and looked away.

"It's a sign of hope," Sky went on.

"What?"

"The sunrise," Sky repeated. "It's a symbol of hope. We survived to see the dawn of a new day."

I nodded, but said nothing; to me, the sun was nothing but a symbol of despair.

"You know," she continued. "The sun is Summer's symbol. Funny that it's the first thing we saw after our victory." She smiled and then added, "So we survived our first war. I can hardly believe it. I thought you were done for when Snowdon took you. I thought we were both done for when Frost caught us."

"How did you find me in the throne room?" I asked her. "I thought maybe Snowdon had..."

She shook her head. "It was a good trick, but I was able to dig myself out. After that, it was only a matter of following his pull through the castle. He didn't think of that."

She smiled, but it was tainted somehow. I knew killing Snowdon hadn't been easy for her, but now wasn't the time to sort through our regrets, our pain. We had to remain strong until we were safely back in Summer.

"What'll we do now that it's all over?" she asked.

"I don't know," I sighed, "return to normal, I guess."

"Normal?" she said. "Isan, there is no normal anymore. You're going to be King."

I shook my head. "I'm only sixteen. The law states that I cannot be crowned until my eighteenth birthday. A regent will be appointed in my stead. Of course, I'll have all the authority."

Sky smiled deviously. "In that case, we'll do whatever we want. We'll go visit Echo all the time, now that everything's over." She gasped. "Isan! We have to go see her soon so she knows we're okay. She's probably sick with worry."

I put a hand on her shoulder. "Easy," I told her. "There will be plenty of time to go see her once everything in Summer is settled."

She smiled sheepishly. "You're right. I'm sorry. I'm just so relieved now that everything's over and..."

She continued to talk nonstop, even as we mounted our horses and rode away from Appalachia. I knew it was her way of coping with everything we had gone through and so I didn't deter her.

I nodded and answered her shortly when necessary, but for the most part, I remained silent. I personally didn't think that everything was over; far from it. As far as I was concerned, the war had only just begun.

Uncle, Frost, and Snowdon may be dead, but Icaria was still out there. She would return to Appalachia eventually and I shuddered to think how she would react to the carnage, not to mention the death of her brother and father. We had stolen much from her and I did not get the sense that she was one to accept injustice.

I could not rest while she remained alive, not if I wanted to live long enough to be crowned King. So the war was far from finished. It wouldn't be over until Icaria was dead and gone, until one of us destroyed the other.

EPILOGUE

Echo

Echo felt the ripple run through Fidalia, felt the trees sway in a non-existent breeze, felt the magic in her veins tingle, and knew her brother was dead.

She sank to her knees on the wooden floor of her treehouse and wept for what once was and what could never be. Her relationship with Snowdon had always been strange and it was ultimately short-lived, but she knew he'd deserved more than this world had given him. Their father had sapped him of his spirit day in and day out, until nothing remained but pain.

Echo knew his death was a mercy, knew that part of the Curse had been fulfilled because of it and the realm was one step closer to salvation, but still she mourned.

When her strength came back, she got to her feet and walked to Isan's abandoned room.

She hated the emptiness of the treehouse now, kept expecting her friends' return with every snap of a branch outside. Isan's bed was still rumpled, as if he would come back at any minute. She knew it only added to her loneliness, but she couldn't bring herself to fix it. She couldn't bear the thought of erasing the last traces of his presence.

It could have been a dream, after all, and if it was, it was one she did not wish to part with yet.

She walked over to the window, grabbing the red scarf off its nail on the way. It was a soft, yet hardy material, an item she had picked up in Tamise the first time she'd visited the market and had not touched since.

Once upon a time, Snowdon had one just like it.

She clutched the fabric tight to her chest for a moment and then she dropped it out the open window, letting the wind take it wherever it pleased, letting her brother go.

When she turned away from the window, she was resolved once more.

One piece of the puzzle had been determined. Now it was up to Isan and Icaria to finish it. Echo did not know which one would prevail, but she knew which one she hoped for. She knew her freedom lay in Isan's hands and she prayed to all the gods that he would handle it with care.

To Be Continued in Winter's Wrath

AUTHOR'S NOTE

Thank you so much for reading!

If you liked *Summer's Revenge*, it would mean the world to me if you could leave a review on your chosen vendor and/or Goodreads. Reviews feed authors and I can't wait to hear your thoughts. Even a rating by itself or a single sentence can help boost rankings.

If you are interested in more content from yours truly, please subscribe to my newsletter. I send monthly updates on writing, releases, and more. Subscription also gives you access to the Content Corner on my website. This exclusive space holds free writing resources for my fellow authors and never before seen content for my readers, like excerpts of unfinished books! You can sign up on my website which I have left below. I can't wait to share more with you!

www.emmacouetteauthor.com

ACKNOWLEDGEMENTS

First, I want to say thank you to my younger sister, Megan for everything she gave to this book. She has always been my biggest supporter for this story and I honestly know it wouldn't be the book it is today without her. Our after dinner chats at the kitchen table were probably my favourite part of the writing process. Thank you for letting me bounce ideas off of you.

Second, to my significant other, Allan who supported me through all the pitfalls and setbacks that this release brought. You gave me the strength to go on when I thought all was lost and this book would never see the world.

Third, to my parents for supporting my author dreams and rooting for me every step of the way. I can't wait for you both to read my first fantasy novel.

I am beyond grateful for my amazing Critique Partner, Ashley, who supported me through all the endless drafts this book needed. This book owes you a lot, Ashley, and I'm glad to have found your friendship. I can't wait to read *Beautiful Curses* in book format someday too!

Thank you as well to my Beta Readers: Emily Weisenburger, Isabella Sandoval, Landri Driskill, Lindsay,

Rachel S, Stephanie M. Whitson, Anakha, Citlalin, and Taylor Wilson :) I can't wait for you guys to see the finished version!

Big thanks to the members of my Street Team for spreading the word about the cover, pre-order, giveaway, and for reading and reviewing ARCs: Crystal Fontanez, Isabella Sandoval, Kimberly Swartz, Tanya Drury, Stephanie Anne, Sumaita Sahriar, and Robin Joyce.

Thank you to MoorBooks Design for creating this cover and exceeding my expectations. It was so hard to keep it a secret until the cover reveal!

Huge thank you to Nicki Richards for being my editor yet again. It honestly amazes me how many mistakes there still are when I send it to her. Thank you for helping me create a polished version.

I would also like to thank Rachael Ward from CartographyBird who designed the stunning map at the beginning of the book. You were a pleasure to work with, Rachael!

Shoutout to the writing community over on Instagram who always inspire me and motivate me to keep going no matter what. I want to give a special thank you to Hannah Richards for her marketing tips, Amie Mcnee for The Inspired Collective, and Viv Kruckow for Retreat.

I am also super grateful for my lovely writer friend, Micah Orth, who was kind enough to let me ship my proof copy to her and mail it to me after some shipping issues. You are a life saver and my proof copy is even more special now!

Last but not least, thank you to my readers for joining me on this new fantasy journey. I hope you liked the realm of Fidalia and are excited to follow Isan and Sky in book two. Thank you for supporting me and my ever growing imagination.

ABOUT THE AUTHOR

Emma K. C. Couette is a Canadian wordsmith whose second passion is woodworking. She has written a few award-winning short stories and dabbles in poetry when the inspiration strikes her. Her dreams include travelling the world, being a mom, and owning a small library. *Summer's Revenge* is her third novel, the first in The Fidalian Chronicles.

Website: www.emmacouetteauthor.com
Instagram: @emmathewriter
Facebook: emmacouette.10
Goodreads: Emma Couette